THREAT

THREAT

RICHARD JESSUP

THE VIKING PRESS   NEW YORK

First published in 1981 by The Viking Press
625 Madison Avenue, New York, N.Y. 10022
Published simultaneously in Canada by
Penguin Books Canada Limited

LIBRARY OF CONGRESS CATALOGING IN PUBLICATION DATA
Jessup, Richard.
Threat.
I. Title.
PZ4.J58Th [PS3560.E8] 813′.54 80-52001
ISBN 0-670-70618-3

Printed in the United States of America
Set in Times Roman

TO
Margaret Handler
Dr. Milton Ratner and
FRIENDSHIP

PART ONE

THE ST. CYR TOWER

He was a young man in his late twenties, but looked younger. He had not lived long enough to have experienced much beyond a very personal point of view about what life really was, or its value. Most of what he knew came from traditional, mid-America–establishment thinking, which after the Viet Nam war was changing rapidly. But he was not changing with it. Nearly all of what he had learned about life stemmed from a military, or para-military, environment, and consequently he thought in those terms. Decisions he made, and the actions that followed were often, if not always, a movement with deadly force toward an objective. If you looked into his eyes, and had a feeling for such things, you might sense that his tensions were those of a neurotic—self-amused, mocking—who sustained himself with an attitude of careless-ness about life; his own, as well as anybody else's.

That morning he walked the length of the subway platform, moving nearer to the wall as the train roared into the station. He was irritated with himself. He had forgotten to take a book with him which he would

3

need that day, and even as the train blew into the station he had not yet made up his mind whether to return to his room for the book or cut the class at Columbia. It was then that he saw the girl. She staggered. Without thinking, he stepped forward and grabbed her by the arm, jerking her back from the edge as the first car roared past, brakes screaming.

"Let go of me!"

Passengers moved into and out of the cars. The girl made no attempt to get on the train. He still held her arm. "Let me go," she said, her voice sounding like the meow of a kitten.

The doors closed and the train pulled away. New Yorkers getting off dispersed quickly, and they were alone in the station.

She looked up into his face. Aside from the red-rimmed eyes, he saw nothing that indicated she might be a junkie. And she was not a girl, but a woman in her early twenties. "I wasn't going to jump," she said, pulling free of him. "And the train is gone, so you can let go of me now."

"Sure." He let her go completely. She staggered. She would have fallen if he had not taken hold of her again. He looked at her more closely. She might have been a hooker, but the clothes were all wrong. Navy pea jacket, knitted watch cap, jeans, sneakers. Her eyes were watery and her nose was red. Blond hair straggled from the edge of the cap. Crying, he decided. Something or somebody had jerked her around a little and she had opened the waterworks. She moved away from him, shoving hard.

He turned his back on her and started to walk away. She walked with him. It was the movement of a stray dog, or a child. He stopped and she stopped. She seemed to have no will of her own. She did not look at him. She did not speak. She stood at his side.

He did not want this, but he could not walk away again, or speak to her roughly, any more than he would have kicked the dog or ignored the child. He knew that he should do these things, but instead, he asked: "When did you eat last?"

"Eat?" She looked away. She made a gesture with one arm, taking in the subway station. Vague. Formless.

"Come on," he said.

He didn't know why, but he had expected some kind of resistance. She offered none and walked beside him trustingly.

They crossed Broadway, pushing against the rain, and down into one of the side streets. The rain slackened for a moment. In the distance, the Hudson River broke strong and wide into view.

He pointed to a neighborhood bar. "In here. I know this place."

They slid into a booth. She looked around. A half-dozen blue collars and neighborhood regulars were nursing morning beers and wake-up shots, and after a quick glance the newcomers were dismissed as crazy street people.

He saw the startled look in her eyes. "It's okay. They serve food too."

The bartender slouched over. "Yeah?"

"Scramble two, ham, fries, and coffee for the lady. I'll have a double bourbon and a beer," he said.

"She drinkin'?"

"Why?"

"I gotta see ID, thas why, Mac."

"She's not drinking," he said. He lit a cigarette, offering her one. She refused. He puffed and studied her. She kept her eyes down, sitting small and tight, like a child waiting to be chastised. "What's your name?"

"Name?" She looked up, surprised.

"Yeah. Your name."

"Eleanor—Eleanor Cassie."

"I'm Tonio Vega. Where do you live?"

"Live?"

Jesus, he thought, this is too tiresome. "Yeah, you know, where's home? The pad? The joint? Where do you sleep?" He did not try to cover up his irritation. Instinct warned him to pay up and get out.

He would have his drink and then leave.

"I lived over near Central Park. Not too far from here. We had a nice place. I painted the bathroom."

"Lived? Had?"

"He didn't come back for five days. He told me not to worry. I waited and waited—"

"Where were you going just now?" Tonio asked quietly. They came to New York by the hundreds and thousands, their fantasies about being a model, an actress, a painter, dancer, writer hanging on their faces like crepe; then when they found the going rough, getting hooked on some turkey who then takes off for one reason or another.

"Look for him."

"Where?"

"He worked somewhere in the Times Square area."

"Doing what?"

"In one of the theaters."

"An actor?"

"No, he wasn't an actor."

"I wouldn't say that." He thought she was about to protest, when the bartender interrupted with the food.

"That's seven seventy-five, pal." The bartender stood over them as if rooted in stone and waited for his money. He had had experiences with street people; they would order huge meals and drink and when he went into the back for something, bolt out of the door Tonio paid. Only then did she move toward the food.

She opened her jacket and he could see small but firm breasts pushing against the cotton turtleneck. She attacked the eggs and wolfed them down without pause or looking up. Tonio did not speak. He threw back the bourbon shot and set his teeth against the rawness of the taste so early in the morning. He chased it with a sip of beer, and lit another cigarette.

"I've got to get going," he said. "Here, this should help a little." He dropped a five-dollar bill beside the plate where she was sopping up the last of the egg and ham gravy with a piece of bread.

He rose to leave and she rose with him.

It had stopped raining but there was still a fine mist, and there was a stiff wind off the river. They stood on the sidewalk and buttoned up.

"Where will you go?" Tonio asked, fighting down his irritation. "Are you going to look for him?"

"I don't know—" She made a gesture with her arm; formless, as she had done in the subway.

Tonio wanted to get away quickly. He was bored. He had been in New York long enough to have seen many incidents like this. He spent much of his time out in the streets at night and that was when he saw a lot. He usually ignored desperate people. "You can't wander around the streets on a day like this. Why don't you go to the YWCA and get a

6

room? Get yourself cleaned up a little. You don't look so hot. Try and find a job." His eyes wandered. All he wanted to do was get away. He moved tentatively, and she moved with him. "Listen, there are city agencies to help people in your situation."

"He took my wallet, with forty-two dollars and my ID. I can't even prove who I am."

"How about your folks?"

She shook her head.

"Friends? You and him must have had some friends you could get in touch with. They might even know where he is. At least you could get your ID back."

She shook her head again.

"You can't," Tonio said stubbornly, "just stand around in the rain."

"I'm okay, really." She bobbed her head. A quick, jerky motion. "Thanks for everything. You know, the eggs and all. I didn't know I was hungry. *That* hungry. And for the money—" She offered her hand.

"Listen," he said intently, "nothing stays serious for very long."

She stared at him.

It was a mystery to him how it happened. The red nose, the waiflike appeal, being alone on the street. He watched her walk off. He thought of the empty room in his building, and then went after her.

"Come with me," he said more harshly than he intended.

"Where are we going?"

"Come," Tonio said impatiently.

They reached the river and swung uptown. The rain gave way to a sharp wind and they both hunched deeper into the collars of their jackets. She strode beside him in silence. Thin. Small, almost like a girl, but not a girl. A woman. Her nose get redder, but her eyes were now sharp and clear. It was amazing, he thought, what a bellyful of ham and eggs will do for the eyes. They swung into the lobby of a gray marble pile on Riverside Drive, one of many in the Seventies and Eighties, huge twenty- and thirty-room mansions, the social ambitions and ego of the owners dying long before the neighborhoods did.

The Riverside Arms, where Tonio lived, was one such mansion that had been converted into furnished rooms and small apartments when Fordham University and The Juilliard School had moved into the Lincoln Center complex. Halfway between Lincoln Center and Columbia University, it was totally occupied by students. There was a good mix of attitudes and sexes, and the institutional atmosphere suited Tonio perfectly.

The enormous marble foyer was empty. Most of the students who had early classes would have been gone long ago, and those who did not leave would stay in their rooms on a bitter day.

The manager's office was empty and Tonio removed one of three keys from the pegboard.

"Do you live here?"

He nodded. "It's a rooming house."

The noise inside the building came upon them slowly as they climbed a marble staircase. He knew most of the sounds and who made them: Mannering and Tulip, the homosexual couple going to Juilliard, had started their morning, as they did every day, with Mozart on their stereo. (He wondered if Tulip, an Indian from Bombay, had another name.) Tubby Engalls attacked his medical books absorbing facts and cigarettes at the same rate of speed, pausing only to blow out the halls with his chronic cough. Laura Roc, another Juilliard student, was vocalizing. At the second level he was greeted with the aromatic scent of grass as someone breakfasted on coffee and a joint. Toilets flushed, doors slammed. A disembodied voice was raised in outrage demanding that Laura Roc SHUT UP! and without breaking her rhythm as she ran her scales, Laura Roc sang FUCK YOU! and continued.

"Who's that singing?"

"A student. Mostly students live here."

"Are you a student?"

"Yes."

"Where?"

"Columbia."

"What subject?"

His impatience with her, and himself, exploded into a deep sigh. "Anthropology. Listen, here it is—" He swung a door open and entered.

"You look kind of old to be a student," she said, entering the room. It was cold and clean. The bed, which was a very old hospital type, was made. It looked very much like a room in a good clinic.

Behind them in the house, Laura Roc moved from scales to a study

8

piece. She had a very good voice and *Un bel di vedremo* soared through the cold halls.

"I'll take care of the rent with Mrs. Coffin—she's the manager—when I come back. I'll leave a note telling her that you're here."

She nodded. The quick bob up and down. "I understand, and I'm grateful. Thank you." Her eyes wandered; looked out of the window, withdrew.

Tonio got down on his knees and turned on the heat, twisting an ancient steam valve with great effort. The radiator began to clank immediately, and then settled down just as she uttered a strangled, half cry.

A bearded, nearly skeletal, figure in rags stood in the doorway. Eleanor turned instinctively to Tonio.

"It's okay," Tonio said, patting her arm. "Go on, Hal. Don't bother this girl now, do you hear me?"

"Sure, good buddy. Ten four." Hal turned and shambled down the hall. "Just lay back, Mama—lay back and say, Ahhh! . . ." He giggled.

Eleanor shivered in her pea jacket. "Is he a student too? What kind of a place is this?"

"He used to be a student." Tonio opened the closet and began pulling down blankets. "Now he's a full-time junkie. Comes from Los Angeles. His family thinks he's still going to Columbia and keeps sending him money, which he uses to buy dope. Been sleeping in the attic for three years. He won't bother you—and—" He turned and spoke pointedly: "Mrs. Coffin doesn't know he's here, so—"

"When will you be back? I mean—" She looked around, her eyes rejecting the sterile room.

"Mean what?"

"Nobody knows I'm here. I could rip things off, you know?"

Tonio studied her a moment. "Some people in this building are very nice. All of them work hard, very hard, for what little they have. I wouldn't advise it."

She turned and warmed her hands over the radiator. "What happened to your eye?"

"Viet Nam."

"You blind?"

"In one eye."

"Why don't you wear a glass eye, like Sammy Davis, Junior, or

9

Sandy Duncan, instead of wearing that patch? You look like a pirate."
She stared at him, waiting for an answer. When he didn't, she sat on the
side of the bed, bouncing on the springs. "Where do you live?"

"Top floor—one above this."

"Why don't you take me to your room?"

"There are reasons."

"Are you a fag?"

"Would it make any difference?"

"I just like to know where I stand," she said with more energy than
he would have expected.

"Right now," Tonio said, "you stand in a clean room, warm, with a
stomach full of ham and eggs and a five-dollar bill in your pocket. You
don't like it, split."

"Then you're not a fag?"

"You're asking what is all this going to cost you, right?"

She didn't answer. She bounced off the bed and spun around the
room, taking possession of it. She turned back with a big smile on her
face. The teeth were white and good. "After what's happened to me,
don't you think I should protect myself?"

"Lady," Tonio said firmly, "I don't know what happened to you. I
have only your word for that."

"Are you questioning my veracity?"

"No," Tonio said slowly. "I'm really questioning myself. And why
in Christ's name I should even consider you, or your problems for a
moment."

A burst of laughter at the door broke into their tensions. Laura Roc
entered, jostling him. She grinned, showing her big, strong white teeth.
She wore baggy trousers ten times too large for her, a T-shirt that hung
to her knees, with TEACHERS DO IT WITH CLASS printed over her bosom
and a Dolly Parton wig. Her face was covered with clown-white makeup.

She hardly glanced at Eleanor and spun around, ending in a grotesque
balletlike pose. "What do you think, Tonio? I'm working with a guy
from Juilliard who's El Blasto on B-flat trumpet—and we've got a deal
for The Plaza fountain. He plays and I sing, see? And dance. All the
schlock stuff. 'Habanera,' and a takeoff of La Strada—"

"Looks terrific, Laura," Tonio said grinning. "Really." Tonio liked

10

the tall, heavy girl with a wide mouth and glittering green eyes that set off her cascading blond hair. Up close she didn't look like much to Tonio, but he had once seen her in stage makeup for a student concert and she had presented a powerful and dramatic figure.

"What do you sing? Rock—country-western?" Eleanor asked.

It sounded innocent enough, but Tonio wasn't sure. He glanced at Laura, who had stopped her foolishness and stood very still appraising Eleanor. Tonio did not know what to expect.

Laura Roc took a deep breath. She took one step backward and planted her booted feet firmly on the floor. Her eyes flashed. And very carefully, chosing her best note and pitch, she opened up. She brought in slow and easy, soft, and then let it swell, opening her mouth wide and really letting go. When she got to the top and they thought she was finished, she poured more into it and let go completely. It was a sound, a single sound, but it was absolutely pure and rich, and in the confines of the marble halls, louder than anything Tonio had ever heard. But she wasn't finished yet. She brought it back down, as smooth as cream and finished easily where she had started.

"Jesus Christ, Laura—" Tonio said, her voice still ringing in his ears.

Laura Roc looked at Eleanor, who appeared to be in a state of shock. "Give my best to Tammy Wynette, music lover," she said, smiling through her teeth. She swept out of the room in her clown makeup and baggy trousers, Good Will boots, every inch the diva.

"Why was she dressed up like that?" Eleanor Cassie asked.

"She pays her own tuition at Juilliard and her own rent and food. One of the ways she earns money is being a street entertainer. She doesn't want anyone at school to know she's doing it, so she wears clown makeup and costumes. I've got to go—" Tonio turned to the door.

"I'll stay," Eleanor said simply. "And I won't rip anything off."

"That's very wise of you. I have to go to work now, after that I have a class. I usually get back around six. If you're here, you're here. If not, that's okay, too."

"Can I go outside the room?"

"Why not?"

"I'll be here. Six, you said?"

"Six."

She started taking off the rain-soaked pea jacket.

At the door of his room, Tonio waited until the hall on his floor was clear. And, when it was, stooped down quickly and peered into the keyhole of the dead bolt lock. The small piece of lint was undisturbed. He removed it carefully, straightened up, and inserted the key. When the door was unlocked, he eased it forward a half-inch. Using a standard seven-inch pocket comb, he inserted it into the crack and caught a strand of surgeon's suture thread in the teeth of the comb. He lifted it up carefully. Maintaining tension on the thread, he moved the door forward enough to get his full hand inside. He reached around, caught the thread, and lifted it up. Inside the room, the large loop at one end of the thread was then removed from a hook on the door. He glanced around and slipped inside.

He followed the thread to a one-hundred-watt light bulb delicately balanced on the edge of a worktable and examined it. His mark was there, a tiny scratch across the brand on the top of the bulb. He turned to the bathroom door, which was stiff and did not close completely. The pin was still on the top across the gap. There was no way the door could be opened, as stiff as it was, without dislodging the pin.

He had only one other trap. He went to the closet and checked the locks. He looked for and then removed with tweezers, a small piece of cotton lint from the keyholes of two locks and placed the lint, which was oily and dark, to one side.

There were no clothes in the closet. On the two shelves, instead of shirts, sweaters, handkerchiefs, jeans, and underwear, was an arsenal of weapons and electronic gear.

On the bottom shelf a one-foot-square box contained a dozen hand grenades; beside it, a Magnum .357, a Sten machine gun, and ammunition for both weapons. On the top shelf there was a large, table model computer, the smallest, full-capacity unit IBM manufactured. Beside the computer, there was a box containing semiconductors, silicone chips, wire, condensers. Everything was as it should be. He looked down at a flat cardboard box containing a dozen books on high-rise construction, the NYC Building Code, and hundreds of architects' working drawings; the edges of the top three sheets were irregularly spread apart, the distance between them measured one-quarter inch, then one-half inch, and one-quarter inch. They had not been disturbed. The traps were foolproof. If anyone had been in the room he would know it.

He closed and locked the closet and turned back to a worktable. He picked up the book he had forgotten and would need for class, then glanced at the wall over the table. A full page from the Real Estate section of the Sunday *New York Times* had been glued to the back of a popular poster, a three-by-five blowup of John Wayne in a scene from *Red River*. The poster had been there when he rented the room and it hung by a string on a nail in the wall. When he was alone, which was most of the time, he reversed the poster; when there was someone else in the room, or when he left, it was an innocent picture of a movie star.

A quarter of the page was taken up by a rendering of a midtown highrise building that had been proposed two years before and had been in construction for nearly as long. The paper was old and becoming brittle. A headline ran across the top. He read it again for at least the thousandth time though he knew it by heart. There were several subhead articles on the page going into greater detail about the various aspects of the building and construction.

ONE-HUNDRED-FLOOR ST. CYR TOWER NEARS COMPLETION;
FIFTH AVENUE HIGH RISE LATEST IN LUXURY-SECURITY MARKET
DELAYED SIX MONTHS BY LABOR DISPUTES;
COSTS WELL ABOVE TWO HUNDRED FIFTY MILLION
SUPERLUXURY HOTEL AND CO-OP APARTMENTS
By Dan Gordon

Want total security in the inner city? Want the convenience of four restaurants? (All at least Three Stars.) A first-rate nightclub? Want a heliport on the roof for easy flights to JFK, La Guardia, Newark, East Hampton? Want a major bank? A major stockbroker? Want *anything* in superluxury living?

It will be available at the St. Cyr Tower, midtown, Fifth Avenue.

In addition there will be four ballrooms, a Galleria Promenade comprising sixteen specialty shops; underground parking; eight banks of elevators; a three-bed clinic, with a separate intensive care unit and a doctor and nurse on duty twenty-four hours a day.

You can have this and more, much, much more at the new, exciting, extravagantly appointed St. Cyr Tower (Co-Ops) St. Cyr Hotel (no singles, only suites, please!) and floor-thru office space. You can have it, but it is going, *is going* to be the most expensive living in the Western world, perhaps in the entire world. And except for the St. Cyr Hotel section, where the mini-suites *start* at five hundred dollars a day, you don't rent at the St. Cyr Tower, you buy. "And only for cash," said owner-builder, E. Joseph Spain, internationally famous real-estate tycoon and financier, who added: "My concept was to offer total security and luxury living in the center of the greatest metropolis in the world. It will be available, soon, but for a price. And I might add that we are ninety-five percent sold. Don't call us, we'll call you. And be prepared to have your background checked out. If you've been given a ticket for speeding, we'll know about it. When I speak of security, I'm speaking about security *from the inside* as well as from the outside."

Asked if there was any significance that he had named his building after the famed French Military Academy, or St.-Cyr-au-Mont-d'Or, the French Police Academy, Mr. Spain smiled and shrugged.

He didn't read any more. He gazed at the newspaper and felt a good satisfying feeling—a sense—of near completion. There was still a great deal to be done, but he was close, very close.

He looked one more time at the drawing of the St. Cyr Tower and then reached out and stripped it from the back of the poster. He curled it into a ball, dropped it on the ashtray, set it afire, and watched it burn.

2 Both he and his twin brother had been wounded in Viet Nam. His twin had taken a bullet in the leg, while he had been seriously injured in the eye and had worn an eye patch temporarily to protect the retina. The injury caused exceptional sensitivity to light, but he was assured there was no permanent damage, that the eye would return to normal, and it did. He had several other wounds, two minor ones and one that was quite severe, but they were well taken care of, and when he was finished with Their War, he was sound and in good physical condition.

They had, like many twins, been inseparable and did almost everything as a team. They decided to join up together and both of them were outstanding soldiers. This was partially true because they had grown up around guns in southern Indiana, where their father had been sheriff of a rural county; and at a very early age they had seen the way men could treat each other.

The twins were always hanging around the jail, and they understood early what criminals were, and that their father and his deputies were on

15

the good side, using force to get another human being to submit to the will of law, and that was the way some things were in life. When it came to war, and time to join up, they gravitated to it without trauma, or any hang-ups, because it was an extension of the way they had been raised. There was a good side, and they were on it. And there was a bad side, and they were part of the machinery, like their father was, that dealt with it.

While he was still in the hospital his brother went back to his unit and was almost immediately reported missing. After months of inquiry, there was no word on his twin—whether he was dead or alive or captured—and it was his persistent search for his brother through Army red tape that had led him to go into Intelligence. It was the best way, he thought, to learn anything at all—because dealing with the fact that his brother was Missing in Action was very difficult for him.

There was no doubt that his early environment around the county jail in the small Indiana township, and the household talk of his father, enabled him to function so well in the interrogation of prisoners. He had heard his father do it hundreds of times and he really had a knack for Intelligence. When they realized what they had in him, they made him a lieutenant and sent him behind enemy lines.

He didn't mind. He saw it as another way of getting information about his twin before it could get fouled up in reports sent back through the chain of command for evaluation.

At first he was terrified at being alone in the jungle, but eventually he overcame this and he became very cold in dealing with his fears. He perfected an internal discipline over himself and a way of staying alone in the forward areas for weeks at a time, eating snakes and rats; burying his fecal matter, leaving no trace of his presence, running, hiding, observing the enemy, and sending back invaluable reports. And always, always, making his own personal inquiries about his twin.

Eventually, too, he became more and more direct, even harsh in his interrogation methods when one of the enemy was captured; and if it was an officer, or better yet, the political adviser attached to a unit, he was unyielding. And while he always had good military information to send back, he also pressed hard for information about his brother.

He was never very successful, and by the time Their War was over, and They decided They couldn't win, and pulled out, he had gained an extra dimension of control over himself and had become self-amused. A deadly loner.

It was close to the very end, when even the Generals were in a panic, and everybody was getting out the best way they could, that he got his first solid piece of information, and proof, that his twin was still alive and held prisoner in North Viet Nam.

At first he was elated with the news, but it was to prove as frustrating as not knowing anything at all. Prisoners returned, and his brother was not among them. Then more prisoners were brought home, and still his brother did not appear. All of his efforts were turned away. The Defense Department had no information on his twin at all; officially, he was still MIA. When he became a pest at the Pentagon, they tried to dismiss him. They were nice about it, but they were also firm. There was no evidence, officially or otherwise, that his twin was still alive or a prisoner of war, just MIA.

They had lost Their War. They had had three sympathetic presidents, a willing and generous Congress, and still They had blown Their War. And his constant, pestering, demanding presence as much as anything reminded them just how badly They *had* blown it. Yet his record in the field was something They could understand, and felt an obligation to deal with. They had even been a little reluctant to see him go. It was Frank Woodies, a captain in Viet Nam who had worked with him, and who was now a colonel, who finally consented to see him in his Pentagon office after having read everything there was in the records on the twins. And it was that conversation, more than anything else, that gave him hope.

They sat in deep leather lounge chairs in the colonel's office, drank coffee, talked of their exploits in Viet Nam, and watched the pale wintry sun die over the Virginia countryside. It was a cold scene, without snow, getting late in the afternoon and from their window they could see the lights of hundreds of automobiles leaving the parking lot as the workday ended. And then in the same calm conversational voice they had been using for over an hour, the colonel told him that there was nothing, absolutely nothing in the records, and he had searched everywhere: there was not a shred of evidence to support the lieutenant's story that his brother was alive—*except* the lieutenant's story.

The colonel didn't expect the sudden hard voice that challenged him

17

in the darkness of the office. All information, the lieutenant responded, that he had gotten from Tien Bha, a Cong political cadre leader he had captured in the jungle, was totally accurate. How could the colonel say the part about his brother was merely *his story?* The colonel had winced under the cover of darkness, and was glad that the lieutenant did not see it.

They talked some more, but the atmosphere had cooled. The lieutenant knew that the colonel had information and was not going to give it to him, and he was at a loss as to how he was going to get it.

In a vicious, criminal war on both sides, much of what the colonel saw, he wished he never had. But there had been moments—moments. The man sitting with him in the dark, drinking coffee, had supplied a few of those moments. When the phrase "deadly force" came up in conversation around the Pentagon, and it did, often, he thought of the lieutenant. He would have been a major now, if he had stayed in. Not bad for someone who had not graduated from the Point. The lieutenant was the best Intelligence officer he had ever encountered, much better than the colonel was. As a psychologist in interrogation, there was none better. He knew electronics and how to adapt them to field conditions. He *understood* communications, not just information, but how to *communicate* it. And he was positively a devil with explosives . . . a devil. But there was one thing above all that the colonel would never forget: the moment he saw the leaflet dropped by the enemy. There were a great many medals handed out in Viet Nam, and most of them well-deserved, but there had been damn few with a price on their heads. It was like a wanted poster from the Old West: The lieutenant's picture and underneath it: TEN THOUSAND DOLLARS—DEAD OR ALIVE. He regretted that he had never kept one. Some of the men had. He wished he had one.

And then the colonel started talking again, with what seemed to the lieutenant renewed vigor; a man with something to say and finding it difficult to get to the point.

The lieutenant sat very still and listened. To almost anyone else, it might have sounded like the rambling of an old friend, but to his interrogator's ear, the tonal inflections, stresses, were like numbers on an interstate highway.

He had always liked New York, the colonel had said. It was like no other city in the world. Among many other things, there were the hundreds, even thousands of fine restaurants of every national character. The colonel was especially fond of Mexican food, and there was one exceptional restaurant near the United Nations that he thought as good as any in the world. But more than any other consideration there was always the possibility of meeting old friends—it always amazed the colonel how one could go almost anywhere in the city and bump into someone he knew. And there were so many refugees in the city, so many different languages spoken, that the city was truly cosmopolitan. Only recently the colonel had been in Manhattan and his electric shaver had broken, and would the lieutenant believe it, not a block away from his hotel on East Fiftieth Street there was a fix-it shop—did the lieutenant remember how clever the Vietnamese in Saigon were at repairing transistor radios and the like? But, the colonel had said, if the lieutenant was partial to Mexican food—when it was prepared correctly—there was none better than El Ranchero.

The lieutenant had sat and listened and waited. When the colonel excused himself for a moment and left the office, he was not surprised to find that the lieutenant was gone when he returned.

Because he was very skilled in such things, the lieutenant did not approach the fix-it shop, or El Ranchero, until he had observed both places over a period of a week, scrutinizing, as best he could, anyone who went in or out. He didn't know what to expect, or what might tie together in his search for information about his twin, but whatever it was, he had not expected to see Tien Bha, the Cong political cadre leader, getting off a bus and walking to work in a small fix-it shop on Third Avenue in Manhattan. Tien Bha was older, and had put on twenty pounds and was quite different from the man the lieutenant had captured and interrogated for several days in the jungle, and who had been the one to tell him his brother was alive, a prisoner of war, but it was the same man.

He did not question Tien Bha's presence in New York. He remembered the man as being very bright and quick when he had questioned him in the jungle. Most of the political cadre leaders were also Intelligence agents. It was not difficult to imagine Tien Bha given orders to infiltrate the flood of refugees fleeing the Communist takeover and make his way to the United States. A fix-it shop only a few blocks away from the United Nations, from his point of view, confirmed an underground contact point.

But Tien Bha had not gotten past Colonel Woodies.

For the next several days he had let his beard grow, had slept in his clothes, and wearing dark glasses he had taken an old electric toaster he bought at the Salvation Army into the fix-it shop to be repaired. Tien Bha himself waited on him, and standing across the counter from the one man who might be able to tell him more about his brother, there was no question of his identity. He was very finely controlled, and kept his fury down and did not grab the little man and try to force information out of him. There would be a row, the cops would come, and, whatever the outcome, Tien Bha would vanish. The toaster would be ready in a week, Tien Bha told him. The lieutenant had thanked him and left, his entire body quivering once he was safely outside.

Not getting anywhere just watching El Ranchero, encouraged that he had found Tien Bha, the lieutenant decided to have a Mexican lunch.

He was less surprised finding Tien Bha in Manhattan than he was to see ex-Corporal Harmon acting as maître d'. Though they recognized each other immediately, neither man gave any indication they had ever seen each other before. He ate a good meal, and when he asked for the check, the ex-corporal himself presented it, and stood waiting while the lieutenant memorized the telephone number written on a slip of paper on top of the check. He had placed a twenty-dollar bill on top of the phone number, thanked the maître d' for an excellent meal, and left.

Later that night, in a quiet second-floor French restaurant on Madison Avenue above an art gallery, the lieutenant did not ask, nor did ex-Corporal Harmon volunteer what his relationship was to Colonel Woodies. The lieutenant explained quickly and briefly about his brother, Tien Bha, and why he was there.

Ex-Corporal Harmon was a small, thin man with a gold bicuspid and skin the color of creamed coffee. A Chicano from Dallas, the lieutenant remembered his speech as being thick with southwestern rhythms. He had adopted the protective coloration of the New Yorker in manner and dress, and without it being too obvious, ex-Corporal Harmon had been successful in shedding his regional identity.

Ex-Corporal Harmon asked a few questions, nodding at the answers,

20

and sipped his wine, barely touching his lips with the glass. The air conditioning whispered against the August heat as he considered the lieutenant's question: Could Tien Bha deal for the twin brother, and if so, for how much?

The meeting did not last longer than a half hour, and when they parted on the street, the corporal, without preliminaries, explained his position. He was going to do what he could, which might be a lot or a little, but whatever it was he did, that was the end of it. The lieutenant was never to get in touch with him again. And then he allowed himself the one speculation that gave the lieutenant hope—real hope. Colonel Woodies had probably known that the lieutenant had saved the corporal's life on three different occasions, and therefore was the one man who might be in a position to do something willingly, unofficially. He would help, the corporal told him, but regardless of what he came up with, he considered his three IOU's canceled.

The lieutenant agreed. He wrote rapidly on a slip of paper and handed it over. Full name, rank, and the serial number of his brother—and as the ex-corporal started to walk away, the lieutenant grabbed him by the arm. There was a bottom line to his brother's identification. As twins, the lieutenant said, he and his brother had done something at a Fourth of July picnic. He wanted to know what it was they did, the names, and what happened as a result. It was something that only the twin brothers knew about.

Ex-Corporal Harmon left, saying that he would call the lieutenant at his hotel when he had something—probably within a week or ten days.

But it was not a week or ten days, it was closer to three weeks before Harmon called him at the Hilton and invited him for a ferry ride to Staten Island.

It was one of the first really cool nights in September, the air was clear, and the lights from Brooklyn and the Jersey shore glittered in the late evening. They leaned against the railing and smoked. There were very few passengers at that time of night and they were not bothered about being overheard. Ex-Corporal Harmon talked slowly and quietly. The lieutenant and his twin brother had been caught screwing the town whore by their father, who was county sheriff. It had been the first woman either of them had ever had, and they had mowed lawns for a month

21

to get the money. When their father caught them, instead of giving them a strapping, he threw down his five bucks and joined in.

The lieutenant had turned away: *His twin was alive*.

That was the good news, there was more, ex-Corporal Harmon told him, and he wanted the lieutenant to pay close attention, and hear him out. There was a lot of action that went on down at the UN. There was every kind of gig one could think of, with all kinds of bad-ass people doing things to each other, looking for the edge, shooting angles, shaving points. Guns, information, precious stones, scag, coke, even people, especially people. People bought and sold as easily as walking into Nedick's for a hot dog and orange juice.

Oil was big right then, ex-Corporal Harmon said, and had been since Iran was blown away. He heard oil deals going down in his restaurant just about every week between Israel and Iran. Nobody is mad at anybody when oil is on the line. And the general population of Manhattan was up to its armpits in spies, ex-Corporal Harmon stated. There were so many spies at the UN he sometimes thought the whole island of Manhattan would sink into the harbor from the weight and numbers. What he was trying to explain to the lieutenant was simple. He had a connection at the UN. He did not work for Woodies—directly—but he did odd jobs now and then, and as a result, any restaurant troubles with the Alcoholic Beverage Control, or the Board of Health would vanish. But even Colonel Woodies did not know the name of his connection at the UN. It was his ace.

Ex-Corporal Harmon's voice became soft as he continued to explain. His connection at the UN had a connection of his own, who had still another connection, and so on, and so on. And everybody at the UN had diplomatic immunity, coming and going by the thousands. Right through Kennedy they brought in, and took out, anything and everything, slipping by customs and immigration, no questions asked. And he had been personally assured that the major source of supply of heroin into the country was brought in by the diplomats with total immunity. It was, ex-Corporal Harmon continued, a license to steal.

That was the background, and the authority of his information, ex-Corporal Harmon declared, but with all of his connections, he could not find out what it was that the lieutenant's twin had done, but it was emphasized in no uncertain terms that North Viet Nam really had it in for him. He had been tried as a war criminal and given life at hard labor. He was a special, ex-Corporal Harmon emphasized, with a twenty-four-hour guard. Getting him sprung was not going to be easy, not easy at all. It could be done, but the price, money in cash, was out of sight.

The lieutenant was more than surprised that a man as politicized as Tien Bha would take money.

Money, ex-Corporal Harmon assured him, would buy anything. Perhaps Tien Bha wouldn't go for cash, but somebody else would.

They had reached Staten Island. They walked out, then around to the other side of the waiting room, and took the return trip to Manhattan.

Suppose Tien Bha was a patriot, a real VC Marxist, ex-Corporal Harmon explained, and suppose he had orders from Hanoi to get the rail schedules out of a munitions factory near Canton? Or perhaps find out how many missiles were aimed at Hanoi, or whatever? That's what *Tien Bha* wants. So, the next step would be to find out *who* had *that* information, and find out what *he* wanted. Maybe the second guy wanted to know how many missile subs the United States had off the coast of China? So find the guy that has *that* information, and get *his* price. Eventually there was the stopper. The one guy that wanted only cash, and with him the deal was struck. The money is handed over, and he then hands over the missile count on the subs for the Canton train schedules, and the train schedules go to Tien Bha, who sends them to Hanoi, who hands over the twin brother. He would get his brother back, healthy, no bones broken, clear-minded, in ex-Corporal Harmon's restaurant two weeks after the lieutenant deposited $4 million, American, in a Swiss bank.

The lieutenant had absorbed the news like a man hit in the back of the head with a baseball bat. But why so much! His brother had been nothing more than a grunt. What could he have done?

Ex-Corporal Harmon was slow in answering. His connection had said they referred to the twin as an animal, and they had wanted him a long time. And wanted him so badly, that they had posted a $10,000 reward on his head, dead or alive.

The lieutenant knew then why there had been no return of his brother along with thousands of other POW's. He understood why there had been no records for Colonel Woodies to examine, why there had been no information at all.

His brother had not been in Intelligence. He had been in a company. A sergeant. They were super-identical twins. His mother and father could hardly tell them apart, and many times they had covered for each other without their parents ever knowing. The military government of North Viet Nam had the wrong man.

They thought they had *him*.

The lieutenant felt an affinity for Manhattan from the very beginning as he began to prowl day and night, familiarizing himself with neighborhoods and districts; the means and the routine of the New Yorker's way, his manner of addressing himself to daily problems. He met cold detachment everywhere. Hustle and con. Strip and run. The indifference, distrust, and disinterest of everyone and in everything, appealed to his sense of logic and order. New York, he sensed, was the essence of the way things are.

You spoke to no one, and no one spoke to you. You were an invisible man. You were simply alone in a city of 10 million; no one knew your name, no one knew where you came from, where you were going, what you were doing, how you were making out, or what your life goals might be. The city, the *entire* city, and its people became his companion. Hot or cold, wet or dry, dirty or clean, dangerous, loud, uninhibited, and secretive, Manhattan possessed all of the necessary parts for his developing plan.

His plan did not come all at once. He was a trained, disciplined, careful observer, and did not bother with hunches. He would conceive a plan, and then after exhaustive examination and review, make the GO, or NO-GO, decision. It was nothing more than he had been taught to do. He was very well trained. The best brains in U.S. Army Intelligence had contributed all of their resources into making him what he was.

He began by reading *The New York Times* from front to back every day for weeks, often sitting alone in his furnished room, sometimes in the cathedral-like reading room of the New York Public Library.

The first step, he knew, regardless of what he decided to do, was to establish a totally new identity. Following a technique he had learned in Viet Nam, which had filtered back by those who had deserted and made it back to the States successfully with new ID's, he began visiting the largest cemeteries in the New York area. He spent days wandering up and down rows of tombstones, reading names, until he found exactly what he was looking for. He copied down the information:

JAIME ANTONIO VEGA
Born May 1st—Died May 1st
1951
Never to see the light of this
world yet instantly the glory
of the next

He dyed his hair jet-black with an inexpensive formula bought at a corner drugstore, had his hair cut considerably shorter than was stylish, and slick-combed it back. He started wearing the eye patch over his wounded eye again, and then shopped the Forty-second Street area until he found a photo shop that would, for five dollars, supply an ID with an official-looking seal on bonded paper, a postage-stamp photograph, and all of his vital statistics sealed in a plastic envelope.

His next step was Birth and Death records of New York City, on Worth Street in Lower Manhattan, where he asked for and was given a certified copy of "his" birth certificate. No questions asked. Armed now with the birth certificate, he applied for a Social Security number, and was assured that it would be mailed to him within a few weeks. No questions asked.

His next step was to enroll in Columbia University for a summer course in anthropology and modern philosophy. But when he was asked for the name of his high school so they could get a copy of his transcript, he mumbled something about not being sure if he wanted to take a credit course or just a noncredit summer course, and left.

But he would need the credit course. He needed full enrollment.

He found 114 Antonio Vegas with telephones in the five boroughs of New York City, and armed with a pocketful of dimes, he located a little-used phone booth in Central Park with a pleasant view and started at the top of the list.

To each number that answered, he asked the same question. "Is this the residence of Tonio Vega who graduated 1969 from Stuyvesant High School downtown on the East Side?"

The first thirty-seven Tonio Vegas he called either did not answer, or

25

had not graduated from any high school. But on the thirty-eighth try, he got a response.

"My husband ain't home now, but he graduated high school in Puerto Rico—in Ponce—who are you, mister? How come you askin'?"

He was enrolled the next day for a full-credit course, pending receipt of his transcripts from Puerto Rico. They anticipated no problem. It was done all the time.

He received a Columbia University ID, again with a photograph. A driver's license was next. After he had rented his room at the Riverside Arms, and felt he was safe with a permanent address, he applied for and received in the mail, a valid U.S. passport issued to Jaime Antonio Vega. He rented a safe-deposit box in that name, placed all of the records of his true identity inside, and emerged from the Dry Dock Savings Bank as Tonio Vega.

Tonio Vega, a dark-haired, one-eyed veteran of the Viet Nam war, was generally liked by his fellow students, but considered a loner. Yet this was understandable because he was getting a late start as a result of Their Fucking War. He was working hard toward a degree in anthropology and his intentions were to work in the field, perhaps in East Africa, following Leakey's basic work. Sound, respectable, though a little dull, and definitely a grind, Tonio Vega was swept into the mainstream of Columbia University life, the Riverside Arms, and ultimately Manhattan without question, or interest, in him or his ambitions.

It was soon after he moved into the Riverside Arms that he read an elaborate story in the *Times* on the labor troubles in the construction of the St. Cyr Tower. Work on the superluxury, supersecure pad for the very rich was at a standstill. In the same issue of the *Times,* there was a fully covered story of an attempted hijacking of an airplane, and a demand for ransom. The hijackers had been caught when they had been outmaneuvered at the payoff.

There was a link between the stories, and he spent three days reading and studying the two reports; he read all of the New York papers and the national news magazines which carried the story, trying to put the pieces together and find the connection.

What had intrigued him? What would be the working procedure? He went downtown to the St. Cyr building site and studied the bare steel.

He took each problem separately and worked on it until he was satisfied with the solution. He then went to the next problem, discarding that solution entirely if it did not fit into what he had already planned and knew *would* work. It was heady stuff and using inductive logic, he built his plan with all of the skill of a dedicated scientist.

His thinking began to accelerate when he figured out the payoff. And after he had spent an entire week examining his idea, and testing it against every possible flaw he could think of, he knew he had the most important part of his project.

It was a payoff that had never been used before, and therefore, there would be no established ways of dealing with it. By the time they figured out the mechanics, *what* he was doing, and *how,* he would be gone.

In the time it took to erect the St. Cyr Tower, to furnish it, and move tenants in, no one was more interested than Tonio Vega. Excellently trained to take advantage of a weakness in the enemy, and with the payoff set, he began his penetration of the defenses.

He had something extra going for him that he had not counted on in the very beginning: You could get away with anything in New York.

He scribbled a note to Mrs. Coffin, reset his traps, locked the door, and hurried out. He would be more than an hour late, but they wouldn't fire him. Delivery boys for delicatessens were hard to come by. Especially Columbia University students who were hardworking and stable, industrious studs on the make. The world, he knew, loved to see young men break their balls on the road to success. Marty's Deli, off Madison Avenue in the East Fifties, was no exception.

He got off the express at Fifty-ninth and walked east on Central Park South, cursing the rain that had started up again, moving with a steady step. The park was shrouded in mist and rain. He was late for work and they were not all that sympathetic. They yelled a lot. But he didn't mind, even when the black cook, who disliked him and knew that he had been in Viet Nam, called him Patch, and delighted in ridiculing him.

"Here comes Patch! The college student. With one eye he gunna tell the world all about the apes and monkeys, and where we all come from! Hey, Patch! Get your ass up to Eight-two-A, the St. Cyr Tower, with this order. Them painters and plumbers ain't going to give you no big tip, you don't hurry. Get it on, sucker, get it mother-on!''

Several people hanging over coffee and rolls at the counter laughed, and waited for Tonio's riposte. And when no smart-ass, hostile answer came back, they dismissed him as a schmuck.

"Okay, Sarge," Tonio said quietly.

He knew the black cook liked his former military rank. He played on it. He began preparing his plastic carrying hampers, reminding himself that it was Friday and he would have to go to Queens that night.

That same morning, Chris Murdoch was pulled out of a deep sleep by the ringing of the phone. The woman in bed with him stirred, mumbled something, and pressed deeper into the covers. The phone rang again. Murdoch fought himself awake, adjusting to the hard fact that he was not going to get any more sleep that morning. There was rain outside the seventy-first floor of the St. Cyr Tower. He fumbled for a cigarette and managed to get it lit as the phone rang again.

"Murdoch!"

"Yes, Mr. Spain," he said, coming awake at the sound of his employer's voice. "Good morning."

"Good morning. Get up here as soon as you can."

"'kay. Be up soon as I get myself together." He dropped the phone and flopped back onto the pillow. "Maggie?"

The woman did not respond. He put his arms behind his head and stared out of the floor-to-ceiling window. Office lights flickered on in

29

Rockefeller Center and the Pan Am Building, emerging through the thick mist. Below him, Fifth Avenue was beginning the day with growling taxis, slamming doors, and the impatience of racing engines, like a low-grade irritation that would last all day. Manhattan, he thought, reaching guiltily for another cigarette, was gunning up for another run. It was late October and the first chilling day of the season. New Yorkers awoke that morning to the full realization that the recent good summer was gone forever.

The automatic clock radio came on. It would rain all day and probably tomorrow. There had been a riot at the Welfare Office in Brooklyn and the cops were called. The massage parlors on Eighth Avenue were distributing flyers on the street advertising sixteen-year-old virgins, and someone had complained to the Better Business Bureau. Another New Jersey congressman had been indicted.

A muscular headlong rush into the rainy, chilling day.

But he was not part of it. Not yet. He was seventy-one floors above it all in a well-furnished three-room apartment, provided with his job as vice-president and general manager of the St. Cyr Tower, Fifth Avenue, New York, N.Y. 10022.

"Maggie?"

"Ummh . . . "

"How'd you sleep?"

"Okay. You?"

"Deep—good."

She adjusted to him and he slipped his member into the hollow of her thighs; there were a few more bodily adjustments and then, just before they became still, she pressed hard with her buttocks against his stomach. She blew a few strands of dark hair out of her face and opened one eye, saw the rain beating against the window and closed her eyes immediately. "Who called?"

"Spain."

"Does he often call you in the morning?"

"Often."

They lay together in silence, reluctant to plunge into the new day and the unknown that it would bring. Not the world they had left the night before. They were both too cynical to expect that a good day yesterday would mean a good one today. They had known each other a little more than six months, and from the beginning there had been an easy, low-key touch to their relationship. Both of them had been married, both were in their thirties—Murdoch was thirty-nine, Maggie Gaston was thirty-four—and they were satisfied with their relationship the way it was. She reached between her thighs and guided him. "Just like this— just like this—" she said quietly.

He circled her with his arm and took her breasts in his hand, responding to her quiet tensions, easing his way forward.

After his shower, Murdoch sat on the side of the bed toweling his hair, watching Maggie pad nude around the room, damp from her own shower, collecting her things. Tall, with a scruff of black hair kept short for ease of daily washing, she slumped a little from years of hanging over a drafting table creating fabric designs. But she was altogether the sum of parts that was totally female. By the time he had slipped the knot in his tie Maggie was dressed, had coffee made, and was seated at the small backgammon table placed against the huge window overlooking Manhattan. It was a view, he thought, that was almost worth the job. She sat, pensive, staring.

"What is it?"

"Remember I told you about Ben Schwartz? My Mozart–Bach-loving old friend who used some of my designs?"

"The one mugged and murdered?"

"It was on a day like this," Maggie said bitterly. "He was so civilized! Goddammit, what a waste. Sometimes I hate this city."

"It wasn't always like this, like it is now." Murdoch had been born and raised in Manhattan. His feel for the pulse, the rhythm of the city, was finely tuned. He knew what the city had been and what it had become. "It used to be terrific—"

"I know, I know. You've told me often enough about how great it was. Well, this is now!" She got up and began to collect her things.

Maggie came from Iowa and her sensibilities were easily bruised. Like many provincials who had moved to New York, they were eager for new experience, but when threatened, clung to traditional values, often characterizing them as "good" or "Christian" or "civilized." Murdoch was patient with her in such moments. He liked his life the way it was and he liked Maggie the way she was. He didn't want anything to interrupt it.

They rode the express elevator to the street level and after he had put her into a cab, he paused for a moment to breathe in the cool, damp chill of the morning. Fifth Avenue was a snarl of traffic, umbrellas, raincoats, plastic hats, darting pedestrians, and cops looking like giant Popsicles in their orange Day-Glo slickers. The lobby was a bedlam with travelers arriving, departing; bellmen staggered under the weight of luggage. New Yorkers using the floor-through lobby as an underpass to escape the rain added to the confusion. It was, Murdoch thought, going to be a hell of a day. And it would start with E. Joseph Spain, builder, owner, and resident of the Tower.

He avoided Stephen Kosinski, the desk clerk, signaling for his attention, sure that the problem was a fouled up reservation. He ducked into a block of elevators and stopped before a polished oak door marked Private. He inserted a key, unlocked the door, and stepped into an elevator with only two stops: the lobby and Spain's penthouse.

He hardly glanced at the penthouse, or the spectacular view of the city, where the taller buildings emerged as shadowy gray figures in the swirling rain. He followed Jimco, Spain's Number One boy, bodyguard, and general functionary, to the roof garden and dashed for a glass gazebo. He broke into the interior breathing hard and flinging water from his hands.

Spain was seated to one side, still in robe and pajamas, talking quietly on the phone. He was not alone.

"What's going on?" Murdoch frowned, wiping his hands and face with a table napkin. Andy Brooks, head of security for the St. Cyr Tower, was heavy-lidded and his eyes were red. He needed a shave and looked as if he had been up all night. One of the orange employee files was on the coffee table. Spain only glanced at him as Murdoch poured a cup of coffee and sat down.

"I'll get back to you," Spain said into the phone. He hung up. "Tell him," he said to Brooks.

"Tell me what?"

Brooks handed him a slip of paper that had been torn from a small common scratch pad. It was typewritten, in capital letters:

THIS PROVES THAT I HAVE
AND THAT I CAN AND THAT
I WILL PENETRATE YOUR
SECURITY. THIS IS NUMBER ONE.
YOURS,
—THREAT

Murdoch read it three times. He went cold with tension.

"Show him the rest of it," Spain said. He watched Murdoch speculatively. Spain was a thickset man, medium height, deeply tanned, with lines running from either side of his nose to the corners of his mouth. He was tough and he was able, and, in Murdoch's eyes, the most devastatingly honest man he had ever known.

"The note was inside the beer can, which was inside the bag," Andy Brooks said. He held a brown paper bag by the top edge, placed it on the table and opened it. "In addition to the note, there were eighteen Lincoln head pennies."

"Pennies?" Murdoch repeated.

"Pennies," Spain said, sitting back, staring at Murdoch with black eyes. "One-cent pieces. Coin of the realm." He smoothed his hair, crossed his legs, and sipped his coffee. He did not take his eyes off Murdoch's face.

Brooks took a handkerchief from his pocket and unfolded it carefully on the table. Murdoch stared at the small pile of coins as if he had never seen any before.

"The note, and the pennies, were inside the beer can?" Murdoch asked.

Brooks nodded.

"Who took them out?"

"One of our maids; she found it."

"Just this? The brown paper bag, with the can inside, and inside the beer can, the note and the pennies? Anything else?"

"That's it," Brooks replied.

Murdoch started to pick up the bag and Brooks cautioned him. "It might have prints on it, Chris."

Murdoch took his own handkerchief and separated the wrinkled folds of the top of the paper bag and looked inside. He used a ball-point pen, reached inside and inserted the pen into the flip-top hole of the can and withdrew it. He held it up. There was nothing significant about it that he could see. An empty beer car, ubiquitous, seen everywhere, like acne on the face of America. He returned it to the bag, looking up at Brooks.

"Where was it found? When?"

"At four o'clock this morning in back of a bank of computers on the seventh floor. That's International Traders, the stocks-and-bonds people."

"So?"

Andy Brooks leaned forward tiredly. He sipped his coffee. "There is only one door into the International's computer rooms. There's a guard on it at all times when it is in use. No one—absolutely no one—gets inside unless he or she is an officer of the company."

"And when it's not in use?"

"Locked door, made of steel, combination lock," Brooks said.

"Why so much security?"

"The computer is hooked into a satellite. When the U.S. markets are closed down, other markets around the world are just opening up, and International's people around the world feed information back to the computer, twenty-four hours a day, which is then encoded. Anyone getting an advanced look on information about a possible new gold strike in South Africa could get a jump on the market."

Murdoch glanced at Spain, who nodded confirmation. "More or less standard procedure with big outfits like International."

"What was a maid—*our* maid—doing at International Traders at four a.m.?"

"Her, and International's night-security man, Manuel Lucas, have been hitting on each other in the ladies' room."

"Why there?" Murdoch raised his eyebrows.

Brooks shrugged. "They have a studio couch—for sick-headache time."

Murdoch picked up the employee file. "This hers?"

Andy nodded. "I got it without your secretary knowing. I figured if you wanted her to know anything, she could get it from you."

Murdoch grunted and glanced at Spain. His employer wanted an older, more experienced man as head of security, but Murdoch had made a strong pitch for Brooks. At the time he had wondered how the New York Police Department could have let such a fine prospect go, but they had, along with hundreds of other cops, during a recent financial crisis.

He shuffled through the file quickly. Estella Malendez: twenty-seven, born San Juan; three years kitchen help at the Hilton; one year kitchen help New York Hospital; two years as night maid at the St. Moritz; then her service at the St. Cyr Tower. Married, two children. One of tens of thousands of service workers in New York with similar or near identical records and backgrounds.

Murdoch hoisted the beer can and turned it slowly, scrutinizing.

"A crazy?" Brooks asked tentatively.

"Or, someone at International who thinks it's funny to pull our dicks," Spain said.

"Or it could be real," Murdoch said. "What do you think, Andy?"

"Mr. Murdoch, I'd have to take it seriously."

"I agree," Murdoch said slowly, looking at Spain, but the owner did not commit himself one way or the other. "I want to speak to Estella Malendez. And get a line on Lucas. Background. Married. Kids. Gambler. In debt—whatever. Spooky sense of humor."

"Spooky?"

"Oddball," Murdoch said. "Practical-joker type. I'll be in the house all day, so make it as soon as you can. And make it quiet with Mrs. Malendez. Routine. Don't frighten her. Remember, she was intelligent enough, and had enough courage to expose her affair with Lucas to let us know about it. The least we can do is to keep her confidence." Murdoch paused. He sat back. He wiped his face. "Who else knows about this?"

"As far as I know, just the maid, and the security man, Lucas," Brooks said. "And the three of us."

"Let's keep it that way," Murdoch said.

Brooks nodded.

"And not a word to anyone," Spain cautioned.

"I understand, sir."

"How many of your people are out? On sick leave? Vacation?" Murdoch asked.

"None at all."

"Are they all in the city?"

Brooks nodded. "Most of them will be here—" he glanced at his watch, "—in about an hour to change shift."

"Set up a meeting for security people from all three shifts in my apartment for ten o'clock."

"Okay."

"I appreciate the way you handled this, Andy," Murdoch said. "So far, there are only six people who know about this. Keep it that way."

"Who's the sixth?" Brooks asked, after making a mental count.

Murdoch tapped the typewritten note. "Threat."

Spain was silent for a long time after Andy Brooks had left. He poured coffee for Murdoch and himself, stood, and began to pace the gazebo. He sat down. He leaned forward, resting his elbows on his knees, and stared at the tops of his slippers. Murdoch waited. He then turned suddenly and folded the corners of the handkerchief over the coins and shook it. The pennies rattled against each other. "These bothered me for a while," Murdoch said.

"Oh?" Spain said. "And you're not bothered anymore?"

"It was to make sure that whoever discovered the can would be curious enough to look inside."

The phone rang. Spain picked it up, listened a moment and hung up with a brief "Thank you." He replaced the phone, pushed a call button on the phone, reached over and tapped the note. "And this?"

"It could be a joker. Someone who has no intention of carrying it any further. A needler. Someone giving you a little shaft."

"I have a lot of enemies," Spain said. "More than your average self-made American millionaire." He looked Murdoch in the eye. "I am not loved," he said deadpan.

The door opened and Jimco stepped inside the gazebo, and waited. He was a tall man, thin and muscular with close cropped-gray hair and a frozen eye.

"That was Kennedy," Spain said. "The plane is ready and the helicopter will be here in five minutes. Are we all set to leave?''

"Anytime."

"The London documents?" Spain asked.

Jimco nodded. "And the Madrid contracts."

"I'll dress on the plane," Spain said. Jimco nodded and left. Spain turned back to Murdoch. "I may be gone a month—more or less. You can always get in touch with me, but before I go, I want to know how you're going to handle this."

"As if we were dealing with a mad bomber. One of New York's crazies."

"And if it is a crazy, as you call him?"

"We wait until he makes another move to determine that."

"Why wait?"

"I didn't mean," Murdoch said confidently, "that there wasn't anything we couldn't do now, or until—if and when—he does make another move. We have a pretty elaborate security file, computer-indexed, on everyone who works here—*and,* everyone who has applied for employment and was turned down. It's going to mean a lot of extra work, a lot of it for nothing, but we start with everyone and anyone who has a connection with the St. Cyr. But the first step would be a special team, a man and a dog, looking for a bomb."

"You think it might be a bomb?"

"I don't think we should take the chance that it isn't."

"You want more manpower, is that it?"

"And," Murdoch said slowly, "I want to bring Jesse Solomon into the picture."

"Who's he?"

"Chief of Detectives, NYPD. He's a personal friend who will give us expert advice and keep his mouth shut."

"Most New York cops I've come in contact with are publicity hounds. *How* do you know he can be trusted?"

"When we staffed our security, I went to him for advice. He worked very closely with me and we got good people. Ninety percent of our security people are ex-New York City cops. He owes me. He'll keep quiet."

Spain thought about that a moment and nodded. "Okay, you make sense."

"I try to," Murdoch said dryly.

Spain started to respond, but the sudden overwhelming roar of the helicopter landing on the roof wiped out his voice. Jimco appeared at the door of the gazebo and Spain stood up. When the rotor noise began to subside, Spain turned back to Murdoch. "Christ! What a world we live in. I build the finest luxury complex in the world, with the latest security, and in fact, that was the main point: security. And here some crazy nut, or worse, a felon, or whatever, comes along with an empty beer car, a fistful of pennies, and signs himself 'Threat,' and we've got to take it seriously."

"The options are thin," Murdoch said. "I'm sorry."

"Get this lousy business over with as soon as possible, Chris. Keep me informed step by step. Find the son of a bitch, and nail him."

Spain dashed across the roof to the waiting helicopter in bedroom slippers, bathrobe flapping in the wind, and within seconds was airborne.

Once the helicopter was gone, Chris Murdoch sat very still in the gazebo watching the rain whip around the glass panels and had another cup of coffee. He had known it was going to be a hell of a day, but nothing like this.

Murdoch entered his second-floor outer office carrying the brown paper bag. " 'Morning, Vicky. Mr. Spain left for London this morning."

"How long this time?" His secretary circled that day's date on her calendar.

"Extended, I would say at least a month. Bring your book, and coffee, please." He walked into his private office, placed the bag on the desk, glanced out at the Fifth Avenue traffic snarl, and reached for the phone. He punched out a number.

"Police headquarters."

"Jesse Solomon, please."

"Who's calling?"

"Chris Murdoch, the St. Cyr Tower."

"His line is busy, will you hold, Mr. Murdoch?"

"Yes."

Vicky Jason entered with two cups of coffee, placed one at his elbow and sat down opposite. She flipped the pages of her book and looked up. "Can I talk?"

Murdoch nodded. "Go."

"Her Royal Highness, Princess Martha, her two children, her husband, Lord Woodford, two security people, a social secretary, and a nanny arrive today. You'll have to meet them."

Murdoch nodded. The police operator came back on the line. "I have Chief Solomon for you now, Mr. Murdoch."

"Chris! How the hell are you? You after more of my people?"

"You're the one I'm after, Chief, but if they ever fire you, I'm packing my bags and getting the hell out of the city."

"I'll go with you. What can I do for you?"

"A private meeting. With you. Right away."

"Oh?" Solomon's voice withdrew.

"I've got something."

"Heavy?"

"Potentially, as heavy as it can get."

"Personal?"

"No."

There was a long silence on Solomon's end. "I have a lunch that I can't break—how about after that?"

"How about before lunch?"

"Can you give me a hint what it is?"

"Not over the phone."

"Let me clear a few things down here and I'll get back to you in a few minutes."

"I'll be here."

Vicky Jason was staring at him. "Close the door, please," he said quietly.

He talked steadily, pausing only to sip coffee. Vicky Jason did not ask him to slow down. She got it all, and when he was finished, having dictated every detail of Threat up to that moment, she looked at him. Her eyes were steady, but as she spoke her voice wavered. "Oh, my God—"

"Set up a special-security file. Everything in triplicate."

"Is it real, Chris?"

"We're treating it as real."

The phone rang. Vicky answered, listened briefly. "Thank you." She hung up. "Princess Martha arrives at Kennedy at one-thirty this afternoon."

"Have the helicopter waiting for her. Keep checking the ETA—let me know when the chopper leaves Kennedy."

"Are you going to tell her?"

"We're telling nobody."

Vicky rose to leave. "That all?"

"There's going to be a meeting of all security at ten this morning."

"Where will this meeting take place?"

"My apartment. And you'd better have one of the maids clean it up right away."

"Shall I get anything?" And in response to Murdoch's questioning look, added, "Coffee—Danish?"

Murdoch thought a moment. "Yeah. But don't use the hotel service. I don't want knowledge of the meeting to get around."

"But—"

"Threat, Vicky, can be anyone at all. A waiter, a busboy, a maid. Anyone. Even you."

She colored. "Even you."

"No," Murdoch said evenly. "Not me, Vicky."

The phone rang. She answered and handed it to Murdoch. Chief Solomon was on his way and would be there in half an hour.

"Where will you be?" she asked, following him out of the office.

"Making rounds. I won't leave the house."

The organized confusion in St. Cyr's lobby was peaking. Murdoch seemed to be the only person there who was not in a hurry, who did not have a look of eagerness new arrivals wore, nor the fatigue of the departing.

He found the man he wanted and tapped him on the shoulder. Sidney Hoag was a big man, as distinguished as any guest, successfully hiding the hard-nosed cop underneath. There had been no question in Murdoch's mind when he hired Hoag that he would make the perfect security man for the lobby.

"Hiya, Chris. What's with the ten-o'clock meeting?"

"I'll explain at the meeting. I'm expecting Chief Solomon in a few minutes. Watch for him. Take him up to my office, quietly, and then forget that he was here."

"Sure, sure." Hoag's eyebrows knitted quizzically. He started to speak and then he clamped his mouth shut. "Well, it's quiet so far."

The early-morning shoppers were out, rain or no rain. The veteran

Fifth Avenue cadres moved ahead with steely determination, occasionally one of them would break ranks and dart into the St. Cyr.

The St. Cyr Tower. It rose straight up from the sidewalks of Fifth Avenue topping off at one hundred stories, and it was not out of plumb an eighth of an inch. A rich and beautiful adornment to the gray and ugly face of Manhattan. Obsidian, with smoky, dark glass sidewalls, it reflected surrounding buildings with the ghostly echo of an old French mirror, cobwebby and pinstreaked, and not quite true. Laced with bronze trim around each window, it reminded Murdoch of a jeweled box that might have been the gift of one king to another. The Tower so dominated all there was around it that venerable St. Patrick's Cathedral a block away looked like a child's gingerbread house.

Murdoch had thought many times that it was not unlike walled cities of the Middle Ages, lacking only pennants flying at the turrets on which sentinels marched the watches. But instead of loyal pikemen guarding the walls, there were Murdoch's clean-shaven, conservatively dressed security guards. Instead of battlements where sharp-eyed lookouts stood, there were hidden television cameras with electronically controlled lenses designed to turn on, zoom in, focus, and scan an area automatically, when anything heavier than a mouse tread on one of the expensive carpets.

Across Fifth Avenue a gust of wind snatched at a black umbrella. The owner fought back. The ribs were turned inside out and sailed out of grappling hands, soaring briefly, like a prehistoric bird, clear across the avenue and landing in a crumpled heap. No one noticed. No one laughed. No one cared.

He continued his rounds, working his way through the Galleria of shops, the huge Monte Carlo Lounge, nodding, smiling. Everything normal, except for the rain. He spent a few minutes with Kosinski untangling a reservation mess, and then continued his rounds leaving the kitchen and his daily meeting with the *grand chef* until last where he would discuss the following week's food budget over his fifth cup of coffee.

In Marty's Delicatessen the phone rang. The cashier, a retired waiter with fallen arches, lifted the receiver and barked a response in a rasping voice. "Marty's Deli, what's-your-order-pleeze? St. Cyr—Mrs. Jason,

41

second floor. One dozen prune Danish, one dozen cheeze Danish, one dozen plain Danish, two large potsa coffee—right away, yes, ma'am. Thank youse for your order." The cashier hung up the phone, and without looking up as he wrote the order, yelled above the voice and dish clatter, "Tonio!"

Tonio closed the book he was reading and shuffled forward to get the order sheet. The front door opened. Wet air swept inside. it would be lunchtime soon. The waiters began to set up the tables.

"Hey, Patch!" the black sergeant yelled irritably. "Let's go, Patch! Stop readin' and start speedin'! Get it on!"

"Okay, Sarge—"

He was curious about the order of three dozen Danish and two large pots of coffee to be delivered to Vicky Jason, whom he knew to be Murdoch's secretary. It would be a meeting, he decided. If they had found the beer can he had left the day before while delivering sandwiches to the receptionist at International Traders, the meeting would be about him.

He felt a slight rise in his tensions; it was happening. All the months of detailed planning, the care, the digging out of facts and bits of information about E. Joseph Spain, Murdoch, not to mention the hundreds of hours he had spent getting into and out of the St. Cyr during its construction without being noticed, all of it was on the downhill run. The beginning of the end.

He slipped around the corner of the St. Cyr and ducking the loading dock of the hotel, climbed the concrete stairs and walked toward the service entrance. He started to push in on the double swinging doors, when the door was pushed open, nearly knocking him down.

"Oh, excuse me—I'm sorry," Murdoch said.

"S'okay," Tonio replied.

Murdoch turned away and then was gone.

Tonio entered the service elevator with three dozen Danish and two large pots of coffee.

After twenty-nine years with the NYPD, Jesse Solomon had developed the patience of Job when it came to dealing with a criminal conspiracy. If answering a call to investigate a domestic fight between a man and his wife was the most tricky and potentially volatile, for the beat cop, unraveling a conspiracy was the one area of crime that put the Detective into Frustration, out of Stagnation by Checkmate. With a murder, the Detective had only to apply three empiricals to suspects. Means. Opportunity. Motive. Was the suspect on, or near the scene of the crime, therefore the opportunity? Did the suspect have access to the means; a gun, knife, club? Did the suspect have a motive? Jealousy, money, hate, revenge? In a conspiracy the odds against finding a suspect who matched all three empiricals, plus evidence solid enough to go to court, were astronomical.

The chief of detectives was a man of average height, but the massive shoulders and drum-tight gut made him look much larger. He peered at Murdoch from beneath bushy eyebrows and took a firmer grip with his teeth on his cigar. The brown paper bag containing the beer can, the pennies, and the note was on the desk between them.

"Until there is a demand for money," Solomon said slowly from around his cigar, "we have to assume that it's a crazy."

"All right," Murdoch said.

"But what *kind* of crazy?"

"Your guess is as good as mine," Murdoch said and poured coffee for both of them, swearing to himself that it would be the last cup that day.

"We had Metesky, the 'Mad Bomber,' a few years back," Solomon said thoughtfully. "Put pipe bombs in luggage lockers. Wanted to get even with Con Ed."

"You think Threat is after revenge?"

Solomon looked up, his eyes boring into Murdoch. "And if he is?"

"Then the target of this—" Murdoch tapped the note "—could be any one of our rich and/or foreign tenants. One of them has the whole ninety-fifth floor. Elusha Delgatov, White Russian, international finance. He must have twenty–thirty million dollars in art. Paintings, sculpture, antiques. Walking through his apartment is like a visit to the Metropolitan Museum.

"Some of the richest, most powerful people in the *entire* world, live here, Jesse. The total worth of this building—considering jewelry, paintings, sculpture, antiques, furs, God knows how much cash and negotiable securities held in their private vaults—could easily come to a billion dollars. Maybe even double that. The point is, we don't turn people like that out into the street for a search of the building if it turns out to be nothing but a practical joke. On the other hand, we have the responsibility to do just that—if we suspect it is a crazy and might try to sneak a bomb in. But there are some people who live here, Jesse, who wouldn't let the president of the United States in their apartments. So we can't even *search* the goddamned building. How the hell do we handle this?"

"Sticking with the crazy theory," Solomon said, "it could be anyone who lives here, couldn't it? The target, I mean?"

Murdoch nodded. "And added to that thought, we have two floors with professional people. Doctors, a whole goddamned floor of doctors, who might have screwed up an operation and caused the death of a loved

one. Or one of the big law firms on the fourth floor, who gypped somebody out of the family farm when they knew there was oil on it.''

The two men stared at each other across the desk, eyeball to eyeball.

"Got many Arabs here?" Solomon asked. "Or, Middle East types?"

"Many. You thinking about oil?"

"If there's a terrorist threat in back of this note," Solomon snapped
his fingers, "they could blow this building apart like that! And there is
goddamned little you, nor I, the entire NYPD, FBI, or the CIA could do
to stop it. We might catch them after the fact, but we can't search every
single person every time he or she enters the building. And how about
the packaged goods that move in and out of a place like this every day?
A bellboy schleps in a bag and takes a guest to his room. Who the hell
knows what's in the bag? A United Parcel Delivery guy comes in with
a dozen boxes for m'lady from Saks—it's hopeless.''

"Anyway, that kind of searching is out," Murdoch said dourly.
"Maybe ten–twelve percent of our people are either United Nations or
have other diplomatic status.''

"So, what have we got?" Solomon asked. "We got a crazy who
could be going after somebody for revenge. And we got terrorists who
might be going after anybody for what reason we can't even imagine,
but let's call it political. What's left?"

"A practical joker."

"That, too," Solomon said. "But there's something else."

"Ransom?"

Solomon nodded. "But that's the least of my worries. Let him make
his threat, then make his demand. We respond and pay off. That's when
we catch him, when he reaches for the money. Kidnapping, hostage-
taking, or whatever form it takes, there has to be a point when something of value changes hands. Money. Diamonds. Plans for the super-X
mystery plane. Payday. Ninety-nine percent of the time that's when they
get caught. When they reach for the money." Solomon drained his coffee and glanced at his watch. "Ever deal with anything like this before,
Chris?"

"Once. In Vegas, before I came here. Why do you ask?"

"You seem to have a handle on it. No panic. Frankly, we get a lot of
this sort of thing against other hotels, theaters, restaurants, all the time.

45

Most of the time the owners or managers make a federal case out of it, start demanding round-the-clock special forces."

Murdoch smiled. "You want the background, I guess."

"You work here too, Chris. No one would have it easier than you—" Solomon was deadpan, not hard, just level, easy. "You'd be in on everything, know everything."

"Born and raised here in Manhattan. Columbia, then Viet Nam. Intelligence all the way, came out a major. Went to Vegas for a blowout when they let me go, had a hell of a time. Gambled just enough, playing it cool, to make a three-month binge last almost a year. By that time I knew a lot of people and when it was over and time to go to work, I hooked on with security in one of the big hotel casinos. I liked it, but I liked the hotel end of it better and made the switch. I made assistant manager in one of Vegas's biggest hotels when Spain's headhunters found me and here I am."

Solomon grunted. "Had to ask."

"Sure you did. Just like you'll have me checked out."

Solomon grunted again, giving away nothing. "Aside from seeing if there is anything to be learned from those—" the chief of detectives nodded toward the brown paper bag and the contents, "—what do you want me to do?"

"Keep it quiet. And help, unofficially, if you can. It's obvious that if this gets out, it would be almost as bad as having a bomb go off."

Solomon wrinkled his nose. "I'll keep it quiet, and unofficial, until and if and when you get a second calling card. That's all I can do."

"That's all I'm asking. If I have to empty the building, I have to empty the building."

"How about Joe Spain? He know you contacted me?"

Murdoch nodded. "He told me to handle it any way I saw fit. But I'll keep him informed."

"What else can I do?" Solomon pulled himself to his feet.

"I need a man who works with a good dog, perhaps you know one. A team. I'll set him up here as a rich, eccentric blind man, and see what he can find."

"I know just the man. I'll have him here soon as I locate him."

"I'm also going to have my own people, under Andy Brooks's supervision, go through the employee files and pay particular attention to rejects." Murdoch looked at his watch. "I'm having a security meeting in ten minutes."

"You going to tell them what's behind it?"

"What would you suggest?"

"Keep it as quiet as you can. It's always best that way. When and if you come up with any possibilities give them to me, and I'll check them against our own private list of coconuts. And if our files can't make a match, I'll check it through the FBI."

At the elevator, Murdoch punched the button. "What's your gut feeling, Jesse?"

"You're making all the right moves. I honestly don't see that my coming into it now would be of any help—"

"But?"

"I don't like the note. If it were a crazy, I think just penetrating your security would give him his jollies. The writer said 'I,' and not 'We,' which closes out some of the terrorist theory, not all, but some. As for revenge, crazies of that stripe rarely come in bunches, 'Let's get together and give Joe Spain, the rich son of a bitch, the shaft.' And there was the threat that this is Number *One*. The implications are clear. He's going to hit again."

"With a demand?"

"I would play it along those lines. That he's going to hit you, and make a demand."

"Money?"

"Not necessarily. But I think a demand is certainly in the picture. 'Deliver one of our Brothers from Attica'; 'Give us the head of the Bowsie-Wowsie delegation to the UN.' A demand."

Solomon stepped into the elevator. "Keep in touch."

The door slid closed.

At the Riverside Arms, Eleanor Cassie had washed her face and began to explore the building. She followed the soprano voice to its source and knocked on the door.

"Hi, I'm Eleanor Cassie. I just moved in with Tonio."

The relationship between Lillene Whalen and her husband, Lou, who was much older than his wife, had never been very good. At its best it

47

was a marriage of mutual need. And Lillene's need at the moment was to escape from the bitter rain and fly to Miami for a long weekend. She hated cold, wet weather, but she knew there was no escape from New York until the racetracks began their winter season in Florida. Acting as lookout for her husband, she sat in a chair in their shop staring out of the front door, past the display in the front window of the boutique and, at noon watched Tonio coming down the block with his two plastic carry-all hampers. Lacquered, cold-eyed, aggressive, and jangling with bracelets, she continued swinging one foot and staring into the street. She yelled, without pausing in her concentration of the street. "Lou! The kid's here with the sandwiches."

"Hi," Tonio said quietly. He started to put the hampers down when she stopped him.

"Don't get the carpet wet, ya jerk! F'chrissakes! Take it ina back— and wipe your feet."

"Sure." Tonio wiped his feet carefully and carried the loaded hampers on through the store to the back room.

"Hiya, Tonio! What's your action today?" Lou Whalen was a small man with bones that stuck out of his chest, seemingly about to pierce the skin.

Tonio sat the hampers on the floor and opened one of them. He read orders stapled to brown paper bags, selected one and put it on the desk. "Swiss on rye, mustard; pastrami, roll, mustard. Two black coffees. Seven seventy-five."

Lou held out a ten-dollar bill, waving away the change. The phone light lit up, flashing a steady sequence. Lou hung over the phone briefly, his eyes closed. "Yeah, Ski, I got it. I got it, I tell ya. A hunnert to win, Beefsteak John, in the fourth. You're down, Ski, you're down." He hung up the phone and turned back to Tonio. "What's your action, kid?"

Tonio handed over two crumpled tens. "Conrad's Favor in the sixth."

Lou nodded and took the money. He closed his eyes. He never wrote anything down. His memory after thirty-five years, was perfect. Not *nearly* perfect. Perfect. "I figure she'll go off at thirty-to-one."

"Whatever," Tonio said casually, reaching for his hamper.

Lou smiled. "You a real horseplayer, Tonio. A real bettor after my own heart. A plunger, firs' class, all the way. Nothing' but long shots, *big* odds, thirty-to-one, fifty-to-one and you down on that horse like Elmer's glue." Lou wiped the back of his hand against his nose. "I hate to see you do it, kid. But that's my business. I take your money, see? Right now, I tell you your horse will run out. Why don't you save your money? You workin' hard to go ta school and all, schlepping around in the rain with sanwiches 'n coffee, and you give it all to me."

"I'll hit one of these days, Lou."

"Not with Conrad's Favor you ain't going to hit. Your horse don't like mud, and it's up to his cannon bones already. It'll be up to his ass by post time." The light lit up and Lou picked up the phone.

Lillene had not moved, nor did she look up as Tonio left.

After his last delivery, still carrying his hampers, Tonio walked to the Rockefeller Station Post Office. It was always crowded at lunchtime, and he dutifully got in line to wait along with others dressed not unlike himself. Young men in jeans, leather jackets, and boots; old men in ratty-looking raincoats. All of them were messengers, or gofers for small professional service shops in the midtown area.

He recognized a few of the faces. He saw them twice a week and knew a little about their lives and their thinking; he had patterned his whole identity after them. Long hair, cheap clothes, loud voices, and eyes that were never quite successful in lying for them. They were going nowhere, but they still tried for excitement and were only rarely successful. And the old men, either winos or Social Security cheats working to supplement their incomes. Eating junk food at hot-dog stands, sleeping where they could.

"Hiya, Tonio." The postal clerk greeted him with a grin.

"Hiya, Joey."

"Litho-Vu, Box 1278." The clerk slapped a two-foot pile of manila envelopes on the counter. "Howsa going, Tonio, kid?"

"Not bad, Joey. Yourself?"

"Making it, ya know. Like, why not?" The clerk helped Tonio stack the envelopes into Tonio's hampers. "All right, who's next?"

An old man shambled forward. "Show-Tech—Box 3426."

"Show-Tech—Box 3426, right here. Show-Tech!" Another batch of manila envelopes were placed on the counter as Tonio moved away.

He walked the corridors of the lower level in Rockefeller Center until he came to a loading area with a huge garbage container. Calmly he ripped the address off each envelope and threw the envelopes away. There were thirty-four of them in different sizes. He had been mailing and receiving the envelopes for eighteen months. His appearance at the post office was as regular and as predictable as snow in January. A thing that happened, that was not important, and if it didn't happen, no one was aware of it too much.

It was the way Tonio wanted it.

Murdoch, following Solomon's advice, had decided not to tell the security staff what he was looking for, or why. There would be time enough if they should get another message from Threat. He looked around. His apartment was really too small to hold a meeting of his entire security force. Most of them were sitting on the floor. "As experienced police officers, you all know, *know,* that if someone really wants to, is intelligent enough, determined enough, and is highly motivated, they can penetrate any security screen. They reached out and got President Kennedy. They got his brother, Bobby. They got Malcolm X, and Martin Luther King, Junior. They reached out further and hit the Olympic Village in Germany. They slipped through some of the tightest security of the day and kidnapped Sheik Yamani at an OPEC meeting in Europe.

"Every one of you also knows a basic thing about police work. When a guy has a cocked, loaded .45 a half-inch away from your brain, you do exactly as you are told, and you do it immediately, and no back talk. I believe we may be in such a situation here at the St. Cyr Tower."

No one moved. There was no nervous lighting of cigarettes. They were all experienced. In the silence the sudden ringing of the telephone broke the tension. Vicky Jason answered, listened a moment, and jotted down information. "Thank you." She looked at Murdoch. "Princess Martha's plane has been diverted to Newfoundland. Something about oil pressure. Nothing serious. They don't expect to get here before six tonight."

Murdoch nodded. He looked at the men. He picked up Xeroxed copies of assignment sheets. "I'm not going to put you on a definite schedule for this stuff. I'm going to assume that all of you will break your back to get the information to me as soon as possible. As I said before, just think of a cocked .45 at your head. This is not an ordinary situation, and I don't want it treated that way—"

The booming voice of Sidney Hoag cut him off before Murdoch could continue. "What the hell are we looking for, Chris?"

"I'm getting to that. Most of this is going to be sheer drudgery, and boring as hell. I am not going to be specific at this time, but I want you to go through every employment application ever submitted to us for a job. Follow any leads, hunches, you can come up with. Use a fine-tooth comb. If you spot anything on anyone's application that you suspect might not be kosher—for instance, a Puerto Rican employee who claims to have worked for the Rockefeller El Dorado outside of San Juan, but other dates on his application don't jibe, check it out. Anything that catches your eye, 'kay?"

"Can you be more specific?" Hoag asked.

"Not at this time. Anybody with a criminal background, obviously, anybody with a mental history, anybody who might have anything but an honorable discharge—you know the drill."

"A kook?" someone asked.

"Especially a kook," Murdoch said. "Anybody, who for any reason doesn't fit into the background he says he has, or is out of the ordinary. You've all heard the expression that this is *not* a fishing expedition. Well, in this case, we *are* a fishing expedition. Personnel has already been alerted and expects you, and computer-time has been put aside for you. I want you to pay particular attention to those applications that were rejected, and the reasons why."

He looked around the room. "Any questions?"

"If you won't tell us what it is we're supposed to be looking for—I don't see how we can spot the one thing that might help you," Hoag said.

"I've told you all I can for now," Murdoch said firmly.

"Is it a dry run, Mr. Murdoch?" someone asked.

"Just keep the cocked .45 in mind. It's real."

The men left the apartment quietly, half of them to start work on the employee files, others to return to their shifts for the day. It was going to be a lot of useless work, Murdoch knew. But it was the only way to be sure they had not overlooked any possibilities.

He stared out of the window. He thought of many things he would prefer doing that afternoon instead of looking for a potential—what—bomber?

It would have to be a bomb, he thought.

THIS IS NUMBER ONE.

"Just don't let it be a crazy," he said half-aloud. "Be a nice, simple extortionist, and make your demand. When you put your hand out for the payoff, I'll be there waiting."

It was the kind of function Jesse Solomon least enjoyed. A banquet luncheon which meant two things: chicken a la king on toast and while everybody else was having a second or even third martini, he didn't dare have one for fear of going to sleep. And, the speeches by politicians honoring a retiring politician were a civilized form of torture; with the commissioner at his table, there was no escape.

When he was a much younger cop he had often thought that he would like to be police commissioner. The reforms he would make would be sweeping, good for the men of the department, as well as offer better service to the community. But he gave up the dream when he discovered that he would have to put at least two-thirds of his friends in jail.

"A message for you, Chief," a waiter leaned and whispered in Solomon's ear.

"Yeah?"

"Diedrickson, from your office."

Solomon brightened. "Diedrickson? You're sure?"

"Yes, sir."

"Thank you, my friend. Thank you." Solomon slipped a dollar bill into the fleshy palm and leaned toward the commissioner. "Something important I'm working on—it might be just the thing I'm looking for. Gotta go."

The police commissioner, a thin, delicately featured man with the best tailor in Manhattan, frowned, and then nodded his reluctant blessing.

Knowing exactly where the public phones were in The Plaza, he hurried through the lobby, was greeted by a few familiar faces, and settled a dime into the slot. "Solomon. Give me Diedrickson in criminalistics," he growled.

"Right away, Chief."

He unwrapped a cigar and bit on it with the pleasure of a man who had just won one.

"Chief?"

"Lieutenant Diedrickson, the next time I start to yell at you, just remind me that I owe you one, okay!"

"Yes, sir, but—"

"Never mind. What have you got?"

"The can was just an ordinary empty beer can, shipped from a brewer in Jersey five weeks ago, and that load was distributed all over the city. The note isn't any help either. Cheap tablet paper you can get anywhere. A million places. And the typewriter—Smith-Corona portable, pica type—which doesn't mean anything either unless we can get the original machine to make a match. And there was a partial on one of the pennies."

"How good a partial?"

"Pretty good, right forefinger, on the back of the penny."

"And?"

"We couldn't match it here in the city, so I've sent it on down to Washington. I treated it routine, like you said I was to treat everything."

"Could *you* make anything out of the partial?"

There was a slight hesitation. "I think *I* could, Chief—"

"But?"

"I'd have to do my own checking."

"In Washington?"

"Yes, sir." The crime lab expert was firm. He knew his value.

"But it's a good partial?"

"It's a partial, Chief, a good one, but still a partial." Diedrickson was sticking to his guns. Solomon grunted. He trusted the man's judgment for that reason. He would not be pushed by Solomon's desire for the right kind of information, or the kind that Solomon wanted.

"You did pretty good stuff, Lieutenant. I'll get back to you about Washington. Like before, it's strictly qt on this one."

Without a backward glance at the oaken doors of the banquet room, Chief of Detectives Solomon hurried outside, signaled his driver, and got away from there as fast as he could.

"Hey, Tony, what's with the dirty neck, huh?"

Tonio was on his knees cleaning up his work station preparing to leave. He looked up at one of the waiters, a runty, sallow-faced man in his sixties. "What?"

"Your neck. It's all dirty. Streaks of dirt down the back of your neck, like from the rain, you know, like don't you take a bath, ever, kid?"

"Up yours."

"Listen to him talk. College professor with a dirty neck! You know what the health inspector say to you, he come in here and find you with dirt and crap on your neck, handlin' food for the public, huh?"

"Up yours, *and* the public's *and* the health inspector's," Tonio said amiably.

"You're a real sweet kid, you know that, Tony? A real schmuck of a sweet kid." The waiter gave Tonio a good-natured pat on the shoulder, buttoned his short red jacket and shuffled off to join his peer group at the front tables by the window.

Tonio did not react immediately. He knew the back of his neck was not dirty. There could only be one explanation. The dye he used in his hair had run—probably through some sort of chemical reaction caused by pollutants in the air brought down by the rain.

He would leave right away, earlier than usual, and take care of it before his first late-afternoon class. He could not afford a slip like that. He was thoroughly at ease, but he would have to be doubly alert now that he had delivered Number One.

It had stopped raining by the time Tonio entered the Riverside Arms at three that afternoon. Students moved freely in and out of the mansion. He was greeted several times, but he just waved and kept moving. At Eleanor's room he pressed his ear to the door. He heard nothing. He started to knock, hesitated, and then started to barge in, and again hesitated. She might be asleep, and he *had* to take care of his hair.

He was rarely at home during that time of day and he had to wait around, stalling in the upper hall until he could get past his traps and enter his room. Once inside, he checked that everything was in order. Nothing had been disturbed, and he spent the next half hour re-dyeing his hair.

When he was finished, he stripped and took a hot shower. Feeling refreshed in clean dry jeans, he cleaned up the bathroom, tossing the dirty towel into the hamper, reminding himself as he did that he would have to use the basement laundry soon.

He still had an hour before he would have to leave for his Columbia class. He went to the closet, checked the locks, opened the door, and took down a box of watchmaker's tools and electronic gear. He turned to the worktable made of a discarded door.

He adjusted the light, set the watchmaker's eyepiece in his eye, and started to work.

From time to time he would sit back, remove the eyepiece and rest, smoking a cigarette. Once he made a cup of Sanka on a hot plate, and then set back to work again. At a quarter to five, when he should have left for his class, he decided that he would cut it. He did not do it often.

Only when he felt it was absolutely necessary. But he was making such good progress, he decided to work right on through. Once he got up and took down the computer, inserted a program and made a few adjustments, programming it slightly differently than he had before, and, satisfied, turned back to the table and continued to work.

Finished, he was pleased with what he had done. He sat back, lit a cigarette, and lounged in his chair. He let his eye pick out critical details. He was superbly professional, but, like any professional, he was reluctant to let the work go until it had been given final and relentless scrutiny. A baseball pitcher wanting a few more warm-up tosses to be dead sure of his control. An airline pilot walking around his ship and kicking the massive tires to make sure of pressure. Secure in his abilities, and confident of finding a flaw if there is one.

His eyes smarted, and he rubbed them, hard, cocking his head to avoid the curling cigarette smoke, still critical in his appraisal. He picked up a watchmaker's tool and felt the tension in the set screw for the tenth time. He tossed the screwdriver to one side. He was satisfied.

The object of his satisfaction, a gleaming, splendidly designed nest of wires, screws, fittings, needed only the charge to make it complete. It was, he decided, the best bomb he had ever made. There was still a great deal to be done, but he was nearly ready to move.

He put everything away, double-locked the closet, and washed his face. He adjusted the eye patch over his left eye, laying the elastic band carefully into the part of his hair. He became aware of the noises outside his room. The majority of the students were on daytime schedules and the house would be full of activity as tensions were worked off.

He inserted the oily pieces of lint into the locks on the closet, rethreaded the light bulb to the hook on the door, and stood waiting for silence before opening the door. When he thought it was clear, he stepped outside, set his trap, and locked the double-fall bolt.

"Well, look at you!" Eleanor Cassie said. She smiled.

Tonio thought for a moment he had entered the wrong room. He took an involuntary step backward. The girl before him was not the same one he had picked up on the subway platform.

Tonio looked around the room quickly, and back to her. Eleanor Cassie stood, a tentative smile on her face, watching him. She wore a flowered granny dress, dirty ballet slippers, her hair was combed back and tied with a ribbon. There were several posters on the wall, Star Trek, with the faces of Spock and Kirk; a famous bullfight scene, and a deep-blue poster with line drawings of a fifteenth-century *abbé* announcing a chamber concert.

"Are you hungry?"

"What the hell is this?" Tonio asked quietly, tensely.

A card table was placed against one wall and set with two places ready for dining. A huge yellow candle was in the center of the table. There was a bottle of cheap wine and two glasses. A chipped serving platter was filled with slices of Italian bread on one end, celery, cold cuts, and cheese on the other. A two-burner hot plate was on the windowsill. An aluminum pot, dented, but serviceable, was simmering just below boil. A second smaller pot bubbled happily with what looked to Tonio like sauce. The window was fogged. "Where did all this stuff come from?" he demanded.

He started to close the door, when it was pushed open and Laura Roc jostled him. She grinned, showing her big, strong white teeth, and pushed past him to hand over two cheap unmatched coffee cups to Eleanor. "This is all I could dig up, Elly. Two cups, two tea bags. No sugar."

"Thank you," Eleanor said, still looking at Tonio.

"Wait a minute, Laura. What's going on?"

"Ask Elly," Laura Roc answered. She grinned. "Enjoy, enjoy!" She closed the door.

Tonio had not moved. He stared at Eleanor, who stared back, the two cups in her hand.

"What are you trying to do?" he demanded.

She made a gesture with her shoulders, the smile fading, returning to the girl he had seen that morning. She put the cups down and sat on the side of the bed, head down, hands in her lap.

"This isn't going to work, you know," Tonio said at last, putting absolutely no inflection in his voice. "I know what you're trying to do, but it isn't going to work."

"You may know what I've done, but you don't know why."

"I live alone. That's the way I like it. That's the way it's going to be. You've wasted your time." He lit a cigarette. "Let's see. You had a sleep. You woke up, and you remembered you had been aced by your former boyfriend, and you figured until something better came along, you might as well make the best of it here. With me. You left the room, wandered around and met some of the others. Laura already knew that you had been brought here by me. And since I have a certain status here as a pretty good joe, but a loner, and thoroughly respected, everybody began to pitch in and help. They do that here. You grabbed at it, and it became a game: Tonio has finally made himself a connection.

"It must have been a very busy day for you. And a lot of fun," Tonio said, dragging on the cigarette, watching her. "Does he like this? Does he like that? What can I do to surprise him? That two-burner plate belonged to a kid on the second floor, I know, because I repaired it before he left to go back home, and he paid off a debt by giving it to the kid in the back bedroom on the first floor. I don't know where you got the pots and pans, and the dishes, but the card table came from the storeroom in the basement. You could only have gotten that from Mrs. Coffin, who keeps a collection of junk there for students to use. So, you made some sort of a connection with her. Did you tell her that I was going to stand in back of the rent? That we were getting it on? And, the rest of it, I don't know. You must have spread yourself pretty thin. You have to have money to buy food. Did you borrow? No, you had the five bucks I gave you—"

"Go to hell, and if you don't like it, split," Eleanor said tonelessly. "You picked me up, remember? I didn't ask you for a thing, not a *goddamned* thing."

"True, but you're asking now," Tonio said. "With a pot of spaghetti, a bottle of cheap wine, a bath, probably, yeah, a bath, and your gratitude. What's supposed to happen, after we eat? Do we go to bed? You going to show me something new? Maybe give me head with the lights on? And by then, you'll hope I'll feel so good about what you've done that we'll really get it on and play house?"

"You son of a bitch! You bastard!"

"Better," Tonio said carelessly.

"I needed something to get me through the next few days, a week maybe—"

"Still better—"

"—Get a job. Oh, I don't know." She threw up her hands. She

switched off the burners on the hot plate.

Tonio sighed with relief. Okay, no harm done. He would cease to play the heavy and let things ride until he could safely ease her out of his life.

It was then that he noticed the suitcase. "Where did that come from?"

"That's mine. I went back to the old place and collected my stuff."

"That was wise," Tonio said, meaning it.

"I found out where he is."

"Who?"

"You know, Chip. Chip Torrance. The one who left me. There's a chance to get my ID back. If he hasn't thrown them away. Why would he keep them?" She stirred the sauce and licked the spoon. "With all the rest, I mean, that you've done for me, if you would help me get my ID back—"

Tonio thought a moment. With her identification, it would be a hell of a lot easier to get rid of her—to avoid her—even if she remained in the Riverside Arms. "Okay," he said quietly.

"Are you hungry? Seems a pity to let it go to waste."

"Why not?" He opened the wine while she made the spaghetti.

They ate in silence. They had nothing to say to each other. When he was finished, Tonio sipped the cheap wine and lit a cigarette. "Where does he live now?"

"Chip?"

"Whatever he calls himself."

"He's moved in with a black girl, Cynthia Turner, on Forty-sixth Street, between Sixth and Fifth. I have the address written down. One of the people in my old building told me. I don't know how they knew."

Tonio knew the area. One block south of the diamond center on Forty-seventh. Odds were, he thought, living so close to Times Square, the black chick was a prostitute. Sixth Avenue in the forties was known for its curb service. And there was not, probably, a pimp involved, since a prossy did not usually shack up with a guy if she had a pimp going for her. Tonio stood up. "Come on, let's go."

"Now? Tonight?" Eleanor Cassie looked up, frightened.

"The only time I have to spare," Tonio said. She hesitated. "You want me to help you or not?"

"Yes. Yes, I do."

59

"Okay, get something to wear besides that dress. I'll be back in ten minutes."

She stopped him at the door. "Tonio?"

"What?"

"Did you enjoy the spaghetti?"

He looked her straight in the eye.

"It doesn't matter."

Her face hardened.

"You got it now?"

She nodded her head quickly, up and down, one time. "Got it. Ten minutes. I'll be ready."

Tonio looked at his watch. No time had been lost. Even a trip to mid-Manhattan and getting her stuff would not interfere with going to Queens later. He had waited two months for the right Friday night before making his move in Queens.

Mrs. Coffin was a gentle soul, who genuinely liked young people and understood many of their problems. She listened to his protests that nothing was going on with Eleanor, looked at Tonio with her sad gray eyes, and smiled. "I don't care what you do, Tonio. You're a fine young man, and Eleanor seems a fine young lady." She handed him a receipt. "If you want to pay a month's rent for her, that's your business."

He climbed the stairs thinking of his brother. He did not think about his twin often. It depressed him terribly and he had not yet learned how to handle it. But he was beginning to feel good about life for the first time in many years.

Eleanor was wearing the same clothes she had worn that morning when she opened the door. He noticed that she had cleaned off the table and stacked the dishes ready to be washed. It wasn't anything important. She could have left them on the table, but she hadn't. It wasn't important, but it was something.

No one saw them leave. The stereos and the Bee Gees were going strong. It would last until the early hours of the morning. They plunged into the Manhattan night. It was raining again. He hoped it would last until he made his trip to Queens. It would make things easier in the rain.

"The man with the dog is here," Vicky Jason said.

"The man with the dog?" Murdoch asked stupidly.

"The man. With the dog. Is here. Now."

"I'm a little tired, Vicky. I haven't had dinner. I need a drink. Maggie hasn't called. I've got a headache. So please explain what it is, exactly, you are trying to tell me."

"The man with the dog, which is trained to sniff things—*that* man with *that* dog, is here."

"Okay, send him in." Murdoch wiped his face with his hands. "Jesus, what a *pissy* day," he breathed.

"I don't appreciate that kind of language."

"Then don't listen to private conversations I have with myself."

"Yes, I'll remember that."

"Hold the calls. Except for Maggie. How about Princess Martha?"

"No word on arrival yet."

"I'm sorry you heard me cuss."

"I've heard it before."

"In that case, you know what it is, and it's nothing new, and I take back my apology." He grinned.

"Yes, Chris." Vicky Jason's voice was weary.

A moment later the door opened and a man entered with a dog at his side. The dog took in the office with one sweep of its large head and then settled on Murdoch and did not blink.

"Morgan Berry, Mr. Murdoch," the man said. They shook hands across the desk. The dog had not stopped watching Murdoch. "And this is Babe."

Murdoch looked down at the dog. It was very large, with a black saddle tapering to beige legs and paws. It was the biggest German shepherd he had ever seen. "Babe?"

"Girl. Three years, one month. Eighty-eight pounds. I got her as a pup and trained her myself after I retired." He puffed on his pipe. "Thirty years, Buffalo Police Department. I've handled dogs from K-9 to the sixties riots and now."

"Married?"

"Widower. But that's an odd question."

"The job I have in mind might not be suited for a family man."

"No problem there. I'm all alone."

"Carry a gun?"

Berry nodded. "I qualify as expert, and I'm a licensed private inves-

61

tigator. I don't like to work much since—" Morgan Berry extended his identification.

"You don't work much since what?"

"I had two dogs. Babe and Jinx. Matched pair. Jinx was bigger than Babe, here, inch and a half more in the shoulder, and eight pounds heavier. A friend of mine has a liquor store on Third Avenue, uptown. Yorktown area. He had been held up four times. He asked me, hired me, to stay with him on Saturday nights. Just Saturday nights, with the animals, of course. I was there four Saturday nights running and nothing. Then they came in. Two of them in stocking masks and one of them had a shotgun. I let the dogs go and the shotgun got Jinx. Tore his head off."

"Jesus Christ!" Murdoch exclaimed.

"But we got 'em. Babe took care of one, and I got the other. I almost killed him—I would have, because of Jinx. My friend pulled me off. So, I don't have the stomach for the rough stuff anymore. I wouldn't want to lose Babe to another junkie." He looked at Murdoch, his eyes twinkled. "I hope this is an easy job—otherwise, I'm not interested. Go to the cops, or get yourself another team."

"What did Chief Solomon tell you?"

"That you needed a team."

"Could you and Babe act the part of a blind man with a Seeing Eye dog?"

"That's almost too easy." Morgan Berry chuckled. "We've done it several times. I won't bore you with the details, or mention the name of the department store, but they had stock going out of the back door as if it were being shipped by express. Babe and me got 'em in four days. Blind man–dog routine."

Murdoch took a deep breath and outlined the problems presented by Threat.

"And the note said: this is Number One? First of many?"

"That's the way we're proceeding."

Morgan Berry thought a moment. "Sounds all right to me, Mr. Murdoch."

"What's your fee on a daily basis?"

"Three hundred dollars a day for me and the animal, on a twenty-four-hour job."

"I want you to move into the St. Cyr Tower with Babe. A blind man with his Seeing Eye dog. I'll arrange for your room, meals, service, everything. You will be a guest. You sign for everything you buy in the shops, or order. Don't be afraid to spend money. You're going to be a very rich man."

"That's a fine job. I might get to like that."

"You are alone. No friends. You get occasional mail. I'll see to that. Be friendly with everyone. Your blindness came from an automobile accident ten years ago, say out West. Arizona, or any town you know well."

"I know Tulsa."

"Good. Imply an oil background, now retired. You're wealthy, very wealthy, or you couldn't stay here at the St. Cyr. Think of some subject that you know *very* well for your current interest."

"I have a perfect picture of what you're asking for, Mr. Murdoch. That's easy. Music. I'm a serious listener. And it fits in with being blind. Who will know about me?"

"My security people, and no one else. No one in the hotel, on staff, maids, waitresses, waiters. Nobody. But, not even the security staff knows *why* you'll be here. Eight other people know about Threat. You'll be the ninth."

"All right, perfectly understood. When do you want me to start?"

"Immediately. I'll have my secretary get you checked in."

"Make it tomorrow night," Morgan Berry said.

"Why?"

"A blind man wouldn't have ordinary personal belongings like anyone else. For instance, wouldn't it be usual for a blind man to have a good supply of Spoken Records? Or even some books in braille? Old classics? Even a Bible? And a special, superradio, with a tape deck, since he wouldn't be able to watch television? Lots of things like that."

Murdoch smiled. He stood up. "Mr. Berry, it's going to be a pleasure working with you. Thank you. Get whatever you feel you'll need and call me when you're ready to check in."

"Estella Malendez," Andy Brooks said. He stood before Murdoch's desk so fatigued, he looked as if he might collapse.

"What about her?"

63

"I've got her tucked away in an empty office off the television-security monitor room."

"Did you get any sleep at all today?"

Brooks waved the question aside. "I'm leaving for home now. But I had to get the men working on the employment-application reviews, and she works the night shift, remember?"

"How is she?" Murdoch asked.

"Nervous as hell at first, but she calmed down when I assured her that we weren't going to fire her, or blow the whistle on her and Lucas—"

"What about him?"

"Touchy there."

"How so?"

"Obviously scared about his job."

"How about his background?"

"Straight arrow. Been in security, night watchman and stuff like that, most of his life. Worked for both Burns and Ace. He checks out okay. So far."

"Why did he leave Burns and Ace?"

"Same deal as this. Private parties with ladies on the job. And you won't believe this—"

"What won't I believe?"

"He's sixty eight—" Andy Brooks broke out into a grin.

"Jesus! What a way to go."

"I didn't press him, thinking we might handle him the same way as Malendez."

"Which is?"

"Not to say anything about their screwing, if he cooperates."

"What about Malendez? Did she add anything to what we already know?"

"I didn't question her too closely. I said you wanted to talk to her, that was all."

Murdoch lit a cigarette. "Did you impress on her the importance of keeping this to herself?"

"Yes, but—"

"What?"

"She's pretty cute. She offered me a deal."

"What kind?" Murdoch raised his eyebrows.

"Not what you think. If we keep it quiet about her and Lucas, she'll do the same about the beer can and the note."

Murdoch grinned. "That's what I like about New York, you always make a deal. You never give anything away. Okay, what can we lose?"

"That's what she said," Andy Brooks replied.

Vicky Jason opened the door, her hat, raincoat, and rain shoes on. "Princess Martha?"

"Yeah?" Murdoch growled. "What now?"

"Latest ETA, Kennedy, is ten-thirty this evening. That puts her here within an hour on the chopper. And Maggie still does not answer her home or studio phone. Good night, all. I'll be in a little late tomorrow, Chris. After a day like this one, I'm sleeping late." She closed the door quickly, firmly.

"That goes for me as well," Andy Brooks said. "Good night."

"How long have you and Manuel Lucas been seeing each other?" Murdoch asked.

"Just about every night since the Tower opened." Estella Malendez was a pretty woman, thin, almost tiny, with jet-black hair. She was calm, and smoked with an offhand manner. "You gonna give me a hard time about morals? I got a man who can't do much, you know what I mean? And I like men."

"I don't care what you do. But not in the St. Cyr Tower, and not on hotel time."

She shrugged. "What harm we do anybody, huh? We have a few minutes together? I do my work. He does his. What harm, eh?"

"I'm talking specifically about a beer can, like the one you found in International Traders—have you seen others?"

"No. No beer cans."

"Have you ever seen anyone act suspiciously?"

"This is a hotel! People come and go and act crazy all the time. They think that as soon as they get away from home they can do anything they want. And they do. I see something suspicious every night, Mr. Murdoch. You a hotel man, you gotta know what I'm talking about. Every night I come to work I see things. Crazy things." She puffed on her cigarette. "Listen, do we have a deal? I mean, you keep it quiet from my old man about me and Manuel, and I keep quiet about beer cans and notes signed 'Threat.' "

Seated in the small office next to the television-monitoring room, Murdoch could see the night man slouched in his chair watching the screens, the plug of a small transistor in his ear. "I could fire you. Right now."

"What about the beer can? And the note?"

"Who would you tell? And what would you tell? And I don't like your attempts to blackmail me."

"What blackmail? This is a good job! Good tips. Lotta rich people in here. Better than The Plaza. I don't want to mess it up. You want me to stop screwing on company time? You got it—okay?"

"All right. Stay away from Lucas, and anybody else. If I catch you away from your station again, or hear talk about you, you're finished. You'll never work in another hotel."

"We got a deal?"

Murdoch nodded wearily. "Yeah, we got a deal."

"Terrific!" She settled back in her chair comfortably and waited.

"If you and Lucas were in the ladies' room—how did you find the beer can in the computer room?"

"Manuel has a key to everything, you know? In case of fire or some emergency."

"But what were you doing there?" Murdoch persisted.

"Manuel has an every-hour, on-the-half-hour punch-in with some office somewhere here in the city. One of the places where he has to turn his key is in that room where the computers are."

"And you went with him?"

"Sure, why not? Who knows I'm there? Who's going to say anything?"

"How did you find the beer can?"

"I kicked it. Scared hell out of both of us—"

"What did Manuel do when you kicked it, and he saw it was an empty beer can?"

"It wasn't empty."

"We know that now, but what happened then?"

"Well, you see, after he made his rounds, which took about twenty

minutes, we didn't have a lot of time to—ah—you know. And I couldn't
stay off my station too long—"

Murdoch nodded. "What did Manuel do?"

"He said that the people who worked in the computer room shouldn't
be drinking in there—"

"But what did he *do?*" Murdoch asked, fighting his rising exaspera-
tion. "With the can?"

"He gave it to me and told me to throw it away. He said he understood why somebody would sneak in a beer. He had often done it, bring
in a pint, and he wouldn't want anybody to get fired because of it."

"Wasn't he curious about what was inside?" Murdoch asked. "After
all, eighteen pennies make a lot of racket."

"We both thought it was garbage."

"Garbage?"

"Yeah, you know. People use an empty beer can to put crap into.
Cigarette butts, the snap-top of the can, and you know, crap. Being
neat."

"Okay, then what?"

"I slipped it into the pocket of my apron, and we went back to the ladies' room."

"And afterward?"

"Afterward, when we finished, you know, I put my clothes back on
and left."

"Taking the beer can with you."

She nodded.

"When did you discover the pennies and the note?"

"When I went to throw it away, a few of the pennies fell out. I jig-
gled it—holding it upside down—and more pennies fell out. Then the
edge of the note."

"And you read it?"

She nodded. "And took it immediately to Mr. Brooks."

"Why did you do that? Why didn't you just throw it away?" Murdoch asked. "Didn't you consider that you might get in trouble—questions asked where you found it, and what you were doing there?"

"Sure, I thought about it. And I thought about throwing it away.
But—I ain't stupid. I knew it was something important."

"Knew, or imagined it might be?"

She pulled herself upright in the chair and sighed. "Like I said, I been a hotel maid before. Things happen in hotels."

"But you didn't find it in a hotel, you found it in a highly sensitive area—a computer room—of a company that had nothing to do with the hotel. How do you answer that?"

"I just had a feeling, okay?" Her eyes flashed. "Look, I told you everything, exactly. Nothing more, nothing less."

"Did it occur to you that it might be a joke? Somebody pulling our leg?"

"No, I didn't think it was a joke. I thought it was serious."

"What made you think that?"

She lit a cigarette and blew smoke out of her nostrils in short bursts. "For the same reason, maybe, that you're questioning me now. A note says it has penetrated your security. What kind of a place is that computer room? Secure, right? They got Manuel going in there all night long to make sure everything is okay. The note is signed 'Threat.' I took it serious."

Murdoch was silent a long time, staring at her. "Okay, okay—I believe you."

"You make it sound like you thought I was a liar."

"No, I didn't mean that at all. I mean that I believe you've told me what happened—and how it happened."

"I did," she said simply. "Listen, Mr. Murdoch, can I go now?"

Estella Malendez stood up and smiled. She straightened her uniform. There was something wild, almost primitive about her. She wore her sexuality like some women wore perfume. He turned away, disturbed by her, and a vague sense of guilt. Her full breasts and heart-shaped hips, sensuous, promising.

She saw him looking at her. In that way. She knew. She threw her head back and laughed. Long and rich. Murdoch stared a moment, and then he laughed himself.

"Go on, get out of here!"

6 Tonio found the address toward the middle of the block and read the names on the letter boxes. Cynthia Turner lived on the fifth floor, rear. There was no bell, no front-door lock, the door swung half-open. They climbed the stairs, the smell of cooking and urine filled the stairwells and stung at their nostrils. The fifth floor turned out to be the top floor. Pausing only to catch his breath, Tonio rapped hard on the metal door with a coin; a demanding, insistent sound that echoed through the five floors of the empty stairwell.

"Who is it?" a voice asked.

"Torrance?"

"Who the hell are *you?*" The male voice was hard.

Tonio didn't answer. He looked at Eleanor. "Does that sound like him?"

She nodded. She looked frightened.

Tonio knocked again.

"I asked who it was!"

Tonio rapped louder, longer.

"I'm not opening that door, goddammit, until I know who it is."

Tonio knocked a full minute, hard, demanding. There was a rattle of the chains and the undoing of locks. The door opened a half-inch, the safety chain still in place. "Who the hell are you! What the shit you want, Man?"

"You have something that belongs to this lady," Tonio said quietly. "She wants it back."

"What the hell are you talking about, man?"

Tonio stepped to one side and pulled Eleanor into view. "This is Eleanor Cassie. You left her and stole her wallet. And her ID. We've come to get them back."

Tonio had eased his foot forward and jammed the door open against the chain.

"Hello, Chip," Eleanor said. Her voice trembled. "I don't want any trouble. I just want my ID back."

"Plus the forty-two dollars," Tonio said.

A female voice rose inside the apartment. "Who is it, baby? What's going down?" Tonio heard footsteps. A black face replaced the white one at the door. "If you're looking for action, I ain't workin' tonight—"

"The man inside your apartment, Miss Turner, is named Chip Torrance. Until recently, he was living with this young lady. He ran out on her, stealing her wallet, her ID, and forty-two dollars—the only money she had. Without her ID, she can't get a job, or even a place to stay. If she's picked up without any identification, she's in for a hassle with the cops."

The black face shifted to Eleanor, then back to Tonio. A quick, sweeping, all-knowing appraisal. The face turned away. "You know where they coming from, baby? I mean, about the ID crap? You cop bread from this little fox?"

Torrance said something Tonio could not understand. The black face came back to the crack in the door. "Okay. You get the ID back, but he say he done spent the money."

"Forty-two dollars," Tonio said, "is a hell of a lot of bread when you're alone on the streets."

"Well, she sure as shit ain't alone now, if she got *you*, cowboy!"

"Then we'll take something that's worth forty-two dollars."

70

"You *what?* You do *what?* You take *what?* Sheet, turkey, get on—"
Cynthia Turner started to close the door. Tonio kicked one time, raising his leg and snapping it forward with amazing speed and power. The
safety chain broke like a string and the door swung open, banging Chip
Torrance on the head.

Cynthia Turner was nude. She looked about twenty. Her body was
shiny and wet from the shower. Torrance, who looked about thirty, wore
only his jockey shorts. He backed away from Tonio, but Cynthia Turner
was unafraid. She came at Tonio with both hands curled into claws.
Tonio stepped to one side easily and threw a short hard right to her chin
and the black whore dropped to the floor and lay still. He turned to Torrance, who stood with his back pressed up against the wall, mouth open,
fear shining in his eyes.

"Get it," Tonio said.

"Okay— *Okay!*" Without looking at Eleanor, he went to a chest of
drawers and opened the top. He took out a wallet. Eleanor ran to his side
and snatched it out of his hands. She examined it hurriedly. "They're all
here." She looked at Tonio and nodded.

"The money?" Tonio asked. He had not once taken his eyes off of
Torrance nor the unconscious woman on the floor.

"Twenty-nine dollars—"

"That'll do," Tonio said.

"That's not my—or Eleanor's money—" Torrance said. "It belongs
to her." He indicated the whore. His eyes glazed. He began to tremble.
"She's got this *thing* about money—"

"Doesn't everybody?" Tonio said. "Is that everything?" he asked
Eleanor.

She nodded. "Yes."

Tonio turned and walked to the door without looking back and started
down the stairs.

He was on the second-floor landing when she caught up with him.
"Hey, wait a minute—" she said breathlessly.

"For what?" Tonio asked quietly. "You got your ID's back, and
most of your money." He swung out of the door, turned left and headed
for Fifth Avenue.

"Wow! You blew my mind back there—"

"And now you want to thank me."

71

"Yeah, sure. Why not? Anything wrong with that?"

When they reached Fifth Avenue, he started uptown, moving at a steady gait with Eleanor not quite keeping up with him.

"Where are you going now? I mean—" She spoke in a strained voice. "If you got someplace special, I can split now, you know."

"Do that," Tonio said quietly. He left her standing on the corner. He did not look back.

At Fifty-third and Fifth he would catch the "E" train for Queens. He glanced at his watch. It had taken more time than he thought it would. It would not throw his timetable off if he missed his rendezvous that night, but he was disturbed that it had happened at all.

He glanced up only once at the St. Cyr Tower, rising from the brightly lit avenue, black surface losing itself in the overcast sky, and dropped down into the subway station.

Tonio sat next to the window with his head buried in the New York *Post.* The rest of the car was filled with rowdy fans returning from a high-school basketball game somewhere in Lower Manhattan. The visiting team from Forest Hills had won a squeaker and most of the passengers got off at that station. The car all but emptied at Van Wyck Boulevard, leaving only a half-dozen passengers, none of whom appeared to be basketball fans, but very tired workers on the way home.

He yawned and stretched, dropping the paper on the seat beside him, and leaned on his elbow and looked at his reflection in the window. He saw movement in back of him. He tensed and turned slowly. A transit policeman stood, swaying slightly with the rhythm of the train. "You finished with the paper?"

Tonio nodded. The cop picked up the paper, and then surprisingly, sat down beside Tonio. "What's with the eye? You in Nam?"

Tonio nodded. "You?"

"Marines. I got lucky. No hits. No runs. No errors."

"And now you got a good job," Tonio said, thinking fleetingly of his brother, not intending it to sound as harsh as it did.

"You sound bitter," the cop said, rattling the paper.

"Why not? It doesn't cost anything."

"Yeah," the cop replied. "It's about the only thing in life that's a freebie."

"What is?"

"Griping," the cop said. "What do you do?"

"Dispatcher—cabs—Manhattan."

"Sounds interesting."

"It isn't worth a damn," Tonio said. "Fighting all day—*all day*—with a bunch of stupid cab drivers."

The transit policeman shrugged and rattled the paper again. "It's better than getting your ass shot off in Nam."

"Did you get your ass shot off in Nam?" Tonio asked.

The transit policeman's face reddened. "Fuck you, Mac," he said, standing and throwing the newspaper onto the floor. He walked away as the train began to slow for Tonio's station.

The people getting off with Tonio hurried toward the exits. The train started to move and Tonio saw the transit policeman standing between the cars glaring at him, and then the train was in the tunnel and gone. The last of the passengers disappeared up the exit steps. Tonio was left walking alone on the station platform.

He paused and then glanced behind him to make sure he was alone, and then ran forward lightly on the balls of his feet. He kept his eye on the tiled wall, and when he came to a place where three tiles were missing, he slipped over the edge of the platform and underneath. He moved up tight inside and below the platform and felt around the back of a girder in the thick dust. He was struck by the silence and the biting smell of ozone. He listened. Silence.

Quickly he unwrapped a length of cotton toweling and a plastic liner inside of it, and removed a .25 automatic, a pair of black cotton gloves, and a woman's nylon stocking that had been cut in half and tied into a knot at one end.

He checked the automatic, which was the best one that High Standard made; he checked the spare clip, and a four-and-one-half-inch silencer. The shells were steel jackets, and the most powerful available. At thirty-five feet, they could penetrate a two-by-four.

He checked the gun, inserted a clip, attached the silencer, and squeezed off a shot down the tunnel into the tracks. There was no more sound than a man might make with a slight cough. He removed his eye patch and scrambled back to the platform. From the moment he had ducked to the track level and was back on the platform, no more than sixty seconds had passed. He walked to the exit and did not look at his watch. He knew within a minute what time it was. He had made a dry run doing this very thing a half-dozen times.

It was not quite 10:00 p.m. when he turned south on Jamaica Avenue and into a steady hum of traffic from cars, taxis, and the roar of motorcycles. The sidewalks were crowded. Men and women, black mostly, walked up and down on parade. This was Friday night and there was a lot of money in their pockets; action money on the street, and everybody looking for an angle. A lot of drugs were passed and there was an appropriate number of unmarked cars with hard-eyed cops. A neon-lit place, a totally manmade place, filled with menace and terror and nothing to keep it from breaking out into open war at any moment.

Tonio blended in perfectly; just another swaggering dude looking for a fix, or a woman. He walked several blocks south and looked at his watch for the first time. He had given himself twenty minutes to get into position and he figured it would be just enough time. He cut into a doorway at midblock. On the corner of the same block, a huge bar-restaurant was getting a big Friday-night play. A gigantic red-white-blue neon sign was across the entrance. PHIL REAGAN'S. The bar was in one of thousands of very old buildings in the area. Once the upper floors had been apartments, but they were all abandoned now.

Tonio made his way to the roof of the building he had entered from the street, crossed over to Phil Reagan's building, and then lowered himself carefully down an air shaft. He entered the upper floor of the abandoned apartments.

He did not to use a light as he walked confidently along a central hall covered with scaly linoleum; paid no attention to the scuttles of disturbed rats and entered a bathroom. He walked directly to the window and looked out.

Below him was a concrete apron and loading area for Phil Reagan's. One floor below him a hundred customers were drinking and laughing and waiting for Skinny Man to show up. They were all in a good mood that night. Besides being payday for many of them, the Knicks had been heavy underdogs to the Celtics in a game the night before and had gone off at good odds. They were all die-hard Knicks fans, and hunch bettors, and they had taken the price and they had won. The bookie, Skinny

Man, was going to pay out heavily that night, and they were happy about that too. It wasn't often that they hit Skinny Man so hard.

The vision in Tonio's left eye had returned to normal and he could see the rear of the building clearly in the dark. A high fence, with heavy steel, double doors, chain-locked and with a rusting steel bar, was at the rear of the loading area.

He pulled on the cotton gloves and very carefully removed the .25 automatic and sprung the clip. He removed each of the shells and wiped them carefully, then he wiped the clip itself, and then the silencer. He reassembled the gun and placed it on the windowsill. He wiped each piece of the spare clip and placed that into his pocket. When he saw the fat little waiter come out of the building, cross the concrete apron, and remove the steel bar from the gate, but not the lock on the chain, he got ready.

Skinny Man took a drink from a bottle of Chivas Regal he kept on the floor, balanced between his feet, and offered the bottle to his driver. "You want one?"

"Not when I'm driving money," the driver, whose name was Percy, replied. He picked up the microphone of a CB radio and flipped it on. "You there, Hardhead?"

" . . . Hardhead hears you, baby . . . "

"We go to Phil Reagan's."

" . . . You move, you covered . . . "

Percy checked a Mercury riding shotgun in back of his Buick. He swung off into a side street and gunned the heavier Buick. The Mercury was right behind him.

"Damn!" Skinny Man said. "Take it easy—"

"What's the matter?" Percy asked. The Mercury was hanging right in back of him.

"You spilled whiskey all over the money—"

"Winners get a little bonus with good whiskey on their money. How much we carry tonight?"

"Forty-seven thousand and change."

"Say on, baby. Lotta bread." He glanced at the rear-view mirror. There was nothing behind him but the hot Mercury. He felt secure now. He headed for Phil Reagan's.

Percy swung the Buick into Jamaica Avenue, his head and eyes moving, searching the sidewalks for potential trouble. He turned into the side street alongside the bar, then into the alley in back of Reagan's, and brought the headlights up against the steel gates. He turned out the lights and as he had always done, waited, searching the shadows, waiting for signs of movement. He saw nothing moving, and taking a .38 from the seat beside him, Percy eased the door open, but did not get out until the hot Mercury had stopped, blocking the alley, cutting lights and motor. Two men got out of the Mercury carrying shotguns.

Tonio watched it all.

When the fat little waiter came out, unlocked and opened the gates, Percy drove straight inside braking sharply only inches away from the loading platform. He did not move until the gate was closed, locked and secure.

Tonio slipped the stocking mask over his head, eased out of the window and dropped to the ground lightly.

Skinny Man was the first to see him and yelled for Percy. The fat little waiter hit the ground and lay still. The bookie made an unexpected move and threw the money bag at Tonio. Tonio saw only movement of the arm and fired. He put three steel-jacketed .25 into Skinny Man's right leg and the bookie hit the ground groaning.

Percy made his move, and Tonio shot four times. One went into his right knee, the second missed; the third and fourth caught Percy in his gun arm. Percy flipped over onto the ground, holding his knee. He began to flop around, as if in a fit, banging his head on the ground. And then lay still.

The waiter found his voice then. "Please, mister. Please, *please*— don't, mister, please—"

Tonio walked to the money bag and picked it up. "Keep your face tight down, man!" Tonio ordered in a sing-song voice.

The waiter dropped his head so fast he cracked the skin on his forehead. Tonio backed off into the shadows, threw the bag through the open bathroom window, scaled the few feet, and was inside.

He picked up the money bag and opened it as he walked back through the apartments. Never hesitating for a moment in his forward motion, he stuffed the money inside his jacket and zippered the front. He tossed the gun to the floor, along with the gloves, stocking mask, and spare clip as casually as he would discard a candy wrapper.

He exited on Jamaica Avenue, using the same doorway he had used to enter the building, and walked steadily to the Long Island Railroad station. He paused only once in an unlighted doorway and replaced his eye patch. No one noticed him. He lost himself in the crowds.

At the railroad station, he caught a taxi, directing the driver to take him to Eastern Airlines at Kennedy via the Van Wyck Expressway. At the terminal, which was the busiest of all the airline terminals at that time of night, he had a drink, then took a taxi back to Manhattan. At Fifty-ninth Street he took a subway back to the Riverside Arms.

He did not think about the two men he had shot ever again. There was absolutely no difference in shooting nameless, faceless shadows in the jungle of Viet Nam and shooting faceless shadows in back of a bar in Jamaica, Queens, New York.

He was not stimulated, nervous, or worried. He had no fear of being caught. New York cops didn't bother all that much with the shooting of a bookie, or gun guards. In fact, Tonio felt nothing at all, except fatigue.

The Riverside Arms was quiet. Most of the windows were dark when he arrived. He went to his room immediately without seeing anyone, or being seen, checked his traps and entered. He put the money into a hole he had made in the back wall of the closet and covered it up with an old suitcase. He didn't bother to count it. It would be a lot of money. Thirty–forty—perhaps as much as fifty thousand dollars. It wasn't how much money he had, but that there would be enough when he made his move.

He stripped and took a hot shower. He had completely forgotten about Eleanor Cassie, and when he did remember, he debated getting up and going to her or not. He had some reading to do, but he wasn't going to be able to do that.

He glanced down and looked at himself. He had an erection. "What the hell—"

He put on his jeans and slippers and pulled on a clean T-shirt, locked up, setting his traps, and went to her room. He tapped lightly.

"Who is it?" She sounded sleepy.

"Me—"

There was a moment and then the door opened. "Hi—"

"Hi—" He closed the door behind him and locked it. He stripped off the shirt and tossed it to one side. "What did you do while I was gone?" he asked quietly.

"I cleaned up. Then I read. And I listened to a fight down the hall."

"Bad fight?"

"Just shouting. Funny as hell. Sounded like two fairies. One of them had a funny accent—not quite English, but Englishy—"

"That would be Mannering and Tulip. They're always at it."

"Very witty. I haven't laughed like that in a long time." She watched him step out of his trousers. When she saw his erection, she shivered.

"I'll take care of that," she said, and dropped to her knees before him, clasping him around his thighs and drawing him into her mouth.

He lay smoking while she used the bathroom. He was impatient with himself. Overcaution could create jeopardy as readily as carelessness. What was happening between himself and Eleanor was perfectly normal. Whatever her needs were, he was, in some way, fulfilling them. And she had certainly satisfied him. It had been a long time since he had had a woman and the torpor he felt at the moment was a luxury he had denied himself for too long.

She brought the rest of the bottle of wine and a glass. "You're still hard," she said, looking down at him.

"True," he said, sipping the wine, liking the raw taste of the cheap red in his throat. "But without enthusiasm at the moment."

She sat on the side of the bed and took him in her hand. She caressed him gently. "I must have come a half-dozen times. And you?"

"Who counts?" He sipped the wine. "Why did you come to New York?"

"Have you ever been to Madison, Wisconsin?"

"No."

Her shrug was eloquent comment. "If you want things that your hometown can't offer, then you go after them. And, if you're lucky, you find them elsewhere. I started looking in New York." She counted on her fingers. "This is October, I've been here since June. Four months."

"How long did you live with the bum who stole your stuff?"

"Chip? About two months. I got a job right away when I first arrived—I was a counter girl at Hertz—and stayed at the Y. I met him in the Village and stayed a weekend, and then just sort of moved in. Hertz didn't pay enough and I switched to being a waitress at Ryan's Steak House over on the East Side. You know it?''

Tonio nodded. "Why did you leave?''

"One of the cooks damn near raped me in the supply room. Tore my dress and bra half off. The manager needed a good cook more than he did a waitress." She shrugged, hunching up her thin shoulders, shivered, and slipped into bed with him and snuggled up close. "By that time I was with Chip and it didn't seem to matter—" she paused.

"Listen," she said tentatively.

"I'm listening," Tonio said.

"I lied to you this morning. I really *was* trying to get up my nerve and jump in front of the train."

"I know."

"How do you know?" She was shocked.

"It's all in the eyes. Back in Nam, guys who knew they had to go out on patrol had the look. I've seen it in the eyes of Cong guys, too. Looking for a way out, and knowing there isn't any, and then working up their nerve."

"That's what I was trying to do."

"I know."

She snuggled up closer and stroked his stomach and down to his erection. "You have a beautiful body."

"It was about time one of us said that," Tonio said evenly.

Eleanor recoiled physically, withdrawing, as if he had threatened her. "Now you sound like you did this morning. And when you came home and found me cooking dinner."

"How is that?"

"Like you're not here. Like you don't even know *I'm* here."

"How old are you?" he asked, sitting up and reaching for his clothing.

"Twenty-two."

"You don't look more than seventeen or eighteen."

"Want to check my ID?"

"So!" Tonio said with an explosive blow through his lips. "You're twenty-two, come from Madison, Wisconsin, split to New York, got

79

hooked up with a punk, almost landed up dead by your own hand, and you've been a Hertz girl, and a waitress. Now you're with me. Did you have any plans at all when you came to New York?"

"No—"

"Didn't want to be a model, or an actress, or a rock star?"

"No. And please, don't be that way. Be nice."

Nice, he thought. "How much education do you have?"

"Two years of college. English lit. I wanted to be a teacher and marry Mickey Service, and later on, have a family with a nice little house, dog, station wagon, bridge on Wednesday, sex twice a week, pot roast and hamburgers on alternate Tuesdays. I didn't have any plans when I came to New York."

"What happened to Mickey Service?"

"What happens to all of the Mickey Services of this world? They go away to college, meet someone else, move to southern California, and live a beautiful life."

"Family?" Tonio was dressed.

"They don't count. I told you that this morning. Do you have to go? Can't you stay with me tonight?"

"I like you enough to sleep with you, and I enjoyed it. I really did. But that's all there is. No playing house. No setups. You want to get it on, I'm easy. But I have a life I'm preparing for. I've been doing it a long time. I don't have the time or the inclination to go further than we already have, so I'm telling you up front. That's the way it is."

She nodded. She swallowed hard.

"Don't try to move in on me. You can't do it. I'm dedicated to my work."

"All right. I accept. But, two questions?"

"Go."

"May I call you Tonio?"

"Why not? That's my name. Second question?"

"Don't you ever take that patch off your eye?"

"Never. Except when I wash my face, shower, and shave."

"Did it hurt? When it happened, I mean."

"Yes."

She lay back on the bed. She smiled. She stretched and pulled her legs down, knees stiff, pointing her toes. "It's going to be all right."

"What is?"

"The way things are. It's going to be easy."

"I'll see you when I see you," Tonio said.

He closed the door.

In his room, Tonio put her out of his mind as effortlessly as blinking his eye. The fatigue he had known before sleeping with Eleanor was gone. The torpor that engulfed him after his multiple orgasms had been replaced with renewed energy. He made a cup of Sanka, went to his worktable, and began preparing Litho-Vu envelopes, tapping out the address on a variety of labels, stuffing them with old newspapers and stapling them closed. When he was finished, he set the alarm on the clock radio for four a.m. and then fell on the bed.

He slept better than he had in months.

7 Chris Murdoch stepped into the damp, wet St. Cyr underground
garage and wrinkled his nose. The raw odor of concrete and
automobile exhaust cut into his nostrils.

"Jesus, am I glad I caught you before you left the Tower,"
Andy Brooks said.

"What the hell is going on?" Murdoch asked, glancing past him
to a crowd of people around the attendant's booth. With some
dismay he saw most of them were reporters. "I thought you
were going home?"

"I *was* going home, on my way out of the lobby, when Kosinski caught me, said I had a phone call. I thought it was you."
Brooks glanced nervously at the crowd. "It was a cop friend of mine out
at Kennedy International who knows I'm working here now. Princess
Martha is bombed out of her skull, staggering drunk, and raising all
kinds of hell. She and her husband, Lord Woodford, had a hell of a
fight. Kids screaming, dirty language, pushing and shoving—the
works."

82

"Oh, Christ, this is all I need. What happened out at Kennedy?"

"Seems she didn't like the way the customs people were pawing through her things. Well, you know those customs guys. Get them mad at you, suspicious, or both, and they can really give you a hard time."

"And they did," Murdoch said grimly.

"And they did. The works. Personal searches, everything. They even searched the kids. That ripped it, and she really went crazy. Anyway, they had to call for help, which produced another confrontation, her security people versus the New York cops. Finally everybody cooled off a little bit and they were hustled into a pair of Cadillac limos and took off."

"Why not the helicopter?"

"Weather's too bad."

"Was Lord Woodford drunk too?"

"My friend didn't say."

"When did you get the call?"

"About twenty minutes ago. They had just pulled out of Kennedy."

Murdoch studied the scene around the attendant's booth and then looked at his watch. "With traffic at this time of night, we should have at least another twenty–twenty-five minutes, more if we're lucky. Get to a phone and call the limo company. They must have CB's in those cars. Tell them to contact the drivers and instruct them to come to the north side, service entrance. If there is any question, the drivers can explain to her people that it's a security measure. And if her security people are with it, they'll dig what's going on."

"If she's all that drunk, and mad, how do you think she'll feel about coming in the service entrance, Mr. Murdoch?"

"I don't give a damn how she feels. I don't want her spread all over the *Daily News* zonked out of her skull, probably throwing another fit of some kind as she enters the Tower."

"Yes, sir."

"I'll stay here and try to ward this bunch off if you can't reach them. Make it snappy," Murdoch said tightly. "Get right back to me."

The crowd around the booth, not getting any answers from the attendant, began to mill around. Several people started back up the ramp to wait in the lobby. Murdoch remained hidden in the shadows.

The television newsman had the camera lights turned off and then looked right at Murdoch, but did not react. He continued to stare, and Murdoch wondered why he didn't come over. Then he realized that the man didn't see him at all and was temporarily blinded by the television lights. Murdoch moved deeper into the shadows just as the elevator door opened and Brooks, red-faced and out of breath, grinned at him. "Got 'em. They should arrive at the service entrance in less than fifteen minutes."

Murdoch breathed a sigh of relief. "Okay, now get over there and convince the gentlemen of the press and television that she's arriving at the Fifth Avenue entrance, that she's steaming, and they might get more of the same she laid down at Kennedy. Got it?"

"Right!" Brooks grinned.

"Then, when you can, sneak away and join me at the service entrance."

Murdoch took his time getting to the loading area. He walked slowly, greeting familiar faces, avoiding the crush of the press and television mob at the entrance of the lobby and arrived only minutes before the two Cadillacs swept into the grubby ports of the loading zones. Murdoch took the arm of a passing waiter and whispered into his ear. "Grab one of the service elevators, and hold it, do you understand? Hold it until I get there, no matter what."

The startled waiter nodded and hurried away just as Andy appeared at his side.

"How're we doing out front?" Murdoch asked.

"The natives are getting restless."

"Maybe we'll get lucky—here they come."

Princess Martha's two security men were out of the cars before they had rocked to a gentle stop, one from each, taking in the area with a quick professional appraisal. Murdoch and Brooks dropped to the ground level as the two security men approached.

"I'm Gregory, and this is Haldstadt, security for Her Highness. Are you the gentleman, Mr. Brooks, we spoke to on the radio phones?"

"Murdoch, manager of the St. Cyr Tower. This is my chief of security, Mr. Brooks. There are reporters and television cameras waiting in the lobby for some of the same that happened out at Kennedy. I suggest your party get into its suite as soon and as quickly as possible," Murdoch said. "I have a service elevator standing by. We can change to an express elevator on the twentieth floor, and have the luggage handled later. How are the children?''

"Right enough. Sleepy, and upset, of course. Long trip, and it wasn't a pleasant situation at your customs, but then that's their job, isn't it? You're right about this, of course, and we appreciate it, Mr. Murdoch. Let's get on with it then.''

They all moved toward the cars. "I hope Princess Martha doesn't mind this back-door approach," Murdoch said under his breath.

"Her Highness is still drunk," Gregory said with quiet authority, "and she may protest, but that isn't your problem. Lord Woodford, on the other hand, will be obliging. It's his nature.''

The exchange from the cars to the elevators went smoothly. Lord Woodford, a tall elegant man, stared into the middle distance, smiled a lot, and stood dutifully to one side as the women and the children were hurried inside to the waiting elevator. The princess remained inside one of the cars. Gregory spoke to her through the open window and Murdoch heard a loud drunken protest.

"She refuses to get out. She wants to go through the main entrance," Gregory said quietly.

"If she goes through the lobby," Murdoch replied, "in the condition she's in, they'll crucify her. They'll provoke her into outrageous behavior. They're expert at that kind of thing. Is there no way to appeal to her? You must have gone through this before, and whatever you do, you had better do it quickly, or the reporters are going to discover they've been had, which will make them sore as hell, and then they will really do a job on her.'' Murdoch had spoken with pressing urgency and expected at any moment to find the loading platform swarming with angry, aggressive reporters and television cameramen.

"She listens to nobody, Mr. Murdoch," Gregory said.

"How does she look? I mean, hair, clothes, stockings—that sort of thing?''

"Her stockings are ripped and her hair is a mess.''

"Let me try and talk to her. Maybe—''

Gregory and Haldstadt nodded in agreement and Murdoch stepped to the open window. Princess Martha was slumped against the cushions. She stared straight at Murdoch. Her voice was thick and slurred. Her eyes blazed.

"What bloody hell do you want?" she demanded.

"I have a private message for you."

She did not move. She waited. "Speak, damn you. What's the message, and from whom?"

Murdoch tightened his jaw muscles. "I'm the whom, and the message is that what happened out at Kennedy was behind closed doors. Official, you might say, and no photographs. Possibly a State Department man there to smooth things over. But not here, Princess. You've no doubt had experience with Italian paparazzi? Well, these boys are tougher."

Murdoch let his voice get hard: "They're waiting in the lobby now, and they're going to see through this trick any second," he paused. "What'll it be, sweetie?" he asked deliberately.

She came forward in the seat, her eyes aflame. *"I am a Princess Royal—"*

"Right now, sweetie, you're a drunken bimbo who's going to get my hotel a lot of ugly publicity. Are you coming, or do I call the television cameras and let them photograph you here with the hotel garbage as background?"

"You bloody bastard," she whistled between her teeth.

Murdoch stepped back, knowing that he had won. He opened the door, glanced at Gregory and smiled. "Yes, ma'am, Your Royal Highness."

When she got out of the car, Murdoch could see that she wasn't as drunk as she pretended. They did not speak during the ride to the upper floor, where they changed elevators to make the big jump to the Tower suite. Murdoch said good night and she slammed the door in his face.

"I want to congratulate you on handling this the way you did, Mr. Murdoch," Gregory said. "They don't need any more bad press."

"I really think," Murodch said levelly, "Princess Martha and her party would be happier at The Plaza or The Pierre. I wish you would tell her that I can have everything arranged by tomorrow morning."

"I understand," Gregory said sadly. "I'll inform Her Highness of your suggestion."

"Thank you. Good night, Mr. Gregory."

"Good night, Mr. Murdoch. Mr. Brooks."

In the elevator returning to the lobby, Brooks smiled. "Congratulations. What did you say to get her out of the car?"

"Simple, I said I would knock out the Royal teeth if she got my hotel into a messy news clip on television," Murdoch said.

"Sure you did," Brooks said, nodding sagely. "Only thing to do. Absolutely."

Murdoch stopped briefly at the lobby desk hoping that there was some word from Maggie. There wasn't. Tired and depressed from the tensions of the day, worried about Maggie—that she might still be upset from that morning, he would make two more stops, and then he would go to bed.

In the room that housed the St. Cyr computers, he watched three of his men studying readouts as they checked through the thousands of employee applications that had poured in when construction of the hotel was announced.

"Anything yet, Braden?" Murdoch asked Andy Brooks's second in command.

"Not even a possible, Mr. Murdoch," Braden replied.

"That's the way it might be for some time."

"Especially when we don't know what we're looking for. That would be a big help."

"I know—I know," Murdoch said wearily. "But not at this time."

"Yes, sir."

Murdoch next visited the television-monitoring room. He glanced at the banks of screens. Two angles covering the main entrance, two more on the garage, three each on the main lobby, the desk, all elevators, and flickering back and forth, the endless corridors of the hotel. A few people entered and departed from the Fifth Avenue entrance; the corridors were empty.

He tapped the security officer on the shoulder. "Don't hesitate to have one of our people check anybody, or anything that doesn't look absolutely kosher," he said to the security officer sitting before the monitors.

He wandered back up to his office and sat behind his desk, started to make coffee, changed his mind and made a drink instead. He kept the lights out and when his eyes grew accustomed to the dark, watched the lights of Manhattan play against the misty black sky.

He picked up the phone and punched out Maggie's home number, and receiving no answer, tried her studio. The phone rang and rang, and finally he dropped the receiver. When she was working against a deadline, he knew that she often turned off the phone so as not to be disturbed.

He made a second drink and resumed his seat. There was really nothing for him to be depressed about; not really. Way down inside he did not believe the note and the beer can. It was someone jerking them off, and even if Threat were real, there was nothing to be done until they received a second notice, or a demand.

He went over his day, step by step, as he often did when he was troubled. Except for Threat, the only truly upsetting thing in the entire day had been the disagreement about New York he had that morning with Maggie. And it wasn't even a disagreement, when you came right down to it. And he saw that she had a point about the city. He had often caught himself resenting changes taking place. Surely that was a sign that he was getting old. He closed his eyes.

Threat.

The note was so goddamned enigmatic. "This proves that I have and that I can and that I will penetrate your security. This is Number One."

If it turned out to be a gag, it would be extremely clever, since it had achieved the desired effect. While the St. Cyr was not yet in a panic, they were certainly in a mild dither.

On the other hand, if it turned out to be real, it would be extremely clever, since it could achieve the desired effect by moving them across the line from dither to panic.

He sat upright. So, he was bothered by Threat, and not by Maggie's silence at all.

This thought depressed him even more, because he saw accurately that he was right back where he started. There was nothing, absolutely, to be done until they heard from him again. Or her. Or them, he thought ruefully.

He stood, stretched, stifled a huge yawn, and rinsed out his glass. The two drinks had worked effectively. He was suddenly so tired he wondered if he could get to bed before falling asleep.

He did not turn on the lights in the apartment but undressed in the dark and did not know that Maggie was asleep in bed until he slipped in beside her. She mumbled something and pressed up against him. At that moment, Chris Murdoch felt a sense of peace and even innocence that he had never known before. He looped one arm across Maggie's nude body and slept.

Tonio awoke a few minutes before the alarm went off. The alarm was really just a backup to the almost infallible internal clock he had developed in the jungle. The Riverside Arms was quiet as he washed and shaved, dressed and, taking the Litho-Vu mailings, slipped out of the house. He knew Mrs. Coffin kept the front door locked at night, but he had found a seldom used basement door. He slipped outside, stood in a small courtyard, closed the door carefully, and paused to listen to a tugboat making its way on the river. He breathed deeply in the crisp predawn air and hurried toward Broadway. He felt good. Alive. Fresh and clean. He thought briefly of Eleanor and knew that sex with her had drained away his tensions.

He walked briskly through the silent crosstown streets. Broadway, as usual, was lit up and restless. He made his mailings at the Planetarium Post Office Station, throwing them onto an already large pile of mail spilling on the floor, and walked on over to Central Park West to catch the subway downtown.

It began to rain. Good. It would be easier in the dark, *and* in the rain. No one hardly ever looked around in the rain. They concentrated on where they were going.

The manhole cover was fifty feet inside Fifty-fifth Street, west of Madison Avenue, and three feet from the curb. Alternate side of the street parking assured him that today there would be no cars covering the manhole and blocking easy access. Pretending to use the telephone in a booth near the Madison corner, he waited until there was no traffic. He would have thirty seconds. It was all he would need to open the manhole, remove the cover, slip inside, and replace the cover.

It was not a heavy cover; the hole was smaller than most to be found on Manhattan streets. And he had done it at least a half-dozen times before. He knew exactly how much weight he was going to have to contend with, both on entering and, the most difficult of all, leaving when he was finished.

The right moment came and he slipped out of the booth and walked quickly to the manhole, dropped to his knee, and inserted the edge of a

89

twelve-inch length of tire iron into the slot and pried upward; the heavy steel cover snapped up easily. He shoved it to one side and dropped down, feeling for the rungs of the ladder. Half-exposed to the street, he pulled at the cover, stepped deeper on the ladder, and slipped the cover into place with a heavy *clunk!*

He snapped on a pencil flashlight and walked carefully over the massive cables, hunched over, splashing water nearly to the tops of his boots.

He did not go very far. About forty feet farther he flashed his light on a hole cut into the side of the bedrock that was, more than any other reason, responsible for the island of Manhattan being the skyscraper capital of the world. Water dripped and splashed around him, and the sound of the water was fused with the sound of the city humming above. He had noticed it before. The steady vibrating hum of tens of thousands of moving parts that kept the city alive; transformers, electric currents, the distant rumble of subways. He snapped off the light. It was as dark as some of the nights in the jungle. He thought of his twin brother. This was what it must be like for him. Isolated. Perhaps in the dark. And then he put thoughts of his brother away and set to work.

He had no idea what the hole in the rock had been used for. But it had been cut to a specific size, was deep, and at the inner edge of a one-foot shelf, there was a drop of about twelve inches. Something that had been essential years before in the life of the underground city, when equipment came in bulky and hard-to-handle sizes and shapes, had rested there. And now it suited his purpose perfectly. Taking his tire iron, he rattled it loudly against the side edges of the hole several times. He had seen rats in the tunnel as large as cats and they were absolutely unafraid of anything.

He paused and listened. There were no wild screams or squeals. He braced himself and eased up to the edge of the hole and felt around inside.

Making a successful wiretap on the most sensitive phone in the St. Cyr Tower had been the toughest aspect of his whole project. But he saw that there was no way around the need for the tap. Every other part of his project could function perfectly, but come to naught without the tap.

Once he had made his installation, checked out the system, and felt sure that it would function, he felt no urgency to check it again. But it had been raining for over a week, day and night, and water and dampness was one of the major reasons for electronic malfunction. He had come down two days before, found the batteries less than perfect, knew that he would have to replace them and left the machine running.

The take-up reel was now only half-filled; the batteries had died. He replaced them with fresh ones and rewound the tape to the beginning.

He also considered that since his first contact had now been made, he might not get another chance to make sure everything was functioning properly. Tonio was supremely confident of his plan and that it would work, but he was also wary of Chris Murdoch.

Chris Murdoch had been schooled by the same people in Viet Nam as Tonio. While most of Murdoch's time had been in administration, he had done his share in the field. He had been trained, had been disciplined in *attack* Intelligence. Force the other fellow to make mistakes. Go against the rules. Look for the seams. But Tonio was determined there wouldn't be any.

The SONY tape recorder was dry, even a little dusty, and the special adapters he had used to install a twenty-four-hour reel-to-reel tape were exactly the way he had left them. The wire connecting to the telephone tap was intact.

He flashed his pencil light on the battery indicator and snapped the On button. The reels started moving slowly, inexorably, silently. The battery needle swung completely over to the green line. The fresh batteries were sound. He turned up the volume on the loudspeaker; the reassuring sound of background tape-hiss sizzled loudly. He was about to turn the machine off when he heard the unmistakable sound of a phone ringing on an open line.

I have Chief Solomon for you now . . .
Chris! How the hell are you? . . .

Tonio tensed. He closed out the sounds around him and listened intently.

. . . How about before lunch? . . .

91

It was Murdoch talking to the chief of detectives. Tonio felt his breath quicken as he snapped the rewind button. He caught it from the beginning and listened to the entire conversation again.

He rewound and listened a third time, started to erase, and then decided to leave the taped conversation between Solomon and Murdoch on the tape. He snapped the entire machine off. The new batteries were all right. He would not have to come back again until he was ready to use the equipment.

They had Number One. He stood at the bottom of the ladder and the manhole cover was above his head. And they were taking it seriously. Very seriously. Murdoch would not have brought in the chief of detectives if he had dismissed the beer can as a joke.

He breathed a sigh of relief when he realized that his first, most important, contact had achieved exactly what he had thought, hoped, it would achieve.

It was time to go to work. He would be early this morning. That would please them. The deli closed at twelve-thirty on Saturdays, but everyone hated coming in on their weekends for a half day, even though they only had to do it every fourth weekend.

He sat in the back of the nearly empty deli and drank coffee, thinking of Threat, ignoring the explosive irritation of the black sergeant, whose turn it was to work the half day.

Murdoch, being the Intelligence *sensitif* that he was, was closing out no options. As Tonio himself would have done. And Tonio was ready for him with options of his own.

Now it began.

He would leave another message—Two—and keep the fires *hot*.

Special Agent Horatio Rota arrived at FBI headquarters in the Hoover Building, in Washington, that Saturday morning with a miserable cold. The cold front that had swept down out of Canada had not moved for nearly a week, dumping chilling rain on the entire eastern seaboard. Rota had done everything possible to keep the cold from getting worse, drank a full bottle of a popular cough syrup and, without realizing it, had od'd on codeine. He signed in that morning feeling rather better than he had in days.

Fortifying himself with coffee, Rota sat with his feet on his desk and read the *Washington Post*'s sports page. A graduate of USC, he followed the Trojans football team faithfully. Rota disliked the weekend watch. But it would not be so bad today. They were playing Notre Dame starting at one, and he had brought his portable SONY.

On weekends there was only a skeleton staff to handle incoming requests from police departments around the country for information stored in the FBI files. Each request was handled as it came in, codes checked against a master file in the memory of the computer, before the request was granted. The time of the request and the origin, and the person making the request were logged, attached to the request as part of the log in memory. All this was done routinely. When the procedure was completed and the information transmitted, Rota would press a button on the console and the query itself added to the data bank.

He was halfway down a column analyzing the USC–Notre Dame quarterbacks when the terminal at his elbow began to clatter.

Rota sat up straight:

−OPEN LINE FOR TRANSMISSION·

Rota hunched over the terminal and typed rapidly:

LINE OPEN STATE CODES·

In New York, Lieutenant Bob Diedrickson was also hunched over a terminal, a cigarette hanging from his lips. He began to type—using the hunt-and-peck system:

−REQUEST CODES ·07
MINUS ·008 1419
PLUS EE PLUS JX·
NYPD DIEDRICKSON·

Rota typed again:

SUGAR ·10 PLUS ·001
ZED GOLD¬ ·01 PLUS ROTA ·/35 FBI·

Rota rested, holding his gaze on the typing line for a few seconds. He yawned suddenly. His jaws cracked. He shook himself, shuddering. He smacked his lips as the terminal began to clatter again.

-CONFIRM IDENTIFICATION. PROCEED.

Lieutenant Diedrickson lit a cigarette, paused, glanced at the material at his elbow.

-BEGIN MESSAGE.
CONFIRM. PROCEED.
-GREETINGS, ROTA. ANY CHANCE OF SUCCESS WITH A PARTIAL?
HELLO, DIEDRICKSON. HOW MANY POINTS?
-THREE. LOOK LIKE A CENTRAL POCKET LOOP.
FORGET IT.
-WILL YOU TRY?
WE HAVE NEVER HAD SUCCESS WITH ANYTHING LESS THAN FOUR
POINTS. SAY AGAIN. FORGET IT.
-WILL YOU TRY?
WASTE OF COMPUTER TIME.
-ONE FOR THE GIPPER?
WILL DO. BUT LOW PRIORITY. STAND BY FOR SIGNAL. TRANSMIT
COORDINATES.
-LINE OPEN FOR SIGNAL. REQUEST CLASSIFICATION FILE CODE.

Rota punched out a code on his console terminal, set the computer memory on DOCUMENT.

YOUR REQUEST FILED STANDARD REFERENCE CODE SUGAR .10
GOLD.
.01 PLUS NYPD 10/27/79 CODE WILL READ OUT 3 PT
PARTIAL.
-UNDERSTOOD.
STAND BY FOR MARK FIVE FOUR THREE TWO ONE MARK.

In New York, Diedrickson began feeding the information via prepared tape into his terminal. The machine printed out the material on his terminal as it fed the information into Rota's computer.

At the instant that Diedrickson depressed his transmit key in New York, Rota reached over to depress the encoding key on his console, and at that moment the codeine acting on his nervous system caused him to yawn again and while he thought he had touched the key, he had missed it. The computer had the information stored in its DOCUMENT memory, but without the codes, it didn't know what to do with it.

```
-THANKS, ROTA.
AS WE SAY IN ENGLAND YOU ARE SO ENTIRELY WELCOME.
-I THOUGHT YOU WERE CHICANO FROM SOUTHERN CAL?
WHO KNOWS FROM GEOGRAPHY. ROTA ./34 FBI.
-DUMMY.
ASK FOR ANOTHER FAVOR, PAL.
-DIEDRICKSON NYPD PLUS EE. PLUS JX.
END TRANSMISSION.
-LINE CLOSED.
```

Dr. Phil Wyeth was about to check out of the St. Cyr Clinic that morning after a busy night. Three cases of acute alcoholic poisoning; one coronary, two suspected coronaries, which turned out to be indigestion, and a broken wrist when a female guest slipped while trying to make love in the bathtub. He made a last-minute check of the charts and started for the door, nodding to the nurse. "Enjoy the weekend, I plan to," Wyeth said.

"I'm stuck. Taking Helen's place on a double shift."

"Poor you." Wyeth slipped into his raincoat.

"I knows you feels for me, baby," the nurse said, and reached for the ringing phone. She listened a moment and handed the phone to Wyeth. "Her Royal Highness, Princess Martha."

"Doctor Wyeth," he said coolly. He listened a moment. "Red spots, vomiting, sore throat," he glanced at the nurse who had paused to listen, "temperature—hundred and four. Okay, I got the picture. How is the other child?"

There was a sudden burst of abuse over the phone loud enough for the nurse to hear. She shook her head. When the tirade was over, Wyeth gripped the phone tightly and replied coldly, "Lady, having never heard of either you or your son, how in hell would I know he should be addressed, even in third person, as Viscount Maximilian? And, lady— *lady*, listen: who the hell *cares*? Now, do you want me to take a look at the child or not?"

There was another tirade and Wyeth dropped the phone into the cradle. He was white with anger. He turned to the nurse. "Get hold of Murdoch. Tell him to meet me on the ninetieth floor in ten minutes. I'm not walking into this one alone."

"Measles?"

"Ten to one it's scarlet fever."

"Here we go again!" Nurse Craik said.

Keep the pressure on, keep tightening the screw, let them know that it's serious and not a joke. It was heavy-handed psychology Tonio was using, and he knew it, but it was also effective.

Suite 82-A was one of the half-floor suites being readied for its owner. Painters, plumbers, paperhangers, glaziers, carpenters had been working on the interior design for over two months. Tonio knew it well having delivered Danish and coffee to the workers a half-dozen times.

At nine-thirty that morning, choosing his moment carefully, when the lobby would be at the peak of activity, crowded with check-outs and check-ins, when the kitchen would be one great bedlam as breakfast orders were filled, he slipped unnoticed into the service elevator with his plastic hampers.

As he expected, suite 82-A was empty. He wrinkled his nose at the pungent odor of fresh paint, moved quickly to a room used temporarily for storage and slipped inside. Deep behind a pile of boxes and litter he pulled out a pair of dirty coveralls and pulled them on. He removed the eye patch, the sweater cap, and pulled on a battered construction worker's hard hat. He slipped on a pair of wrap-around glasses which were only slightly tinted, and lowered the plastic face shield, which was discolored and scruffed, and difficult to see through. With the shield in place and the tinted glasses behind it, it was almost impossible to distinguish his features.

Taking a clipboard from the hamper, he glanced over it briefly. The top sheet was one he had prepared himself:

SELIGMAN & SON
Electrical Contractors
789 Broadway

There was a graph, and the long sweep of an exponential curve he had drawn on it, with meaningless numbers written in at random points along the curve line.

Lastly, he removed a voltage-test meter, and Number Two from the hamper. He shoved the beer can into his pocket and made his way back to the service elevator.

He rode to the second-basement level without stopping, which was unusual considering the hour, and stepped outside, checking first for the building engineer he knew would be on duty before the control board. There was no fear of making a noise. The roar of the machinery overwhelmed any other sound. The man moved back and forth across the hugh panel of dials, lights, and meters, his attention focused entirely on his job. Tonio slipped off in the opposite direction quickly.

All of the elevators in the building were computer-controlled, programmed to react to demands with the least amount of waiting regardless of the time of day. It was a beautifully designed system with double-backup fail-safe checks against accidents.

Tonio opened the door of the panel housing the circuitry for the entire system, placed Number Two inside, and threw the circuit breaker on a bank of four lifts.

Above him four high-speed elevators jolted to a stop throwing the passengers to the floor.

On the other side of the power vault, the engineer nearly went into shock when he saw the red emergency flasher indicating malfunction in the elevators. He punched at an override fail-safe button freezing the elevators into place, turned, and sprinted toward the circuit-breaker panel.

Tonio ducked behind a building column as the man raced by him and continued on to the service elevator. The ride back to the eighty-second floor took more than five minutes as waiters crowded in with tables laden with food for room service. But he was not perturbed. He kept well out of the way. He spoke to no one and no one spoke to him. He might not have been there at all.

Within five minutes, the lobby-security man, Hoag, who was the first to respond to the elevator emergency, notified Murdoch that he had found something unusual, and that it might be tied in with the extra work they were doing.

Reluctantly, Chris Murdoch assured him that it was.

He then dialed Jesse Solomon at his apartment in the Riverdale section of the Bronx. "We just collected another beer can," he said.

"I'll be right down," Solomon replied.

"Was anybody hurt?" Solomon asked.

"None seriously. Few sprained ankles and wrists," Murdoch replied.

They sat in Murdoch's office, both of them unshaven and wearing casual Saturday-morning clothes. The beer can, the pennies, and the note, an exact duplicate of the first with the exception that the word One had been replaced by the word Two.

"Is the hotel full?" Solomon asked, scratching his day-old beard.

"To capacity."

"What would have happened if, instead of the beer can, it had been a bomb? If he had blown out the whole panel?"

"My best guess is, that with the backup fail-safes in the system, the cars would just lock in place."

"But you're not sure?" Solomon asked.

"No. But the elevator people are here now, if you want to ask them."

Solomon shook his head and stared out of the window. He looked at Murdoch. "How many people were in the four cars that got stuck?"

"Altogether, seventeen."

"They could have been killed."

Murdoch remained silent.

"Is he, or isn't he?" Solomon mused.

"What?"

"A crazy. What do you think?"

"I *don't* think it's a joker, somebody out to dick us around—"

"I'm talking psychotic-crazy—somebody who has lost contact with reality. Bananas."

Murdoch was quiet for a full minute. Both men stared out of the window.

"Well?" Solomon demanded.

"No, I don't think it's a crazy."

"Why not?"

"So far, he's just showing off," Murdoch said slowly.

"Okay, what else?"

"Telling us he can do, what he says he can do. Penetrate our security."

"All right, you're saying he's lucid. But I've talked to nuts who are as clear as me or you until something snaps—and then they go funny right before your eyes."

"What're you chewing on, Jesse?" Murdoch asked quietly. "Are you thinking about evacuating the building?"

"It's sticky, Chris. Crazy or not, he's proven he can get in and out of the most sensitive areas."

"Want to hear what I really think?"

Solomon nodded slowly. "What's his motivation? Why is he doing it?"

"Psychological warfare."

"Bullshit." Solomon continued to scratch his beard.

"I have no say-so in this, Jesse. We made a deal. You'd keep quiet until we heard from him again, and we have, but although it's only twenty-four hours that I've lived with this thing, I'm already convinced he wants a payoff. His psychology has to be that he softens us up and when the time comes, we *will* pay off. And if I'm correct, we don't have anything to worry about until we get a demand. But ripping people out of the building now, especially on a day like this—"

"So, of course it's all on me if I get their precious butts out in the cold," Solomon said angrily.

"You want 'em out," Murdoch shouted angrily, "I'll give the order! But I ought to tell you that Princess Martha, a Royal bitch if there ever was one, has two kids up on the ninetieth floor with scarlet fever in quarantine. And we got one coronary that can't be moved to a hospital."

"That's a shitty point to score, Chris, and you know it."

"Shitty or not, it's a fact," Murdoch said, cooling off. "And have you thought about where you're going to send the rest of 'em? There's St. Patrick's, that oughta take a couple of thousand. And St. Thomas down the street for some more, and the underground promenade in Rockefeller Center—"

"Okay, okay, you made your goddamned point," Solomon said testily. "And before you say it, before you even think it, I'm not hesitating about this to cover my ass."

"I know that, Jesse," Murdoch said. "But what do we do now?"

"We leave it alone," Solomon said, "play it by ear—and wait and see." He thought of the partial print at the FBI. "Maybe we'll get lucky before anybody gets really hurt."

The following Monday afternoon, Lieutenant Diedrickson received a message from Special Agent Rota that the computer response to the three-point partial had been negative. In fact, the computer had not even confirmed a trace of the central pocket-loop fingerprint. There was, Rota concluded, nothing else he could do.

PART TWO

CHRIS MURDOCH

It was dawn on the day before Christmas and a threat of snow hung over the city, presaged by a kind of cold that is dead and still. Eleanor listened as Tonio, leaving, closed the door. She glanced at the clock: 5:00. Then silence. She knew he was going to his room to study. He did it so often, early in the morning, late at night, that she had begun to refer to his room as "the study." And in this way she understood why she was never invited there. He had established the limits of their relationship, and while he practically lived with her in her room, his room became off limits because it was "the study," and she accepted that.

She did not move. She remained in bed and stared at the sky. She thought she could detect the first signs of gray, but was mistaken. Someone in a rear building across the courtyard had turned on a light and she had only seen the reflection.

For several weeks she had felt something approaching contentment with Tonio at her side every night, preparing his breakfast and dinner, sitting together, with Tonio eating so casually, as if even food had no interest for him, describing scenes at the deli, or at Columbia.

Once when she was alone she had glanced through some of his books. She was particularly interested in what he had underlined. There weren't many such passages. She sought them out, flipping the pages rapidly. Many of the underlined passages made her wonder why this or that particular thought appealed to him, and she tried to match the thought with what she knew about him.

She shivered. The early-morning bitter cold slipped into the room and she went back to bed thinking about Tonio. There was something wrong and she could not quite define it. She lay a long time listening to the noises of the Riverside Arms as it shook off the night and braced for the day of cold, and possibly snow. Laura Roc began vocalizing. For the past two weeks Eleanor had been working with the singer, performing on street corners in the midtown area. Dressed as nuns, Eleanor played Schubert on a battery-powered tape recorder while Laura sang "Ave Maria." They had made a lot of money, and had not yet been hassled by the cops. Today would be the last and while they had been averaging well over two hundred dollars a day, they hoped to double it. Laura's voice soared through the halls. No one yelled at her. Everyone knew how much she needed what she would make that day.

Eleanor was distressed by Tonio's attitude toward love, and she struggled to remember an underlined passage in one of Tonio's books, a volume of essays by Montaigne.

If you press me to say why I loved him, I can say no more than it was because he was he, and I was I.

She smiled in the dark and closed her eyes and listened to Laura's powerful, absolutely pure voice dominate all other sounds in the building, not having any way of knowing that the passage Tonio had underlined referred to his twin brother.

In his room, Tonio collected the stack of manila envelopes he had prepared the night before to be mailed to Litho-Vu and left the Riverside Arms by the basement door. At this hour there were few people out on the cold streets. He kept glancing up at the sky, worried about snow. Snow could really make trouble for him. But if it came, he would deal with it. He swung into an almost empty Broadway and headed uptown a few blocks, then east toward Columbus Avenue. At a deserted mailbox he mailed what he knew would be the last of his newspaper-filled Litho-Vu-addressed manila envelopes.

The all-night attendant at the small garage was drowsing over a magazine in his tiny office. A steam radiator hissed. A radio was tuned to a rock station. Tonio tapped the glass. The attendant, who was black, looked up, one hand seeming to hang loose at his side in a body position that suggested total fatigue, or even sleep, but Tonio knew the man was holding a .38. On seeing and recognizing Tonio, the attendant released his grip on the gun and it slipped back into the slot he had made in the well of the scarred desk. He grinned and got up to open the door.

"Tonio! Them dudes got you out making a trip on the day *before* Christmas?" The black man and Tonio slapped hands. "You going to Philly, Jersey, or Bridgeport?" Tonio moved to the radiator, warming his fingers, rubbing them together.

"That's the bottom line. Mr. Glotzman called me at midnight and told me. Just like that. Bridgeport tomorrow. Woke up the kids. It's a good thing I answered the phone. My wife would have blown the fucking Christmas bonus right then and there. I never heard her so mad—" Tonio lit a cigarette.

The attendant unlocked a wooden cabinet on the wall, dirty and greasy from a hundred thousand openings, revealing a Peg-Board and over two hundred sets of automobile keys. He selected one, and tossed the keys to Tonio.

"Say she got pissed, huh?" He laughed and sat down in the spring-back office chair. "Sheet! That same thing happened to me. I was working over a few years back on the East Side, doing the same thing, with a little mechanical work on the side—"

Tonio cut in. "Listen, Simon, I haven't got much time this morning. Mr. Glotzman told me to pay you for next month, and here's a ten for Christmas." Tonio dug the money out of his pocket and counted out the bills carefully.

"You got me coming off the *wall*, Tonio. Your boss give *me* a ten, for Christmas! Sheet—that's some boss you got. Here, man, take a shot of this good stuff before you take off."

"What'cha got?"

"Good cream, man. One of the customers give me a Christmas bottle. Jack Daniel's—sweet—*good* whiskey, man. Cream." The attendant pulled a bottle from the desk and handed it to Tonio. While Tonio drank the attendant pulled a worn receipt book from the top drawer of the desk. He lined up the carbon and wrote slowly and carefully, forming his letters with great care:

Received of Spoc's Tool and Die Company $100.00.

The receipt was stamped PAID and then passed over to Tonio, who folded it carefully and put it in his pocket. Tonio handed the bottle back.

"Go on, man, take another pull. It's going to snow sure as shit covers a chicken yard and you get stuck on the New England Thruway—"

"Thanks, but that's enough. Well, I gotta shove off. Merry Christmas, Simon."

"Same to you and the family, Tonio." They slapped hands. "Your van's on the fourth floor."

He had stolen the VW van in Hartford a year and a half before and repainted it twice, shifting it to three different garages in different parts of the city, until he was satisfied that it was secure. He rode the elevator down, keeping the engine going though he was not supposed to, getting a good hot blast out of the heater, waved to the attendant, and bounced out into the darkened street.

He headed east, rode Amsterdam Avenue straight north, and then swung east again on 125th Street. There was more activity up here in Harlem than there had been on Broadway. Bundled figures walked fast in the cold. He passed a patrol cruiser with the cops giving him the once-over and then he was approaching Third Avenue. Delivery and service trucks from all parts of Manhattan were headed north, as he was, for the Bronx. He swung in back of a huge, red Consolidated Linen Supply truck and hung there, crossing the Harlem River into the Bronx. The traffic was thickening. Delivery trucks of all kinds, shapes, and sizes were making final deliveries on the last day before Christmas. Big and little shops all over the Bronx would make as much as ten percent of their annual sales on Christmas Eve, and they couldn't do that unless they had last-minute goods on the shelves.

At Third Avenue and 149th Street, Tonio pulled over to the curb, parked the VW van, and walked back to an all-night diner that catered to inner-city truckers. He had been stopping there two and three times a month and he was known by some of the regulars who greeted him cheerfully. He ordered coffee and a prune Danish and ambled to the rear of the diner, where several men sat in a booth. They looked no different in dress and manner than any of the others in the diner, but they *were* different.

"Ahh! Tonio, baby! Here comes my Christmas bonus! Tonio bets short money on sure things, and then he makes his big-money bet on the long shot, and that's like finding money in the street. Merry Christmas, spik!" The bookie stuck out his hand and they shook briefly.

"Merry Christmas, Brandy."

They got right down to business. Brandy pulled out a roll of bills. "You wint eight bucks on your five horse yesterday ina sixth. You win a hunnert and forty and change on the two horse in the second. That's two twenty and change, and you blow two hundred on the twenty-to-one long shot in the seventh. Making a grand total of twenty bucks and change I owe you."

The other men in the booth said nothing. They watched the money pass hands and took a long hard look at Tonio. They always did when money changed hands. "What'cha like today, Tonio?"

"Twenty to win, Possum's Lady in the first. Fifty to win Show-Me-Now in the fourth, and five yards on Sampson's Cool in the sixth—"

"Tonio! I love you, baby. *I love you!* A twenty-to-one horse. Sampson's Cool," Brandy said to the two other men, "couldn't win this race if they had one of them big moon rockets shoved up his ass!"

Tonio shrugged. "I stay even. Make a few. One of these days I hit big, but will you pay off?"

"Kid, I pay off. But you ain't never going to hit playing dogs like Sampson's Cool."

"You don't like my action, Brandy, I take it elsewhere."

"Tonio, baby, what's the story, huh? Don't go hard on me, Tonio. I like it, I like it."

Tonio peeled off the money and dropped it on the table, Brandy gathered up the $570 and applied it carefully to his roll, very much like a man wrapping an Ace bandage. Nothing was written down. It was all in Brandy's head.

"Say hello to the wife and kids, Tonio. And Merry Christmas, ya schmuck! You schmuck spik, ya! You going to Bridgeport today?"

"I tell my wife, yeah," Tonio said. "Bridgeport. Wouldn't you know. I take even money I get my ass stuck on the thruway in the snow."

Brandy laughed. It was not a merry laugh. It was the kind of giggle a man will make when he sees someone else in jeopardy and he knows he's safe. And it was the first time his two bodyguards had made a sound as they laughed also. But they cut it off quickly. They did not like too much humor when business was being conducted. It was a distraction, and they had heard what had happened in Queens to Skinny Man and Percy. One of them indicated a nearby stool at the counter. A tall, sleepy-eyed black in a Sanitation Department uniform was waiting patiently to approach the booth and make his bet.

"See you, Tonio." Brandy turned to business. It was not a cold or unfriendly dismissal. After all, Tonio was a good customer, but so was the black. But he was nervous just the same, even if Sampson's Cool was a dog. Five hundred on a twenty-to-one shot could beat the hell out of him.

Park Avenue in the Bronx was not the same as the Park Avenue in Manhattan where the rich and important lived their lives of luxury and ease. Park Avenue in the Bronx was block after block of four-, five-, six-, eight-, and ten-story apartment buildings, where tens of thousands of the quiet, patient middle class of the city lived. That was forty years before.

Park Avenue in the Bronx on which Tonio drove northward that morning had begun to change right after World War II and the change was radical, rapid, and thorough. It was not long before the area was a ghetto. Buildings began to decay. Plumbing was ripped out of empty apartments and sold to get a fix; children were not safe on the streets; women were not safe on the streets; and eventually there came the time when even the cops were not safe on the streets. Landlords abandoned ownership of their buildings, cut their losses, and wrote them off, never to return.

Block after block of gutted apartment buildings, open windows gaping like eye-less sockets, torn, ripped, defeated structures in the last stages of decay were covered with graffiti in bright primary colors, expressing hate and contempt for society in four-letter words that were often misspelled. It reminded Tonio of photographs he had seen of German cities at the end of World War II, and in fact it was known as the "bombed-out section" to those who were familiar with the area. And when the people moved out, the rats and the cats and vermin took over.

Tonio had chosen this building very carefully. It was a sturdy, stone structure with a steel skeleton, hardwood floors, thick walls; exactly what he needed.

Traffic was beginning to quicken to a steady hum. Daylight would not be long in coming. He parked the van on a side street near the corner, got out, and pretended to be checking the engine. He made a careful survey, and particularly the nine-story structure set on the corner of the block. Once-clear sidewalks were now filled with brick rubble, twisted pipe, and cracked toilet bowls gleefully ripped out and tossed from the upper stories. Bags of kitchen garbage discarded from passing cars were fought over by stray dogs. Broken glass like the glaze of a baker's icing overlayed everything with a fine patina.

When Tonio was in this part of the Bronx, he acted with the same life-death caution he had used in the jungle. It was not exactly a war zone, but he treated it as such and he came spectacularly armed for what he considered to be the most dangerous part of his project against the St. Cyr Tower, carrying two six-inch throwing knives, a .38 automatic, and a live hand grenade. He knew exactly where he was and what kind of enemy he would face, should there be one. They roamed in large gangs. But he was, he felt, prepared.

This would be his last trip to the old building. It had taken him six months to complete what he thought of as Phase Two of his project.

He removed the rotor from the engine, locked the van, and moved quickly to the doorway fifty feet away. The door hung lopsidedly on one hinge. He took one more look around, saw no one, and moved inside. He paused and listened. It was black and silent. He did not need a light. All of his previous work in the building had been done almost exclusively without light and by touch alone. He flipped the eye patch upward and let it rest on his forehead. He waited for his vision to adjust, then moved on, turning into the first door on his left.

The ground-floor apartment was littered with human feces, newspapers, empty bottles, milk cartons, discarded clothing, and the inevitable carpet of broken glass. Traffic rumbled outside on Park Avenue. He glanced at the nakedly open window and saw the first murky daylight coming up through the snow clouds over the East Bronx, the East River, and farther on, Hell's Gate. He would have to hurry. Twenty minutes to a half hour at the most, and then he would be gone.

He moved into the kitchen, stepped over a mattress, and felt along the wall inside of what had once been a utility closet. Down on his knees, his head and shoulders inside the closet, he felt around the baseboard, found a finger grip, and pulled the baseboard away from the wall.

He did not have to use a light yet. He reached inside and felt around. The mass of plastique explosives and the high-intensity thermoincendiary bomb attached to one of the steel girders, bulging out like an awkwardly applied bandage on a person's leg, was exactly as he had left it. He checked the wiring and the detonator; he found the timer, which was nothing more than a Silent-Ticking Baby Ben alarm clock. The crystal had been removed from the face. Being careful of the connecting wires, it was now that he used a light for the first time. He snapped on a pencil flash, covering it as much as he could with his body and looked at his wristwatch. It was 7:30 a.m. exactly. He set the alarm for 7:30 p.m., twelve hours later.

Careful not to run over the alarm, he set the minute and hour hand at 7:25, and then very slowly, wound both the main spring and the alarm. He snapped off the pencil flash and he was in darkness again.

When the clock started ticking, he slipped it back into the hole and placed it next to the detonator, checked the wiring one last time, slid back on the filthy floor, replaced the baseboard, and remained perfectly still, not breathing, listening for the tick of the Baby Ben. He heard nothing. Anyone entering the closet could not hear the clock on the other side of the wall. He eased back and stood upright in the kitchen and listened again. He heard nothing but the traffic outside.

The whole operation had taken him less than three minutes. He had eight other timers to set, and he would be finished.

Like most apartment buildings built in that period of growth in the Bronx, the structures were simple in design, with a single hallway running down the center of the building, dividing the building "front" and

110

"back." Two self-service elevators were placed in the middle of the building and on each side of the elevator shafts were fire stairs.

He left the first apartment and moved across the hall to the apartment directly opposite, which occupied a similar corner location as the first. He was finished setting the alarm on the second charge in less than three minutes, and he moved on down the ground-floor hallway, holding one of the throwing knives in his right hand and the .38 automatic in his left. He did not want to have to use the gun unless it was absolutely necessary. He wished now that he had bought the silencer his weapons supplier in Bridgeport had offered him. But he had seen no use for it at the time and had refused.

Tonio had placed two charges at the base of the elevator shafts, which required his going into the basement. All of the equipment to operate a functioning apartment house had been removed long ago. The entire elevator apparatus—cables, drums, switching panels, and the cars themselves—had been gone for years. The furnace and boiler and major electric paneling had all been bid on, sold, and removed when the landlord had given up on his property.

He bent to his work and set the alarms on all the charges, climbed back to the ground-level floor and set the alarms on the remaining corners of the building. It was bitterly cold in the open building, but he kept moving, not really feeling it.

Finished with the ground floor, there remained only the last charge on the top-floor corner apartment. This charge was different from the others, having a much larger quantity of thermoincendiary explosives. He was absolutely sure the building would collapse, but he wanted a corner of the top floor to not only blow out but burn spectacularly.

He climbed the concrete fire stairs three at a time, lightly, still holding the knife in his right hand and the .38 automatic in his left, reached the top floor, and turned down the hall to the corner apartment. There was less litter on the upper floors, but the destruction by vandals was just as extensive. He glanced only briefly out of one of the windows onto Park Avenue and the steady stream of lights moving north and south. The traffic was at its peak in the morning rush hour. He entered the apartment where he had placed his last charge, dropped to his knees in the broom closet, and pulled out still another Baby Ben. He checked his

111

wristwatch, set the alarm and time, wound them both and returned the clock to the hiding place. He replaced the baseboard. Finished.

"What the fuck you doin' in there, turkey?"

He turned, bringing up the gun and the knife in one movement, and in the dim light, saw one of the biggest men he had ever seen in his life. He was well over six feet six, with a stocking cap pulled down over his ears, but the hat was not enough to contain the mass of red hair. The pasty white face was blotchy. He wore an overcoat that was old and dirty and swept the floor. He also looked as if he had been sleeping off a drunk. He wavered slightly on his feet, keeping his hands deep inside his pockets. He looked mean and dangerous.

Tonio could have taken him right then, but he had prepared a plan should such a situation arise. "I got a .38 on your gut, *turkey!*"

"Say what?"

Tonio stood up and brought the gun around so the man could see it.

"Man, what is this shit!"

"Don't talk. Don't think. Don't even breathe. Take your hands out of your pockets slowly and empty."

"Man, you crazy! I'm looking for a bottle to wake up and you—"

"I said don't talk."

The big man pulled his hands out of his pockets, empty, and raised his hands over his head.

"Turn around and stand perfectly still," Tonio said.

"Man, let's get something *on,* I mean, I don't *care* what you got going down, but don't pull no fuckin' iron, man. I'm bad, real bad, but not against heat—" The man turned around.

Tonio moved forward and prodded him in the back with the gun. "Walk down the hall, slowly, and if you don't, I'll drop you with two quick ones in the brain before you can sneeze."

"Man, you gotta listen. You *gotta* listen to me! I just walk away and never even think about you again as long—"

"Shut up and move," Tonio said tonelessly. "Any other time, maybe, but not this morning—not here."

The big man stumbled slightly, and walked down the hall before Tonio. They reached the fire exit near the elevator shafts. "Up—straight to the roof."

"Man, please—just give me a bottle, that's all. I'm that bad off. Just a bottle. I got a brain so soggy, I forget I ever was in New York—"

"Shut up," Tonio said.

"What you going to do with me?"

They climbed one flight to the roof. The snow clouds seemed to be no more than a few feet above his head, and it was growing lighter by the second. Tonio knew they would be skyline silhouettes to someone who might look in their direction.

Tonio moved swiftly and silently up close behind the big man and brought the gun down hard on his head. The hair and the stocking cap softened the blow and the man only stumbled forward on his knees and lurched to the back edge of the building. That was all Tonio needed. He stepped in quickly and lifted and rolled the man over the parapet into space.

He raced down the fire stairs to the ground floor, approached the exit carefully, and did not go out until he had made sure no one was stopping on Park Avenue. No one was yelling. He brushed himself off, flipped down the eye patch, and stepped outside.

In a few minutes he had joined the flood tide of early-morning traffic, another commercial van heading for one of the bridges and Manhattan.

He did not get to the deli until a quarter of nine. But no one said anything. After all, it was the day before Christmas and there was a good spirit in the air. Everyone was too busy, really, to notice; the deli was jammed with office workers and tradesmen taking their time that morning.

One of the waiters tapped Tonio on the shoulder and jerked his head for Tonio to follow. They walked to the rear and into the dressing room used by the employees. The waiter offered Tonio a drink of very fine whiskey. "Good stuff—"

"What's this?" Tonio asked, taking the bottle. "You never even answered me when I said hello before, how come you offering me drinks?"

"Shaddap and take a toss, kid, f'chrissake, it's almost Christmas, ain't it?" The waiter nodded to himself as if agreeing that he was doing the right thing and was pleased with his charity.

"Sure—" Tonio took a small drink, thanked the waiter, and returned to the front of the deli.

"Merry Christmas, Patch," the black sergeant said with a grin.

"Yeah, Merry Christmas, Sarge."

"You behind in your orders, but ain't nobody going to get up tight today."

"Yeah, that's right," Tonio said, preparing his carrying hampers. "They won't hassle me today."

9

"Good morning, and Merry Christmas," Murdoch followed Jimco into Spain's office overlooking the city from the south Fifth Avenue corner. It was so dark from the threatening snow that all the lights were on. "And welcome home. Long time away this trip."

"Merry Christmas, Chris, and thanks." Spain stood. They shook hands. "Coffee or a drink?"

"It's going to be a long day, with lots of Christmas cheer, I think I'd better stick to coffee."

"Make that two, Jimco," Spain said. "How long have we been after Threat now?"

"Fifty-nine days."

"And?"

"And we don't know any more about him than we did when we started. We've eliminated a lot of junk areas, prospects, and suspects—" he sipped his coffee, "—and come up with nothing. We know only that he has access to the Tower. Easy access. That narrows it down to about

115

thirty thousand a day. Our psychological profile of him amounts to zilch. We don't know if he's screwy, a joker pulling our leg, or someone getting their rocks off. We have two empty beer cans, with two almost identical notes, the only difference being that there is a progression in each note: This is Number One; this is Number Two. Same paper for the note, same typewriter. Same brand of beer. And we have a stack of thirty-six Lincoln head pennies, eighteen in each can.''

Murdoch sipped his coffee. He stared at Spain. The man was fit. He did not look as if he had been racing all over the world in his private jet making deals. He was trim and tanned.

"What else do we know?'' Spain asked.

"Most importantly we know that he hasn't made any demands. And until he does, I think that everything that could be done, has been done.''

"I believe you,'' Spain said. "That's not a compliment; it's a statement of fact. You know your job.''

I hope it's true, Murdoch thought, studying the snow-laden skies outside the window. He had read and reread everything he could get his hands on about bombings and the techniques used to back up extortion demands. The very early work of the Jews in Palestine against the British; the Irgun, Stern Gang, and the Hagannah. The IRA in Ireland, including the restaurant bombings in England, and the workers' buses in the Midlands. The Japanese Red Army, the PLO, the German-Italian Red Brigade, the Weathermen in the United States. He had studied them all, tried to understand their motives, and though he used computers and manpower with zeal and determination, he had come up with no pattern of motivation that would fit, and lead him to Threat. He pored over every scrap of information he could place his hands on with details about kidnappings, hijackings, blackmail, and extortion with a ransom demanded, and the payoff; how many payoffs were successful and how many were frustrated, ending in capture. Night and day for almost two months he had tried to find a clue in the wording in the notes; the beer cans; the pennies, for some obscure symbol that would help him determine if Threat were a hoax, or real. He vacillated between dismissing it as a gag, and waking up in the middle of the night, drenched in sweat after a nightmare in which the St. Cyr Tower was blown apart with huge gaping holes in its sides.

When a run-through of the employees on the computer had been completed, including all those who had been hired, fired, and originally rejected, or had quit, Murdoch switched teams, and sent in another group of his men to cover the same ground with a fresh eye. He was satisfied that both teams had done a thorough job when the second team came up with an almost identical list of names to be investigated.

With the help of the commercial tenants in the St. Cyr, they had gone over the employment applications of everyone in the lobby bank, and every employee in the Galleria shops. They had checked and cross-checked every guest who had been in the hotel during both weekends the two beer cans had showed up.

They checked, very carefully, every workman who had spent time installing and decorating the hotel suites, the co-op apartments, their bosses, the contractors, *and* the decorators.

Nothing.

Tens of thousands of applications were checked and rechecked. Estella Malendez was questioned a half-dozen times—and threatened to quit. Nothing. Her husband, Roberto, was checked on the off chance that he might have known about his wife's relations with Manuel Lucas and was taking his revenge on the St. Cyr. But he was innocent of the affair, and Murdoch's men, keeping Estella Malendez's trust, did not let him suspect it, saying only that she was being considered for a much more important job. Her lover, Lucas, was checked again. Nothing. Finally, Murdoch put all three under a twenty-four-hour surveillance on the possibility that they might be in on it together. Nothing.

There was no one else to check, so Murdoch had Andy Brooks check the St. Cyr Tower security forces themselves on the theory that no one would be in a better position to know what was going on than his own security team. Nothing.

And then *he* checked Andy Brooks.

When everything came up negative, Murdoch began to have nightmares about explosions in the Tower.

Nobody saw anything, knew anything, heard anything. If it had not been for the pennies inside, they would have dismissed it. But they hadn't, and Murdoch had two signatures.

But what did Threat want?

Spain had listened to Murdoch's account of what had been done, silently, as he always did, never taking his eyes off the face of the speaker.

"I don't know what he wants, Chris. But I'll tell you this: my position remains the same. Find the son of a bitch and nail him. You've done a hell of a job keeping this quiet. Keep it that way. As for what he wants? Who the hell knows."

"But, maybe it's time to go to the cops. They've got more manpower. As a matter of fact, Jesse Solomon has been of tremendous help. He's checked out any suspicions we've come up with—that's one way I'm reasonably sure that if there were something more to be known, we'd know about it."

"No, no cops," Spain said emphatically. "Not until I find out what the son of a bitch wants from me—or if it's a goofy. And when I think you've spent too much time on this operation, I'll call you and tell you. Until then, keep going, and do whatever you think is necessary. Okay?"

Murdoch said wearily, "Yes, sir."

It was the time of the year that Special Agent Horatio Rota enjoyed most. Christmas in the northeastern United States was *Christmas*. There was snow, hoary breath, bitter cold, and real log fires as opposed to sunshine, Christmas trees on the beach, date palms, and fake logs concealing a gas jet in a fake fireplace, all of which he had grown up with in Los Angeles. He was, in fact, in such good spirits that he did not even mind working the morning watch on the day before Christmas. It was a slack time for his department; requests for searches in the bureau files dropped off eighty percent. It wasn't that things criminal were not happening in the world; they were. But inquiries from the hinterlands for fingerprint identification were put off until after the holiday. Nobody wanted to work on Christmas Eve when one day more or less was not going to matter to a felon sitting inside a cell.

Special Agent Rota planned to use the free time to clear his logs and free the computer's Document Memory of requests, putting them either into Answered, Unanswered—Search Continuing (meaning the computer needed more information), or Hold for Further Inquiry.

The computer had been programmed to do this, and if there were any errors, or enigmas, the computer was coded to kick them out and bring them to the unit operator's attention. It rarely happened. In fact, in the eleven months that Rota had been on the assignment, it had never happened.

That morning, however, the bell rang.

When Rota got over his initial surprise, he saw that it was Diedrickson's request of nearly two months before, and that it had not been encoded. He checked his logs, rechecked the computer, asking it again to give him a search on the three-point partial central pocket loop, and again the computer kicked it out.

Rota then encoded correctly, asked for the search, and in the few seconds that it took for the computer to fill the request, with the answer filling the display, Rota wondered how it could have happened.

He studied the display screen, asked the computer how many of the 11,757 names with a three-point partial central pocket loop were still alive, and began working:

```
-51%.
HOW MANY LIVED IN THE NORTHEAST CORRIDOR?
-11%.
MALE/FEMALE?
-23% FEMALE. 77% MALE.
AGES 20 THROUGH 45?
-10% FEMALE. 39% MALE.
HOW MANY WITH ONE CONVICTION OF FELONY?
-3% FEMALE. 28% MALE.
TWO FELONIES?
-1¹/₂% FEMALE. 11% MALE.
THREE FELONIES?
-¹/₄% FEMALE. 3¹/₂% MALE.
HOW MANY MALE-FEMALE ALL FELONIES PRESENTLY
INCARCERATED?
-88%.
```

Rota continued, weighting his questions, narrowing down the list of names. It was not the kind of personal attention he would ordinarily give to a request, especially one with so little chance of turning up something meaningful. But he felt guilty about the error—and he was sure that it was his.

It was the week he had had the bad cold, had taken the cough medicine with the codeine. He remembered that very clearly, because he had nearly fallen asleep at the wheel while driving home.

The computer kicked out the final list. There were twenty-two names culled from the more than eleven thousand. Five were in the New York City area. He sat down at the terminal hoping to contact Diedrickson personally so that he might explain. The lieutenant had gone to an early lunch. Guiltily, Rota sent the names on up to New York anyway.

```
HOLLAND, TAMAR ELISE A/K/A KITTY
HOLLOWAY AGE 37 W F 5'2" 115
762 WEST 52ND ST. NYC.

KEPHART, RICHARD LYLE AGE 41
W M 6' 175
14-27 72ND AVE. QUEENS, NYC.

MARELL, VICTORIA REGINA
AGE 33 W F 5'4" 110
809 101ST ROAD QUEENS, NYC.

TAPLIN, PHILIP JAY A/K/A TAPS TAPPY
AGE 44 B M 6'5" 220
3830 VINTON AVENUE THE BRONX, NYC.

WITHEY, HAROLD MILTON A/K/A WHITEY
AGE 41 W M 5'1" 130
235 PIER AVENUE, CONEY ISLAND
BROOKLYN, NYC.
```

Maggie Gaston stood in her East Side apartment and from her bedroom watched the snow clouds build up over the river. It was not only going to be a white Christmas, but a white Christmas Eve as well. Dressing carefully, as always when she was going to meet Murdoch or any man for that matter, she anticipated they would go to bed. There had not been that many men in her life, and in fact, that was one of the reasons she was leaving New York. She had married while still in college and discovered too late that what her husband had wanted was someone to sleep with, to do his laundry, keep house, and help pay his way through school. He had had no intention of continuing their marriage once he finished his residency in a major midwestern hospital. There had been no bitter scenes, no acrimony, he had simply come home, packed his bag, and left that evening to board a round-the-world cruise ship, having signed on as ship's doctor.

Maggie had not gone into a tailspin. Suddenly, and with brutalizing clarity, she knew exactly what the world was all about and how it operated. The most significant thing Maggie learned from her marriage was that she would have to make her own decisions, decisions *she* could live with, and then let others adjust. She had made the mistake of moving her life according to the wishes and decisions of another, and she was *never* going to do it again. Now she had a firm proposal from one of the major networks to move to Hollywood and supervise the art direction on network shows, and she had accepted. Acting by her husband's code, she had arranged her affairs, was packed, had plane reservations for that afternoon, though from the look of the snow clouds and the threat of bad weather, she wondered if she would get away. She had not yet told Murdoch.

His near obsession of the last two months with the person called Threat, who left beer cans and pennies, had effectively closed her out of his life: she saw that her life was once again revolving around someone else's decision making—only in this case it was not her partner, Murdoch, but some abstraction called Threat.

And she was not going to allow her life to be ruled by empty beer cans, pennies, and threatening notes.

It had not been an easy decision for her to make. She hated leaving Murdoch, but he had become so unreasonable since Threat had appeared in their lives, that, coupled with her intense dislike of the grime, fear, and frenetic pace of New York, plus the appeal of the climate of southern California, she had accepted the job offer.

She selected a gray wool skirt, light-blue silk blouse with navy trim, and a navy blazer. She transferred the contents of one bag to a black leather shoulder-strap model and ran a brush through her hair. She pushed her feet into a pair of boots, touched her lips lightly with lipstick, and rang for the doorman to get her a taxi.

Tonio was pleased to see the snow. Coming down as heavily as it was, it would not take long to cover the body of the big man lying in a

121

heap at the rear of the building in the Bronx. He stood in the rear of the deli filling his hampers with coffee and Danish. It would be his fourth trip since coming to work.

"Got you humping this morning, huh, Patch?" The sergeant smiled lazily.

"Yeah, Sarge." Tonio knew he had been sneaking drinks in the kitchen.

"Lotta tips?"

"Not bad."

"Tell me something, Patch, you ever think about the old days, back in Nam?"

"No." Tonio was startled and curious. "Do you?"

"I don't know, just asking, you know?" The cook wiped the counter with his hands, cleaning off imaginary crumbs. "It was such a good time for me. Back then."

"*I* was in a war, Sergeant. I don't know where the hell you were."

"Yeah, well, wasn't war always. Not for me anyway. I had some of my best times. The last year and a half I was on special duty. Every night it was New Year's Eve."

"Yeah?"

"Had me a couple of good deals, man. I was there for three years, see, and they pull me off the line and give me this special duty. A couple of the old boys, they set me straight, see? We just passed on a little gasoline now and then. Nothing big, not like some I know, you know, into scag, and stealing whole boxcars full of stuff. Naw, we just had a little thing going, enough to make the *night right* for drinkin' and fuckin' and—"

"Why didn't you stay in?"

"I thought I could do better outside." The sergeant looked around the deli like a man searching out a desert island that had already been explored a hundred times. "But I was wrong." He turned away.

Tonio watched him go and continued packing. When the carrier was filled, he reached under the counter where he kept his supplies and took out a flat package wrapped in a paper bag which he had dug out of the garbage and secured with a rubber band. He very carefully placed the paper bag in a half-torn Saks Fifth Avenue shopping bag he had also taken from the garbage. He had not touched either bag with his bare hands. He placed the Saks bag on top of his take-out orders and pushed his way through the crowded deli, out of the door, and into the swirling snowstorm.

The loading platform at the service entrance of the St. Cyr Tower was jammed with delivery trucks, most of them from United Parcel, loaded with boxes, gifts, packages for St. Cyr guests.

Tonio stepped inside the service area and paused by a steel, mobile garbage container. Standing just inside the entrance, it was filled nearly to the top and dusted heavily with snow. Bending over as if he were adjusting his carriers, Tonio slipped the Saks shopping bag out of the hamper, glanced around, and when no one was looking, shoved the bag down, deep into the rear right-hand corner. He then picked up the carrier and continued on down the street and his delivery rounds. He paused to look at his watch. A snowflake blurred the dial. He wiped it with his finger. It was five minutes to twelve.

Tonio had never seen a customer in Whalen's Boutique, so he was not surprised to find it empty. Lillene sat like stone, swinging one crossed leg, concentrating on the street. He wiped his feet carefully and walked through to the back, and after a warning knock, entered.

For a split second Tonio froze. A man stood with Lou. He was short, stocky, wore a raincoat, and was as easily identifiable as a detective as a fire hydrant.

"Hiya, kid. I see it's still snowing," Lou Whalen said.

The cop stared at Tonio with the flat expressionless eyes of all cops all over the world; suspicious of everything, all the time.

Tonio knew the look. He not only remembered his father's deputies but he had seen the same personalities in the military. Most of them complained bitterly that they were misunderstood. Maybe it was because they knew that when they took off their badge and gun, they were less than what they thought they were and did not like it. He dug out sandwiches and coffee and put them on the corner of the desk as he always did. "Seven seventy-five, Lou," he said.

"Action? Little action, Tonio?" Lou chided. "I got horses running in Florida and California—" He rubbed his hands together vigorously, then handed Tonio a ten-dollar bill, waving away the change. "What'cha like today, kid? Got any hunches, huh?"

Very deliberately, Tonio hesitated and looked at the cop. He wanted the cop to know, and for Lou to also know, that *he knew,* it was a cop. And that it was Christmas Eve and therefore, the cop was 99.44 percent sure to be there picking up his take money.

Lou glanced nervously at the cop and then back to Tonio. "Don't worry about it, kid, you know what I mean?" He winked at Tonio. The cop had not changed his expression and continued to stare. He did not like what was happening, and reflexively he used silence and his steady unrelenting gaze as a weapon of fear.

Tonio knew what the cop was doing, and let him do it; he lowered his eyes. When he looked up again, the cop had relaxed.

Lou liked that. He said to the cop, "Tonio's one of my regulars. Plays consensus and a long shot. Every day the same thing. Stays even with consensus and hits now and then for a long shot." He patted Tonio on the cheek. "Student at Columbia. Workin' his way through. Studyin' anthropology. Studyin' monkeys, ain't'cha, kid? I tell him, Rocky—I tell him—"

The cop interrupted hard, "Watch your mouth."

Lou Whalen jerked up as straight as his bony chest would allow him. He blinked. "Oh, yeah, Sarge—sure." He looked at Tonio and indicated a light shrug. "I tell him to keep his eyes open right here in the city and he sees all the monkeys and apes and gorillas he wants or needs!"

The cop made a gurgling sound in his throat, and grinned.

Only then did Tonio pull out his roll of bills. "Gimme ten to win on Running Orange in the fourth, and twenty across on Frying-Pan-Shoals in the sixth, and two hundred to win on Phil's Dan in the eighth." Tonio put the money on the desk beside the coffee and the sandwiches.

"Yesterday, all your horses run out, kid. I owe you nothin' for yesterday."

"I know."

"You bettin' Florida, right?" Lou intoned, and then repeated the bet Tonio had just made.

Tonio was about to pick up his carriers when the rasping voice of the cop stopped him.

"Pretty big fuckin' bets for a deli delivery boy—"

"He stays even, you know—" Lou smiled and wiggled his hand. "He's in and out—"

Tonio bent to pick up the carriers again.

"Where'd a deli kid get money to make bets like that? You skipping numbers, Tonio?"

Tonio could not avoid it now. He turned and faced the cop. The eyes bore into him. He dropped his eyes and used body language. He began to dissemble. "Not me, Sergeant."

"I hear there's a lot of action here midtown. Maybe you're a big man, huh?" The cop had begun to press in his voice. "You'd be in a perfect position, wouldn't you say so, Tonio? You all over midtown."

"Yes, sir," Tonio said, bringing up his eyes briefly, and then dropping them again.

"Open up the hampers," the cop commanded.

"Rocky, f'christ's sake, leave the kid alone—"

Tonio waited to see if Lou was going to have any weight in the matter. He looked up again at the cop. Lou was out of it.

"The hampers, kid. Let's see what's in there besides sandwiches and coffee."

"Nothing in there, Sergeant Rocky—just like you say, sandwiches and coffee—"

The voice came out hard, mean, "Open the fuckin' hampers."

With a great show of reluctance, Tonio picked up the hampers and put them on Lou's desk. One by one he removed the brown paper bags and opened the ends and showed them to the cop. The cop was not perturbed that he had not discovered anything.

"Empty the pockets."

Lou was completely out of it now. He had backed over to one side of the office and watched the power play. Tonio continued his shambling attitude, moving with a shuffle, even in the confined space, and emptied his pockets. He had nearly two hundred dollars of the deli money, which he always kept in a separate pocket, a cheap wallet with his Columbia University ID, handkerchief, and comb. He placed everything on the desk.

Still not satisfied, the cop moved, grabbed Tonio by the arm and spun him against the wall. "Take the position—"

Tonio spread his legs and arms while the cop patted him down.

"Okay," the cop said and stepped back.

Tonio turned around. He started to remove his belongings from the desk when the cop reached out and picked up the thick wad of money to be turned in to the deli cashier. "What's this?"

"Money I collect for the sandwiches and coffee and stuff. I turn it in to the cashier when I get back."

The cop threw the money back down on the desk. "I'm going to be watching you, Tonio. I know you spiks run numbers. All of you do. You lucky I didn't catch you—and if I do, I'll break your balls. You hear me, Tonio? Say you hear me."

"I hear you, sir," Tonio said.

"What's the last name, Tonio?" The cop reached over and picked up the ID and read everything on it.

"Vega, sir."

"Get outa here." He tossed the ID back onto the desk and turned away.

Tonio gathered his carriers and left. Lillene was seated in her usual place, swinging one leg over the other and watching the snowstorm. She did not look up as Tonio opened the door and eased outside.

Sergeant Rocky—*Sergeant Rocky!*

On one of the crosstown streets near Madison, he found a telephone booth unoccupied, a minor miracle. He tried a dime and found that it was working. Another miracle. He glanced at his watch: 12:29. He would call at 12:30. That would give Murdoch plenty of time.

He held the dead receiver to his ear and occasionally made a movement with his lips as if he were talking, warding off anyone who might want to use the phone. But no one came near. At 12:30 exactly he took a deep breath, dropped the dime, and dialed the St. Cyr Tower.

"Murdoch's office," he said, using a hoarse voice and heavy New York accent.

"One moment, please. I'm ringing."

He waited, smoking, watching the pedestrian traffic.

"Mr. Murdoch's office," Vicky's voice flowed over the line.

"You got a pencil and paper, lady? I'm only gunna say this one time—"

"Who is this?"

"This is *Threat*."

"How do I know?" Vicky responded coolly.

"I'm sending you a third beer can with eighteen pennies."

"I understand," Vicky said calmly and efficiently. "What is your message?"

"In the big garbage container in the service entrance of the hotel, in the rear right-hand corner, there's a wadded up Saks Fifth Avenue bag. Inside is another brown paper bag. Inside the brown paper bag is something you people better pay attention to."

"Is that all?"

"Say it back to me exactly," Tonio demanded.

Vicky read her shorthand notes perfectly without stumbling. "Is that all?"

Tonio hung up the receiver. He opened the door of the booth and picked up the carriers. The coffee would be cold and the Danish as hard as a rock, but who would complain today?

It was nearly noon, Murdoch had missed all of his morning meetings, skipped his daily rounds, and ignored the intermittently ringing phone. But he didn't care. Maggie smoked idly and studied the falling snow. They lay side by side, exhausted from their lovemaking, quiet, staring out of the window.

She had told him quickly, at one breath. After he had absorbed the initial shock, and accepted her decision to leave, she started crying. He held her close and assured her that he understood—he didn't like it worth a goddamn—but he understood. Going to bed after that was the only natural thing to do.

Murdoch got up and took a bottle of champagne from the refrigerator and poured two glasses. He got back in bed. They sipped the champagne and stared at the snow.

"Won't they be looking for you?"

"Yes. Probably."

"And you don't care?"

"I care, but there isn't anything I can do about it."

After a long silence, and not looking at him, but at the snow, she said: "What would you say if I asked you to come with me?"

"I'll come visit you. Week or two, maybe. Laze about in the California sunshine. Spend some of your Hollywood money."

"And then come back to work."

"And then come back to New York."

"Threat?"

"Threat and other reasons."

"Tell me some of the other reasons."

"You're carrying your liberation shield a little too high for me."

"That doesn't bother you, not really."

"No," he said thoughtfully. "That doesn't bother me."

"Not really," she agreed. "And I certainly don't want to live in a hotel."

"You would," he said, letting it come out slowly, "if that was what you had to pay to get me, hold me, keep me. If you wanted me."

"Not for you, not for any man."

"I know. So, don't ask any more foolish questions."

She snuggled up against him, quivering, but she was not cold. "I would loathe myself if I bruised your ego."

"I would loathe you to."

"Are you going to catch this man who calls himself Threat?"

"As soon as he makes his demand."

"Do you think this man—Threat—do you think he really made a private deal with himself?"

"Where did you get that idea?" Murdoch looked down at her sideways, frowning.

"It's not mine. It's yours. You were speculating about Threat one night, that if it were one man, what would he be like? Isolated, alone, alienated, surviving without moral restraints—trusting no ideas, or having a belief in anything."

Murdoch got out of bed, poured another glass of champagne, and stood in silence before the window looking out at the storm.

"Don't leave me just yet. Come back to bed—"

"All right." He nodded, paused a moment longer and stared into the snow, but did not see it. He went to his jacket, took out a notebook and wrote rapidly.

Viet Nam Vets. Demo experts.

Green Beret? Intelligence?

Murdoch thought a moment, and then added:

Loner? Behind enemy lines?

"What did you write?"

"Note on something I have to check." He sat on the side of the bed and ran his hands over her body. She watched his face, his enjoyment, and it gave her pleasure.

He saw the Threat notes as clearly as if tattooed on her naked stomach:

I will penetrate your security
I—I—I—I—I . . . I . . . I. I. I. I. I!

One man used to operating alone. Why hadn't he thought of it before?

"What are you thinking?" he leaned over her.

"Looking at you standing beside the window—I—I thought I would cry."

"Why, for God's sake?" he asked puzzled.

"Because at some time in the future, you're going to be a part of my past. A memory. And I don't ever want you to be anything but what you are now—then—standing at the window in thought. Or anywhere except in my arms, hovering over me with your good strong self ready to make love to me."

He took her in his arms. "Don't leave—"

"I wish I loved you enough to live on your salary, cook dinner, and muck about a hotel apartment waiting for you."

He moved over her.

"Tell me not to go."

"Maggie, don't go. Stay here with me."

"I've got to go," she said desperately.

There were no overtures. It was the roughest he had ever been.

10 Murdoch and Maggie walked through the lobby unashamedly holding hands. The air was filled with Bach's Greatest Hits coming from a stereo in the background. He wondered how Bach would feel about having hits. They did not even glance up at the twenty-five-foot Christmas tree that had cost nearly two thousand dollars to install and decorate. Ladies in minks and sables hurried breathlessly through the Fifth Avenue entrance, arms laden with Christmas-wrapped packages. The bar in the Monte Carlo Lounge was doing a land-office business. He thought about suggesting a last drink, but they had said their farewells.

Outside, Murdoch caught the eye of the doorman and indicated that he wanted a taxi, and that he wasn't going to wait in line. They stood at the edge of the crowd and watched as the doorman snapped at car and taxi doors with a hearty "Merry Christmas!" while his half-frozen paw closed around tips with the deftness of a Kodiak bear snagging salmon.

130

New Yorkers rushed along the sidewalk, bouncing off each other without so much as a glance. The skies overhead were almost totally black, car lights were turned on. Salvation Army lasses, their Gimme Bells clashing tonally with the clink of tire chains, shifted from one foot to the other. It was New York at its finest, on Christmas Eve, and desperate to care about something.

The doorman was very skilled at his job. He wanted to make points with Murdoch, but he also wanted the tips he would surely get from the mob waiting for taxis. The next taxi in rank rolled down. The doorman spoke briefly to the driver and then turned to the crowd. "Who ordered the taxi for Connecticut?" He looked at Murdoch. "Special for Connecticut? Your taxi, sir."

There was some grumbling in the crowd, but Maggie swept forward and was in the taxi and gone before Murdoch realized that it had all happened.

There had not even been a quick kiss and good-bye. She was just gone. The way death removes any hope of reward.

Murdoch stepped out onto the sidewalk and was caught up in the crowds. He walked and walked. He walked heedlessly, and though only a very short time had passed, it seemed to him like hours. He had come out without his coat and gloves and he was covered with snow. He was chilled. He would have to get inside quickly. He headed for the bar in the Monte Carlo Lounge. Someone yelled at him, but he didn't look up.

"Where the hell have you been!" Spain exploded as Murdoch stepped into his office. "We've turned this place inside out looking for you."

"I've been busy, Mr. Spain," Murdoch said easily.

Spain thrust a sheet of paper at him. "Look at this!"

Vicky had typed out Tonio's message, stamped the time and date, and then initialed it. Murdoch read it once quickly, and then as his heart began to pound, he read it again slowly.

"Well, let's go see what our friend has left in the garbage for us," he said with some sense of relief that something might at last be happening.

Spain started out of the door in a lunge, tweed coat flying.

Murdoch hesitated and turned to Vicky. "Find Chief Solomon. Track him down. Don't let anyone know why you want him, just find him, and when you do, read him this." Murdoch returned the message. "Maggie is taking flight 600, TWA, to the coast, see if you can get a message to her—'' Murdoch hesitated.

"Come'n, Murdoch," Spain commanded.

"Saying what?" Vicky asked.

"Just—oh. Love, Chris."

"Will you come *on!*"

Murdoch turned, took a pair of gloves from a drawer, and dashed out of the door after Spain.

In the lobby, Murdoch looked around for one of his men, and signaled Sid Hoag to come with them. He spotted three more and waved for them to follow.

There were great bursts of laughter in the Monte Carlo Lounge as Spain pushed past waiters and diners, brushing aside everything and everyone as he plunged through the swinging doors into the chaos of the kitchen. With Murdoch, Hoag, and the others close behind, he swept onto the loading platform. The cold air blasted them as they leaped to the pavement and proceeded to the garbage container. Spain plunged his hand deep inside before Murdoch could push him away.

"Stop!" Murdoch shouted. Spain staggered back from the unexpected shove.

"What the hell's wrong with you!" Spain demanded.

"Suppose they're after *you?* And suppose it isn't what he says it is? Suppose it's a booby trap? And all you have to do is dislodge it and up you go, with the garbage. Now get back and stay out of here!"

It was a command of authority and Spain knew it. He backed away. Murdoch turned to Sid Hoag: "Clear the area. Get those people off the platform and inside. And keep them away from the doors."

Murdoch turned to the other three men who stood shivering from the sudden change in temperature. "Get out there in the street and keep people from crossing in front of the opening."

"But what'll I say?" one of the men complained.

"Tell 'em anything. Show 'em your badge. Tell 'em you're a cop. But keep them back. Move! And you—" Murdoch pointed to the others. "Stop all traffic—everything."

He approached the garbage container. "Get up there with Hoag and help keep the people back," he said to Spain.

Spain moved.

132

Murdoch approached the container again. He looked outside, and then inside, for any wires. The snow was thick on top of the refuse and did not look as if it had been disturbed for at least an hour.

Behind him pedestrians began to complain as they were being shuttled across the street. Traffic began to back up and horns were sounded. Spain and Hoag watched Murdoch as he edged his way around the container.

Murdoch hesitated. Perhaps he should call the NYPD and their experts in the Explosive-Arson Squad. But he was reluctant to involve them unless it was absolutely necessary. And he wouldn't know that until he knew what was inside the Saks Fifth Avenue shopping bag. He walked to the right-hand rear corner and looked in. He saw nothing. He glanced around. The crowd was jamming up and so was the traffic. People argued with his men. He had to make a decision: call the NYPD or reach inside. He pulled on his gloves.

He stepped to the edge of the container, pushed the snow to one side briskly, and saw the corner of the shopping bag. He reached for it, pulling gently, carefully, a quarter of an inch at a time, his eyes searching for wires or attachment. It was not heavy, in fact it was light, almost as if there were nothing inside but the brown paper bag as stated in Threat's message.

He lifted it up carefully and looked at it. If it exploded, he knew he would be dead before he would be conscious of the explosion or pain. And the thick steel sides of the garbage container would more than take the major part of the explosion, protecting anyone in the street.

Murdoch put the Saks bag on the ground and opened it carefully. He looked inside and saw the soggy brown paper bag. He eased it out, prodding it gently with his finger. It could still be a letter bomb, but he was committed and he went on. He opened the brown paper bag and looked inside.

He forgot everything for a moment and frowned. It looked like a set of blueprints. He heard the distant wail of an approaching police cruiser. He reached inside the bag, removed the blueprint, and unfolded it gingerly.

It was just that: a single sheet, a two-by-three foot blueprint of some sort. He looked inside the Saks bag, and the brown paper bag. They were both empty.

133

He looked up at Spain and Hoag who were watching his every move. He shrugged. He gathered up the two bags and the blueprint. He leaped up to the platform and hurried toward the kitchen.

"The cops are coming and they're going to be mad as hell," Murdoch said to Hoag. "Tell them one of the guests had thrown out a half-million dollars in jewelry by mistake and we had to get it back. Tell 'em Mr. Spain is springing for Christmas dinner for them and their wives—tell 'em anything, got it?"

"Does this have to do with what we've been searching for?" Hoag asked.

Murdoch nodded. "When you're finished here, send those other three back to the floor, and you come to the office. To *everyone*, it's lost jewelry, 'kay? It's the kind of story everyone would want to believe about the St. Cyr and its tenants anyway."

Hoag grinned. "I like it myself."

"Come inside, Vicky, please, and make me a drink. I'm going to start shaking any second. Did you locate Chief Solomon?"

"I left word. They're tracking him down."

Spain looked at Murdoch sharply. "You all right?"

"I will be in a few minutes." Murdoch, still wearing gloves, spread the blueprint out on his desk, unfolding it carefully. "Please don't touch anything. There is always the chance there *might* be fingerprints."

Vicky joined them, handing Murdoch his drink. He took several deep swallows and leaned over the desk. In the lower-right-hand corner, in a six-by-three-inch box, separate from the actual drawing, he read the legend:

THE ST. CYR TOWER NINETIETH FLOOR APT. B SECT. 3
112357 -B modified 11/8/77 NYC CODE PAGE 248(a)
342-2 (CODE 7 c&d inclusive) PERMIT NO 2176-11
COOPERMAN & DAWES
Architects
Stratton & Sontag
Builders

Murdoch searched for the compass sign, found the arrow indicating north and studied the whole print for a moment. "This is the northwest corner. I'm not sure, but this looks like the second kitchen." He glanced up at Spain. "Some of the Tower suites have a small service kitchen and bar off the main living room."

Spain nodded. "I know. Ninetieth floor. That's Lady George's suite—"

"No. Opposite her, ninety B. Princess Martha."

"Oh God—" Vicky said under her breath.

"What does that mean?" Spain glanced at her and then looked at Murdoch for an explanation. "What has she done now?"

"Do you know her?"

"Her, *and* her reputation," Spain said. "I didn't want to let her in, but she had a lot of pressure put on me."

"The day you left on your trip, she arrived, dead-drunk."

Spain grunted. "And?"

"The next morning both of her children came down with scarlet fever."

Spain's voice became more sympathetic. "How are they now?"

"The boy's deaf, and the girl has a heart condition."

"Christ!" Spain said bitterly.

"Dr. Wyeth wanted to hospitalize both of them, but she was arrogant, demanding that Wyeth treat them here—she has practically a whole hospital set up in her suite."

"And she's been there all this time? With the kids?"

Murdoch nodded. "She's not quite the lady she was before."

"Yeah? How's that?"

"No expense has been spared," Murdoch said. "But she's still with the children—day and night. Or so the nurses tell me. She doesn't leave the suite for weeks. I've only seen her a few times myself. She's very thin, even haggard. Hair straggly. Not quite the same lady."

Spain continued to study the blueprint.

"We're going to have to get inside and take a look," Murdoch said. He turned to Vicky. "Call 'em up, Vicky," he said slowly. "Make it sound like a routine Christmas Eve goodwill thing. Wish them Merry Christmas, that sort of thing. Get a reading on what's going on up there." The secretary nodded and hurried to her office.

Spain jabbed at the blueprint. "That red star, over there, marking a wall or something."

"I saw it," Murdoch said. "It could be anything. This print is dirty enough to have been a working sheet. One that the construction crew might have used. That could be any kind of a marking. On the other hand—"

"What?"

"Our friend may be making his move."

"What the hell could be in the Princess's kitchen wall?"

"A bomb," Murdoch said quietly.

"Inside the wall? But how—"

"He's telling us," Murdoch said, controlling his tension, "that he had access to the building while it was being constructed."

"But how is it possible?"

"Excuse me—" Vicky stood in the doorway. "I spoke to Princess Martha herself. They're busy trimming the tree, she seemed quite calm. Appreciated the call—"

" 'kay," Murdoch said, pursing his lips. "Get hold of Kosinski on the desk. And Dr. Wyeth. Block out a suite, and as many rooms as Wyeth thinks they'll need. I don't care who Kosinski has to cancel out—get that space and have Wyeth ready to move those kids in less than a half hour."

Vicky nodded.

"Be very careful about this, Vicky: call back up there, and ask for either Gregory or Haldstadt. It doesn't matter which one you speak to, but I want one of them in my office in a half hour."

Again Vicky nodded.

"When Sid Hoag gets here, just tell him to stand by. Also get hold of Morgan Berry and have him bring his dog. And Andy Brooks. All of them to wait in your office. I don't want to be disturbed, and hold all calls."

"What the hell is this, Chris?" Spain demanded. "Let's get up there and find out if there's something in that wall!"

"Threat is making his point," Murdoch said quietly, ignoring Spain. "But what does he want?"

"Let's go—"

"No!"

"What the hell do you mean, 'no'?"

"I think it's time to call in the troops," Murdoch said reluctantly but firmly. "This part of the operation has to be placed in the hands of experts, the Explosive-Arson Squad. They're probably the best in the world."

"Then we're right back where we started," Spain said bitterly. "All the effort to keep it quiet goes out of the window."

"Not necessarily. Who do you know in City Hall?"

"The mayor."

"Call him. Tell him what's going on," Murdoch said. "Impress him with what will happen when the bomb-disposal truck shows up and the specialists start walking around the lobby in their flak suits. He's got to control his cops, and he's the only one that can do it, or you'll have people bailing out of the St. Cyr as if it were the *Titanic.*"

"Jesus! And on Christmas Eve—"

"And there is always the possibility that instead of just a threat, he might go ahead and do it."

"*Do what?*"

"He could have wired it with remote control. Rigged it in such a way that, say we don't do what he wants, all he has to do is send a signal, and boom!"

"But what can he gain by telling us where it is?"

"It's another hook in our balls. And because there is a lot of work and know-how in this," Murdoch said slowly. "But we're wasting time, I think you had better make that phone call to the mayor."

"What do you think Chris? Crazy or not?"

"I think, that there is going to be a demand, probably money. It's too planned. Too perfect, so far."

"And when he makes his demand, we grab him."

"The odds are on our side. I've done everything I thought was necessary, and that I could, and we still have the problem."

"I know what you've done. Don't take it on your shoulders for living in a fucked-up world. I'll call you as soon as I've got things set up. One way or the other. You'll be here?"

"Right here."

The technique so far was flawless, Murdoch thought, staring at the blueprint. Threat had had them running around, knowing that a lot of manpower and effort would be wasted, and the odds in his favor that they would never catch him. Well, so far, Threat had been successful.

But until a demand is made and the payoff arranged, we're still in the ball game.

He lit a cigarette and looked at his watch: one-twenty. His back ached, the familiar sign that he was under tension. He picked up the phone. "Vicky, order me a sandwich and a cup of coffee. If you have to go powder your nose, get someone to relieve you. Set the tape machine up for silent recording."

"The tape is already set to go, and everyone is here."

"Send 'em in."

Andy Brooks, Sid Hoag, Morgan Berry and his dog entered the office. Babe bounded around the desk to greet Murdoch. Vicky came in, closed the door, positioned herself near the phone, and took out her steno pad. "The tape is on automatic," she said. "Any call that comes in is recorded."

They all stood before Murdoch's desk and waited for him to speak.

"Remember that cocked .45 I spoke to you about a couple of months ago, when we started our search for oddballs? Well, it's got a hair trigger with a two-ounce pull—and if somebody breathes hard—*Blam!*"

Hoag was the only one present who did not know about Threat and it took only a few words to explain to the street-wise cop.

"Threat has made phone contact." He indicated the blueprint. "That red X may well mark the spot. Spain is on the phone to the mayor trying to keep a lid on it. But either way, we're going to have to call in the Explosive-Arson Squad. If they find anything where this X is, and depending on what they find, we may have to evacuate the building—"

"Good Christ!" Andy Brooks sighed.

"But, in this weather!" Hoag said.

"That's it," Murdoch said abruptly. "No arguments. If the cops order an evacuation, then we evacuate. But, if it happens, you're still security for the Tower, its guests, and their property. I'm giving you each an area to protect in case the order should be given. Sid, I want you to take charge of the cashiers. Andy, I want you inside the vault room."

Vicky took down the assignments, and Murdoch continued going through the details. One man for every two shops on the Galleria Promenade. One man behind the bar in each of the dining rooms. One man for each bank of elevators. Three men on each door to the street.

"If the word is given," Murdoch said slowly, emphasizing each word, "people are going to grab their furs, jewels, money, anything and everything that's valuable to them, and run for the hills. They're going to abandon their usual precautions, and many of them will forget to lock their doors, some may even leave them standing open. You never know what people will do in a panic. And this is a potential panic situation. Now, *if* we have to bail out, there will be a lot of assistance from the police. The place will be swarming with cops. Your primary job is *not* to stop anybody from looting. That's for the boys in blue. You just spot them and point them out. When people panic, or when there is an emergency situation as this one might turn out to be, we must anticipate the snatch, smash, grab-and-run crowd will always try to take advantage of it. And if you see anyone looting, and there's no cop nearby, shoot the son of a bitch.

"If a lady is caught in the shower, and has her fifty-thousand-dollar necklace on her dressing table and she runs out in a panic, forgetting it, it's going to be right where she left it when she gets back.

"I'm going to be with the Explosive-Arson Squad when they arrive. Sid, you and Andy speak for me. We still keep it quiet until, and if, we get the order to bail out? 'kay, let's go."

Morgan Berry stood to one side. "What do you want us to do?" Berry patted Babe.

"Take a look at this." Murdoch indicated the blueprint. "Recognize it?" He pointed to the red X.

Berry nodded. "That's the service kitchen in one of the half-floor suites in the Tower. Ninetieth floor. That would be—let's see—the ah— Princess." He looked at Murdoch for confirmation.

"Right." Murdoch put his finger on the red X. "Can Babe sniff out something behind a sealed wall?"

"I'd like to give her a try."

"I want to get you in there before the cops arrive."

"I'll wait in Vicky's office," Berry said.

Murdoch picked up the blueprint, again wearing his gloves, and folded it carefully. "Did you get all that down, Vicky?"

She nodded, closed her notebook, and stood. "And I ordered a chicken sandwich and coffee. I hope it gets here before Mr. Spain calls."

Murdoch stared out of the window. "If we have to evacuate the building in this weather," he said thoughtfully, "there will be thousands of people who will need a place to go. Call Cardinal Cooke's office and find out where he is. Just find him. Should we need St. Patrick's, the mayor can explain it to him. Call the people at St. Thomas's also, find out who's in charge, and get their number, and where they can be called. You'd better do that now. There's no telling when we'll have another chance.''

He sat down at his desk and studied the hasty scrawl he had made in his notebook: Viet Nam Vets. Demo experts. Green Beret? Intelligence? Loner? Behind enemy lines?

It was not impossible—but improbable. Yet he recognized certain patterns to the approach. First, create a disruptive atmosphere behind the enemy lines by demonstrating that he is vulnerable. Second, exploit this capability psychologically by introducing into the enemy thinking the possibility of an agent who might *be one of them.* Third, when the enemy is so sure that there *is* an inside man, make a devastating strike of such sureness that it convinces the enemy that there *was* a traitor in his inner circle, thus making zilch out of the mathematical possibilities of detection.

Vicky appeared with his sandwich and coffee. "Lunch, and Mr. Gregory, of Princess Martha's staff, is here."

"Send him in." Murdoch started wolfing the sandwich.

"Hello, Chris." Gregory came forward, smiling, his hand outstretched, and then quickly withdrew it, seeing that Murdoch had a sandwich in one hand and coffee in the other.

"We have a problem," Murdoch said at last, swilling down the sandwich with coffee.

"Concerning Her Highness?"

Murdoch nodded and then quickly, briefly, sketched the broad outlines of Threat, bringing Gregory up-to-date. "How would Her Highness accept moving herself, the children—the entire staff—to other quarters here in the Tower so that we might take a look at that kitchen wall. It may be nothing at all—let's hope that is the case. But one way or the other, that wall is going to have to be examined."

"Could it be done while she remained in the suite?"

"Unrealistic," Murdoch said. "Within a very short time, the police are going to come in here with a bomb squad—men in flak suits, the works—I'm hoping it can be done without hysterics."

"It's not her so much," Gregory said. "These bomb things have come up from time to time—"

"I'm expecting a call from Dr. Wyeth, if you're thinking about the children."

"Yes, the children, of course. But—she's quite a different person now, you might say. The children are everything—*everything*."

"I haven't seen her," Murdoch said. "But I've gotten information about her attitude. It's either she moves on her own or the police will move her."

The phone rang. Murdoch picked it up, listened and then hung up. "That was Dr. Wyeth. He's ready for the move—what about it?"

Gregory stood up. "Have Dr. Wyeth meet me at the elevator."

"You don't have much time," Murdoch said.

"Are you going to evacuate the building?"

"Not until, and if, we find anything behind that wall."

"Good luck," Gregory said, and hurried to the door.

"And the same to you."

Murdoch sank into his chair and swallowed the last of his coffee as the phone rang again. He snatched at it. "Murdoch—"

"Captain Hansen of the Seventeenth Precinct here, Chris, and what the bloody hell was all that business about stopping traffic, and pushing people around, and some bullshit about jewels thrown into the garbage!"

Vicky opened the door. "Spain," she mouthed silently, pointing to the phone.

"I've got to go, Captain. Merry Christmas."

"But what the hell—"

Murdoch cut the captain off and punched in for Spain. "Murdoch."

"They're on the way. The mayor's going to play it our way until his men on the scene decide how serious it is, and if it is, then they take over," Spain said.

"How about the bomb trucks—guys in flak suits?"

"Standing by, ready to roll, and won't show up and start a panic, unless we find something. If that's the case, then we still bring them in through the kitchens. Though why, I don't know. If they find something, who are they going to keep it from?"

"Moot point. How much time before the cops arrive?"

"Any minute now. Why?"

"I'll meet you at the Princess's apartment." Murdoch threw the phone down and raced for the door, yelling at Morgan Berry. "Let's go."

And even as he raced to the elevator with Babe leaping happily at his side, Murdoch wondered where the hell Jesse Solomon was.

While Berry held the dog back, Murdoch approached the door of Princess Martha's suite cautiously; the door was open a few inches and as he was about to push inwards, it swung open and he was face-to-face with Her Highness.

The change in her was so radical Murdoch did not recognize her at once, and for a moment thought she might be a maid. Her hair was combed but was uncared for, her face was blanched white, no makeup, her small frame and an obvious loss of weight made her look like a waif inside a sweat shirt and jeans. Murdoch was genuinely shocked.

She looked at him, hesitated a moment as if she didn't quite place him, and then put her hand nervously to her hair. She pressed her back against the doorjamb and dropped her eyes. She sidled, moving crablike, past him. Murdoch was not sure, but he thought she said: "Thank you—" And then she was gone, moving quickly down the corridor toward the opposite side of the building.

Murdoch raced through the apartment to the service kitchen. Babe had paused on entering and issued a low, threatening challenge. Berry spoke one of his command words. Babe tensed, and began to quiver, alert.

"Let her go first," Murdoch said. "It should be behind that refrigerator." He placed the blueprint on the nearest counter.

Morgan Berry dropped to one knee and spoke into the dog's ear, smoothing the sleek head as he did. The dog relaxed. He took off the choke lead. "Easy, girl—easy."

Murdoch stood in the doorway watching the dog move nervously around the kitchen, the flush-floor cabinets, two dishwashers, sink cabinets, refrigerator, and a crystal cabinet filled with what seemed to Murdoch thousands of champagne and cocktail glasses. Babe made another tour of the kitchen urged on by Berry. "Fetch, Babe—find it, girl—fetch, Babe."

The dog began to concentrate on one end of the kitchen and then slowly she had eliminated everything but the refrigerator. She stepped back and barked one time and pawed at the gleaming surface of the refrigerator door. Babe barked again.

"What do you think?" Murdoch asked.

"I think there's something behind that refrigerator."

They both stepped forward, gripped the sides of the huge box, and began to press it outward to pry it from its position. They did not hurry. As soon as the refrigerator was away from the wall, Murdoch shoved his head around the back, reached down, and pulled the plug. Babe was as interested as they were and eagerly pushed her nose into the opening trying to get in back of the box.

"You'd better restrain her," Murdoch said.

Berry spoke to her firmly. Babe did not respond. "She's excited," Berry explained. He spoke again, putting harshness in his voice. The dog looked up at him. He spoke again, and it turned away, head down, and walked to his side. Berry pointed to the doorway. "Stay, Babe. Stay."

The dog sat down and watched them. It might have been a statue, Murdoch thought, glancing at it, as they heaved the box away from the wall and rolled it out of the way.

The wall was blank, an undisturbed, smooth painted surface. "Try Babe again," Murdoch said.

Berry spoke the release word, and Babe came bounding forward to his side. "Fetch, Babe. Fetch—"

The dog leaped at the wall and began to bark and paw at the floor in a digging motion, claws slipping on the waxed surface, ears pointed and stiff.

Berry and Murdoch looked at each other.

"She's got something," Berry said.

"Call Babe off," Murdoch said quietly. "Stay here. I'll wait for the others at the front door."

Murdoch had just made it to the front door when the bell rang. He yanked it open, expecting to be flooded with cops and men in flak suits.

"I've got something," Jesse Solomon said.

"So have I," Murdoch replied.

143

11

"The FBI gave us a list of five names in the New York area for a possible matching of a partial print we found on one of the pennies from the first beer can," Solomon said. "I've got a team checking out each name now. We should know soon."

"And we've had a phone call from Threat."

"Did you get a tape?" Solomon asked quickly.

"No, but we have what he said," Murdoch said. He handed over Vicky's typewritten transcription of her conversation. As the chief of detectives read, Murdock began filling him in on the blueprint and what had been done until his arrival.

Solomon looked up from the paper. "He's going for a payoff."

"I figure," Murdoch said.

They started to reenter the suite.

"Just a minute!"

Spain hurried down the corridor toward them. He gave Solomon a quick look and spoke to Murdoch: "Find anything?"

144

"We don't know yet. Chief Solomon—Mr. Spain," Murdoch said. The two men shook hands.

Spain kept his gaze on Solomon. "The brass is coming," he said.

"Which ones?" Solomon asked.

"All of them. The mayor, police commissioner, chief inspector, chief of intelligence—"

Solomon grunted. "That's four of a kind to draw to."

"What did you find?" Spain asked.

"The dog went bananas right where it was supposed to," Murdoch said.

"Let's go see—"

"Seventeenth Precinct—McHugh."

"I wanna speak to Detective—Sergeant Rocky," Tonio said in his best nasal New York accent.

"You mean Sergeant Roccaforte?" the police operator asked.

"Yeah, yeah, that must be him. Short, stocky—he speaks with a funny gargle in his t'roat, Y'knowwhadImean there?"

"Hold the line, please," McHugh said.

Tonio waited through a series of clicks.

"Squad room, Roccaforte—"

Tonio heard the gurgle in the throat.

"Never mind who this is, Rocky," Tonio said, haltingly, in a raspy voice, "but you did me *good,* one time back, man."

"So?"

"I'm going to lay a good one on you."

"Lay what on me?" He was getting bored.

"You know them street people, singing and dancing to that Fifty-ninth Street corner at Bloomingdale's?"

"Who is this?" He was interested again. Cops, Tonio knew, loved details.

"Hear where I'm coming from, now. They is this big blond fox, dress-up like a *nun,* singing songs, man. Only she ain't no nun, she is *passing,* man. Under that black thing she wearing, she laying down more scag than come in JFK in one week!"

"What's her name?"

Sergeant Roccaforte, Tonio would bet his life, was writing rapidly.

"Man, you *bust* that phony broad, you *learn* her name! At three o'clock, a jive dude going to come up to her and collect on what she already *passed,* and give her a refill, and you *be* there, Sergeant, and you got *two* for Christmas!"

Tonio hung up.

He was not at all sure the detective would go, but it was worth a chance. He did not like the idea of having to improvise, but after the roasting Roccaforte had given him—he had no alternative. There had just been no way he could have avoided the cop's demands. The single most damaging part of the whole incident was having to hand over his Columbia ID. He knew about cops, and their memories. It would surface, somewhere along the line, and Roccaforte would put it together.

He trudged through the dirty snow making his deliveries. The office parties had started in many of his regular stops. He was making a small fortune in tips, and in three offices that day he had been kissed on the mouth by half-drunk older women. After all, it was Christmas Eve.

A dozen cops, in and out of uniform, stood about in small groups. If he didn't know what to look for, Murdoch thought, he wouldn't be able to detect any sign of nervousness. But it was there, he knew. It was the way they looked at him, not moving their heads, using eyes only, as if any movement might trigger a hidden mechanism and blow them apart. They were frightened, but they were disciplined men.

The refrigerator had been moved out of the kitchen. Morgan Berry and Babe stood to one side. Spain was in the kitchen talking to the mayor and the commissioner. Two cops were being assisted into body-armor suits while the three chiefs, Chief Inspector Libby, Chief of Intelligence Reddy, and Chief of Detectives Solomon talked with Sergeant Andonian, bomb and explosives expert for the department.

The commissioner was smooth-shaven, handsome, wearing a tailored top coat, homburg, and gloves. The mayor was short, fat, and jolly-looking, even when he was troubled. The only difference in the three chiefs was their size. Solomon was the smallest of the three. And all of them had eyes that reminded Murdoch of some of the gamblers he had come to know in Vegas. Flat, hard, expressionless; a dead stare, taking in everything, revealing nothing.

The two men getting into the flak suits began to test communications equipment built into their helmets, talking to a monitor and a closed-circuit television system set up in another room. A crayon had been used to mark a square area around the wall where the refrigerator had stood. One of the bomb men turned awkwardly and spoke to the commissioner: "We're ready, sir."

"Let's get out of here," the mayor said to everyone in the kitchen. He waved to the flak men. "Good luck, gentlemen."

"How are we going to approach it?" Solomon asked quietly.

"Skil saw around a six foot area," the commissioner replied. "Cut through the plaster and then open it up and see what we've got. Any better ideas, Chief Solomon?"

"Sounds okay to me," Solomon said.

"Glad it meets with your approval," the commissioner muttered, "considering you've done all the thinking until now."

Everyone but the flak men left the kitchen and took up a position in the television-communications center on the opposite side of the building.

"We're ready to go," a voice announced over the speaker. The television monitor showed the interior of the kitchen and the two bomb men. A video tape was running. If there was an accident, there would be a record right up to the time of the explosion. Sergeant Andonian, the explosives expert, turned to the commissioner, "Ready, sir."

The commissioner nodded.

"Okay, start your tapes," Andonian said. While everyone present could hear the bomb men in their operation, Andonian had made a rule that only one man would speak to the men on the site. He smoked, nervously. "Starting tapes—audio and video," the monitoring officer said into his mike. "Okay, you're on your own."

" . . . Starting Skil saw . . . approaching area. . . . Starting the first cut . . . across the top . . . cutting nicely . . . no resistance. . . ."

"You've kept records of your work, I hope, Murdoch?" the commissioner asked.

"You can have copies anytime."

"What about the originals?"

"Mr. Spain has them."

" . . . Okay . . . we're finished cutting. . . . Going in now with rubber-head chisel and mallet. . . ."

Everyone but Murdoch and the commissioner was crowded around the television-monitor screen.

"You played with fire on this one, Murdoch," the commissioner said. "That was pretty cute, going after the blueprint in the garbage can yourself. Suppose it had been a letter bomb?"

"Two beer cans, two notes. Both threats. There was no reason to believe that this was any different, and that he wasn't jerking us off again."

"True. But we have experts."

"And clear the building on a day like today? Bringing in your bomb-disposal trucks, scaring hell out of anyone within a block—and all on Christmas Eve?"

"But—"

"It was a fast decision to make, Commissioner, and I made it in the best interest of people, *all* the people, and in the interest of my city."

"Your *city?*"

"Smaller than yours. Only about fifteen thousand people, but still a city, within four walls and a hundred stories."

"I hope, for your sake, that you kept good records."

"That all depends."

"On what, Murdoch?"

"What you're nit-picking for, Commissioner."

The commissioner waited a long time before answering, looking Murdoch straight in the eye. "I'm at the top of my field, Murdoch. I don't need publicity."

"And I'm at the top of mine and do everything I can to avoid it."

"Okay." The commissioner grinned. "I'm not needling you. I've heard from Chief Solomon, Captain Hansen at the Seventeenth, and from a few of the boys you picked up when we had to make department cuts. Sid Hoag, Andy Brooks. I can't say that in your position I would have done things much differently."

"*Any* differently," Murdoch said, putting it all on the line. "I did it all."

The commissioner looked at Murdoch a moment and finally nodded. "Maybe."

"*All,*" Murdoch said. "Bet it."

" . . . Getting a light inside the wall . . . can't see anything so far. . . . We're going to enlarge the hole. . . ."

Solomon walked over and nodded toward the kitchen. "What do you think?"

"I think we're going to find something," Murdoch said.

"Then you don't think it's a crazy?"

"No. I think he's making a major move. The demand should come soon."

"Money?" the commissioner asked. "Terrorist? Let somebody out of jail or else?"

"I say money," Murdoch replied.

"The Mob?" the commissioner asked.

"Not their kind of operation," Solomon said.

"I agree. But tell me why you say money?" the commissioner asked Murdoch. "Why not the Red Brigade? Hitting the United States for the first time and making a big splash out of it?"

"It's too well-thought out. Planned in detail, and he's working psychology on us—he's in or has been in psych-warfare," Murdoch said. "It doesn't have the gung-ho shotgun feeling of a terror group. And a crazy would just blow a hole in us and snicker as the Fire Department rolled down Fifth Avenue jerking off under his overcoat. So, I think it's blackmail and this is the first move, to prove his point, toward his demand."

"I hope you're right," the commissioner said. "We can deal with a blackmailer, whether it's for cash or a terrorist deal. Crazies, on the other hand, give me the shits."

" . . . Okay . . . we're down far enough for a good look now. . . . We're putting the light back into the hole for a look-see. . . . Let's see . . . we got a steel girder. . . . We got . . . Oh, oh . . . bingo! Sergeant! We got something!"

All three of the chiefs, charging like bulls, made for the door.

"*Hold it, goddammit!*" Sergeant Andonian yelled. "Stay the hell out of there. And that means *everybody*—"

The three chiefs stopped and looked at Sergeant Andonian as if he had just gone out of his mind. He hurried past them and down the corridor toward Princess Martha's suite.

The commissioner stepped forward. "Sergeant Andonian *is* the expert, gentlemen. He's perfectly capable of telling us what the situation is."

Murdoch walked over to Morgan Berry where he sat to one side with Babe. "You can do more good in the lobby, in case we have to bail out of here. And you can drop the blind man routine."

"Right."

Sergeant Andonian's voice broke through the murmur of excitement around the television monitor: "We got about seventy-five—maybe a hundred pounds of plastique explosives, Commissioner. It's wired, with a timer. The timer is the most elaborate I've ever seen. And goddamn professional. Looks like the inside of a computer. . . ."

There was no holding anyone back when they heard that information.

They were met at the door by Sergeant Andonian. "Screwiest thing I've ever seen." He held out an elaborately made electronic device on a piece of cloth in the palm of his hand. "The damn thing wasn't even connected! Look, here are the leads going from the timer to the batteries, see? Then the relays, and then these go to the charge. Everything was ready to go, but it just wasn't connected."

"Are you sure, Sergeant?" the mayor asked nervously.

"You think I'd be standing here with the damn thing in my hand if it wasn't! I'm telling you, all you have to do is plug these two things into the charge and she's ready to go. He didn't leave it unconnected by accident. And why, I don't know, because the guy who made this knew what he was doing. Yes, sir. This son of a bitch is the best. The *best!*" Sergeant Andonian turned and looked at the hole in the wall, the plaster and dust all over the floor.

The two bomb-squad men, who had taken off their helmets, were wiping sweat and smoking. "You agree, Hubie?" Andonian asked the taller of the pair.

Their hands still shaking, the two men nodded. "In twelve years, Sergeant, nothing like this," Hubie said.

"From the blueprints," Andonian said, "this is one of the main structural columns—core elements—a part of the steel skeleton. The charge is just below the column joint, at the gusset plates, where the beams come together forming a six-point junction. Up and down, right and left, and then right and left again.

"If it had been connected, and if it had blown, the charge would have blown all the bolts at the junction of columns, which is the weakest point in the building. The floor would have dropped in this part of the building onto the floor below. There are ten floors above us, all of them pushing down, and that is a hell of a lot of weight. This whole corner would probably have been blown out for seventy-five to a hundred feet along each side of the building.

"Now, with the amount of plastique the guy's got packed in there, he could have sent three–four floors down onto the *next floor,* and the weight coming down would be like dominoes, sending, God only knows, how much of the building down into Fifth Avenue.

"I can't be sure until I send some of it to the lab, but I think it's high-intensity stuff, the best of its kind, and as far as I know, offhand, only three or four places in the country make it, mostly because it's so volatile. It doesn't control very well. But there's something else—"

"Nu?" the mayor asked in a voice that was not too firm at the moment.

"There is another load of thermoincendiary explosives in there. This guy wasn't going to be satisfied with just blowing hell out of this place, he wanted it to burn as well."

"Oh my God!" the mayor said.

"Okay," Solomon said around his cigar. "It's obvious that this thing was put here during the construction of the building. How did he disguise it from all the workers that followed *after* the building was roughed in? I mean, they got inspectors that check these things. Telephone guys, electric guys, plumbing guys, and Christ only knows who else! Then the carpenters, the guys that put up the wallboard, the plasterers, all that *before* the wall was closed in. Months had to go by with dozens, maybe hundreds of inspectors and foremen in here—how come No Goddamn Body noticed it!"

Sergeant Andonian smiled at Solomon tolerantly. "You don't know your New York construction workers, Chief. All those guys are specialists. They have one job. They do that job. Nothing else. If they pick up the wrong tool, they're crossing into another union's jurisdiction. Once the structural steel has been checked on the lower floors, the other guys, rising up from below to the next floor above, just keep coming up after them. The plumbers, the concrete guys, the tin knockers, everybody,

151

they don't look at anybody's work but their own. There must be a million changes made in the building blueprints as they go along—it happens all the time. Especially in a custom building like this, with so many different rooms, so many different layouts. Christ, the rough plumbing for the bathrooms alone, and the kitchens, and the changes in them, when the lady of the house comes in and says: put the john over there, and the bathtub over there, and rip out the sink and put it somewhere else. They're not going to pay attention to anything that isn't strictly theirs to attend to. They wouldn't pay attention to this hunk of gunk stuck on a junction I beam anymore than they would anything else that wasn't their responsibility."

"But my God," the mayor exploded, waving his short fat arms, "couldn't they just see it!"

Andonian shook his head. "You don't understand, Your Honor, all steel beams are sprayed with liquid asbestos—guys come in with hoses and under fifty or sixty pounds per square inch, they cover the beams with fire-retardant—"

"Okay—okay," Solomon said, his voice rising with frustration. "How about the phone wires, and that thing you have in your hand—how come that wasn't discovered when the asbestos guys came in to spray?"

"Chief, in a high-rise building like this, they have dozens of temporary phone connections with guys talking to other guys fifteen–twenty floors apart. Those wires usually run up the columns. When they move out, they just leave them there, because it costs more to remove them than leave them. When the asbestos guys come in, whatever is there, they assume is okay, and they spray it."

"Okay," Solomon said heavily, "it's a construction worker."

"Not necessarily," Andonian said, shaking his head slowly. "It could be anybody with a little knowledge about high-rise construction, which he could get out of a book—"

"But, but, how the hell could he do it and get away with it, with hundreds of other guys on the job?"

"Weekends, Sundays," Andonian said.

"But security—" Solomon said.

"Come on, Chief," Andonian said. "I've spent my entire life in the mid-Manhattan area. Born in Polyclinic, and raised on West Fifty-fifth.

Went to school right here, not more than an avenue block away. Then to work on the department. And in all that time, there has never been a period when there wasn't construction going on somewhere."

"What's your point?" the commissioner said loftily.

"Let him *talk,*" the mayor said.

"Now, if you know the midtown area, you know that on Sunday—and most of the time, Saturday—no work is done in construction. A building, like this one, has an access to it on three sides—the avenue side, and down both crosstown streets. And there's one watchman—one—who's there to keep kids out, and to see that hijackers don't come in and try to rip off big loads of copper and brass. There is a building going up over on Lexington, and I'll bet anybody a hundred bucks the watchman is sitting in his shack watching television, or listening to the radio, and I can walk into the building—crawl all over it—and neither the watchman nor anybody else will know about it. But let's say I'm discovered? What am I doing? I got on a hard hat, rough clothes, a tool belt, probably freezing my ass off and I give the watchman a line of gripes about working overtime—I'm *working,* see? Not trying to steal anything."

"How do you know so much about this, Sergeant?" the commissioner asked.

"Two uncles and my old man were all in high-rise work. The two uncles fell. So, instead of following them, I got onto the cops, sir."

"And into the Explosive-Arson Squad," Solomon said ironically. "Go on, Sergeant."

"All right, the guy's got this explosive in place. And he didn't connect it. But how was he going to detonate it if the wall was sealed up? This is no punk, Commissioner. See these contact openings right there?" Sergeant Andonian pointed to a line of open contacts on the device. "Basically, the thing I'm holding is a telephone receiver. See this green wire here, the one with the alligator clip on the end, *that* spooked me. He had scraped back a half-inch of plastic sheathing on the telephone wire inside the wall and attached this alligator. He dials an exchange, to get up here to this phone, then for the last four digits, he dials four zeros, or four ones, or four whatevers, since that's not a number the phone company would give a subscriber. They give the exchange number, like 987-1234, or -5678 or anything like that, but they don't give out 987-0000. It's got to be 987-1000. Or -3000. Seven digits. But then, you see that last contact there. An eighth one? That was his control. A last number to make the series work. So, 987-1234–9. Or 8. Or 5. The contact closes. The batteries send the juice flowing to the detonator, which goes to the charge, and you're out two–three floors and two hundred feet of high-rise building, with an incendiary fire which no sprinkler system in the world can contain, and a goddamn big chunk of your building goes down into Fifth Avenue.

"Here, I'll show you." Sergeant Andonian walked to the wall phone.

"I figure he used zero for his four-digit number—and then any other number for his control."

"Are you sure that damn thing is disconnected?" the commissioner asked nervously.

"Nothing can happen, but the contacts will close." The sergeant picked up the phone, punched the exchange number, and then started punching four zeros, and when nothing happened, disconnected and started again; then again; again. He hit it on the fives. The contacts began to close.

They stood watching the contacts close one at a time. Andonian punched out the code. The metallic clicks seemed as loud as anything they had ever heard. The last one snapped closed. "If it had been connected to that pile of gunk in there, Commissioner, you'd be visiting with your great-grandmother now."

Solomon was the first to break the silence: "So, we're dealing with some kind of evil genius," he said aloud, staring at the device in Andonian's hand. "And if there are others? Hooked up in the same way? And somebody dials a wrong number? A kid playing with the phone out in Brooklyn, or in Queens. What if we change the exchange number?"

"Which exchange, Chief?" Andonian asked. "If there are other bombs, how do we know they're hooked up to the same exchange as this one? A building like this can have many exchanges, not just one. Or that he hasn't built in an override—creating an exchange of his own?"

"'kay," Murdoch said, "we accept that he's brilliant, and he's worked it all out in advance. But what does he want? And what's more, how is he going to collect it? If he's been working on this trip for such a long time, he's got to have the payoff figured also."

They all turned to him.

"This was just a warning," Murdoch continued. "He was sending us a message. He can do it. We know now that he *can* do it. And when he makes his demand, we'd better meet it. This is the ninetieth floor. How many more of them could there be in the last ten floors?"

"How do we know this is where he started?" Andonian asked.

The silence was broken by the mayor: "Chief Solomon, use any man in the department, and as many as you need. I want you to direct this yourself, personally." He glanced at his watch. "It's a quarter of three, Christmas Eve. Mark that time as official."

"Yes, sir. I understand," Solomon said.

"What about evacuating the building?" Spain asked.

"It's sticky, Joe," the mayor said. "It's not just beer cans with threatening notes. We've found enough explosives to start World War Three and a means of detonating it."

"But he's not going to do anything until he makes his demand. That's his big item. He knows that *we* know he can do it. I think we're safe until he leans on us," Spain argued.

"I know I work for Mr. Spain," Murdoch said slowly. "And I have no official capacity, or say-so, but I've lived with this thing for two months now. He *wants* a payoff. I'm convinced of it. He just made a big bet that we're *going* to pay off. I think ripping the people out of the building, especially on a day like this, well, it's not my decision. But that's the way I feel."

The mayor looked at the others. "Jesse, I just put you in charge. What do you say?"

"I go along with Murdoch," Solomon said. "I think he's right."

"Commissioner?"

He nodded, reluctantly.

"All right, gentlemen, we hang tough—for a while." The mayor looked at Solomon. "Where will you set up your command post?"

"Right here in the Tower." Solomon looked at Murdoch. "Your office will do temporarily—can you arrange for something larger?"

"We can find you space."

"Then let's move," Solomon said. "Andonian?"

"Yes, sir."

"Get communications down here. I'm going to want at least a half-dozen phones, with roll-over numbers, installed by yesterday. And you'd better call home and tell them Santa Claus is going to be late. I want every man on the Explosive-Arson Squad down here. Tell 'em to be quiet about it, and to use the service entrance.''

"Yes, sir.''

"Get hold of every dog in the department that's been trained to smell out contraband, then call security at Kennedy airport and La Guardia. See if they have any dogs they can loan us." He turned to Murdoch. "We'll use your man Berry to coordinate the dog details, since he knows the building.''

"Okay.''

"Andonian!''

"Chief?''

"Leave that hole in the kitchen open, and the hot stuff untouched until the criminalistics people have been here. We might get lucky with fingerprints. And I want the dogs to get a good whiff of that explosive so they'll know what they're looking for. Okay, gentlemen, we go to work. I'll be in Murdoch's office until we get set up.''

Murdoch's office was filling up with policemen now; moving about with a serene sense of purpose, authority and power. These professionals poured their concentration into whatever assignment was handed to them. They listened, telephoned, spoke in low voices, and made polite requests of Vicky, Andy Brooks, Sid Hoag; the special teams had slipped into the mainstream of his professional life, and in a very short time had assumed control. He watched this quiet takeover of his authority, answering their questions, directing them into areas they wanted to check out, or research, without any resentment. There was almost a sense of relief that he had, at last, major help in countering Threat.

Chief Solomon was also parking in Murdoch's office, sitting at his desk reading the voluminous file that had been kept on Threat, answering the phone, directing his men.

"You did a hell of a job, Murdoch," Solomon said, thumping the thick file. "I can't see anything you've missed.''

"Except who it is.''

"That'll come," Solomon said. "Pretty cute, switching teams and having them go over the employees' records a second and third time.''

"Excuse me, Chief," Vicky stood at the door. "Mr. Kosinski called. Suite 2500 is ready."

"Thank you," Solomon said. "Andonian!"

"Right here, Chief."

"We're moving—set up the command in suite 2500. That's where we all live for as long as it takes."

Sergeant Andonian's craggy face broke out into a grin. "Not bad— not bad at all. Beats an unheated church basement in Brooklyn, or a Harlem tenement."

"Don't get used to the rich life for two reasons, Sergeant."

"Yeah?"

"One, we move out when we catch him; two, he might blow us away before we do."

"You make life hold such promise, Chief," Andonian said with a grin. "Oh, by the way, Lieutenant Diedrickson called. Said he was on his way down."

"Son of a bitch!" Solomon slapped his forehead. "I forgot all about him! Thanks, Sergeant."

"Isn't that your criminalistics man?" Murdoch asked.

Solomon nodded.

"That reminds me of an idea I had earlier today," Murdoch said. "Can you check with the Pentagon, Army, Veterans Administration, perhaps, and get a line on Viet Nam vets with electronic, explosive, or Intelligence backgrounds? Say, anyone in this area. The northeast corridor. Can't be too many of them."

Solomon agreed: "Good idea." He pulled the phone around and dialed a number. He spoke briefly, in low tones, ordering the search to be made on Viet Nam veterans with backgrounds as Murdoch had suggested. He hung up and tapped the Threat file. "I should get my butt out of here and read this—"

But he remained sitting.

Murdoch paced the office.

"You got any family?" Solomon asked. "It is Christmas Eve."

"An aunt I'm pretty close to, out on Long Island . . ."

They were both stalling and they both knew it.

"Think he might have something?" Murdoch asked.

157

"Diedrickson is a very careful man."

"And you wouldn't be surprised—" Murdoch said, finishing the cliché.

They talked some more. They had a cup of coffee. They switched places. Murdoch sat down and Solomon paced.

And then Diedrickson was there. He had entered the office quietly and closed the door behind him. He was a tall, gangly man, with a large Adam's apple, bony wrists and the wildest-looking blond Afro Murdoch had ever seen.

"Chief?" He glanced at Murdoch questioningly.

"It's okay—what'cha got?"

Diedrickson came forward and placed a manila envelope on the desk before Solomon, who ripped it open quickly.

"I've checked and double-checked, Chief. It's real. You got a *flat guarantee.*"

"Who is it, for Christ's sakes!" Murdoch exploded.

"Name Marell mean anything to you?" Diedrickson asked.

"Marell—Marell," Murdoch repeated. He shook his head.

"I didn't think it would," Diedrickson said. "That's her maiden name. Now she's Jason."

"She?" Solomon asked, looking up from the data Diedrickson had given him. "A woman?"

"Victoria Jason."

"Vicky," Murdoch said to Solomon. "My secretary."

12

"Isn't this some trip!" Laura Roc laughed quietly.

"I love it!" Eleanor said under her breath. "It's unbeliev-able."

They had discovered another world for themselves when they had donned the nuns' habits. They were given seats on the subway, they were allowed to go to the head of the line when they grabbed a bite to eat in one of Bloomingdale's restaurants, and even the cops treated them with a consideration usually reserved for crippled children. In the ladies' room of the department store, they had been passed to the head of the line. Laura washed her hands. "What time is it?"

"Nearly three," Eleanor replied. "How much do you think we made?"

"I tried to keep a running account in my head, but I stopped at three hundred—that was four hours ago."

"Jesus!" Eleanor breathed.

"Come on, let's get back. I don't know how much longer my voice will take this," Laura said. "The snow has soaked me through to the skin. But as long as those fat little ladies keep dropping fives and tens into your basket, I'm staying."

"I don't know how you do it," Eleanor said with genuine admiration. "Sometimes when you're singing, I get so involved in listening, I forget where I am, and what I'm doing."

"Only sometimes?" Laura shot back. "Listen, Elly, there is one thing I promise you. After today, if I *ever* sing Schubert's 'Ave Maria' again, I'll slit my own beautiful throat."

A tentative knock sounded on the door, and then a small small voice inquired. "Are you about through, Sisters?"

The two nuns looked at each other and grinned. "Shall we let the suckers in to pee?" Laura asked.

"Why not?"

"Ready?"

"Off on deuce—"

"Me, Mean Joe Green," Laura said.

"Me, Too Tall Jones," Eleanor replied.

They slapped hands.

"Set—"

"Hup one. Hup two—"

They composed their faces, folded their hands inside their sleeves, and opened the door, smiling sweetly.

The two nuns didn't have the Bloomingdale's corner all to themselves. There was competition to the right and left, spreading away to the corners. Backed up against the curbstone, the hot-item hustlers hawked their wares, accosted pedestrians, fought among themselves for space, selling watches, leather goods—wallets and handbags, transistor radios, televisions, and stereo components. Most of it was stolen. But nobody cared.

Laura, with her big voice, blew it all away. She soared above the Italian sausage on a roll, the pastrami on rye, the hot dogs, pizza wedges, and slabs of greasy pork on onion rolls roasted at 4:00 a.m. in Central Park. There were racks of clothing for both men and women, designer dresses, skirts, jackets, raincoats, moved about on especially designed tubular dollies for quick break down and storage in the trunk of a car. Boots, fur hats and gloves, silver flatware; and as many accents as there were vendors. Twenty different tongues described their wares in broken English, their voices heaving up and down like a restless surf covering the fast-hands artists who could count change for a twenty and palm a five right before your eyes. The other vendors liked having Laura and Elly on their corner. And while those nearest the nuns were solicitous, they needed no prodding to take advantage of the customers distracted by the big-boned sister belting out Christmas songs.

Again and again pedestrians would step forward and press a bill into Eleanor's or Laura's hands, mumbling "God bless you," and moving off into the crowds.

It was, Detective Roccaforte thought, watching the black-robed pair from across Lexington Avenue, as neat a take-down as he had ever seen. The part that made it work, he knew, was the fact that the big broad could really sing.

He studied them for a long time, searching the crowds around them for a spotter, and saw none. They were good, as good as Roccaforte had ever seen. He had watched the bills flash when they were pressed upon the two nuns, but he hadn't yet seen anything that might be scag pass hands.

He stood smoking, letting the tide of Christmas shoppers move him, not resisting, going with the flow, occasionally getting away from the curb when one of the huge Transit Authority buses swept down at great speed, rocking to a stop with a hiss of compressed air.

He watched and waited. He wanted to be sure of the information, he wanted to see something *pass*. He wondered who the tipster that had called him might have been, and then dismissed it. It was no doubt someone who had been aced out of the action in some way, perhaps he had been thrown some bad stuff and this was his way of getting even.

He was in no hurry. He bought a wedge of sausage pizza and stepped into the protective entrance of the Dry Dock Savings Bank. He continued his observation, ate his pizza, and listened to "Ave Maria." He shook his head sadly, wondering about the way things happen when a kid with a voice like that could get hooked into dealing. He sighed. It took all kinds.

But he still had not seen any dope passed. He really didn't want to bust two nuns without being dead-sure. He lit a cigarette, turned his collar up against the snow, and moved for a better position near the curb.

Tonio removed his eye patch and bought a red, white, and blue knitted ski cap from one of the street vendors on the Third Avenue side of Bloomingdale's and slowly worked his way along Fifty-ninth Street to Lexington.

After waiting for ten minutes and not seeing either Roccaforte or the girls, he began to search the crowds, peering into the shop windows. He was reluctant to believe that the detective might have acted earlier, and already picked them up. He moved along the edge of the crowds, watching, waiting, and then he saw the two nuns come out of Bloomingdale's and take up a position on the curb. Laura started singing "Silent Night," and feeling a sense of relief, Tonio started his careful search of the crowds for the cop.

Just don't be sitting in a car, Tonio thought. But he didn't see how that was possible. Lexington Avenue was one-way downtown and a parked car near the bus stop, which would be close enough for the cop to observe the nuns with any confidence, would be too conspicuous.

And then he saw him. Roccaforte has bought a piece of pizza and moved back into the entrance of the bank. Good, Tonio thought.

He moved quickly to get into position.

Eleanor was cold. She, like Laura, was soaked through to the skin, and the heavy serge habit weighed a ton. They had worked it all out in advance. Since Laura had gone to a Catholic school, she knew about such things: nuns always traveled in pairs. So, while there wasn't anything for Eleanor to do but stand there and play the tape while Laura sang, just being there and not doing anything was part of the scam. But she grew tired and bored. Laura had to be careful in her singing so as not to injure her voice, and had that to concentrate on, so Eleanor let her eyes wander over the crowds. It was exciting at first, the eager faces, the snatches of conversation, the quick rush of the mass, and then the cold reached her and she wished it were all over with so she could have a long hot shower with Tonio.

And then she thought she saw him. But how could it be? There was no eye patch—and the hat was not Tonio's common navy-blue knit.

She stared, hard, and then lost the figure as it crossed with the light to the Dry Dock side of Lexington. She brought her attention back to the front: nuns were not supposed to twist and turn, searching the crowds.

But she couldn't resist. She stamped her feet lightly and made a half-turn so she could see.

It wasn't Tonio—but was it?

She continued to stare. The figure moved along the sidewalk, head averted to the windows. How could it be Tonio, when he was supposed to be working? And while she wasn't absolutely sure, it didn't make sense that he would be delivering deli food so far over on the East Side, so far away from Marty's.

She had decided that it couldn't possibly be Tonio, when the figure looked up, straight at her.

Goddammit, she said to herself, it *is* Tonio.

On his side of the street, Detective-Sergeant Roccaforte saw the smaller of the two nuns turn and search the crowds. She's looking for her connection, he said to himself. He glanced quickly at his watch: 3:20. He felt confident of his tipster now. He'd better call in for backup. He would move in when the pass was made and action went down. He kept his gaze hard on the two nuns as he stepped back to avoid the snow splash of a bus sweeping down to the curb.

"Excuse me," he mumbled. He tried to move to one side and back. He was blocked again. He pushed harder. He couldn't move. The bus was nearly on him—he pushed hard, ramming his elbows backward to get away from the press of the crowd on him. He felt himself jolted in the small of his back. Even through his raincoat, it was like he had been hit with a sledgehammer. He felt himself jackknife forward—he heard a scream and then fell forward just as the bus caught him broadside, flattening him against the front bumper like an insect.

It was Roccaforte who had screamed as he realized he had been set up—and then, nothing.

Across the street, Eleanor saw Tonio deliver the blow to the man's back, saw him fall, heard the thickening thud of bone and flesh against steel, screamed, and ran across the street.

By the time she had cleared the bus, and pushed her way through the hard clot of violence around the crumpled man in the dirty snow, the figure in the gaily colored ski hat had vanished.

"*Stay out of it!*" Laura said in her ear.

"But—I saw him pushed!" Eleanor said.

Laura took her by the arm and half dragged her away to the subway entrance. "Listen to me!" she hissed through her teeth, shoving Eleanor down the subway stairs, "this is *New York*."

"But—"

"*Nobody cares!*"

It was dark by the time they arrived at a famous theatrical costumers where Laura had gotten the nuns' habits for half price. They changed into street clothes in the fitting rooms. "Don't bother to put them back into the boxes," Laura said. "Just let 'em stay on the hangers. I'll tell Dom they're just a little damp, and that way he won't charge us for having to have them dry-cleaned."

Eleanor nodded quietly, and did as she was told. She had not said much since their flight from Bloomingdale's. Even when Laura, half nude and unable to wait any longer, counted out their take. She looked up at Eleanor, her mouth open. "My God! Nearly six hundred dollars! With what I've already made, my share is enough to pay next semester's tuition, and have a hundred bucks left over. Elly, we did it!" She jumped up and danced Eleanor around the small room.

"You know what we are?" Laura said in a voice that was beginning to crack. "You know, Elly?"

Eleanor shook her head. "No—"

"We're survivors, baby—in a hard town, we *survive*." Laura Roc kissed Eleanor on the cheek. "Come on let's get the hell out of here before they discover those rags are practically ruined. I'm starving for a corned beef on rye."

They finished their dressing hurriedly.

"Did you see it too?" Eleanor asked. "Is that why you ran?"

"See what? The guy and the bus thing? No, baby, I didn't. But we were phony nuns, dig? And I didn't want to answer any cop's questions. Besides, it wasn't anybody we knew. Come on, let's split."

But it was, Eleanor thought. She was absolutely sure it was Tonio.

Chief of Detectives Solomon looked at Murdoch. His eyes hooded down. "It's happened before," Solomon said in a voice as hard as flint. "But I'm surprised you didn't check her out."

"Just—just wait, Jesse—" Murdoch said, his voice and hands quivering. "I had Andy Brooks check our security people—"

"So? They could be in it together."

"And *I* checked Andy."

"And *we* just went through the file. Nowhere is there a record that your secretary had been checked out—in fact, everybody has been, except you and her."

"Don't start that crap," Murdoch said harshly.

"It's not *crap,* Mr. Murdoch," Solomon said levelly. "And as far as I'm concerned, she's a prime suspect—how else could her print have gotten on that penny? And before you answer, follow me closely.

"The maid, and her lover, find the beer can. They hand it over to Andy Brooks. He shows it to Spain, who calls you. You in turn come down here and dictate a detailed account—" Solomon slapped the file,"—of what has happened until then. You call me. I come down and we have a meeting. I take the beer can, the note, and the pennies to Diedrickson. Nowhere in that sequence does your secretary have an opportunity to touch anything."

Murdoch stared at him.

"And *I* checked *you* out—and that leaves only her."

"I don't believe it," Murdoch said quietly.

"*Don't* believe it, or don't *want* to believe it?" Solomon asked. "She's the only one that has had Means, Opportunity. Means: she could have gotten an empty beer can, eighteen pennies, and typed the note; Opportunity: she could easily have gone to International Traders on some pretext, after all she was your secretary; Motive: we don't know yet, but I'm beginning to smell money—"

"Okay, okay," Murdoch said hoarsely. "What do we do now? Drag her in here and give her the third degree? If it *is* her, *and I don't* believe it, and I don't want to believe it, then she has to have a confederate, or confederates—"

"True," Solomon said mildly.

"—and since that confederate is most likely to be a man, because

165

there is no way you're going to get me to believe that a woman could have planted that stuff we found in Princess Martha's kitchen wall.''

"So?"

"How about putting her under a twenty-four-hour surveillance, get a court order for a tap on her phone, and keep her isolated from what develops—what's going on here in the office, in the Tower?''

Solomon had gradually broken out into a grin as Murdoch talked.

"It's her confederate, if there is one, that we want. The outside man—the guy that can blow us apart.'' Murdoch paused. "What the hell are you grinning at?''

"The first time I ever worked as a plainclothesman, I had a old harness dick as a partner. One of his rules was never to knock the way a man makes a buck, or how he finds his way to reason.''

"Then you'll handle Vicky my way?''

"I didn't say that.''

"Then what did you say—or mean to say?''

"Suppose she's innocent . . .''

'' 'kay.''

"There is no denying that it is her print we found. How did it get there?''

Murdoch stared at him. "How?''

"We question her. We tell her the facts, and reassure her that she is not under suspicion, and then we get her help since she's the only one that *can* help us.''

"And?''

"In the meantime, we put a tap on her phone, and watch her.''

Murdoch had never felt anything for his secretary beyond the fact that she had come to him with excellent references, was positively a whiz at typing and shorthand, and thoroughly dependable.

But all that had changed with the knowledge that her fingerprint was on one of the Threat pennies. She knew everything, every move that had been made—had sat long hours with Murdoch since the first beer can, talking about Threat over coffee. There was not a single idea or thought or move that had been made during the entire time that Vicky Jason was not a part of, or knew about.

Solomon, on the other hand, viewed her in the cold professional light of a prime suspect. His years of training and experience had taught him that when he had two of the three empiricals—Means, Opportunity, Motive, in this case, Means and Opportunity—the third was not far behind. And while conspiracy was not as cut and dried as a simple felony investigation, it was more than odd coincidence. If Murdoch was treading water because it was his secretary and felt the flush of betrayal to expected loyalties, Chief of Detectives Solomon was eager for the plunge. He glanced at his watch. "It's four-fifteen. Can you hold her here—I mean on some excuse—for a couple of hours?"

"It's Christmas Eve, Jesse."

"Can you?"

"I'll think of something. What have you got in mind?"

Instead of answering, Solomon picked up the phone and punched out a number. He drummed his fingers on the desktop impatiently. "Hello. This is Chief Solomon, let me speak to Deputy District Attorney Duval, please. Okay, then let me speak to Assistant Rosen."

"What's going on?" Murdoch asked.

Solomon held up his hand. "Hello, Herbert? Jesse Solomon. Listen, I've got a problem. Yeah, yeah, I know it's Christmas Eve, but this won't take you very long, and I *need* a favor—a wire tap. Who? Judge who? Yeah, I know him. Okay, where is he now? That's right around the corner. Okay, Harvard Club in half an hour—and thanks, Herbert."

Solomon hung up and looked at Murdoch, gathering up the Threat file and Diedrickson's report. "We're in luck. Judge Diamond—he *hates* criminal conspiracies." Solomon headed for the door.

"But—"

"Just keep her here until I get back."

It was still snowing when Tonio put his carriers away, had a last drink with the black sergeant, who was by now quite drunk, and left the delicatessen to a chorus of good wishes for the holidays. Once outside he moved through the Christmas shoppers with the security of a shadow, pushing into the subway for a quick ride uptown and the parking lot where he had left the VW van. If he did not get held up in traffic, he would make it to Bridgeport and be back in the city by seven. He was not at all concerned about the snow, having allowed extra time.

He narrowly missed being held up by an accident on Bruckner Boulevard, but managed to get past and cruised the New England Thruway at a steady fifty-five, pushing it just a little. There was a lot of traffic and there were hard patches of packed snow that had turned to ice in the bitter cold. He had to concentrate on his driving as he sped north, and just beyond Westport, but before Fairfield, he pulled the VW van off the thruway into a Howard Johnson's.

He went to the rest room, washed his face and hands, and stood in line for a phone. Out of a double bank of six booths, only two were working. He did not mind the wait. He closed out his surroundings as children slipped and chased and slid on the snow-wet terrazzo floor and "Silent Night" was played again and again on the PA system. His turn came and he slipped into the phone booth ignoring the stale smell of body odor and dialed a Bridgeport number.

"Toledo Parts—"

Tonio recognized the voice instantly. "This is Ace," he said quietly. "I need some stuff."

"Jesus Christ, man—it's Christmas."

"You think I don't know it's Christmas? I need some goddamned stuff, man!" Tonio said.

"Where are you? In the city? If you in the city, then forget it. I gotta get home. I promised my wife—"

"Lay back, man, I'm easy. I ain't in the city. I can meet you at the place in less than a half hour."

"Yeah? A half hour, huh. All right—okay. What'cha want?"

"You know that sweet little .32 with the silencer you had the last time?"

"Yeah?"

"That," Tonio said. "And shells."

"That's a cold piece, man. So's the silencer. For that, I take out five bills."

"I ever argue price in two years?" Tonio demanded.

"No, but—"

"I know, I know, it's Christmas, and you need the money for the wife and the little kiddies. Okay, five bills. At the place. Inna half hour."

"Deal."

Tonio hung up and looked into the face of a very tired-looking young woman with her hair in curlers. "'Scuse me," he said politely and moved around her.

He bought a double container of black coffee and was on the road again running past Fairfield in a perfect, clear winter night. It had stopped snowing. Ahead of him the lights of Bridgeport rose out of the darkness. He glanced at his watch. He would make his appointment with Toledo and have time to spare.

He swung the van off at the first Bridgeport exit and descended the ramp cautiously, and even in low gear, the VW slid the last thirty feet. He narrowly missed smacking into the rear of the car ahead of him.

He turned right and moved into the dark and forbidding streets lined with red-brick buildings. He headed for the warehouse and foundry district near the water and parked at an abandoned loading platform. There were no lights. It was dark, cold, and silent except for the hum of passing trucks on the thruway.

There was a movement from around one corner of the platform and Tonio tensed, ready to move, until he recognized Toledo.

"Where are you parked?" Tonio asked.

"Two blocks away—why?" Toledo answered. He was a short, thick man with a shock of black hair covered by a knip cap and wore a fleece-lined car coat.

"I thought I saw a car. Security maybe? Coming in here?"

"Blue car? With a CB antenna?"

"Yeah, looked like it," Tonio lied.

"Crazy Jake. Night watchman that patrols this area sometimes. I'm surprised he's here. He's usually bombed out of his gourd. You got the bread? Five bills."

"Where's the piece?" Tonio demanded.

Toledo unbuttoned his coat and pulled out a Smith & Wesson .32 with a four-inch barrel and a three-inch silencer. He handed it over, along with a box of shells. Tonio handed him five one-hundred-dollar bills.

While Toledo snapped the bills, Tonio took the box of shells Toledo had given him and loaded the pistol. He turned, sighting a rusting tin can nearly covered with snow. He snapped off a shot and grunted with satisfaction when the can plowed backward into the snow. There was no sound, except that of a wintry, dry cough. "Nice. Very nice."

"See? I told you. Nice goods. Came in from Canada."

"I didn't ask for no pedigree," Tonio said easily. "You don't ask me. I don't ask you."

"That's right," Toledo said. "That's one thing I learn back in Nam, right? Don't ask no unnecessary questions. And when I make the connections, and get into this business, you be surprised the customers I got, man! Some of the stuff I ship out, you wouldn't believe. *I don't ask.*"

"That's right," Tonio said. "You learn that in Nam. But I bet you wondered a little, huh, Toledo?"

"Sure I wondered. Like everybody else, I got curiosity. Nine hundred pounds of high-intensity stuff, incendiaries, Thermos, radio stuff, arsenal of guns, grenades, ammo. I think maybe you going to try and blow up the whole world. *But I don't ask.*" Toledo buttoned his coat. "I gotta get the hell outa here. So long, Tonio. Merry Christmas."

"Yeah, Merry Christmas, Toledo."

Toledo paused and looked up at the sky, which was clear and fixed with stars. "Back in Nam, I don't bet no odds I get my ass back home for *any* Christmas. But I screwed the mothers. I made it."

"Yeah."

Without another word Toledo crunched away in the snow and at the end of the loading platform, just as he was turning around the corner, Tonio shot him in the back. He hit him once more before he hit the ground. He emptied the chamber into his neck.

He walked a few hundred feet to a rotting pier and threw the gun into the water as far as he could.

No, you didn't ask, Tonio thought, as he drove up the ramp and onto the thruway south and heading back toward the city, but you knew. You were the only one, and you knew too much. You knew it all, except the job. And after tonight you could have figured that out.

He glanced at his watch. He settled into a steady fifty-five miles per hour. Even if it started to snow again, he could still make it back to the city with time to spare. He would give them an hour. He would make the call inside the Bronx city line, that would give Murdoch an hour.

Murdoch was very good and dependable. He would be able to make it in an hour.

Bridgeport dropped off behind him, unchanged, still saturated in ugliness. Still pretending to be a city.

In the world of Vicky Marell Jason, divorced, living alone in a two-room apartment in Queens, there was work, the winter vacations, one year skiing in Vermont and the next year a Caribbean cruise, male friends who were small-time lawyers, retail-store managers, middle-level employees in civil service, and occasionally one-night stands with a swinger on his way to the top with no time for steady relationship, let alone marriage. She was not content with her world; neither was she ready to accept the fact that she was out of the race and the spectacular win of someone very nice. She had, when she first went to work for Murdoch, done more than just wish. She had made it very plain to him that she was interested, but the chemistry just was not there. He was kind, considerate, thoughtful of her feelings, her work, did not make demands on her, and paid her well, even extravagantly; and she was learning a great deal about hotel management. It was something that she kept to herself, and hidden away, My ace in the hole, as she thought of it. If by the time she was thirty-five, there were no really good prospects around, she would dedicate her life to a career in the hotel business. The prospects were excellent now that things were beginning really to open up for women at management and even policy levels. She had made a few contacts and had been encouraged by Murdoch.

She had watched with envy as Maggie made all of the right moves with Murdoch. She was cynical enough without bitchiness to see through and even admire Maggie's going to California. And though it had only been a half day since Maggie had left, Vicky was alert to a change in Murdoch's behavior. If they only didn't have the awful problem of Threat to deal with; still, the field was open, and what the hell, who knows, and why not?

At five forty-five Solomon returned. A few minutes later Murdoch asked her to come in. She surrendered her desk to Sid Hoag, made sure he knew how to start the tape for recording the calls, picked up her steno book, and entered Murdoch's office.

From that moment on, every move Vicky Jason made would be watched, timed, and evaluated, and anyone she met or called would be checked out, and if there was anything suspicious about them, they too would be put under surveillance.

Vicky sat down, opened her steno pad, and looked up, waiting.

"You don't need that," Solomon said quietly.

"Oh? Okay." She closed her book. "What's this all about?"

"We're just cross-checking some information, Vicky," Solomon said. "You've been privy to everything that's gone on here, with regard to Threat." Solomon smiled. He tapped the Threat file on the desk. "Typed this all by yourself, so you're the only one that knows and probably recalls every detail."

"Probably."

"We'd like to ask you a few questions."

"Shoot."

Solomon nodded. "Okay—and since I don't know as much about you as Chris, here—tell me a little about yourself."

Vicky frowned, glanced at Murdoch standing at the window, and then shrugged. "Born and raised here in the city. Queens. Forest Hills. My father was an automobile salesman. For a while, I wanted to be a tennis star—but that changed to an actress. Then—" She smiled suddenly. "Do you really want this kind of stuff—I mean, does this help?"

Solomon nodded. "Fine."

"Are you looking for something specific? I mean, maybe if you'd give me a hint, I might be able to zero in on it?"

Again she glanced from Solomon to Murdoch.

"Did you go to college here in the city?" Solomon asked.

"Two years at Hunter—but then I met Neil and dropped out to get married."

"Neil Jason?"

Vicky nodded. "It looked good at the time."

"In what way?"

"His father had just died. Mr. Jason was a dental technician and owned his own lab. Neil had to leave school to take over the family business. There was another brother and a sister, and of course his mother."

172

"I would say it looked very good. What happened to sour it?"

"Usual things. In-law trouble. If I wanted something, I would usually get it, but only after he had talked it over with his mother. There was enough money. If we wanted to take a winter vacation—we'd make the plans, a cruise in the islands, but Mrs. Jason would either come down with something or she would use the younger brother or sister as an excuse."

It was easy, relaxed, with Solomon never pressing any particular point.

"How about some coffee?" Murdoch suggested.

"Okay. Vicky?" Solomon asked.

She started to rise, but Murdoch held up his hand. "I'll get it." He slipped quietly from the office.

Solomon had spent half of his life questioning people in one way or another, and he had an exquisite ear. Murdoch had made the right move at the right time, and if there were going to be any results from the interview, they would come while he was out of the room.

He took his time. Murdoch would not return with the coffee too soon. He lit a cigar, pulling himself together, resisting rising inner tension before beginning the most delicate part of all, the hard questions.

"Can you think of any reason why your fingerprints would be on file with the FBI?" Solomon asked.

"Are they?" Vicky thought a moment. "I guess they would be."

"Why?"

"I have a passport."

Solomon nodded.

"And once I made application for a job as secretary in the State Department. While I was still at Hunter College. That may account for it. I'm sure they ran some sort of security check." Vicky shrugged.

The questions became a little sharper, asking for more and greater detail; they were still related—always—back to Threat. Solomon emphasized this by tapping the bulky file on the desk when such a question came up—always back to Threat. But he was getting nowhere, and he knew it.

By the time Murdoch returned to the office, Solomon had not yet decided if she were completely innocent, or terribly clever. Murdoch served the coffee and took up his position at the window again.

"Where is your former husband now?" Solomon asked Vicky.

"I don't know."

"Don't know?"

"I haven't heard from him in three years."

"Did he contact you? Or you him, three years ago?"

"He called me. He said he was on his way to California and wanted to know if I needed anything."

"Was he always so solicitous?" Solomon asked.

"He had his thoughtful side."

"Did he go to California?" Solomon asked.

"I don't know. That was the last time I heard from him."

"And he was himself a dental technician, aside from owning the lab you say?" Solomon asked.

Vicky nodded. She took a cigarette pack out of her skirt pocket. Murdoch snapped his lighter. She sat back, exhaling, cocking her head to one side, blowing smoke nervously.

"Where, where was it—the lab—here in the city?"

"Downtown, West Thirty-third—there are a lot of them in that area."

"Do you remember the name?"

"Of course."

"Would you give it to me, please?" Solomon asked.

"United Labs—they also did the lab work for silversmiths," Vicky said.

"Did he ever indicate to you that he could make a lot of money? Become superrich?"

"That he wanted to, yes; but never that he could," she said.

"Wanted to—in what way?"

"In a way that most of us want to make a lot of money: that way. Nothing conspiratorial."

"Nothing that would indicate he would attempt something like Threat?" Solomon asked very softly.

Vicky leaned forward and stuffed out her cigarette. She glanced at both of them, slowly, moving from one long look at each of their faces, and settling on Solomon. "Is my ex-husband under suspicion?" she asked directly. "Am—I?"

Vicky took a long breath, picked up her steno book, flipped the pages.

She wrote rapidly a few seconds, and pencil poised, she looked at Chief Solomon. Neither of the three moved for a long time.

"What's that all about?" Solomon asked, indicating her steno pad. "What did you write?"

Vicky read her notes: "December twenty-fourth, 6:02 p.m.—office of Chris Murdoch. NYC. Present: Chief Solomon, Chris Murdoch, Victoria Jason. Interrogation of Victoria Jason by Chief Solomon and Chris Murdoch. Subject: Threat." She lowered her pad and looked, again slowly, from one face to another. She then read again. "Question—Jason to Solomon: Have you, at any time in the previous hour and a half of questioning, read me my rights?"

She again looked from one man to the other, pencil poised.

"No," Murdoch said. "No rights were read to Victoria Jason."

Vicky scribbled the answer hastily. She stopped and looked up, waiting.

Solomon turned to the window. It had stopped snowing. He did not want to be there, but at home with his wife and daughter in their Riverdale apartment trimming the tree and having Christmas drinks. When he turned around, Vicky was writing again. She looked at him and read: "Question—Jason to Solomon: Is Victoria Jason under suspicion, or is her husband under suspicion, in the conspiracy of Threat?"

He had played out the string, Solomon knew, and he would have to inform her of her rights, and he believed, he *knew,* that she would ask for a lawyer, and clam up.

On the other hand, if he asked for her cooperation, telling her what they knew about her fingerprint being on the penny, and she *were* involved, it would effectively close down any possibility of the truth.

All of his instincts warned him to oppose her. Everything he had ever learned cautioned him to go by the book, to read her her rights, and if she refused to cooperate, then book her and put her away. But which option would produce Threat, or an effective means of stopping him? Which, after all, was what he wanted most.

The potential loss of life and property was too overwhelming for him to consider anything but the obvious. There were guidelines set down for just such situations. He had no alternative.

Murdoch and Vicky were staring at him, waiting.

175

"You have the right to remain silent," Solomon said slowly, reciting the words mechanically.

Murdoch looked at his secretary. Her face went white. Her hands began to tremble as she tried to write. The pencil point snapped and she threw it to one side. She looked up at Murdoch. Her face twisted as she began to cry.

Chris Murdoch looked away, out of the window and down on the gay and festive Fifth Avenue street scene. Christmas Eve. Peace on Earth. Goodwill to men. He thought of Maggie. She would be in Los Angeles by then. Behind him he heard Solomon continuing the questioning, but he closed it out. He felt he was losing as surely as men fall in battle; a slipping away of his courage. It was a new experience for him. Meaningful things in his life were being taken away and he was powerless to prevent it.

A snowstorm in New York City is cruel to the outer boroughs. Expressways and boulevards and main traffic arteries are swept clean of snow, but side streets and neighborhood areas are the last to be cleaned. Tonio knew this and had counted on it once it had begun to snow. He drove the Cross Bronx Expressway and began to examine the north-south arteries. He chose Third Avenue and got off the expressway and headed south. Driving slowly looking for a phone booth. He pulled up to a service station. "Fill 'er up, Mac, and check the oil."

He did not expect an immediate answer from the operators on the St. Cyr Tower switchboards. He counted eighteen rings and finally a weary voice answered.

"The St. Cyr Tower, Merry Christmas."

"Murdoch's office," Tonio said, dropping his voice to a dead monotone and talking through his nose.

"One moment, please."

"Murdoch's office." Sid Hoag's voice was cold, impersonal.

"I'm sending you another beer can with eighteen pennies," Tonio said. "You dig, man?"

Tonio gave the street number of the Bronx apartment building. "It's on a corner, man. Abandoned, you know? There ain't nothing you can do but clear the building and stand back, you hear where I'm coming from?"

176

"Keep talking," Sid Hoag said tightly.

"Deadline is seven-thirty. Don't try to find nothing. All you can do is stand there and watch that mother go sky-high, man. Boom! You dig?" He hung up. He didn't have to repeat—after this morning's call they would have a tape on all calls.

Tonio stepped out of the booth, looked around, and walked back to the VW van. He paid for the gas, got in, and drove off without anyone noticing that he had ever been there. He eased into traffic and headed south.

A few blocks from the mined apartment building, Tonio found exactly what he was looking for. He reached down and turned off the ignition, put the gear in neutral, and coasted. Still coasting, he turned into a partially cleared side street and parked as close as he could to a five-foot bank of snow piled up at the curbing. He removed the rotor and sat punching the starter, grinding the battery down until finally it would no longer turn over.

He got out of the van and walked back to Third Avenue, where two bars, cater-corner from each other, were lighted with Christmas cheer. Both were doing big business. He chose the largest of the two, and once inside found hardly enough room to move. No one noticed him. Laughter and shouts fought for attention against blaring television evening news.

The phone hung on the wall at the far end of the bar and Tonio dropped a dime and dialed the Time number. He signaled the bartender and mouthed the word "Beer" and then turned his attention to the phone.

"Hello, Spino? It's me, Sal," Tonio said loudly to the mechanical voice repeating the Time. "Where the hell do you think I am? In the Bronx and the battery went dead on me. . . . How the hell should I know! Listen, Spino, I'm going home to Marie and the kids. . . . Yeah. . . . You think I care? Spino, listen to me. The van is off Third Avenue here in the Bronx—" He cupped the phone and spoke to the nearest man at the bar, "What's the name of that street out there?"

"Milgrim. Third Avenue and Milgrim."

"Third Avenue and Milgrim. . . . What? Not for twenty bucks, not for fifty. Not for nothing, Spino. I leave the keys with the bartender here in the—" he cupped the phone again. "What's the name of this bar?"

177

"Yankee Clipper," the bartender said.

"Yankee Clipper. Yeah. Got baseball pictures all over the wall. . . . Yeah, the same to you, Spino—up yours. And Merry Christmas."

Tonio slammed down the phone and picked up his beer. "Stupid schmuck," he said to no one in general. "I tol' him to buy a new battery, but the cheap bastard—Ah, what the hell."

He finished his beer, dug the keys out of his pocket, and handed them to the bartender. "Spino, he's most likely the one to come. Short, heavyset guy. Always needs a shave. It'll either be him or a black dude named Edwards. The van is up in a snowbank halfway up the block. And here's five for your trouble."

"Sure, kid," the bartender said, dropping the keys into the register.

Tonio thanked him and walked back to the VW van. There were only a few things he had to take. He went over the interior carefully for anything he might have forgotten, took the registration and identity papers. He got out, locked the door, and made a show of testing the doors and then, hunching his shoulders against the cold, walked off toward Third Avenue.

He knew that he should be hearing the approach of the cops soon, and then he did hear them. Only one siren at first, and then growing in intensity, the first was overlapped by a second and then a third, and within minutes the air was filled with their sound.

From two blocks away, he could see the building, the lights, and the activity of the cops. Even from that distance he could see that the cops were causing a lot of excitement. People began to appear from the darkness. Firemen began to arrive, and more people. He went no nearer. Two blocks was close enough.

"What's going on over there?" someone asked at his shoulder.

"That many cops," Tonio said and shrugged, "somebody musta mugged Santa Claus."

Powerful shafts of blue-white light began to play on the abandoned building. Traffic on Park Avenue was detoured away into snow-clogged side streets. More people began to arrive and stood around watching in the frozen darkness.

He would like to have stayed, but spectator was not the role he had assigned himself. He knew it would go off on schedule. He hailed a taxi.

"What's with the cops?" the taxi driver asked as Tonio climbed into the back.

"Probably cornered some junkie stole somethin'," Tonio said.

"Yeah. Probably. Where to, Mac?"

"Manhattan—and see that bar up ahead?"

"Yeah, I see it, but I don't make stops, Mac."

"Just slow down a bit, that's all. I want to see something."

"Slow down I do. Stoppin' I don't do. This afternoon another cabbie did it, stopped, you know, fare goes in and robs the joint and comes back out and gets into the cab waving a gun, tells the cabbie to take off. Slow down I do. Stoppin' I don't do."

It was dark halfway up the block, but Tonio knew exactly where to look. There was just enough light from the corner for him to see that all four wheels had been removed from the van. He settled back. Within two hours it would be stripped. Even the engine and the transmission would be gone, removed, hauled away, and sold in various parts of the city. Without a complaint, there would be no investigations, no checking of motor numbers, no fingerprints, nothing.

Solomon didn't book Vicky Jason; he released her on her own recognizance as he and Murdoch had planned, and went home. It would have been difficult for her to make bail on Christmas Eve, and the psychology was to give her a sense of relief that she was not in jail over the holidays and thus instill a false sense of security. It was hoped that, if she *were* involved with Threat, she would make a slip. It was a hard thing to do to her, Solomon admitted, even shitty, but they had no choice. From the moment Solomon allowed her to leave, the surveillance teams were on her and Judge Diamond's approval of a phone tap working. There was nothing to do then but watch and wait.

The invasion of the St. Cyr Tower by the special police teams had gone so smoothly that not even the bellhops, notorious for being nosy, were aware of what was happening around them. The entire security force of the St. Cyr Tower knew, and all the senior managers in key positions, but no one else.

Murdoch could detect no suspicion that anything irregular was going on.

It was Christmas Eve and there was still a huge building to operate. The lobby was boiling over with activity and the Monte Carlo Lounge was going strong. But Murdoch knew it would thin out soon. At about nine o'clock there would be very few people left. Almost everybody had someplace to go on Christmas Eve, and those who didn't, would hang over the bar isolated, full of sentimentality, or bitterness.

Jimco had told him that Spain had left the Tower, but would return within a few minutes. After such an incredibly hectic day, he found himself temporarily displaced and he stepped into the Monte Carlo Lounge for a drink. A moment later he was touched on the arm. "Mr. Murdoch."

"Hello, Andy. Where's Sid?"

"On watch up in the office with Sergeant Andonian. They're playing gin. Everything's quiet. Soon as the dogs get here, Sid's going to work with Berry and the handlers on dog patrol, then Braden'll take over the office watch."

"And you?"

"I'm going home."

Murdoch nodded again. "Of course you are. What the hell is Christmas Eve without— Are you a dad, a father, or papa?"

"Papa."

"Have a drink, Papa."

"There's a pretty wild party in Sixty-seven–B."

"How wild?"

"Well, they're spilling over into the halls. Braden's been watching them on the television monitor. Says it looks like a porno film. They're hitting on each other in the halls."

"Can you take care of it before you leave?"

"Sure."

Murdoch signaled the bartender to give Andy a drink, and the security officer ordered a brandy. As head of security, Brooks would have to know about Vicky, and he filled him in quickly.

"Do you *really* think she has anything to do with it?"

"Solomon can't take any chances."

"You feel the same way?" Andy Brooks asked.

Murdoch put his drink down firmly on the bar. He turned and faced his young security chief squarely: "You're the cop in this stately pleasure dome, what do you decree?"

"As a cop, I'd have to go along with the chief."

"And not as a cop?"

"I don't see it—I don't see her in it at all."

"Neither do I," Murdoch said.

They drank. The bartender answered the bar phone, brought it down to Murdoch, and placed it in front of him. "Front desk, Mr. Kosinski."

Murdoch ordered another round of brandies and picked up the phone. "Yes, Stephen?" He listened a moment. "Okay, I'll be right there."

He dropped the phone. "Another complaint about the party—"

"I'll go now."

"Finish your drink. And then get something for your breath before you go up there. We can't have drunken cops rousting our rich clients."

"I wonder what Threat really wants?" Andy asked thoughtfully. "Is he really going to try and put the arm on us for dough?"

"I believe it, and I'm beginning to think Solomon does too. If he thought it was a crazy, he wouldn't have leaned on Vicky."

"But, if Threat's smart enough to work this thing out so far, wouldn't you think he knows that when he reaches for the money, we're going to be ready for him, regardless of what it takes? I mean, we've got all the manpower we need. NYPD. FBI, even, as soon as he makes a demand and it becomes extortion. What then? An overseas drop? A numbered account in Switzerland? Or parachute the money into the Atlantic Ocean and they pick it up by submarine? We can follow the money to Switzerland, and we can get the Navy to go after a sub, so what could it be?"

"If you figure that out, Andy, you can have my job. You won't even have to ask. Spain will give it to you." Murdoch stood. "I gotta go."

They separated in the lobby. Andy went off to dampen the wild party and Murdoch walked over to the desk.

Kosinski was a tall, immaculate man in a double-breasted blazer, perfectly groomed, and with a manner that could charm old ladies and children, and if necessary, slice up a demanding guest with surgical skill. He placed a Telex envelope on the marble desk before Murdoch. "I think it has to do with our new problem in the kitchen wall."

Murdoch ripped it open:

PLEASE CONTACT THIS OFFICE AT ONCE REGARDING EMERGENCY SUITE
NINETY—B.

S.V. LEONE
MERCHANTS INTERNATIONAL

"Son of a bitch," Murdoch said under his breath. "I forgot all about
insurance."

"I reacted differently, Christopher. I said: This could be pissy." Kosinski shrugged his shoulders exquisitely.

"Is our brilliant young Harvard law graduate, Mr. Sotine, still here?"

"The entire legal department had an office party, beginning at noon,
and, by one o'clock, were all drunk and went home," Kosinski replied.
A phone rang behind the desk. "Kosinski. Yes, Mr. Spain, he's right
here."

"I'm on my way up," Murdoch said into the phone.

Chief of Detectives Solomon was assisting his married daughter and
her husband trim the tree between trips to the kitchen, where his wife
was being helped by their youngest unmarried daughter. He walked into
the kitchen, freshened his drink, stole a shrimp, and walked back
through the living room. He examined the tree critically, made a suggestion, and paused at the sliding glass doors to his terrace. The terrace was
one of his favorite places in the whole world. On the seventeenth floor,
it overlooked the Hudson River and the Jersey shore. He unlocked the
glass doors and stepped out over the ridge of snow in his shirt-sleeves.
It was bitterly cold, but he didn't intend to stay more than a moment. He
watched as a tug nosed a string of barges upstream. He was about to turn
back inside, refreshed, when his daughter tapped on the glass, panto-
mimed the telephone, and pointed to him.

His shoulders sagged. He knew, he just knew. The evening had promised to be too perfect. No one looked at him when he went to his den.
They went on about their activities as if they were alone. In a lifetime
they had gotten used to the phone calls that took him away. He closed
the door and picked up the phone. "Yeah? Whatever it is, it had damn
well better be good. Talk."

"Sid Hoag, down at the St. Cyr Tower, Chief. We just heard from our friend Threat. I have it on tape. It's all set to go, want to hear it?"

"Of course I want to hear it!" Solomon growled. "Turn it on."

The entire conversation between Tonio and Sid Hoag hummed in Solomon's ear. "Is that it?" he asked tightly when it was finished.

"That's it."

"Call the Forty-seventh Precinct—Captain Ness. Tell him I want the entire area cleared for a block—block and a half. And that means cleared of everybody. Who else knows about this?"

"I told Murdoch—he was in Spain's penthouse, so Spain knows, and your crew in suite 2500. Other than that, nobody."

"I'll hold on while you call Spain and ask him if he can use that chopper he has on the roof—and if he can, to bring Sergeant Andonian with him."

"Gotcha!"

Solomon paced the floor of his den impatiently with the phone pressed to his ear.

And then Hoag was back. "They're taking the chopper—and Andonian is going with them."

"Okay," Solomon said. "Give me that address again."

Sid Hoag repeated it. Solomon knew the section. He had once been Bronx Borough Commander. He calculated his time and distance. He could do it in twenty minutes, less, if he didn't get hung up in snow traffic. "Okay, I'm off."

Solomon was on the street in less than a minute, driving the family car which was equipped with a siren. He picked up the radio mike and flipped the switch. The car was immediately filled with the sounds of radio static and the voice of the dispatcher. Driving expertly with one hand, Solomon broke into the broadcast channel. He identified himself. "I want to speak to Captain Ness, of the Forty-seventh—"

"I'm right here, Chief," Ness's voice broke through the radio noise.

"What does it look like, Nessy?"

"I have ten men searching inside," Ness responded. "It's one of those abandoned shells—nine stories. Hasn't been lived in for years, or so the people standing around here say. Used mostly by junkies and bums."

"You have thirty-five minutes to search it and make sure no one is inside."

"That's cutting it close, Chief," Ness responded. "Can we depend on the seven-thirty deadline being firm?"

"You can't depend on a damn thing, Nessy," Solomon said. "This is only a piece of a bigger puzzle we've been working on. So, make it twenty minutes. Give yourself a good ten minutes to be on the safe side."

He dropped the mike and touched the siren. Christmas traffic melted before his approach, clearing the way for him.

"Jesus Christ, Mr. Spain!" the helicopter pilot exclaimed. "I never saw so many fire trucks and police cars at one time in my life. Where do you want me to land?"

"Get as close as you can without hitting anybody," Spain replied.

"Holy shit, here comes *another* helicopter!" Sergeant Andonian shouted.

"Probably the commissioner," Spain said, stretching around to look.

The commissioner's helicopter was allowed to land first, coming to rest on a rubble-strewn empty lot across from the building, while they circled. Spain's pilot began his approach. He turned on his lights.

"Clear the area! Clear the area!" the pilot barked over the bullhorn as a warning to those on the ground.

Murdoch glanced at his watch. It was exactly seven o'clock.

Traffic was rerouted off Park Avenue. Patrolmen shouted back at cursing drivers, while trying to get others to keep moving and stop rubbernecking the scene. There were scattered blocks of occupied buildings still remaining in the "bombed-out" section that had not been entirely abandoned, and from these came the onlookers. Dressed against the cold in thick jackets, knit hats, coats, boots, and gloves, they laughed and talked and shouted and drank from bottles hidden beneath their coats. Someone had discovered an old oil drum and built a fire. Police and firemen stood about and waited for something to happen, or for orders, as huge searchlights played against the abandoned apartment building across the street.

From within the building, through the dark holes that were once windows, dark-suited figures could be seen racing through the building, their flashlights probing dark corners, winking on and off as they searched for anyone who might be inside.

"It's seven-twenty, Captain Ness," Chief Solomon said. "Get 'em out of there—*now!*"

The precinct captain nodded grimly and adjusted his bullhorn. "This is Captain Ness speaking. Clear the building! Clear the building. All police personnel clear the building at once. Attention! Attention! *Clear the building!*"

"How many went in?" the commissioner asked. He stood with Spain, Murdoch, Andonian, Captain Ness, Solomon, and Battalion Chief Ipolito from the Fire Department.

"Ten," Captain Ness said.

"Then you make goddamn sure ten come out."

But it wasn't necessary to coax the men to leave the building. They came tumbling out of doors and windows, pounding awkwardly across the snowfield as if pursued by demons while the crowd cheered.

"Find anything in there?" Captain Ness demanded of the puffing and heaving sergeant in charge of the detail.

Nothing had been found.

Television reporters and their cameramen began to arrive and unpack gear.

"How the hell did they get here?" the commissioner muttered. "And so fast—"

Solomon shrugged. "Who the hell knows. Tell 'em it's a ruptured gas main."

"Good idea. Pass the word—that's the story—a ruptured gas main. Jesus Christ! What *do* you expect to happen, Jesse?" the commissioner asked.

"Commissioner, you know as much as I do," Solomon replied. "What about it, Andonian?" he asked.

"If this guy," Andonian said, breathing moisture in thick clouds from his mouth and nose, "used the same materials he used downtown, and he used enough of it, there ain't going to be a hell of a lot of that building left."

"And fire?" Battalion Chief Ipolito asked.

"A lot of fire, Chief. Thermoincendiary, probably."

"Son of a bitch! What the hell's going on here? Why doesn't some-body tell me something?" The fire chief spit on the ground and flapped his arms to warm them, stamping his boots in the snow.

"Now you belong to the party, Chief," Solomon said. "And you know as much as we do."

"Seven twenty-five," Murdoch announced, looking at his watch.

The officials became quiet and turned to look at the building. Police-men, firemen, television and newspaper reporters saw them, and react-ing to the quiet, turned to face the building.

"Start rolling," one of the television reporters said quietly to the cam-eraman.

"But nothing's happening—"

"Start rolling, dammit!"

"Okay, okay, but it's a waste of film, and if something *does* happen and I have to reload, it ain't my fault."

"Start that fucking camera!"

In the distance the city hummed and moved on, unaware of the drama that was taking place on Park Avenue in the Bronx.

At seven-thirty the four charges in the elevators went first. The entire center of the building rose straight up, like the top of a surging sea, up—up—up and up and still more, cresting against the black Christmas sky, and then, slowly, it began to fall in a slipping, sliding motion toward the ground. The top-floor corner charge with the heavy load of incendiary exploded, taking out three floors, expelling a ball of fire that lit up the sky brilliantly. Almost immediately all four charges on the ground-floor corners exploded in series: *one—two—three—four!*

Both ends of the building were brought up and away from the foun-dations with a mighty heave, and, as if in slow motion, the ends began to fold downward and inward toward the empty center and collapse into a huge pile of concrete, rubbish, twisted steel, and all of it blazing with incendiary white heat.

Shock waves swept back. Cars were rocked. People were knocked off their feet. Hundreds of windows in the surrounding area were cracked or shattered. The air was filled with flying rocks and chunks of concrete.

And then it was over. The blazing ruins of the building, fanned by the back-draft of the implosion and, coupled with the intense incendiary elements, created a fire storm that burned with the pinkish white of a sparkler.

"I knew it!" Sergeant Andonian said with the conviction of a professional. "Ammonium nitrate, TNT, aluminum powder—mix very carefully, and boom!"

Murdoch turned to look at him. He knew it could have been the St. Cyr Tower on Fifth Avenue just as easily.

Slowly, as if coming from a great distance, there began a roar as the crowd reacted. In seconds the roar became a howl. Those few who knew most about what had happened, and why, stood perfectly still in the snow, their faces lighted up by the flames.

Solomon looked around him, at the crowds, at the empty hulks of abandoned buildings, at the fury of the blaze. "It's a war zone," he muttered angrily.

"War," Murdoch said quietly to himself. "War in the city."

The officials began to move away. The building had been worthless before, and it was too far away from any other building to present any danger. There was nothing for them to do.

The two helicopters revved up and disappeared into the sky. The firemen moved in on the burning rubble and the cops began to untangle the traffic snarl. Slowly the stunned onlookers dispersed.

Tonio had taken a hot shower, shaved, put on fresh clothes, and was stretched out on the bed watching an old black-and-white television he had bought secondhand, when Eleanor came in. She was exhausted, but smiling through her fatigue, her arms filled with bundles and packages. She collapsed against the door and took a deep breath. "Hi—I don't believe I made it!"

"Watch this," Tonio said, sitting up, staring at the television. She walked around and stood beside him. The newsman's voice narrated the scene. It was photographed poorly, but there was enough light for Tonio to see Murdoch and Spain among the many harried faces. The picture focused clearly on the building seconds before it exploded.

"My God, what was that!" Eleanor asked.

"Someplace up in the Bronx," Tonio said. "I saw it before, on another channel. Gas main ruptured because of the weather, they say."

"But the people—" Eleanor said with genuine concern.

"Nobody hurt. They cleared the building before it went off."

The building was a pile of flaming rubble now. The firemen and the cops were brought out of their temporary trance and exploded into a frenzy of activity.

"That's it," Tonio said, as the news went on to sports. He reached over and turned the set off. "Here, let me help you with the stuff. What'd you buy, f'chrissake?" he asked good-naturedly.

"We did more than six hundred and fifty!" Eleanor said with excitement. "What did you make in tips?"

"Close to two hundred."

"Oh my God, we made more than *five hundred dollars!*" Eleanor cried. She threw the remaining packages on the bed and collapsed on top of them. "I'm not even tired anymore."

Tonio began opening packages and looking into bags. Most of the contents were groceries, but there was a bottle of wine and a cake.

Eleanor lay sprawled on the bed looking up at him, examining his face. "I saw a man killed today," she said quietly.

"Yeah?" Tonio looked down at her. "How so?"

Slowly, watching his face, Eleanor told him what had happened on Lexington Avenue, and how Laura had dragged her away. The whole time she talked he put the groceries away.

"Laura's a pretty wise head—she was right," he said. "Don't get involved."

"Were you over near Lexington today?"

"Lexington? What the hell would I be doing in that part of town?" He paused. "Why?"

"Because," Eleanor said quietly, "I saw the man who pushed the other man in front of the bus—I could have sworn it was you."

"Lotta guys look like me in New York, ever think about that? Was this guy wearing an eye patch too?" He grinned.

"No, he wasn't. He was wearing a funny ski hat."

"So?"

"Other than that, he was absolutely a twin."

"Was it snowing?"

"Yes."

"And it was across the street?"

She nodded.

"There were times today, Elly, when I couldn't have recognized my Aunt Tilly across the street. And she weighs three hundred pounds. I nearly got hit by a taxi on Madison—the guy swore he couldn't see me, and I believe him."

"Well, it rattled hell out of me all day—and I'm sure glad it wasn't you."

"New York's a funny place, Elly," Tonio said. "Funny things happen here all the time with no reasonable explanation, you know?"

"I know," she said tiredly. She sat up and leaned forward on her knees and stared at the floor. "I was propositioned at least a half-dozen times today—can you imagine! *One* guy came right up to me, as if he knew me, handed me a twenty-dollar bill, dressed very well, you know, and leaned over as if he was going to say something nice, and asked me if I would like to—"

"Like to what?"

"Never mind."

"No, come on, what'd he say to you?"

"It's so disgusting, I don't want to repeat it."

"But you took the twenty—didn't you?" Tonio said coldly.

She looked up at him as if he had slapped her.

"See what I mean, kid? That's New York."

"But I was dressed as a nun, f'God's sakes! He didn't know that I *wasn't* one!"

Tonio didn't say anything for a while, letting the doubt that it had been him, reinforced by her own story of the proposition, soak in.

"Feel like going to Laura's party?" Tonio asked.

"Anywhere, as long as I can sit down."

"How about taking the wine and the cake?"

"Anything you say, just let me rest a minute."

"Sure," Tonio said pleasantly. "Why don't you take a shower? It'll make you feel better."

"I would, but I can't move. Undress me," Eleanor said, staring straight up at the ceiling. "How was your day?"

"Rough. Lot of moving around. But it's over now." He bent over the bed and started undressing her. When she was nude, he covered her with a blanket and went into the shower and adjusted the water. He came back to the bed, slipped out of his jeans and drew her out of the bed.

They took a hot shower together, soaping each other until they could stand it no longer and then made quick and violent yet satisfying love.

They got dressed and went to Laura Roc's party with a dozen others in the Riverside Arms, including Mrs. Coffin, and ate pizza and submarines and cake and drank wine. They lay on the floor and smoked grass, and Tommy Weeks, who had gotten drunk and had not gone to Boston for Christmas with his parents, showed up with a beautiful Chinese girl. About one in the morning, Mannering and Tulip began to feel very emotional about the Birth of Christ, and with Tulip playing on Laura's old upright piano they sang Christmas songs so beautifully that everyone cried a little, including Tonio.

At two in the morning, Mrs. Coffin, filled with wine and sentiment over her "student children," began a real crying jag and Eleanor and Tonio said good night. They returned to her room where both of them slept as if they were dead.

At eleven o'clock on Christmas morning, explaining that he was going out to get the morning paper, Tonio took the subway down to Times Square, used a pay phone in one of the busy subway corridors called the St. Cyr Tower, and asked for Murdoch's office.

"Murdoch—"

"This is Threat, man," Tonio said, using a heavy New York accent with slight Spanish overtones. "Did you get my message in the Bronx last night?"

"We got the message. What do you want?" Murdoch demanded coldly.

"I let you know, man."

"Are there any more packages like the one on the ninetieth floor?" Murdoch asked, hoping against hope that Threat would reveal something.

"For that kind of information you have to pay, man!"

"We'll pay. How much and where and when?"

"I tol' you man, I let you know."

Tonio hung up.

It was almost over now. He walked back uptown through dirty snow

191

to the Stage Delicatessen and like many New Yorkers that morning, bought lox, cream cheese, bagels, and whitefish for Christmas breakfast. He picked up the *Daily News* and took the subway back uptown.

It was a beautiful day. Bright, clear, and cold. He would like to take a drive up into the Connecticut countryside and stop in some out-of-the-way inn and have dinner. But spending the day in bed with Eleanor watching television wouldn't be so bad either.

PART THREE

TONIO VEGA

The New York Police Department, or any police department for that matter, becomes almost paranoid in their suspicions when a veteran member of the department is killed; special attention was given to the death of Sergeant Roccaforte.

Mr. Maggione was the bus driver. He saw Tonio hit and shove Roccaforte in the back. He *saw* it. When the cops heard this, when they started digging into Roccaforte's background, and since the cops who worked Vice were *always* suspect, they peeled back the protective coloration of Rocky's shield and were not surprised at what they found.

Sergeant Rocky had $100,000 in various savings accounts and had paid off the mortgage on his home. He was also putting three children through college.

Not on his salary, he wasn't, NYPD Internal Affairs concluded.

Sergeant Rocky was also known to be short-tempered, cynical, and quick with his hands, if his pigeon didn't pay off, or pay enough, when Sergeant Rocky thought otherwise. The investigators didn't get any signed statements, but they got enough to know that Roccaforte had been on the take for a very long time.

Solomon read the confidential report, and while it filled him with disgust, there was really nothing more to be done. To pursue it further, to bring it out in the open would have been punitive to Mrs. Roccaforte and their children, and, reluctantly, he swept it under the rug. Rocky had obviously pushed someone on his sucker list a little too hard, and they had pushed back, and with much better timing.

The report was going to go in as it was, but for his own satisfaction, Solomon called Mr. Maggione and set up a meeting over a cup of coffee in a Ninth Avenue cafeteria, wanting to see and hear for himself if Maggione was relating what he saw, or what he thought he saw.

"What makes you think Sergeant Roccaforte was pushed?" Solomon asked the thin, blue-eyed little man.

"Ina first place, I been pulling down to bus stops in the city for twenty-t'ree years, all kinds of weather. And even the toughest of them waiting, step back, see, *away* from the curb when they see me coming in. Now the cop, pardon me, Sergeant Roccaforte, was *trying* to step outa the way, but there was this guy who was blocking him, and when I'm about twelve feet away, he gives the cop a shove in the back, musta used something hard, cause the cop shot off the curb like a rocket, and there was no way I could stop. Not in the ice and snow, there wasn't. No way. And I ain't saying this to avoid nothin' for myself, I'm clean. My record as a driver is clean, but you asked, and I'm telling you, the cop was pushed."

"What else did you see?"

"I'll tell you what I *didn't* see. I was outa that bus in t'ree seconds flat, the bus's still moving when I'm at the door, and the guy with the funny ski hat, the one that pushed him, is moving down the street, very cool, not running, like nothing happened, and I *don't* see his face. And then I don't bother anymore, because there are women screaming and people yelling and the cop's brains is dripping off the front bumper of my bus."

Solomon thanked him, reassured him that there would be no further questions, and that he was clear of any involvement.

It was, Solomon knew, a professional hit. What galled him was that there was nothing to be gained by doing anything about it. Even if he could. But he did not like having one of his cops, even a crooked cop, murdered for *any* reason.

He let it go, and slouched beside his driver fighting crosstown traffic en route to the St. Cyr Tower, where he had an appointment with Spain and Murdoch, and mulled over the latest information produced on Threat.

He searched for a connection, some one piece of information that would link up with another piece of information that in turn might give him a place to start.

The Vicky Jason angle, which had held out such promise of a breakthrough, had so far not paid off. Murdoch's secretary, not even bothering to say good-bye, had taken the subway home and had not been seen or heard from since. The phone tap was useless because she had not just taken her phone off the hook but had cut her phone wire. No calls came in and none went out. And she herself remained locked inside.

Solomon had talked to the DA and they considered getting a search warrant, but the DA did not think there was enough evidence in Solomon's suspicion to get a judge to sign a court order.

There was no question that she was alive. The surveillance teams saw her at the window two or three times a day. Whatever game she was playing, Solomon told Murdoch, she had successfully closed down any possibility, so far, of learning anything from her. But he did not alter his surveillance.

They found the man in the rubble of the building Tonio had blown up in the Bronx three days later, and though it gave their pursuit of Threat the added pressure of suspicion of murder, it was just that, pressure, and nothing more. They turned their full attention to looking for more bombs.

Using nine dogs, borrowed from various security agencies around New York working under Berry's supervision, and ultra-sophisticated electronic-sweeping equipment Andonian had borrowed from the Army, literally every square inch of wall, ceiling, and floor space of the St. Cyr Tower had been examined. Seventeen times they thought they had discovered something and seventeen times it proved to be nothing, and seventeen times they left holes where either the dogs or electronic gear indicated there might be a bomb. Like victims of Chinese water torture begging for the next drop, Murdoch, Solomon, Brooks, Hoag, Spain,

197

and Andonian waited for Threat's demands. They heard nothing. They paced and waited. They grew sarcastic, and lost their tempers with each other, and waited. No idea was too farfetched to examine and explore. They played devil's advocate with each other and always came to the same point: What did Threat want, and how was he going to take the payoff?

They found no bomb, but they found other things:

Sammy-the-Doorman was running a ten-thousand-dollar a week book on everything from football to Florida dogs.

Kenneth Sotine, chief legal officer of the St. Cyr, was sleeping with three different women residents of the Tower. One of them was quite old and had already changed her will.

The chef of the La Parisienne Dining Room was getting a kickback of one percent from hotel suppliers.

They found large quantities of grass in the guest rooms.

They discovered a gang of first-class stick-up men who were planning a 3:00-a.m. hit on the safe-deposit boxes.

They found a runaway teenager, who looked and acted older, and who had been screwing the bellmen and room-service waiters night and day, and whose daddy had flown up from Dallas to take her home; whereupon Daddy became so enraged when he learned of his daughter's behavior, he had belt-whipped her into unconsciousness and was arrested by Solomon for aggravated assault.

They found a lot of things, but they found no bomb. Or evidence of one.

Sixty-five percent of the guests had moved out and five percent of the employees from all departments quit cold. Each of the employees who quit was interviewed at length for his reasons for quitting. Each departing guest had his luggage searched without knowing it. Each guest who *remained* was subjected to the same search of personal belongings without his knowing it. And still no evidence of Threat was found.

The associates and employees of lawyers, doctors, and commercial companies had their backgrounds checked again. Customers who frequented International Traders daily, those regulars who traded directly off the tape, were investigated for very large stock losses. No connection was made and no bomb information developed. No one was immune; no one even remotely connected or associated with the St. Cyr Tower, past or present, was passed over.

Chief Solomon's men went over every detail and every angle that had been developed by Murdoch's staff and came up empty-handed. The Explosive-Arson Squad sifted through the ruins of the Bronx building looking for anything that could give them a lead on the identity of Threat. And as they had done in the midtown neighborhood of the St. Cyr Tower in Manhattan, they fanned out over the Bronx neighborhood near the bombed building questioning residents, shopkeepers, and anyone who might have seen something suspicious before the explosion.

The residents laughed. There was always something suspicious going on in that neighborhood. Heroin sold. Hot articles sold. The cops got nowhere. A twelve-year-old girl summed up the attitude: "It's the city, man. You don't even know we're alive until something happens, so go home, turkey."

But there had to be something, they reasoned. Sergeant Andonian, basing his opinion on the bomb they had removed from the Princess's kitchen wall in the St. Cyr, estimated that nine charges of the size and power used on the Bronx building would have taken at least a week, perhaps ten days to install, even by a trained professional like Threat. And to do it quietly, secretly, without leaving any trace at all, would have taken at least three times that long. Threat had spent a lot of time in the building.

But the building had been used by so many derelicts, drunks, junkies, and prostitutes as a sex crib, that no one in the area paid any attention to who went in, who came out, or when. The cops questioned dozens of drunks, but none of them remembered anything except people of their own kind. They questioned the children who had played in the area and in the building. Another blind alley. If possible, the kids were more hostile than the adults. They questioned as many junkies as they could find, which was quite a few.

Nothing.

The only thing they found was the big man Tonio had shoved off the roof. But they got no help there. The body was so badly mangled no identity could be established until they got a report on fingerprints, which were sent to Washington. What was established was that he had cirrhosis of the liver and that he was probably drunk when he died, and suspicion of murder was formally added to the case file.

And then there were the tapes.

They had been labeled the Murdoch Tape and the Hoag Tape since they were the only two who had spoken to Threat while the tape machine was running.

Murdoch and Solomon listened to the tapes more than a hundred times; copies were made and given to the other detectives on the case for their own private listening, on the theory that someone might hear something everyone else had missed. They had voice experts listen to the tapes; linguists listened to the tapes; psychologists and psychiatrists listened to the tapes.

Murdoch and Solomon had gone through—off and on—four days of this.

"What do you think?" Chief Solomon asked when the last of the experts had departed.

"I think," Murdoch said, "that they're all full of shit. They added nothing. They took information we already had and gave it back to us in their language. They did nothing to help us do the one thing we wanted."

"Which is?" Solomon asked.

"Catch the son of a bitch."

"I agree."

Cots were brought into suite 2500, while a dozen phones had been installed and manned as street teams of detectives reported back with, or requested, information. A fifty-cup coffee urn had been brought in from the kitchen; half-eaten sandwiches, and the remains of food were strewn about, and though the St. Cyr housekeeper sent maids in every day to keep ahead of the mess, it didn't help very much.

There were simply no hard facts. No name. No photographs. No fingerprints. Not a scrap of information leading toward an ID. Nothing came from the streets, even though Solomon pressured everyone. Every cop on every patrol, on every beat, every detective in every precinct in every borough was ordered to put the word out on the street and push their informants as hard as necessary to come up with something, anything, upon which Murdoch and Solomon could begin to use the incredible machinery of the NYPD at their disposal. Every known political activist organization that had any history of terrorist activities was reviewed—again. Those organizations in which successful undercover penetration had been achieved by either the FBI or the NYPD, the inside man was asked to give Threat priority over anything else they might be working on. There was no deadline—and yet, there was. They all knew that Threat could make his demand at any moment—and they would have to respond.

Some cops were sure that it was a Mob operation. It was such an elaborate plan, with parts of it thought out, planned, and executed so far in advance, requiring the cooperation and the help of so many people that it would *have* to be the Mob. No one else had that kind of manpower. It was too professional.

There was an equally vociferous group that argued it was the work of terrorists, using extortion to finance their operations. And they too argued it was too professional, too well planned for one man alone.

There was no feedback from the streets, from informants, or from the undercover men. There was simply nothing to go on. They knew nothing about him, where he came from, what he looked like—and, most important, what he wanted.

The payoff. The demand. The takeout. *That* was what they were all waiting for. Give them that, and they were primed. They were ready. They felt confident that when Threat reached for the money, their powerful resources could be brought into play and they would take him.

"How's Vicky? What did you find out?" Murdoch asked Dr. Wyeth. He lounged against the back of the elevator. "I'm surprised you got in to see her. The way she dropped into this depression, isolating herself the way she has, it's almost like the swings of a manic—is that the correct use of the word?"

Wyeth laughed and nodded. "Correct, but where did you learn that one?"

"I've been listening to psychiatrists argue over the voice tapes we have of Threat's phone calls. I learned a lot of new words."

"Oh?"

"Most of them either beginning or ending with bullshit."

"To answer your questions, Vicky is fine. I found out that she's pissed at the world for being suspected—and she let me in because I convinced her I was only interested in her health."

"And?"

"She doesn't look so hot—" Wyeth paused. "And speaking of that, you don't look so hot yourself. When's the last time you had more than a few hours sleep?"

"Who the hell knows." The elevator stopped at Murdoch's floor. "I've got to get out of these clothes, take a hot shower, and shave. Want a drink?"

"No, and you don't want one either. What you need is twelve hours' sleep, get up and eat something, and then back to bed for as long as you want."

"I'll take it," Murdoch said. "Meantime, I'll settle for a double on the rocks and clean clothes. I haven't been out of these for two days. See you, Doc. Thanks for going out to see Vicky. I didn't believe it then, and I don't believe now, that she has anything to do with Threat, but I had to go along with Solomon."

"Of course you had to do it," Wyeth said. "And oddly enough, Vicky understands that."

"She does?" Murdoch was curious.

"That's one of the reasons she's so pissed off. She can't do anything to fight back."

"You believe that, Doc?"

Wyeth nodded deliberately.

Murdoch stepped out of the elevator and turned to get an answer and Wyeth had stepped out with him. "I've changed my mind about that drink," Wyeth said. "And since you won't get some rest, I'm going to give you a shot."

"I don't like that stuff, Doc. Makes me groggy. It keeps me awake, but I can't think clearly."

"It's not speed, my friend. It's B-12. You're a candidate for the flu."

Murdoch shrugged he was too tired to care. And then he thought of Vicky. Somehow it pleased him to know that she hadn't just gone into a funk—that she had the instincts to fight back.

They both had a drink, then Wyeth gave him a shot of B-12 and left. Murdoch stepped into the shower and began to prepare himself mentally for the meeting with Spain and Solomon. Nothing would come of it.

There wasn't a damn thing left to be done that hadn't already been done, and the meeting would be a rehash.

With a great deal of effort he dried himself off and began to shave.

Vicky, he thought as he scraped away.

So she was pissed. If Wyeth's judgment could be depended on, being *genuinely* outraged was the behavior of someone who knew themselves to be innocent.

But how did the partial fingerprint get on the penny?

He dressed without haste, sipping his drink carefully, knowing that in his condition he could easily fall asleep. The shower refreshed him, but he could not fight off the fatigue.

He decided to lie down and close his eyes for a few minutes.

He slept nineteen hours.

If Tonio had known that he was officially wanted on suspicion of murder, it would have made little difference to him. He did know that they were looking for Threat. The atmosphere had so changed in the Tower that he was sure they would start asking questions around the neighborhood. And it was inevitable that someone would remember the one-eyed guy from Marty's Deli. Why not? He was in and out of the building two and three times a day. He was not worried about it, and he had prepared for it.

The day after Christmas he had gone to work as usual, but less than a quarter of the usual orders came in since most of the business people in the area took the long holiday weekend. The black sergeant was off, replaced by one of the luncheon cooks, and only half the waiters had come in. Tonio made two trips and spent most of his time in the back studying.

He was preparing his luncheon orders, using only one of the carriers, when he saw them come in, flashing their shields even as they asked questions.

"Hey, Tonio! Come'ere!" the cashier yelled.

"Ina minute!" He continued preparing his carrier.

The detectives nodded to the cashier and walked to the rear of the deli. Tonio kept working, wrapping napkins around plastic knives, forks, and spoons, checking orders already packed away in brown paper bags against the cashier's order list and addresses.

"Your name Tonio?" one of them asked. He was flat-eyed and short and looked tired. His partner could have been a twin except that he was thinner and nearly bald. Both were in their middle forties.

"Yeah."

"Like to ask you a few questions, Tonio."

"You cops?" Tonio kept moving.

"Detective Fitzgerald, I'm Detective Karl. You got an ID, Tonio?"

"Sure." Tonio paused in his work and dug into his back pocket and flipped out his wallet. He tossed it casually to Karl. He went back to his work.

"What's the last name, Tonio?" Fitzgerald asked.

"Vega."

"How long you been working here?"

"About two years, yeah—about that."

Detective Karl examined the wallet, pulling out cards. "You a student at Columbia?"

"Yeah."

"Night courses?"

"Full credit. Carrying the hump."

"What subject?"

"Anthropology."

"This your address? The Riverside Arms?" Karl asked. He read off the street number.

"That's it."

"How long you lived there?"

"About two years."

"And Columbia? How long you been going?"

"Same," Tonio said. "Excuse me a minute. Hey, cookie, I got two more roast beef, rye, mustard coming. Two pickles on the side, and an order of cole slaw."

"You deliver stuff to the St. Cyr Tower?" Karl asked, when he had finished copying down the address.

"Every day, practically. Sometimes two and three times a day."

"Who to, mostly? Anybody special?" Tonio pocketed his wallet as Karl put his pen away and leaned on the counter and stared at Tonio's face.

"Everybody—you know? Guys painting new apartments, plumbers putting in bathrooms. You know, some rich jerk up there is putting in solid gold handles on the toilets and the sinks. I saw it with my own eyes. Rich people, man. Rich!"

"Who else do you deliver to?"

"Everybody. Nurses, receptionists, Mr. Murdoch's office."

"You've delivered to Murdoch?" Karl asked.

"Sure. The biggest order I ever had went to him once. Two hundred and four dollars. And that secretary gives me a lousy five-buck tip. Ina restaurants, you run up a two-hundred-dollar tab and try to get out with a five-buck tip. You get knifed by the waiter!"

As Tonio expected, the two cops relaxed; it was not obvious, they were too professional for that, but Tonio was looking for the effect his Murdoch story would have on them.

"Ever see anything funny going on over there?"

"Like what?"

"I don't know, you tell us," Karl said.

"I don't know what you mean, Mr. Karl. I see lotsa funny things over there. Give me some idea what'cha looking for maybe I can help, y'know? I know *something* screwy is going on. . . ."

"How do you mean?"

"The joint is practically empty. A blind man see that walkin' ina lobby and feeling the breeze from people checking out. I heard somebody say something about a bomb. Is that what you looking for? A bomb? I-don't-know-nothing-about-no-bomb. I ain't seen nothing. And I don't wanna know nothin'."

The two detectives looked at each other. It was over. Nothing. Zip. Karl glanced at his notebook again. "You be reached at this address, Riverside Arms, Tonio?"

"Either there or here, or Columbia. One of them three places."

"What's with the eye?"

"Viet Nam."

"Tough."

"Some guys got their balls shot off, you know." Tonio shrugged. He closed his carrier and watched them leave. He glanced at his list of addresses, and seeing one halfway down, smiled to himself. His second stop was the St. Cyr Tower. Three corned beef on whole wheat, mustard, cole slaw, and coffee. But his first stop was Whalen's Boutique.

"You got no luck, kid, ya schmuck ya. No luck at all," Lou Whalen said, watching Tonio open his carriers and take out the sandwiches. He was paid with the usual ten-dollar bill and the change waved away. "My uncle dying out in New Jersey with cirrhosis of the liver, he's got more luck than you. You know the long shot you bet?"

"Yeah."

"The horse goes off at twenty-to-one. You got two hundred to win, right? The horse comes in, you got yourself real money, but, kid, the horse finishes the race seventeen lengths—last.

"He's so far back, they already paid off the winners. The horse is so slow, the trainer asks for Medicare for him and the horse. Your horse, Tonio, ya schmuck ya—" Lou was enjoying himself. "Your horse—the jockey, the jockey got a hat pin *this long!* They give the horse two goof balls, and a big shot of marijuana—the horse—this horse don't win, but he's the happiest horse in the race!" Lou doubled over with laughter at his own joke.

Tonio chuckled and waited for Lou to straighten himself out. Lou blew his nose and shook his head. The telephone light exploded and he took a complicated bet over the phone, hung up, closed his eyes and memorized the bet to himself. "Okay, kid, what's your action today?"

"Big surprise for you, Lou."

"Yeah?"

"I want the one-plus-one at the Big A."

"Don't make the bet, kid. It's pouring your money down the dirty. Every hunch bettor ina country makes that bet. More money lost on that bet than any bet ina whole world. I get people call me from the cruise boats ina C'ribbean on vacation, making that bet."

"One-plus-one-plus-one," Tonio said, taking out his money. "For one large—"

Lou slapped his head. "He not only wants to make the lousiest bet ina whole entire world, he wants to play a grand to win. Tonio, lissen to me, I like you. Don't make the bet."

"I got a hunch," Tonio said, counting out the money. He placed one thousand dollars on the desk. "One grand on the one-plus-one-plus-one, at the Big A."

Lou hesitated.

"You going to take the bet?"

"I'll take the bet. A grand. Ona one-plus at the Big A. How long you have to save to make a grand?"

"I got a lot of big tips over the holidays," Tonio said, picking up his carrier. "By the way, that's my whole bankroll, so I won't get into any other action until after the race. Big A opens in a week, right?"

"I used to think you were just another meshuga bettor, a crazy kid, messing around trying to score, maybe—but I know now."

"What?"

Lou's voice hardened: "Anthropology my ass! You just like any other sucker whose money I take. Columbia? Shove it! You ain't no more gunna finish college and go digging up bones in Africa than I am."

"One grand. One-plus-one-plus-one—Big A—to win."

"I got the bet," Lou said coldly. "Go on. I'm busy." He took the money and counted it rapidly.

"Sure," Tonio said, and eased out of the door. Lillene sat as she always did, staring into the street and did not look up.

Tonio had learned a lot about bookies in the last two years. Who were the Mob syndicate bookies, and who were the major independents who paid off the Mob *and* the cops with a piece of the action like Lou Whalen, Skinny Man, and Brandy, allowing them to operate.

It had been the independents from the beginning that he had been interested in—from Bridgeport south, and including all of New York, New Jersey, and down into Philadelphia. It was a big territory, but it wasn't hard to learn who belonged to the Mob and who was independent.

He wanted no part of the Mob. They were a government and a law unto themselves and, like the CIA, operated in such a tightly controlled manner that no one ever really knew if the man you might be doing business with was *in* or *out*.

He had always been careful to make his bets with independent bookies in the presence of other bettors, heavy players, so that the bookie would not be tempted to welch on him. It was to their advantage to pay off a big winner and they used the same psychology used in Vegas and Monte Carlo. Pay off the big winner in the presence of television cameras, then step back, and watch the suckers line up and try to do the same, only to lose their shirts. They didn't enjoy paying off the big winners, but they covered themselves by advertising the winner.

Theirs was the nongambling style of a certain kind of man Tonio had seen all over the world. They wanted it all safe. The Civil Service worker, customers men in brokerage houses, real-estate salesmen, automobile hacks, judges unable to compete in the open market as lawyers, district attorneys who, even if they lost the case, lost nothing of themselves. They were the sidemen in society who took a piece of the action off the top. They were the generals who never heard the sound of guns.

They were the real winners in life.

That Friday, when he quit work early because of the lack of business in the deli, he went to the Rockefeller Center Post Office Branch, picked up his Litho-Vu mailings, ripped off the addresses as usual, and threw them away as usual. He then walked to the Holiday Inn on West Fifty-seventh Street and after looking through the motel guide, he selected a Holiday Inn west of Rochester, New York.

"I'm only going to be there for one night," Tonio said to the clerk, "and I need a guaranteed reservation for the night of January second."

"Let me check and see if they have anything available for that night."

A reply came back within a few minutes. "One person, one night, one room—you're lucky, they have space."

"I'll take it."

"Credit card?"

"Cash."

"Name?"

"Algernon Chayefsky."

"Hiya, Algie, what'cha want this time? The Ford or the Chevy?" The gas station owner watched Tonio approach.

"Gimme the Chevy—the Ford didn't run so hot for me last month."

"Chevy'll do nice for you. Just put in new points and plugs."

"We'll see," Tonio said.

"How long this time?"

"I'll pick it up about noon, tomorrow, and bring it back next week," Tonio said. "And gimme a break on the price. I'm running thin on dough."

"I'll do the best I can, Algie," the owner said sympathetically. They moved to the interior of the station, where the owner dug out his rental book. "How's she doing?"

"Not so good," Tonio said.

"Jesus, you know, when I was a kid, lotsa people were always going up to Saranac Lake for TB. Now you don't hear about it so much anymore. How old is your mother?"

"Close to seventy."

"How do you spell your name again?"

"C-h-a-y-e-f-s-k-y."

"A hundred bucks even is the best I can do for a whole week, Algie," the owner said.

"That's not so hot, is it?" Tonio said.

"It's the best I can do."

Tonio paid over the deposit and took his receipt.

"Hope she's feeling better," the owner said solicitously. "How long has she been sick?"

"How long have I been renting your crummy cars?"

" 'Bout a year and a half."

"That long," Tonio said.

15 Tonio began to put his affairs in order on Saturday the twenty-seventh of December. He went about it with the same deliberate care and concern as a man would who had been told he was about to die and had a limited time to function before he would be bedridden.

He knew almost to the hour when Tonio Vega would cease to exist and preparing for the death, real or imagined, of an individual requires a great deal of attention to detail. This was true of Tonio, though his objectives were the exact opposite of the ordinary man in such a situation. Perhaps afraid of his coming doom, the ordinary man sets about establishing material things to be remembered by: money trusts, marble halls, art foundations, stone busts.

Tonio Vega wanted to be forgotten. But he knew this would not be the case. A great many people would remember him and be vitally interested in every aspect of his life, so he set out to destroy all traces of Tonio Vega.

As careful as he had been, he was surprised at the quantity of possessions he had accumulated during his stay at the Riverside Arms. He had, little by little, since setting the last bomb in the Bronx building, gradually stripped his room of all the equipment and tools he had used for his project and threw them in the river. The only thing left was the money he had accumulated from hitting nine different bookies in various parts of the city, New Jersey, and Connecticut over the last two years. He had kept a rough accounting in his head, but he had never been curious enough to count it. He did not know exactly how much it was, but he knew it would be enough for what he wanted to do.

Telling Eleanor that he was going to study for a while, he went to his room, checked his traps, and entered. He locked the door and turned on the radio as he had done hundreds of times before. But he did not study. He took out two quart bottles of a strong cleaning detergent and a bath towel. He tore the bath towel into smaller pieces, filled a pail with hot water, and starting in the bedroom, began to wash the room.

He took his time. There was no hurry. He listened to symphonic music on WQXR, and starting with the walls, began washing them down. He washed the chairs, his bed, and the legs and frame of the bed. He washed his workbench, the closet, and inside the closet. He was very particular about areas that had gotten heavy traffic, door handles, and around locks on the door. Anyplace where grease or oils from the human body might have accumulated. He worked steadily, scrubbing and washing and polishing. He did the bathroom last, taking special care around porcelain surfaces.

He walked into and out of the bathroom a half-dozen times, pretending he was going to the john, to wash his hands, to shave, shower, moving and touching everything that he might have touched in an ordinary unthoughtful way. He washed and scrubbed the walls, ceiling, and floors. He washed the windows and the radiator. Behind the radiator.

It took him nearly four hours, but when he was finished there was no surface in the entire room that held a single fingerprint.

There was only one reason for him to ever return to his old room and that would be to get the money and the weapons he would need for the finish. If he wore gloves all the time, the danger would be past. From the very beginning he had recognized that more than any other single factor, his fingerprints could destroy everything. He would do the same thing to Eleanor's room when the time came, but not yet.

When he was thoroughly satisfied that he had scrubbed and washed down every square inch of surface in the room, he went to the closet, opened the door, and pulled away the baseboard. There had been times in the past two years when he did not have enough room to store all of his equipment and it seemed strange to him now that it was all but empty.

He removed a heavy-gauge aluminum toolbox, two feet long, nine inches wide, and seven inches high from the hole. There was just enough light in the closet and he sat on the floor, opened the box, and began counting the money inside.

It did not take him long. There were mostly hundreds. When he was finished, he had $151,870. He put it all back except $9000 which he would use later that day. He had not thought it would be that much, his estimate would not have been more than $125,000. He was pleased that it was as much as it was.

Late that afternoon, accompanied by Laura Roc, Tonio and Eleanor went down to the East Side and shopped the stalls, small stores, and examined stolen goods on Orchard Street. Tonio was able to buy a factory-new RCA nineteen-inch color television for $75.00—described as being so hot it was radioactive. Laura borrowed $30.00 from Tonio and with $20.00 she had budgeted from her Christmas singing money, bought a luxurious $400 leather coat, stolen from Saks on Christmas Eve, for $50.00. Eleanor concentrated on household goods and kitchen appliances: a GE toaster-oven for $10.00, three Revere Ware copper-bottom pots for a dollar each, a SONY digital clock radio for $5.00, two lamps for $7.50 and a $120 North Star woolen blanket for $20.00, and two new down pillows for $3.00 each. Tonio and Eleanor bought Laura a new pair of fine leather boots to go with her new coat as a Christmas present, and finally when they were so burdened with their loot that they could no longer walk, and making a last buy of some really good grass, they called a cab and rode happily, and in style, back to the Riverside Arms.

Eleanor's room was soon filled with a small crowd as the word got around the Riverside Arms about the new acquisitions. They hooked up the television and somebody bought a gallon of red wine and all of the girls tried on Laura's new coat and boots; and then everyone turned on with the good grass. Tonio slipped out without being noticed, or missed, and headed downtown.

Tonio made nine stops and made nine bets, making sure there were witnesses, and he had a story prepared to explain his early bet on a race that wouldn't take place for nearly a week.

"I gotta go to Montreal. My dumb father got himself screwed up. All his life his idea of exercise is getting up for another beer while watching the ball games, you know? So he goes on a little skiing trip with some young chick, younger'n me, and has a heart attack. Never been on skis in his life. Strange, ain't it, what a woman will do to a guy. I don't know about the heart attack. If it came from the sack or skiing. Probably both. I'll be back after the race to collect. I gotta strong hunch on this one."

Only one of the bookies was surprised at the size of the bet, but he took it. They worked on the biggest handle of the year on that particular race. One-plus-one-plus-one, the great sucker-hunch bet of all time. They all knew Tonio for a plunger, a genuine sucker and compulsive bettor, and they took his money happily. All nine bets were placed with bookies in the Times Square area, and it took him less than an hour to get his money down.

Since Tonio was always slipping into and out of his room to study, no one thought anything about his not being at the impromptu party, which was over by the time he returned. Elly had fallen asleep watching television, and considering her fatigue from the shopping spree that afternoon, the wine and the grass, Tonio was pretty sure she would sleep the night through.

He went back to his room and, checking off the names of those bookies he had already visited from a master list he had compiled over the past two years, studied those remaining, selecting the ones he thought he could get to that night without any problems.

He went to his cache and counted out the amounts of money he would need. There were thirty-two bets to be made in Manhattan, and he had made nine, leaving twenty-three. There were twenty-two bets to be made in Brooklyn. He decided to finish the bets in Manhattan, move to Brooklyn the next day, and if there was time, move on into Queens where he would drop seventeen more bets. There were fourteen in the Bronx.

But he would do what he could that night. He removed $21,000 from the toolbox, locked the room, set his traps, and, after checking that El-

213

eanor was still sleeping, left the Riverside Arms using the basement door.

Once he had moved out of the city, where he could get around on the subway quickly, it would be more difficult and take more time, with sixteen bets to be made in Connecticut, twenty-nine in three different parts of New Jersey: Jersey City, Newark, and Hoboken, and fifteen bets in the Philadelphia area, including Camden, he would be doing a lot of driving. He hoped that the Chevy Impala would hold up.

He had been careful to group the bookies for their operational schedule as well as their locations. Many of them were specialists and catered to gamblers in specific trades, and the working hours, the changing of shifts in those trades and factories, dictated when the play took place.

Brandy in the Bronx operated primarily from four-thirty in the morning until eight or nine, and was back at the diner at 1:00 p.m. to start paying off the winners, and would stay until seven-thirty or eight in the evening. Most of the bookies who did an over-the-counter business to go along with their phone operations had developed hours to accommodate the special needs of their clients, and Tonio had simply adjusted his needs and plans to the working hours of the particular bookies he wanted to play. Not one bookie questioned his bet on the one-plus-one at the Big A. They loved it. They adored it. It was the sucker-hung bet that produced dreams of retiring to Miami.

Tonio got more or less the same reaction from all the bookies. No one gave a damn about his father's heart attack. Not one of the bookies who knew him, and whom he knew, could hide their greed over the size of the sucker bet. They revealed it in their eyes, their nervous laughter, in a quickness with which they folded the sheath of bills into their possession, slipping it into their pockets, and then leaning on the table, or desk, or counter, or bar and looking pleased. It was money in the bank, as they say. He was a sucker. He was hooked. He was the fantasy of every bookie. Some of the bookies in New Jersey and the Bronx, who were black and who lived more than ordinarily dangerous lives, had as many as three or four bodyguards. But Tonio had an established reputation. He paid cash. He was a cool daddy who did not talk much. His money was *good*.

By New Year's he had placed one hundred and forty-two bets in the tri-state area, and he had $6000 left in his cache. It would be more than enough for the finish. He parked the Chevy in a Kenny parking lot on the East Side near Grand Central Station and went shopping.

At Macy's he bought a medium-priced suit off the rack; a fine pair of dress gloves, a half-dozen shirts, several ties, a wind-breaker golf jacket, and a pair of slacks; he bought underwear, socks, handkerchiefs, a raincoat, a Remington electric shaver and the necessary toilet articles; he bought several pairs of glasses, with different frames, some clear lens and others with different colored dark lens, and finally he bought a large, expensive suitcase with good locks and put all of his purchases inside.

He arrived at his bank just before it closed and emptied the safe-deposit box of all the papers and his real identity, put them into the suitcase, and checked it at the baggage check in Grand Central Station.

There were only three things left for him to do now, and it would be over.

One more warning phone call to Murdoch.

He had to clean Eleanor's room, washing it down as he had done his own, and destroy all material from Columbia that might have his handwriting or prints on it. He had used a typewriter on all of his papers, but he knew eventually they would trace his handwriting on applications he made as Tonio Vega, but by that time it would not matter.

And finally, the last phone call, and his demand.

After a short, wild, and very loud New Year's Eve party at the Riverside Arms, Tonio and Eleanor relaxed in bed smoking grass, both of them passive and quiet after sex that had lasted much longer than usual.

"Tonio?"

"Yeah?"

"Do me a favor?"

"If I can."

"You can," she said, moving closer to him, pressing as much of her body against him as she could. "You're the brightest and most cynical person I've ever known. You know so much—"

"What's the favor?"

"Give me some advice on what to do, how to think, to cope, after

215

you leave me. You're the best friend I've ever had, or will ever have. I don't think I will ever trust anyone else as much.''

"Who says I'm leaving?"

"I don't mean tonight, or tomorrow. But you will. Sometime. I don't want it all to be just let go of, you know? I mean, what you and I have had, I want to take the best of it. And keep that. And not let your leaving me have too much meaning. Like, how do I take the best, and keep *that,* and let the rest of it just fade away like that general said about old soldiers.''

He considered what she had said a long time. He did not believe she knew anything about his plans. And he did not believe in premonitions for himself or anyone else. He thought about her question; and her need was sharp, and right to the point. He was not surprised.

"It would be easier for me to tell you what *not* to do than what to do. The doing of something comes from inside yourself.''

"All right, tell me what not to do?''

"Don't look for stable values. There aren't any. If you try, you'll only be disappointed.''

"Oh boy, do I ever know that.''

"If you know that, then you know most of it,'' he said quietly. "Judge everything very harshly. Everything. One of the surest ways to wind up in depression—melancholy—is to realize too late that you were too charitable in your evaluation of others. Or believed a promise too much.''

"Am I to trust anything? Believe anything?''

"Yeah, your own motivation. There isn't anything else.''

"Explain that one to me.''

"Do your own thing, but *know* what you're doing. Know the price you've got to pay. The dangers involved in doing it. The possibility of rewards. But most importantly, do it because *you* want to do it. Find motivation for doing something, and let the rest of the world dig dry wells in the desert and pray for rain. Don't let what other people say, or think, affect you or your being. Or take time away from you. That's the most precious thing we have—time. We're all strangers. The only thing we have is ourselves. One being in time and place.''

"What else should I avoid?'' she asked after a long silence.

"Charity. If it smells of charity, judge it quickly and harshly.''

216

"You mean like the Salvation Army?"

"No, I don't mean giving somebody something to eat or a place to sleep. *I mean giving of your time, your presence.*"

"Dreams?"

"Don't ever dream. Plan meticulously, but don't ever dream. Dreams rob you of your sense of now."

"I won't," she said in a small voice.

"What?"

"I promise I won't ever dream," Eleanor said, and rolled over and without his being aware of it, cried herself to sleep.

"You were up several times last night," he said, sipping orange juice.

"I couldn't sleep too well," she said. "Tonio?"

"What?"

"Does happiness always have a limit? Does happiness have a life of its own?"

He put his orange juice down and took her hand. "You're not the first, nor will you be the last, Elly, to see your happiness crushed."

"But I don't want it crushed!" she cried.

"What's the hurry, Elly? Why the desperation? We're here, now, together. *Enjoy* that. Don't dream. Don't project."

"Please, Tonio—give me something I can mark it with, something that I can hold on to forever."

He stood up and walked about the room. He was into something he wanted no part of.

"Tonio?" she said softly. "Please?"

"Emily Dickinson wrote this." He came to her side, pulled her up out of the chair. " 'Sweet hours have perished here; This is a mighty room; Within its precincts hopes have played, —Now shadows in the tomb.' "

She clung to him, her nails biting into his flesh. Tonio held her and stroked her hair and rocked her back and forth in his arms like a child.

After a while her sobs and heaves eased off and she grew quiet, and he grew quiet with her.

Chief of Detectives Solomon woke up in his Riverdale apartment with a terrible headache. Champagne had never agreed with him and he wondered why he drank it. His wife lay on her stomach, one arm dangling

217

over the side of the bed. A sure sign she too had too much to drink. The phone rang and he closed his eyes, but it did not help. The phone rang again.

"If that's our daughter calling so early in the morning to wish us a Happy New Year, so help me—" He grabbed for the phone. "Yeah!"

He listened. "Pick me up in twenty minutes." Solomon hung up the phone, his headache forgotten. "It isn't much, but it's something. It's a way to travel."

"You'll have to take this journey alone," his wife mumbled. "Where are you going?"

"Bridgeport."

"Isn't that the way things go sometime," Mrs. Solomon said, and went back to sleep.

Tonio spent most of the day cleaning Eleanor's room while she worked luncheon at a fancy East Side restaurant, famous for its New Year's Day brunch, filling in as an extra. He was slow and thorough as he had been with his own room, but it took much more time since there was a lot more to be done. He half-watched—half-listened to the New Year's Bowl games and when he was finished, he paused long enough to make a cup of Sanka and an egg sandwich. He then started on his clothing, cutting out all of the labels. He had never sent anything to the cleaners, so there were no laundry marks to be concerned about.

The Riverside Arms was quiet all afternoon, but he could hear movement outside the door now and then. At four-thirty, Laura Roc tapped on his door telling him she was going out for the evening, and that Elly had called, saying she was also working the dinner at the restaurant, and to pick her up at eleven. He set up his typewriter and began addressing two sets of labels of different sizes. On the larger label, which was at least two inches wider on all margins than the smaller, he wrote:

MR. TONIO VEGA
THE RIVERSIDE ARMS
168 RIVERSIDE DRIVE
NEW YORK, N.Y. 10024

and on the smaller label, he wrote:

LITHO-VU
POST OFFICE BOX 1278
ROCKEFELLER CENTER
NEW YORK, N.Y. 10020

He glued the smaller label very firmly to a ten-by-fourteen-inch manila envelope and double-sealed the label's edges with cellophane tape. These small labels addressed to Litho-Vu were nearly all of different commercial makes. It had taken him months to collect them. There were some duplicates, but he reasoned that it would be more likely that common commercial types of address labels would be used by many people and firms.

He then took the larger label addressed to himself, and without using glue, attached it with Scotch tape on the four corners only, completely covering the first label. On each envelope he stuck five dollars in postage and rubber-stamped the envelope FIRST CLASS. On all of the envelopes he used the Litho-Vu box number as a return address. There were a hundred and fifty envelopes and he was finished by 9:00 p.m. He took all of the empty envelopes and put them into a cardboard carton by the door, tied it securely, and left it as if it were a package ready for mailing.

Taking the typewriter with him, he left the Riverside Arms at nine-thirty and took the subway down to Times Square. He was a few minutes early for his call to Murdoch and using a street-corner phone booth he called the restaurant on Madison Avenue and asked to speak to Eleanor Cassie, and told her he would pick her up when she got off work.

At exactly ten-thirty he dialed the St. Cyr Tower.

"Murdoch's office." Tonio used a very slow rhythm of speech with nasal overtones as if he had a cold. He knew they would be putting his call on tape and he was not at all disturbed by the delay in making a connection.

"Mr. Murdoch's office," Andy Brooks said.

"This is Threat, man, you better dig my jive cool. You hear where I'm coming from?"

"I hear you. Keep talking."

"Jest two things, turkey. You got another package like the one you

219

got before, you hear me, man? Like the big one on the ninetieth floor? Like man, you take yo' ass up to the top floor and look, like in the duct work under the helicopter pad and there be one big New Year's surprise for you.''

"Is it another bomb?"

"Daddy, you are one smart son of a bitch! Is it a bomb? Sheet, man, this be *the* bomb!''

"What else?" Brooks asked.

"I'm gunna lay it on you tomorrow, man. Tomorrow you goin' do it *all* for me.''

"Do what?"

"I tell you tomorrow, daddy. In the a.m. say 'bout nine in the a.m., how's that grab you, daddy?''

"You'll call tomorrow at nine a.m. Okay, what else?"

"You impatient mother, ain't you? Now listen cold, man. You better lo-*cate* the governor of your fair state, you dig? Find that turkey, 'cause he the only *one* got the *big* balls to do what you gunna *do*. You got me, turkey?''

"Okay, the governor. What else?"

"Why, happy New Year to *all* you mothers!'' Tonio laughed over the phone hysterically, crazily. Let them try and figure that one out. He hung up.

He stood a moment in the booth and looked around through the glass panels at the movement in Times Square. He left the typewriter in the phone booth. Like the VW van he had left in the Bronx, he knew it would not be very long until it would disappear. He walked a half block, turned, and went back to look. The typewriter was gone.

Twenty minutes later Tonio was using another phone booth, one he had used before, but he did not make a call. He was waiting for the right moment to move to the manhole cover and start the tape recorder. After almost twenty minutes of waving his arms and acting as if he were making a very long phone call, he saw his chance and slipped out of the booth, expertly pried up the manhole cover, and dropped down into the tunnel.

He started the tape recorder and sat down to wait for a call to be made or received and make sure it was working. He did not have to wait long.

It was Spain. He was yelling to someone. ". . . on the top floor? Under the goddamn *roof?* beneath the helicopter pad? . . ."

Tonio turned the volume all the way down. He listened. There was a faint hum of the motor-driven reel inside the unit, but it was no more than any other sound that filtered through to him. It would run twenty-four hours. It was more than enough.

He had a much easier time getting out then getting in, and five minutes later he had hailed a taxi and rode straight up Madison Avenue to pick up Eleanor.

"*If* it's under the helicopter pad, then it *has* to be somewhere along this air-conditioning duct, from here to there—" Sergeant Andonian jabbed at the blueprint Hans Kabe, the building engineer, had supplied.

"Why only there?" Murdoch demanded.

"I'm thinking about his means of detonation. If he followed the same pattern with this one he did with the first, he's hooked up to a phone. This is the only place he could do that, and still be under the helicopter pad, without running his wires all over the place.

"This section of the duct, from here to there, is only about twenty feet. And well within the reach of getting to that phone terminal there, or anywhere along the line." Andonian traced out his theory with a forefinger heavily stained with nicotine. "And that section of the duct runs right across the ceiling of this room." He pointed skyward with the same finger. They were standing in Spain's bedroom.

Involuntarily everyone looked at Spain. With the reinforced-concrete helicopter pad just above the ceiling, the explosion would be blown downward into the bedroom.

While it was not Spain's decision to make, Solomon deferred to him. "We'll have to tear out the whole ceiling," he said quietly.

"Do what you have to do," Spain said tightly.

"I suggest," Andonian said, "that we go in from another room. The next one over, or perhaps the bathroom. I'd hate like hell to jab a tool into a mass of the kind of stuff we found before, now that I know how unstable it is. I talked to the manufacturer. It was a bad batch, too unstable for commercial use, and it was supposed to be destroyed. But somebody along the line got ideas and it wound up in the hands of the bandits, and our little Viet Nam veteran in Bridgeport."

"You weren't so touchy about the first batch in the kitchen, going in, I mean," Solomon said.

"I didn't know what was behind that refrigerator," Andonian replied coldly. "Now I do."

"Aside from getting the stuff out of there," Solomon said, glancing at Murdoch and Spain, "we're back to an earlier decision."

"Which is?" Murdoch asked.

"Do we evacuate the building?"

"I say no," Murdoch said instantly.

"Why?" Solomon asked. "Convince me."

"He hasn't made his demands yet. This is still psyche time. He's still letting us know that he's got us by the balls. He's raising his bet against a nine-a.m. deadline in the morning. When we hear his demands, what he wants, how he wants it, where he wants it, then we have to decide if we can, and if we will, give in to him. If we do or if we don't meet his demands, we still have time to get every one out. It will be daytime. And a hell of a lot easier, therefore less chance of panic."

"It's not our decision to make, Chief," Spain said. "But what Chris says makes sense to me. I go with him."

"All right," Solomon replied. He turned to Andonian: "Get your people started and get that stuff out of here."

The two cops looked at each other. "Have fun," Solomon said in a light whisper, his eyes hard and tight.

"I'll let you know if anything goes wrong," Andonian said, casually lighting another cigarette. He turned to his men who were preparing to don their flak suits while the television monitor lines were being strung out and hooked up to the cameras already in place.

"I want to hear the last tape," Spain said as they all left.

". . .You impatient mother, ain't you? Now listen cold, man. You better lo-*cate* the governor of your fair state, you dig? Find that turkey, 'cause he the only *one* got the *big* balls to do what you gunna *do*. You got me, turkey? . . ."

Tonio's voice rasped out in the silence of suite 2500 as the entire team sat or stood and listened to the tape.

"Play it again," Solomon said.

The tape was rewound and played again.

"What is it that the governor," Solomon said to them, "and only the governor could do? All right, Threat is making his demand. We know that. But where, what, how, and when? I want a list of every department, agency, board, commission—the works, on which the governor is the head, or appoints the head. I have a hunch it will be in one of the areas where he has executive powers. Any comments?"

"What about that screwy laugh at the end, the joke about Happy New Year?" Brooks asked. "I've tried picking out and isolating the background noises. They're faint, but if you put it all together, the background noise, the laugh, the way he talks on this tape—well, it could be—Harlem—125th Street and Seventh Avenue, or Lenox Avenue—"

"I think that's a put on," Murdoch said. "Don't forget this guy has used phony accents before."

"An actor?" Spain suggested.

"I would say no," Solomon said. "It's not the kind of professional characterization an actor would try. If he *were* an actor, he would try *not* to sound like one. No, this is a smartass with a good ear who can do it just enough to throw us off. He's got one more phone call at nine a.m., tomorrow. I wouldn't be surprised if he didn't drop a French accent on us."

Murdoch kept glancing at the uniformed officer who sat with an open telephone line, nodding and speaking quietly, taking notes. He paused and cupped the mouthpiece. "Excuse me, Chief, but Andonian says they're through the ceiling. They went in through the bathroom. So far, they haven't seen anything."

Solomon nodded. "Okay, get onto that list of the governor's," he said to the telephone officer. "Have you located him yet?"

"Only that he's in upstate New York on a mountain with his skis," the officer replied. "His people wouldn't give me any information until they had checked with him."

"Did you tell them," Solomon asked heavily, "that the phone call was from me, and that it was a fucking emergency?"

"Yes, sir. Just like that. I said it was a fucking emergency," the officer replied with complete sincerity.

There was a pause and then everybody, including Spain broke into uproarious laughter. Murdoch laughed so hard he had tears in his eyes.

They became a crisply functioning squad again. The two-man teams of detectives Solomon had put on the frozen streets, chasing down fragments of leads, came in and made their reports, which were coded into the computer. The phones rang constantly as still other detective teams reported in from the street, or asked a question, or wanted some name or license plate checked out, or came up with hunches.

But it was not all catch-as-catch-can. Since getting the information on the murder of Toledo in Bridgeport and his identification as an armorer, and a Viet Nam veteran with a background of electronics and explosives, Solomon had his teams running rechecks.

"We can't go shot-gunning anymore," Solomon explained to Murdoch. "With an absolute tie-in by Andonian that this Toledo character was selling the same kind of stuff, from the same rotten batch that Threat placed in Her Highness's kitchen wall, we have to run the Viet Nam veteran angle until it dries up, or produces something. And so far, it's produced the one solid thing we have."

Murdoch agreed. There was only one problem that dampened enthusiasm for both of them: there were over seven hundred names of the thousands that had been interviewed who were either veterans of the Viet Nam war, or had been there in a civilian capacity. But as long as the list was, both Solomon and Murdoch knew they had to continue.

Solomon's men and every man Murdoch could spare were put out on the street checking names. Knocking on doors, talking to neighbors, the detective teams slogged through the dirty snow-covered streets of Brooklyn, Queens, the Bronx, Manhattan, and even Staten Island.

On Friday at three-thirty in the morning of January second, Sergeant Andonian very carefully snipped the wires connecting the detonator with the timer; he slipped the needle-nose pliers into his pocket and inched his way backward to the opening in the ceiling and was helped to the bathroom floor.

He held up the detonator, a twin to the one he had found in the kitchen wall. He tossed it casually to Solomon. "Present for you," he said, his voice hoarse with fatigue, too many cigarettes, and sheer nervous exhaustion. "Same thing as before. A phone job. Ring a special number, the contacts go off in series. There's only one difference between this one and the first one. . . ."

Murdoch, Spain, Solomon, and the others looked at the sergeant and waited for him to continue.

"What's the difference?" Solomon asked.

"There must be two hundred pounds of the stuff up there. One phone call and the whole top—*the whole top*—of the building would have gone up another five hundred feet."

"What was the difference?" Solomon asked again.

"This one was connected," Andonian said. "Whatever this guy wants, give it to him."

"I'll note your comments and recommendation, Sergeant," Solomon said dryly.

"And I'll put it in *my* report," Sergeant Andonian responded in the voice of a man wise in the ways of protecting himself in bureaucratic jungles.

"Just a minute!" Spain said sharply. "Why do you suggest we give Threat what he wants, Sergeant?" He ignored Solomon.

Andonian hesitated.

"Well?" Spain demanded.

Sergeant Andonian looked at Solomon. The chief of detectives would overlook one indiscretion, but not two. He held Sergeant Andonian's eyes with his own and then very slowly nodded. "Go ahead, Sergeant," he drawled, "we'd all like to hear what you have to say."

None of this was lost on Spain. "Cut this crap!" he said coldly. "I want information. Sergeant?"

"Okay," Andonian said. "We've had the best electronics gear available from the Defense Department sweeping this building looking for a bomb and we missed. We've had the best dogs and their handlers, and they missed. We've chopped seventeen holes in seventeen different places and found nothing. Now we get a phone call and the guy tells us where it is. And it's there. Just like he said. I don't know about you, but it scares the hell out of me just thinking how smart this bastard is. That bomb sitting up there, underneath a slab of concrete, wasn't placed there because it was a handy place. *This guy knows what he's doing.* He demonstrated *that* when he dropped that concrete apartment house in the Bronx like a smashed egg crate. Now, if he has other bombs in this building, and all he has to do is make a phone call, if you're thinking about *not* giving him what he wants when he makes the nine-o'clock phone call, then I suggest that you empty this building right now. This minute.''

Sergeant Andonian spoke slowly and emphatically: "I think I'm the best man in the world at what I do. But this building and everyone in it," he added quietly, looking at Chief Solomon, "is in his hands. And I don't doubt it for a minute.''

It was a defeat for them and they were emotionally and intellectually unwilling to accept it. All the work, all the effort, all the manpower, all the expertise and resources at their disposal were brought down to an undeniable fact: they would have to meet his demands and hope to catch him when he reached for the money.

There was no doubt now in anybody's mind that it would be money.

They had hoped against hope; they *believed* they could and would catch him. But they hadn't.

They were running out of time.

16

At the Riverside Arms students returned from holidays to the routine of their daily lives. Ahead was the drive toward mid-term exams. Many of them had early classes that morning and Tonio awoke to sounds that had become a part of him. Eleanor was curled up against his side, sleeping heavily. After working a twelve-hour restaurant shift, she was exhausted.

As he had done so many times he lay still and listened. The sounds came to him in recital, the pseudofamily noises he would probably never hear again.

Tubby Engalls' vicious cigarette cough. Laura Roc vocalizing. Someone telling her to shut up. Tommy Weeks, who had successfully convinced the Chinese girl to move in with him, was the first to reach a point of desperation, screaming for Laura to SHUT GODDAMMIT UP!

He slipped out of bed, showered, and shaved quickly. Dressing quietly without waking Eleanor, he wiped everything clean that he had

227

touched, picked up the carton with the addressed manila envelopes, and stepped to the door. He took one last look around: was there anything he had missed or forgotten? There wasn't.

He glanced at Eleanor and paused for a second. He could stop the whole process right then. All he had to do was get back in bed and sleep through the nine-o'clock call to Murdoch, and it would be over. Totally. Beyond recall. Finished. He would still have better than a hundred thousand dollars. Probably much more. It was a lot of money for a man who might want to go to Africa and continue Leakey's basic work. Even if he could only get to half the bookies and they took 20 percent, or more, off the top for returning the bet before the race.

And then he thought of his twin brother.

He looked at Eleanor Cassie, and then closed the door firmly. Have a good life, kid, he thought, and walked away.

When Tonio Vega left the Riverside Arms that morning a little before seven o'clock, there was absolutely nothing of himself remaining.

He took the subway downtown to Grand Central Station, checked the carton containing the manila envelopes, returning uptown and arriving at work on time. There was not much conversation that morning. Everyone was drawn into himself as they thought about the coming year, working back into their routines, facing the bleak months ahead until spring, and then, far, far away, summer.

The black sergeant was sullen and sarcastic, yelling at waiters, the cooks in the kitchen, and slamming things around.

"Let's go, Patch! Get these mother orders out of my way! You way behind. Catch up, Patch. Catch up! New Year's over. *Gone.*"

"Yeah, yeah. Okay, Sarge," Tonio said and began to prepare his carriers.

A waiter shuffled by and administered a pat on the shoulder. "Happy New Year, ya schmuck."

"Same to you," Tonio said.

At five minutes to nine that morning, Governor T. Clay Cavanaugh had not returned the repeated calls from Chief Solomon, the commissioner, or Spain. The governor would, they were informed, return the call as soon as he was free to do so. Suite 2500 in the St. Cyr Tower was filled with anxious, tense, and very tired men. Every precinct in New York had all of its patrol cars and men on alert, ready to move into any section of the city within minutes, should Threat's demands be of such a nature they might be able to catch him. But they really did not believe this. It would, they were sure, be something elaborate and tricky. But there was always hope.

At nine the phone rang. Solomon looked at Murdoch and nodded.

"Chris Murdoch speaking."

"I want," Tonio said in a steady, firm voice, but still heavily accented with New York vowels and rhythms, "the first horse, in the first race, the first day of racing at Aqueduct to win and pay odds of thirty-to-one. I will repeat. I want the first horse in number-one post position, in the first race, today, Friday, January second, the first day of racing, to win at odds of thirty-to-one. If this does not happen I will drop the St. Cyr Tower into Fifth Avenue the minute the results are announced. Don't think about cutting all phone service into the building. It won't help you. Sergeant Andonian must know by now that I can do it."

In suite 2500 of the St. Cyr Tower, the line went dead as Tonio hung up.

In the absolute silence that followed not a man moved except to breathe. "A horse race, he wants to *fix a horse race!*" Solomon said.

"A guaranteed win," Murdoch said. "And he picks the greatest hunch bet on the sucker list to cover himself. One-plus-one-plus-one. In Vegas the bookies called it the Good Fairy Race. They made so much money on that particular race it was as if the Good Fairy had brought the money overnight."

"How do you," the commissioner asked, his face congested, "fix a fucking horse race *legally?*"

"That's why he warned us to get the governor," Spain said. "He's the only one that would have the power to do it."

"But do you realize what's *involved?*" Solomon said. "It ain't that easy—"

"Beautiful—" Andy Brooks said. "Just beautiful."

"Sen-sational!" Sid Hoag grinned. "Jesus! What a slant!"

"Far out—" Andonian said.

"Easy or hard," Spain said to the commissioner, "we're going to do

229

just what he said." He started for the door, signaling Murdoch to follow him. He paused and turned back to face the unbelieving men. "He beat you," Spain said. "He beat the best you had to go against him. He's beaten you at every turn. *He's not going to beat me*. That race will be run exactly the way he wants it, and at the price he wants. I'll talk to the governor, I'll talk to the president of the United States if I have to, *but that race is going to be fixed*. You've all had your shot at him, and you missed. Now stay out of it. Don't get any grand ideas—"

Solomon took a step forward. "The New York Police Department does not respond to blackmail or threats. That's official. Now what is not official, *Mr*. Spain—you speak to me, or my men like that again and I will personally beat the living shit out of you."

Spain smiled. Cold, hard, black eyes frosting over. "Chief, don't make the mistake of taking out your frustrations over this defeat, *your* defeat, on me. I'm not your enemy. Threat is your enemy. This one particular Threat happens to be brilliant, but there are a lot of little Threats running around mugging old people, who are not so brilliant, and you can't catch them, either. You've lost your city, Chief. It doesn't belong to the cops anymore, it belongs to the street people. And when you're jammed up, as you are now, and the heat gets close, *real heat*, like me, *I'm real heat*, you have a ready answer. You'll beat the living shit out of someone. That makes you stupid for not recognizing that the time has come for compromise. It makes you dangerous—because you allow your arrogance to take over your well-trained, and possibly brilliant, mind. Finally it makes you worthless to the community you're supposed to serve. All of you are much too wise and cynical not to recognize, as they say in the streets, what's going down. I don't doubt for a minute that all of you worked your ass off doing your job, and that your personal and professional integrity is beyond reproach. But understand this: *you lost this one*. I'm not going to take a chance of your screwing this thing up, and trigger something in Threat's crazy head, and blow up the St. Cyr Tower, which he has already proven he can do, and that your own expert, Andonian, says that he can't stop."

Spain took a step back into the room and faced them all. He might have been facing a mob, or he might have been making his case before some emperor. He might have been an exhausted fighter finding his second wind. "Take some of your own advice, gentlemen, the kind you've given to citizens recently, holding seminars in church basements, citizens you're supposed to protect, and I quote: 'When approached by a mugger, or you surprise a burglar in your home, be a cooperative victim. Don't resist, give him what he wants. Money isn't everything; save your life. Live to fight another day. *Be a happy mugging victim.*'

"Gentlemen, it would seem to me that your suggestions should apply to yourselves. Be a happy victim. And don't be in such a hurry to beat the living shit out of someone."

Spain paused and looked Solomon in the eye. "You got about twenty-five pounds on me, but I'm probably in better shape than you are. But don't invite me outside. I still remember dirty tricks from the Lower East Side that might surprise *you*."

The commissioner stared into the middle distance. He wasn't going to buck a potential political power. He had a career to think of.

Solomon did not move. He worked his jaw. Small knots of muscle tightened.

"I'm going to my apartment now," Spain said, "and speak to whoever it is that can arrange this race to be won the way Threat wants it to be won. I'll probably have to get the mayor into it too, and of course the governor. I don't know about the FBI, since there may be something about horseracing being interstate, making it a case for the Feds, along with the bomb threats and extortion. But I'll deal with that when I come to it. I would like to be able to say that I have your full cooperation, Chief Solomon, when I speak to the various people necessary to fix the race. May I tell them that?"

"Of course," Chief Solomon said with a grin. "My fullest cooperation, Mr. Spain."

"Thank you, Chief." Spain glanced around the room. "Gentlemen—" he smiled cynically. "Back to being a happy mugging victim: what's the old saying, if rape is inevitable, relax and enjoy it? I might add that if you keep this fixed-race thing very, very quiet, I don't see any reason why you can't get down a few on one-plus-one-plus-one. How many times does a sure thing come along in life? And, gentlemen, take my word for it, this is a sure thing. *Threat wins.* Come on, Chris."

Solomon turned to his men. They did not know what to expect. Spain had just challenged his authority as well as invited him outside. But if Solomon had any feelings about the matter, he wasn't going to show

231

them. "We close down this operation in suite 2500, as of now. It's finished. You can all go home."

"Commissioner?"

"Yeah?"

"A hundred to win isn't going to hurt anybody," Andonian said. "Except the bookie."

"If I hear about a single one of you making a bet on this race," the commissioner said, looking around the room with a totally blank expression, "and this is official, I'll have that man's ass tied in knots." He walked to the door pulling on his gray doeskin gloves. He looked back. "And I mean what I say. If I *hear* about it. You coming, Chief?"

The room was silent as the two men left. Andonian looked at Hoag. "What time do the banks open, Sid?"

"Open now. Why?" Sid Hoag grinned. "Thinking about making a withdrawal?"

"I wouldn't think of it. You heard what the Commish just said," Andonian replied, slipping into his coat and heading for the door.

"I'm under no such restrictions," Andy Brooks said grinning broadly. "Here's where I pay off the mortgage."

"I think I'll make a few myself," Sid Hoag said.

At 10:00 a.m. Spain had not yet been able to reach the governor. He did not seem overly anxious, and Murdoch was interested in the way the man could continue to do business, making one phone call after the other about major financial decisions and not have the tensions generated by Threat cloud his thinking. They sat in the gazebo and sipped coffee.

Spain finished a call and dropped the phone. He sat forward in his chair, elbows on his knees, arms dangling. He remained that way for several minutes. "Well, I've done all I can at the moment. I haven't had too much experience fixing a race."

Murdoch nodded. "However it's done, it's going to be damned interesting."

"Thinking of making a bet?" Spain asked casually. "Why not? It's sure money."

"No," Murdoch said with a slight shake of his head. "I'm cynical, but not that way."

"Conscience?"

232

"Not at all," Murdoch said and laughed.

"Then why?" Spain asked. "I would, if the positions were reversed."

"There are certain things that belong to me," Murdoch said slowly. "And they can't be bought or bartered for. They're mine. They can only be given. If you ask for them, you'll be turned down. They're not part of me, these things, they *are* me. And if I give them away too freely, or too often, they tarnish, and their value diminishes."

"Integrity? Character? Honor?" Spain asked.

Murdoch was not sure, but he thought he heard a note of disdain.

"Certainly all of those," Murdoch said, implying there were more. "If I made a bet and took advantage of the situation, I wouldn't be any better than Threat. I don't mean that I'm smug, and feel morally superior, but he's trapped by what he does. Perhaps he thinks he's inspired, I don't know—

"The point is: what he does is not what I do. And what you would do, if the positions were reversed, does not interest me."

Spain sat back and smoothed his hair. "Any qualms about fixing the race?"

"Not at all!" Murdoch shot back. "Threat is ultimately unimportant. There will always be situations like this. It's how you deal with them that counts. Knowing when to fight, and when to give in. It's a great art—and often a misunderstood one."

"What is?"

"Compromise. The world turns on it—"

The phone rang. Spain snatched it up. "Hello—yes. Yes, put him on, please."

He looked at Murdoch and nodded.

"Good morning, Governor. I'm sorry to interrupt your holiday, but I have a little problem. You've probably heard about the situation we've been having here at the Tower. We finally received his demands. . . . Yes, this morning at nine. Chief Solomon has been on top of it from the beginning, and we have Threat's demands down on tape, which you can hear for yourself. Now, here's the situation, Clay. It's going to be sticky, so hang on to your cock, because I'm about to request your balls."

———

233

Governor T. Clay Cavanaugh lay back in a chaise in the solarium overlooking the indoor heated pool; beyond the large panels of steamed glass a foot-thick carpet of snow covered the Lake Placid ski slopes. He wriggled his toes. He had big feet and long toes; tiny blue veins traced out a pattern beneath the dead-white skin. They were, he thought wrinkling his nose, really ugly feet. He looked out over the pool, where beautiful young women and slim young men cavorted. It had been a long time since he looked like one of them. He looked away. Big white ugly feet and beautiful young girls, sadly, do not mix. He patted his stomach. He should, he really *should* get to the gym more often, and cut down on the calories.

He closed his eyes.

How the hell could he fix a horse race?

That goddamned Joe Spain—and that *police commissioner,* the dumb fuck! He couldn't pour piss out of a boot if the directions were on the heel.

He picked up the phone. "Please come in, Jacoby."

A slim young man in ski clothes with modish-cut hair, a pair of steel-rimmed glasses, and flat eyes, entered the solarium quietly. He sat beside the governor and waited.

Clay Cavanaugh glanced up from still another examination of his ugly feet and studied the younger man. At twenty-four he was very much younger than many executive assistants in statehouses around the country, but Cavanaugh genuinely admired him. He had the most devious mind of anyone he had ever met.

Quickly and quietly, in short sentences, Cavanaugh outlined the problem.

"What do we get out of it?" Jacoby asked instantly.

Cavanaugh's eyebrows shot up. "What do we want?"

"That upstate utility deal, for one thing," Jacoby said.

Cavanaugh smiled. "That's right. Joe Spain's got the real-estate background on all that, hasn't he?"

Jacoby was already moving toward the door with quick, long strides. "I'll get to Jimco on this right away."

"Who the hell is Jimco?"

"Spain's man—in such matters." He reached for the door.

"Wait a minute—"

Jacoby glanced at his watch. "We don't have much time, Governor."

"But how the hell are we going to do the other thing—fix that race?"

"Oh," Jacoby said lightly. "That part's easy."

"How easy? And who else will know?"

"Very easy—and only one man."

"Can we get to him?"

"He owes us. Yes, we can get to him," Jacoby said in the same manner that he said everything. Uninflected, like a doctor delivering an opinion to a nervous patient.

"Who?"

"I'll handle it—"

"No, goddammit, not this time, Milt," Cavanaugh said. "I want to *know* what you're doing, and how're you going to do it, and who—"

"Why? It's so unnecessary, Governor—"

"Just tell me, please?"

"Anton Cabot."

"Cabot! But—but he's one of the richest, he's got stables, he's Thoroughbred racing itself—with a Triple Crown winner a few years back— he's the biggest since Alfred Vanderbilt!"

"That's why he can do it without anybody suspecting," Jacoby replied.

"How—will he do it? Does he have a horse running in the first race?"

"It doesn't matter," Jacoby said. He glanced at his watch again.

"But you *know*, don't you?" Cavanaugh insisted.

Jacoby was silent.

"Tell me."

Milton Jacoby walked back into the solarium thoughtfully. He picked up the phone. "Find Anton Cabot for me. Try his town house first, on East Sixty-fifth in the city, then the club at the Big A, and if he's not there, find out where he is. Tell him to get to a public phone and call me immediately."

He dropped the phone and sat down beside the chaise and lit another long brown cigarette. "When a horse wins a race, they test that horse to see if it has been hyped in any way."

Cavanaugh nodded.

"They don't test the losers. They're just taken back to the barn and handed over to a hot walker—the horse ran out. Nobody's interested."

"Go on."

"Cabot goes down to the barns before the race. Nobody's going to question his interest, or his right to give the nags the once-over. He feeds them a lump of sugar, or whatever, with some stuff in it to slow them down. He gives it to all of them except the one-plus-one-plus-one horse."

"And nobody knows?"

"Nobody—not the jockey or the trainer, nor the guy that makes the tests afterward. Even if they suspect, who's going to lean on Cabot?"

The phone rang. Jacoby snatched it up. "Yeah—get the number of the phone—check with our man in the phone company. Make sure it's a public phone."

He looked at the governor. "I've got to get Jimco." He ground out the brown cigarette. "Terrific," he said quietly.

"What is?"

"The guy that thought up this whole thing. Nice. If he weren't a felon, or about to be one, he's the kind of man I'd like to open an office with in D.C. But we'll probably never know—"

"What?"

"Who he is."

Murdoch sat in his office with his feet up on his desk. The conversation with the governor—at least Spain's side of it—had been as rough as he had ever heard as a man. There was nothing now to do but wait and see if the race would be fixed, and if not, Solomon had already issued orders to evacuate the Tower and two blocks on either side of it, they would see what Threat would do.

There was no point in looking for more bombs. If they had not found the one under the helicopter pad after searching for a week with the best dogs, men, and electronic equipment available, there seemed to be nothing they could do now.

The phone rang and Murdoch snatched it up. He listened, glanced at Solomon, and frowned. "Hold on a minute, Vicky—"

Murdoch held his hand over the mouthpiece and looked at the chief.

"She's calling from a pay phone and wants to know if she can come in and examine her telephone logs—she thinks she has an idea."

Solomon sat forward. "What've we got to lose—tell her I'll send a car up to get her."

Murdoch relayed the information and hung up.

"Now that we're getting close to the deadline, she might be having second thoughts," Solomon said.

"I think you're wrong," Murdoch said quietly.

Solomon shook his head slowly, the big cigar in his mouth moving in a wide arc. "It's a major conspiracy, and she might still be a key figure in it. I've had a hunch from the beginning that that might be the case."

"I disagree," Murdoch said.

It was the first time since Tonio had gone to work for Marty's Deli that Lou had not ordered sandwiches from them. Passing Whalen's Boutique, he saw a slight Puerto Rican youth in white trousers and busboy's jacket enter with a brown paper bag. Tonio knew that he was the delivery boy for a quick-food restaurant on Madison Avenue. It was going to be interesting to watch the bookie's face when, within a half hour, he went in to collect. Would Lou do another reversal, Tonio wondered, and be happy that Tonio had made a big score?

Tonio returned to the deli at noon after his last delivery and went about cleaning the carriers, as he had always done, and putting them away. Only this time he was especially careful not to leave his prints. Under the pretext of cleaning up his work station, Tonio had spent most of his free time that morning doing just that; wiping anything and everything that he might have touched.

When he was finished, he went into the men's room, locked the door, stood on the toilet seat, reaching up to a large, grimy ventilating fan. He unscrewed the brackets carefully, removed the fan, reached down behind it and took out a .38 automatic, spare clips, and two hand grenades. He shoved the weapons into his jacket pockets, replaced the fan, wiped his fingerprints away, and stepped down. He wiped the door handle and the lock, and then the knob outside and walked back toward the front of the deli.

"See you tomorrow, Patch," the black sergeant said.

"Yeah, Sarge."

THREAT

"How you do today, kid? Make a lotta tips?" the waiter asked.

"Not bad, about thirty bucks."

"That ain't bad, kid. No, that ain't bad at all, ya schmuck, ya."

"Yeah."

Tonio walked to Madison Avenue, and then downtown toward Grand Central Station. At a Fiftieth and Madison music store he bought a good transistor radio for thirty-nine dollars, and with the mini plug stuck in his ear, continued on down Madison listening to WINS news, broadcast twenty-four hours a day. He cut through the short block on Forty-fourth and was approaching Vanderbilt Avenue when he stopped and listened.

". . . WINS newstime, one thirty-four . . . results of the first race at Aqueduct just in, and all you hunch bettors on the first horse, in the first race, on the first day of racing, the one-plus-one-plus-one-bet as it is known, are in for a surprise. The winner, *Steel Pit—Steel Pit* the winner, paying a whopping sixty dollars, twenty-nine twenty and sixteen forty. That's *Steel Pit*, OTB letter A, a big winner in the first race today at Aqueduct. . . . Second, *Back Space*, OTB letter G, paid twenty-five seventy and twelve twenty. . . . Third, *Last Page*, OTB Letter D, paid ten-eighty. . . . WINS newstime, one thirty-five."

He removed the earphone, crossed Vanderbilt and entered Grand Central Station. There was not much activity at that time of the day and the huge central concourse was nearly empty. He went to the baggage-claim counter under the stairs, presented his two claim checks, retrieved the suitcase and the box of envelopes. He remounted the stairs to Vanderbilt and climbed into the back of a taxi.

"Kenny Parking Lot over on Third and Thirty-ninth, please," he said to the driver.

17

Detectives Fitzgerald and Karl had not called in for several hours and were still on the street. They were working down a list of veterans, and getting nowhere.

At a quarter to two that afternoon they had just finished checking out a suspect, a plumber's helper who had worked on the construction of the St. Cyr Tower. But as soon as they had entered the Columbus Avenue apartment they knew he couldn't have been involved: the man who had answered the door sat in a wheelchair. He had been in an automobile accident eleven months before and had a crushed spine. They hadn't even bothered to ask him any questions.

"What's the next one?" Karl asked his partner.

Detective Fitzgerald began flipping through his notebook pages. "That's everybody on the list Solomon gave us," he said. "Unless you want to check out that Tonio Vega."

"What Tonio Vega?"

"The kid that delivers for Marty's Deli. The one working his way through Columbia. The vet with one eye?"

"Oh, yeah. Is he on our list?"

"No. But since we're in the neighborhood . . ." Fitzgerald said.

"Okay. We check out Tonio Vega and then we go back in. I'm so goddamned tired I could go to sleep standing up," Karl said.

They walked back to their car. "It's almost two o'clock. Think we could get him at the deli, or try catching him at home?"

"Where does he live?" Karl asked.

"Right here, practically. Over on Riverside Drive."

"Let's go there first. Maybe we can get a look around, then to the deli."

"Yeah."

"We already talked to him once, why again?" Karl asked.

"Why not? He's a Viet Nam vet, ain't he," Fitzgerald said tightly.

"Okay. And don't get so snotty."

"I'm just as tired as you are," Fitzgerald said, easing out into the traffic.

"No you're not. Nobody could be."

Tonio parked the Chevy Impala in a lot in the midtown area on the West Side and removed ten of the empty, addressed envelopes from the box in the trunk of the car. He tossed the keys to the attendant. "Don't bury it, pal. I won't be very long. And here is a large one-dollar bill for your trouble, and kindness."

"All *right!*" They slapped hands and laughed.

He kept one envelope in his hand, shoved the rest under his jacket, and headed for Whalen's Boutique.

Lillene sat as she always did, swinging one leg and looking out into the street. She glanced up at him and then away. It was the first time he had ever been inside without delivering food.

"Lou in?" he asked.

She jerked her head toward the back and returned to her stare out of the window.

He walked to the back of the store and knocked softly.

"Yeah?"

"Hello, Lou," Tonio said pleasantly, smiling. "I finally made a win, huh?"

Lou Whalen looked at him from behind his desk. Without a word he opened the drawer and took out a large white envelope that was thick and heavy. He tossed it on the desk. "Why don't you let me keep it for you, Tonio? You'll only piss it away."

Tonio reached for the envelope, opened it, and counted it very rapidly. When he was finished, he stuffed it inside his own self-addressed manila envelope, licked the flap, sealed it, and then withdrew a roll of Scotch tape. He sealed the flap again and stood up straight.

"Wyddya say, Tonio? You'll only throw it down the dirty?"

"Thanks for the thought, Lou," Tonio said. "See you." He started out of the door.

"Tonio—"

"Yeah?"

"I believe ya, you know? I mean, I know I probably won't see you again 'cause you'll get a long ride off the win. I hope you make it, you know, with the African bones."

"Sure, Lou. Thanks."

On the street, Tonio ripped off the top label addressed to himself, revealing the Litho-Vu address. From the door of Whalen's Boutique to the mailbox was no more than fifteen feet. He dropped it inside. He pulled another envelope from under his jacket and headed for the next stop.

It was going to get hairy now. He had known from the beginning that collecting his winnings was perhaps the most dangerous part of the project. He was not dealing with an OTB window cashier, or gleefully throwing his tickets in at the track window. He did not doubt that the bookies would pay off. It was the people around a bookie and what they might try to do when they saw him walk out with a big win.

But he wouldn't walk far. He knew to the foot how close he was to the nearest mailbox at each stop. He made his second collection in the back room of a bar in the theater district, near Sardi's Restaurant. It was a large room and always crowded. "I win the one-plus for a grand," Tonio said. "Gimme."

"Sure you did, Tonio. Lot of money to carry around. Want I should send somebody along with you for protection?"

Tonio opened his jacket and let the bookie see the butt of the .38, and waved the envelope in front of the bookie's nose like a fan. "I got protection, Mike." He patted the .38. "This gets me to the mailbox, and Uncle Sam protects it from there. Gimme the win."

The money was counted out and shoved across the desk. "Every guy with a pecker goes down on one-plus," the bookie whined. "I never been hit so hard in my life. You going to give me some of that back? What'cha like in the feature, Tonio?"

Tonio sealed the envelope flap and applied the Scotch tape. "I like the Chase Manhattan savings, Mike. To win."

He walked out, conscious of the stares, aware that almost everyone there was looking at the envelope, trying desperately to figure out some way to get the money before it went into the protective custody of the U.S. mail.

On the street Tonio hurried to the mailbox and looked back. They were watching him. He waved, smiled, and tore off the top label. He dropped the manila envelope inside.

It went very quickly, and there were no gyps, no come-back-tomorrow, no heavy attempts to stop him and take the money. He was in and out. They didn't like it. They *hated* it. But if they were to stay in business, with the others looking on, their regular suckers, they would have to pay off. It was maddening for some of them. One short, fat bookie was so nervous he missed the count twice and had to start over again. Another bookie gasped and breathed so hard Tonio thought he was going to have a heart attack.

It was the bodyguards that Tonio was most wary of. They itched for any kind of excuse, any sign from the bookie that something was not kosher, so they could stop him from shoving the money into the envelope, licking the flap, sealing it, sealing it again with the Scotch tape and leaving.

He returned to the Impala, drove to the East Side of Manhattan and parked, taking seven envelopes. He was back in an hour. He drove back to the West Side and made his pickups in the rough section of the luxury piers, where the stevedores made their bets, and for the first time felt threatened. He walked out of the bar with his hand on the .38, the envelope under his arm, and holding a grenade in his jacket pocket.

When he was finished with Manhattan, he moved into Brooklyn, where he anticipated that it might get rough, and it was. In Brooklyn, he had to pull the gun for the first time. They followed him outside, and when they saw him drop the envelope into the mailbox they became so enraged they started to rush him in spite of the gun and he had to pull a grenade and show it to them. That stopped them long enough for him to get into the Impala and escape.

In Queens it was easier. He made all the stops, pickups, and mailings without interruption; nowhere did he find anyone who greeted him with cheers that he had made his big score.

Vicky Jason was formal and direct when she arrived at the St. Cyr Tower. The change in her was nearly as drastic as that in Princess Martha. She had lost weight, her hair was covered with a kerchief that she never removed, and she wore old slacks and a sloppy sweater under her raincoat. Murdoch felt more than a tinge of guilt when he saw her.

"Why should we believe anything you say?" Solomon asked, challenging her in a subdued voice. "You have not been very cooperative. Want to tell us about your part in this now? Maybe you're just, *maybe,* a pawn who has been used by your boyfriend. Tell us what you know, it might be easier on you later."

Her response was correct, but chilly: "I'm here voluntarily. I will not answer any questions, and will not do anything except what I told Mr. Murdoch over the phone. I may be able to help *myself,* not you, by looking through my telephone logs."

"Tell us about your boyfriend," Solomon said.

"Mr. Solomon, can't you see that by helping me, you get helped?"

"Never mind what *you* want," Solomon said. "Tell us about your boyfriend."

"Watch your mouth," Vicky responded calmly.

Solomon slammed his palms down flat on the desk. "You want to get locked up, I'll accommodate you." He picked up the phone.

"You're losing your cool," Vicky said quietly. "Do you want my help or not?"

Solomon glanced at Murdoch. "Get her out of here."

Murdoch shook his head slowly. "No, Jesse, you want her out of here, you do it."

Solomon turned, facing Murdoch. He did not try to hide his anger. "*Her fingerprint* was found on one of the pennies. *How did it get there?*"

Murdoch held Solomon's stare and then slid off to look at his former secretary. "What's in the logs that makes you think you might help, Vicky?"

"I've had nothing to do for a week but try and figure how my print got on the penny."

"And?"

"Somebody here in the Tower had to give it to me."

"Who?"

"I don't know. But I do have nearly total recall, when my memory is jogged into a specific moment. Let me look at my logs, maybe I can remember something—"

"How do we know that what you remember isn't a clever maneuver to avoid suspicion—and get out from under?" Solomon demanded.

"Then you'll have to get off your derriere and prove a connection, a conspiracy, won't you?"

Solomon began to tremble. Murdoch had never seen anyone so enraged, and at the same time controlled, in his entire life.

Solomon could hardly speak. There was a strangle in his throat. He was red in the face. The big-shouldered man and the too-thin woman glared across the desk, their eyes expressing pure, venomous hatred.

"Mr. Solomon," Vicky said icily, "which of us is the worse? Me, because my fingerprint was found on a coin and is connected with an extortion attempt on the Tower, or you, for being what you undeniably are, a skilled, professional hustler of human garbage, *so* professional that *everyone* is garbage to you."

Vicky stood. She looked at Murdoch. "Am I going to be allowed to look at the logs?"

"Go ahead," Murdoch said quietly.

Vicky stepped out of the door.

"If you had struck her, Jesse," Murdoch said, "I would have laid you out with this chair."

"I know that," Solomon said. He looked up. He managed a weak smile. "Let's hope she stays raging long enough to find what she's look-ing for."

"Listen a minute, will you?" Detective Karl argued. "The girl, Cas-sie, said he often went out at night, down to the Rex Cafeteria to meet with other students. And she said that he had picked her up at the res-taurant late at night to escort her home. Here we sit freezing our ass off, waiting for him, f'chrissake!"

Detective Fitzgerald sat slumped behind the wheel of the car parked across the street and a hundred feet from the doorway of the Riverside Arms. "I want to see him," Fitzgerald said. "I want to know where he was today."

"The guy is as steady as a *rock!*" Karl shouted. "You talked to the blond singer, Laura Whats-er-name, and the manager of the building, Mrs. Coffin, and the black cook at the Deli, and they all said the same thing. Please, Pat, let's call it a day. I'm tired and I got to get some sleep."

Fitzgerald was just as tired and just as cold, but there was something eating at him about Tonio Vega, and he couldn't find a word for it.

"I tell you what," Karl said, yawning so hard his jaws cracked, fol-lowed by a shiver of cold. "Now, we checked that old waiter, and the black cook, and they both said Tonio had never missed a day's work since he started, right? So, Monday we go to the deli, first thing in the morning. If he doesn't show up, then we go to the chief and tell him what we got, and what you suspect. Personally, I don't suspect a damn thing. Is that agreed? Huh, agreed? Come'n, dammit, Pat, I'm tired and cold and out on my feet. *I'm going home!*"

"All right! All right, dammit! But I think you're wrong."

"I'll be wrong tomorrow," Karl said. "Just take me the hell *home!*"

The car eased away from the curb and rolled past the entrance to the Riverside Arms. The door was opened and several students came out, pausing to button their coats, and then hurrying down the street.

He was falling a little behind schedule. At eight he crossed over into the Bronx and it was at Brandy's at the diner that he had to use the .38 for the first time.

He had not noticed the two men sitting near the door when he entered and walked to the rear where Brandy sat with his guards.

"Oh, Jesus Christ, Tonio! Couldn't you have at least waited until to-morrow!" Brandy moaned.

"Gimme the win," Tonio said. He held out his hand, and leaned in over the table of the booth, letting his jacket fall away so the two body-guards could see the gun stuck in his belt. "I give you one grand on one-plus-one-plus-one. I win. I want it," Tonio said. He held out the envelope, opened the top, and followed the count as Brandy totaled the bills and slid them across the table. Tonio picked up the money and shoved it into the envelope, double-sealed it. "Thanks, Brandy, it's been nice doing business with you."

They glared at him with such hatred he thought the guards would jump him right in the diner. He backed off a few steps and deliberately dropped his hand to the butt of the .38. He did not notice that the two men at the door had slipped out. He backed off a few steps, turned quickly and got out of there.

He had a half-block to the mailbox. He glanced over his shoulder. No one was following him. He ripped off the top address down to the Litho-Vu address and curled his own address into a ball and tossed it casually into the gutter.

He was fifty feet from the mailbox when they approached him in the classic mugging maneuver: one coming straight at him, one sneaking up behind. He recognized the one in front of him. There was no mistake.

He dropped to the ground, pulling the automatic, and shot the one in front of him in the knee, spun around and caught the second man high in the gut, just below the breastbone. The second man had been running and in spite of the .38 slug, his momentum kept him going until he sprawled at Tonio's feet a yard away, his hands outstretched, reaching for the envelope. His eyes were open, he tried to speak. His jaws worked.

Tonio checked the first man, twisting and rolling around on the sidewalk in agony, scrambled to his feet and ran for the Impala, swerv-ing out into the homeward-bound traffic.

No one called out, no one tried to stop him. He got a few loud blasts of horn and left some drivers screaming as they braked to avoid his sling-shot swerve into the moving traffic, but that was all. It was New

York. It was cold. It was time to get home. It was the Bronx. No-man's-land. No one asked questions. Or even cared to know what had happened.

He dropped Brandy's envelope into the mailbox nearby his next pick-up on Tremont Avenue, working his way eastward and the New England Thruway.

It was easier than he thought it would be in the Bronx. He had allowed himself time for traffic, but because of the intense cold, the streets and avenues were nearly empty. It was in the Bronx that he got his only sincere offer of protection. "Smart move in this town, man!"

"What's that?" Tonio asked, sealing the flap of the envelope with Scotch tape.

"Having Uncle Sam escort your money." The black bookie, named Champ, waved to three of his men sitting to one side in the back of the restaurant bar. "I'll get you to the mailbox. Ain't no dude going to go up against my people."

"Thanks, Champ," Tonio said. "But I have resources."

"That little thing you got in your pants? Sheet, Tonio, my cock do more damage than that .38."

Tonio pulled out one of the grenades and tossed it up and down as if it were an apple. Twenty people in the bar hit the floor. Only Champ did not move.

He laughed and slapped the top of the table. "I would surely like to see some of these bad street people, walking around saying how they so mean and all, just what they *do,* you bring out that goddamn thing! Resources! Classy—*classy,* Tonio. My man, you-are-a-fuckin'-*army!*"

"See you, Champ."

"Spend my money good, baby. Spend it rich and good. And come back to see me. Don't stay away just because you got a good hit, man!"

"I hear where you coming from," Tonio said and backed out of the restaurant, holding the grenade. Only a few heads were raised.

He drove steadily on the New England Thruway to Bridgeport. And again, because of the intense cold, the traffic was light. He pushed the big Impala just enough to keep it at a little more than fifty-five, but less than sixty, and was in Bridgeport at ten minutes of ten.

It was easier in Bridgeport. The streets were almost totally empty and he was able to make his stops, drop his envelopes, and get back on the road south, heading for New Jersey by 11:00 p.m. He was right on time when he crossed the George Washington Bridge, picked up the New Jersey Turnpike, drove steadily in the cold, clear night without thinking. Moving ahead to the next stop, working in a rhythm that was as stable as his pulse.

It was 10:30 p.m. by the time the information about the shooting at the Bronx diner filtered back to Murdoch at the St. Cyr Tower.

"Some guy who had a reputation for betting on long shots," Solomon explained to Murdoch over the phone. "He bet a thousand bucks and wins thirty. Not too unusual. He had done it before—but then it's not your ordinary five-buck bettor. Anyway, the cops who investigated the crime came up with the usual answers—"

"And they are?" Murdoch asked.

"Nobody ain't seen nothing, no-how." Solomon's voice was tired.

"Where are the men who were shot?"

"Morrisania Hospital—up ina Bronx." Solomon paused. "Why? You thinking about talking to them?"

"Why not? I've done everything else trying to catch this bastard—unless you have any objections?"

"No no—but I really think it's a waste of time. Every indication is that these two, the guys who got shot, were hanging around the diner waiting for one of the horseplayers to come in and make a big collection."

"Did anybody talk to the bookie?"

"Yeah, but you know what you get there." Solomon raised his voice in register: 'Waddya mean, bookie? I'm in here having a cuppa coffee with my friends!' That's the kind of answers you get. They don't carry betting slips anymore. They memorize everything. We have to actually see money change hands before we can nail 'em—or get 'em on a wiretap."

"What was the name of the guy they tried to rip off?"

"Same deal," Solomon said. "Nobody don't know nothing. But somebody said they thought they heard Brandy, that's the bookie, call him Tonio."

248

"Tonio what?"

"Don't know that either. But Tonio, in a place like the Bronx, is like looking for Paddy in Dublin."

"Let's go see the guys who were shot."

"You getting squirrelly, Murdoch. Those guys are tough stick-up people. They wouldn't tell you if it was night or day."

"I might as well try," Murdoch said.

"One guy is in pretty bad shape. The one who got it in the gut. He's still unconscious. His name is Mazzie. The other guy lost a kneecap, name of Garth, from out West somewhere. Did time in Utah. You want somebody to go up there with you?"

"Andonian is still here, cleaning up the odds and ends from suite 2500."

"Okay, tell him I said to help you any way he can. I gotta go, Murdoch. But you're wrong about talking to these two. This is a Mob operation. I'm convinced of it down into my balls, and this Mazzie and Garth were just looking for something easy to hit on and make a score. Only they picked the wrong guy—"

"That's part of what I mean," Murdoch said. "This Tonio What's-his-name seems to have been prepared and very cool."

"Okaaay!" Solomon said on top of a long sigh. "Tell Andonian I said to go with you. I gotta run, see you, Murdoch."

"Yeah."

"One more thing—" Solomon said.

"What?"

"Did your secretary come up with anything?"

"Not yet—she's still looking."

"I didn't think so."

"We'll see," Murdoch said.

There was a long pause on Solomon's end of the wire. "I'm giving a little eight-to-five she comes up empty-handed."

"I'll take that eight-to-five—your eighty to my fifty," Murdoch said, grinning. That'll teach the tough old bastard, he thought.

"Christ, you spent too much time in Vegas."

"That's where I learned it."

"Learned what?"

"Take advantage of a sucker."

"You think she's going to come up with something, really?"

"I'll give *you* eight-to-five," Murdoch said, "and double the bet."

"Call me if you learn anything in the Bronx," Solomon said.

The phone clicked in Murdoch's ear. He grinned. He looked up at Vicky through the open door. She was leaning on her desk, studying the phone logs, pausing, leaning back in her chair, closing her eyes and recalling.

The phone rang. He snatched it up. "Murdoch."

"Maybe you got an idea," Solomon said quietly. "I'll meet you and Andonian at the hospital."

"Why should I tell you anything?" Louis Garth said. He lay in bed, his right leg sealed in plaster. The kneecap had been removed and he would be crippled for the rest of his life.

"You're wanted in Utah for jumping parole, Garth," Solomon said. "And you're going back. A kind word from the NYPD might help."

"Okay. I'm sitting there have a cuppa coffee me and Mazzie talking about being broke—"

"I don't want your history, ya stupid schmuck!" Solomon said roughly. "Tell me about the guy that shot you."

Murdoch and Andonian stood to one side, quiet, listening.

"What did he look like?"

"He was a punk. A *punk*. About thirty, younger maybe, and he had a bad eye—"

"What do you mean, a bad eye?"

"He wore a patch over his left eye. Like the general in Israel."

Solomon looked up at Murdoch. "Ring a bell?"

Murdoch shook his head. Solomon turned back to Garth. "What else?"

"Who the hell knows? f'chrissakes! I'm down, and he's got Mazzie in the gut and I'm going outa my mind with pain. But—"

"But what?"

"Before he starts blasting he takes something off a big yellow envelope he's carrying, and tears it off like, balls it up, and throws it into the gutter."

Again Solomon looked at Murdoch, who moved in closer to the bedside. "He did what?" Solomon asked.

"He's carrying a yellow envelope, one of those big kind they use in offices."

"Manila," Murdoch said.

"Yeah, manila envelope. He takes something off it, like a piece of paper, balls it up and throws it into the gutter. Right after that he pulls out heat and starts blasting."

"Ever see him before?" Solomon asked. "Maybe by the name Tonio?"

"No. But—"

"What?"

"You catch the son of a bitch. Don't do anything to him, leave him to me," Garth said. "I'll catch up with him."

"Garth," Andonian said, "if this is the guy we're looking for, the safest place for you is back in the Utah State Pen. And if you should see him again, *vanish*."

"What do you think?" Solomon asked, as they drove through the cold dark streets of the Bronx.

"That if there is any chance at all, I'm in the mood to try it," Murdoch said.

"Chance for what?"

"Find that crumpled—whatever it was he threw into the gutter."

"And the eye patch."

"So far, it doesn't mean a thing to me," Murdoch said.

"Well?"

"Let's go to the diner and take a look."

"Why not?" Solomon said. He reached over and pulled out the radio-microphone. "This is Chief Solomon."

"What now?" Murdoch asked.

Solomon flipped off the switch. "If we're going to do a ground search at night in the gutter, we'll need some help."

"What's Tonio?" Andonian asked.

"A name somebody gave one of the detectives who investigated the Garth shooting," Murdoch said.

"Doesn't mean anything to me."

"Me either. But it's something."

There had been no problems with the New Jersey collections and Tonio had gotten lost in Philly, finally having to stop a cruiser and ask a cop how to get back to the New Jersey Turnpike. The cop had been very friendly and told Tonio to follow him, and took him on a shortcut down a one-way street and headed in the right direction. Near the turnpike entrance the cop pulled over and stopped. They talked between the cars.

"What happened to the eye? You in Nam?"

"Yeah. You?"

"Yeah. I still got a sprung back. Marines. Took a load in the Tet Offensive. I almost didn't make it onto the cops. But they made allowances. Take it easy going back to New York. And keep it down to fifty-five. Those Jersey troopers on the turnpike are smoking speeders lately."

"Thanks, I will." Tonio waved to him and drove away.

He did take it easy returning to New York, not because he was afraid of the turnpike troopers, or speeding, but because he was so tired he could hardly keep his eyes open. He stopped for coffee and popped two Benzedrine pills and waited for them to start to work before getting back on the road.

He got into the truck traffic beating its way into the city for early-morning deliveries, crossed the George Washington Bridge, and a half hour later feeling sharp and clear from the Benny lift, parked on a side street near Madison. The only traffic was moving uptown, and there was hardly any crosstown movement at all. He did not have to wait long before getting his chance to open the manhole cover and slip inside the tunnel.

He walked to the hole and felt around in the darkness and touched the reels. If everything had gone smoothly, the right reel, the take-up reel would be full. It was.

He glanced at his watch. He had plenty of time and he wanted to make sure the tape recorder had functioned. He snapped the rewind button and sat down to wait. He wanted a cigarette but was afraid to light one because of the wild gas in the underground tunnel.

252

When the machine stopped, he set it to fast forward, stopping and starting, listening to various conversations, dismissing them, until he heard Spain's voice:

SPAIN: Hello, Governor. What's with our little deal?
GOV: Hello, Joe, I know you're going to . . .

Tonio listened intently to the entire conversation and then rewound the machine to the beginning of the conversation, dropped a cassette into the window, snapped down the Play and Record buttons, adjusted the volume, and taped the entire conversation, playing it out until the two men had hung up; two clicks and the steady unbroken hum of the dial tone.

He rewound the reel-to-reel tape, removed the master reel, slipped it into an envelope, and shoved it inside his jacket.

He slipped the cassette into his pocket and set about departing. It was still dark and cold and there was hardly any traffic at all. He had no difficulty getting out of the manhole and hurrying over to the Impala.

In the Bronx, Solomon, Andonian, eight uniformed policemen, and Murdoch picked up, turned over, and examined every scrap of paper they could find; every empty milk carton, empty beer can—rattling it, probing it with flashlights, every crumpled cigarette package, discarded newspaper, in fact, everything they could find that was manmade for two blocks on either side of the avenue.

They had been searching for several hours when Murdoch thought he saw a piece of paper sticking out from underneath a crushed orange peel. He moved it with his toe, stooped, and picked it up.

When he read it, he felt himself grow hot and then cold. He began to sweat. The label was soggy, but clear and distinct.

MR. TONIO VEGA
THE RIVERSIDE ARMS
168 RIVERSIDE DRIVE
NEW YORK, N.Y. 10024

It wasn't just the name Tonio—it was the typewriter.

Solomon watched Murdoch lay the precious piece of soggy paper into the leaves of a notebook. They stood in the gutter looking at each other.

"We got a name," Murdoch said.

"And an address."

"And there's a connection with a big-league bookie—and a thirty-thousand-dollar win on the one-plus—"

Solomon spun and cracked out an order. "Get Diedrickson's ass out of bed and down to the lab! Let's move it, people!"

Vicky Jason, who slept for a few hours when Murdoch left with Andonian for the Bronx hospital, awoke refreshed, washed her face, made coffee, and went back to studying her logs. She had started exactly a year before, and took each name entered, concentrated on it, and closed her eyes; it was not difficult for her to remember the telephone call—but it was what else she was doing at the time that she wanted to recapture.

It was a terrible strain. But she was doing it, and she was satisfied that she was not missing anything.

Little by little, piece by piece, each name she looked at would bring up the next moment in that day's work routine.

"Jonathan Ludlow, Altman's decorators, will call back: 10:37 a.m.," she would read half-aloud to herself, and then try to associate.

". . . Mr. Murdoch was interviewing people for staff that morning and couldn't take the call," she said to herself aloud. "The housekeeper had quit, and was being replaced. There were seven, no, eight women sent over by the agency—and one who had come in on her own. . . ."

And then she rejected the moment, and the incidents, because no money had changed hands.

She went to the next name, starting all over again.

It was well onto eight o'clock and she still had two months of log entries to consider. Maybe she was wrong. Maybe she couldn't remember *everything*—and something had slipped by her.

She was exhausted. She was doubly frustrated because she believed, she *knew*, that her fingerprint could have only come from someone in the Tower.

She got up and walked around the office, washed her hands, made a fresh pot of coffee, and went back to her logs. She began flipping pages of the remaining two months rapidly—names leaped out, and memories with them.

Princess Martha: 11:07 a.m.

She stopped. She sat down quickly and closed her eyes.

She had been surprised to get the call from the princess personally. All other contact with Her Royal Highness had come through one of the two security men, Gregory or Haldstadt.

The princess had sounded hesitant, remote. There were long silences between her remarks with Vicky. She had tried to put the princess at ease, she remembered that very clearly.

It was about the children. They were bored—and Vicky had listened to a guilt-ridden mother, albeit a princess, describe the difficulties the children were having adjusting to their confinement—one deaf, and the other with an unstable heart—they were tired of the hotel food, and as children will do, they wanted the hamburgers advertised on television.

Vicky had gently suggested that the fast-food chain stores were not always the best, and under the circumstances, since it was for the children, she could recommend a very good place, and the children would never know the difference.

Vicky had ordered double hamburgers and French fries from Marty's Deli—and they had been delivered by Tonio.

And then she remembered Tonio, and the many times he had brought sandwiches. They always made change.

He was the *only one* with whom she had ever handled money while in the Tower. It had to be him, and it could not possibly be anyone else.

She sat down. She closed her eyes. She summoned up the scene:

But the first beer can had been discovered the same day that Princess Martha arrived, therefore the penny with her fingerprint on it had to come from an *earlier* transaction with the deli delivery boy.

But when?

Vicky opened her eyes and returned to her examination of the telephone logs, moving backward through the pages. She found it four days earlier.

"Maggie/Chris/lunch/Italian Pavilion Café."

There was a double line drawn through the entry. The lunch had been canceled and Murdoch had worked through, and being tired of the hotel food, had sent out for a sandwich. She even remembered his joke: "I'm a typical New Yorker, Vicky. Once in a while I've got to have my fix— a hot pastrami on rye from a kosher deli."

Tonio had delivered the order; because of the city sales tax, the amount due had required pennies in change. She had counted out four of

255

them, taking them from her desk drawer where she kept odd change mixed in with the paper clips and pencils for just that purpose.

At the Holiday Inn on West Fifty-seventh Street, Tonio walked in with his new suitcase filled with his new clothes. The same clerk who had assisted him before had just come on duty at seven. He looked up, surprised. "Hi," he said, grinning. "You're supposed to be in Rochester."

Tonio dropped the suitcase on the floor. "I was. You can't believe how they've been jerking me around. I didn't even get a chance to check in up there. My company set up meetings here in the city without telling me. So, instead of sleeping up there and then driving like hell to get back here on time, I decided to come on down now. The bottom line, pal, is that I need a room for the weekend."

"No problem," the clerk said.

"Any chance of getting any dough back from the other Holiday Inn?" Tonio asked.

"I'm afraid not," the clerk said. "You guaranteed the room."

"Well, doesn't hurt to ask."

"Here you are, Mr. Chayefsky. Four-twenty-seven."

"Fine." Tonio registered.

"What kind of business are you in, Mr. Chayefsky?"

"Aluminum siding. You know that crap people get suckered into putting on the side of their house?"

"Yes."

"That crap."

The clerk laughed. "Have a nice day."

In his room, Tonio took his boots off, loosened his belt, and stretched out on the bed. He could not go to sleep right away. The Benny lift was still with him, and he used the time, as he stared at the ceiling and felt himself relaxing, to go over everything that had been done. Had he missed anything? He didn't think so. Everything had gone exactly as he had planned. He had only to wait out the weekend, and it would be over. The wait would not be difficult. He felt that he could sleep until Monday morning.

Saturday morning was another bright, cold day. The sun broke through the steam jets escaping from underground pipes, oil-burner soot,

256

automobile exhausts, and fumes released from utility plants.

"Has he ever stayed out all night before?" Murdoch asked.

"No," Eleanor said. She sat on the side of the bed in her nightgown and housecoat. "He's stayed out very late, many times, but I always heard him come in, even if he went to his own room to study." She looked around at the faces. "Will you please tell me what this is all about?"

"Just a few more questions, Miss Cassie," Chief Solomon said. "You've been living with this Tonio Vega since October?"

She nodded her head.

"And he never told you where he came from?"

"No."

"Did you ever ask?"

"I never thought of it," Eleanor said honestly. "It wasn't the kind of question you asked Tonio."

"Why not?" Murdoch asked.

"He was so private—I mean, apart."

"A loner?" Murdoch asked.

"Very much so. And yet, he wasn't. I mean, look what he did for me? You don't know what it is to be so desperate that you want to jump in front of a subway—and he stopped me. Will you please tell me *why you're questioning me this way!*"

"Did he ever mention," Solomon asked calmly, ignoring her outburst, "what outfit he was with in Viet Nam? Or how he lost his eye?"

She shook her head and turned away from them. There was a tap on the door. Andonian opened it and stuck his head in. "Can I see you a minute, Chief?"

Solomon nodded and turned back to Eleanor. "You'd better get dressed, Miss Cassie."

"Why? Where are you taking me? Am I under arrest?"

"It would be better," Solomon said firmly, "if you just get dressed. Please?"

Eleanor Cassie nodded.

Murdoch and Solomon stepped outside and faced the stares of Laura Roc, Mrs. Coffin, and a half-dozen half-dressed sleepy-eyed students.

"What is it, Sergeant?" Solomon asked.

"Here, I'll show you," Andonian said.

They followed him to Tonio's room, and as Solomon started to step inside, Andonian restrained him on the arm lightly. "Nothing of what I was looking for. No tools, no electronics, no papers, books, nothing."

Solomon and Murdoch stuck their heads inside the door and looked around the bare room. "You see anything?" Andonian asked.

"No—am I supposed to?"

"No, as a matter of fact you're not. This room has been scrubbed down. Ceiling, walls, floors, windows, bathroom—everything. This guy bailed out, Chief. And he knew what he was doing. Every trace of anybody living here has been wiped out."

"And did you notice her room?" Murdoch said. "The same thing. It's just been scrubbed down too. I could see the cleaning marks on the walls."

Solomon pursed his lips and looked sideways at Murdoch. "You think she's in it with him?"

"I don't know," Murdoch said. "But I'd certainly like for you to hold on to her—if you can."

Solomon nodded, turning to a patrolman. "I can. Where the hell is that matron?"

"Should be here any minute, Chief."

"All right, you stay here," Solomon said, "and wait for the matron. Take her in as a material witness."

"Where shall I take her?" the patrolman asked.

"The Seventeenth Precinct, Captain Hansen. And get hold of Karl and Fitzgerald. And let me know as soon as Diedrickson has information on that label." Solomon looked over at the group of students and Mrs. Coffin. "Get a statement from these people about Tonio. Anything you can."

The cop nodded.

"Do you think we should tell Spain?" Murdoch asked.

"What for? What can he do to help us now?"

"There could still be another bomb," Murdoch said. "And even though we're onto something that looks good, Threat—or Tonio Vega—could still blow a hole in the St. Cyr with a telephone call."

"So?"

"We may still have to evacuate the building."

"Maybe now, more than ever," Solomon said.

There was not much talk on their ride back downtown. Without the other knowing it, both men were acutely aware that they were at the very beginning again: there was still the possibility that Threat—Tonio Vega—could make a phone call and blow up the St. Cyr Tower.

Detectives Karl and Fitzgerald sat at the counter in Marty's Deli and drank coffee and ate prune Danish. It was eight-thirty and they had been there since seven.

"What you say Patch's done?" the black cook asked.

"Just want to ask him a few questions," Karl said.

"Patch sometimes late," the black cook said, glancing up at the big-faced clock on the far wall, "but he ain't never missed a day."

"Ever been this late before?" Karl asked.

"Come to think of it—no, he ain't."

"Look what's coming in the door," Fitzgerald said.

Murdoch, followed by Chief Solomon, entered the deli and glanced around. Detectives Karl and Fitzgerald looked at each other. They left their coffee and prune Danish and hurried over.

The look that passed among the four men needed no talk.

"Vega?" Karl asked.

Solomon nodded.

"He hasn't showed up. This is the first time in two years."

"The two of you stay here," Solomon said to the detectives. "I doubt he'll show up, but you never can tell. What time do they close?"

"Twelve-thirty on Saturday," Karl said.

"Stick around until they close and then come over to the Seventeenth Precinct," Solomon said under his breath and turned to the door abruptly.

Entering Murdoch's office, the two men stopped, startled to see Vicky was still there.

She rushed toward them a few steps. "It's the deli kid, the one who delivers sandwiches!" She looked from face to face. "Don't you understand, he's the *only* one I've ever changed money with here in the hotel. Don't you see? Giving him change is the only way my fingerprint could have gotten on that penny. His name is Tonio. I don't know his last name. He works for Marty's Deli over on—"

"We know," Murdoch said, going to her.

"You *know?*" Vicky glanced past Murdoch to Solomon.

The cop returned her look with a steady gaze. Slowly he nodded confirmation.

She stepped back. Her face hardened. "Ohhh no! No, you don't!"

"Don't what?" Murdoch asked.

"Tie me in with him!"

"We're not trying to do that," Solomon said. "You're free to go." He walked past both of them into the inner office. "I'll call Spain," he said. "Just in case we have to get out of here."

He closed the door.

Murdoch put his arm around her shoulders and pulled her toward the door to the corridor. "You've confirmed everything we already know," he said. "Your part . . ." he hesitated. "Well, it's over. For you."

He felt her slump against him. She started crying. "I'm going home."

"I'll have someone take you."

She shook her head and wiped her face. "No, I don't need that."

Murdoch took out his apartment key and tried to press it into her hand. "Please, take this and use it. No one will bother you."

She refused the key and shook her head.

"Vicky, take it." Murdoch said as firmly as he dared. "Let me do *something* for—for—what has happened."

Holding back her tears, like a child who has been hurt and not understanding it, she turned away from him. Murdoch watched her walk down to the elevator, thin, vulnerable, yet as tough as anyone he had ever met.

He turned back into the office, wondering why he had never noticed how really attractive she was.

18 Working out of the Seventeenth Precinct, Solomon commandeered the precinct captain's office and plunged into the track-down of Tonio Vega with all of the energy and determination of an enraged bull. An All-Points Bulletin was flashed. The very best surveillance teams in the department were sent to observe the Riverside Arms and Marty's Deli. Because he felt that Eleanor would not give a reliable description of Tonio, he ordered the police artist to work with Mrs. Coffin and Laura Roc. When the sketch was finished, it was shown to the black cook and the waiters at Marty's Deli. They all agreed that it was an accurate likeness, and Solomon ordered three times the usual number of copies to be distributed. Both Tonio's and Eleanor's rooms at the Riverside Arms were sealed until the laboratory and criminalistics teams could go over them.

Solomon had been unable to catch Threat at the payoff, which had always been his ace-in-the-hole; he had been outsmarted, outwitted, and made to look foolish, but now he had a name, he had facts, he had details, he was overwhelmed with information whereas before he had had nothing. But he was working on *his* turf now, he was a detective and he knew all of the resources at his command, and how to use them. And last but not least, he had the greatest asset a policeman possesses: he had time. Time to examine and sift the facts as they were known again and again; to shuffle them like a deck of cards. It was what he did best, and he was one of the very best in the world.

"Where's the girl now?" Solomon asked Captain Hansen. "You didn't lock her up, did you?"

"She's here with the matron. In one of the offices." Captain Hansen said.

To one side in the large office, Murdoch finished filling Spain in on the developments.

"It's incredible, but as you tell it to me, it makes sense. A deli delivery boy—Jesus! Who the hell ever looks at them? And he was in and out of the Tower as much as I was during and after the construction," Spain said. "Do you think there is another bomb?"

"I honestly don't know."

"How will we ever find out?"

"Threat is the only one who can tell us that."

"If we catch him," Spain said.

"If we catch him."

"Don't you think we will? After all, we know a great deal about him. How many one-eyed guys—"

Murdoch cut him off: "And if it's a disguise? And the name Tonio Vega is a phony? He scrubbed down the room of the girl, and his own. They've examined the things he left. Shaving gear, toothbrush, comb—everything has been wiped clean. What does that tell us? That the one way we can absolutely identify him, and track him down, is with his fingerprints. And he's made damn sure we don't find one."

"His books—you said he was studying at Columbia. Maybe you could lift one there?"

"Sure," Murdoch said. "But where are they?"

Murdoch was silent a moment. "But there is one thing," he said half-aloud.

"What?"

Murdoch looked up and saw that Solomon, Captain Hansen, and Andonian were listening.

"What one thing?" Solomon asked quietly.

Murdoch took a deep breath. He stood. His voice was rough, gravel-
ly, and hard. "I've had this son of a bitch on my back for over two
months. And if it *is* Tonio Vega—or whatever his name is—we know,
from the two bombs he directed us to in the Tower, that he was clever.
We learned that it wasn't cleverness when he had us fix the race for the
payoff. We learned then that he was brilliant. Now, we have a name, a
figure, a background. He's so fucking anonymous he's like a blade of
grass in Central Park. Another face, another figure—not personality, *a
figure*—among millions here in the city. And then he becomes even less
than that. He becomes a deli delivery boy." Murdoch paused and looked
at them. "He's delivered sandwiches and coffee to my office!"

Detective Fitzgerald spoke up: "He told us that himself."

"Okay, now," Murdoch continued. He began pacing the floor. They
all watched him, letting him weave his narrative. "He's put himself into
a perfect picture. He's an ex-GI working his way through college by taking the most menial job in our society. Who is going to argue with that?
Nobody, not today, not with welfare cheats, muggers, street crime. We
admire that kind of old-fashioned, hard-working upward mobility.
Threat has wrapped himself in the safest possible cover story, and at the
same time one that allows him complete and absolute freedom. He can
go anywhere, especially in this city, anytime, and no one suspects him.

"Okay, so much for his cleverness and his brilliance. He's worked
this whole thing out into a two-year project. He doesn't drop the Tower
into Fifth Avenue, he drops an abandoned apartment building in the
Bronx, while we watch, as easily as a child knocking over building
blocks. He demonstrates that he can do it. He then directs us to the
bombs in the Tower and we become prime suckers for his *Threat*.

"Ahh! we say, but we'll get him when he reaches for the money. The
payoff. And what does he do? He forces us to fix a goddamn horserace,
and he *wins* his payoff from illegal bookies! And the race he has us fix?
One of the greatest action races of the year, when, maybe millions of
people put down a five or a ten or a twenty on the one-plus-one-plus-
one. I've done it myself. No doubt some of you have. So, even when he

wins, he becomes just another guy who has had his hunch bet pay off. But what kind of payoff is he expecting for the years of effort, planning, and effectively planting bombs in a major building in the heart of Manhattan? I tell you this, it isn't going to be twenty cents.

"So, what was his bet? And with how many bookies? It would have to be substantial, because getting the equipment and the explosives he needed to implant those two bombs in the Tower cost plenty. A substantial bet. What is a substantial bet? When the guaranteed odds are thirty-to-one, a substantial bet that would not be too noticeable would be a thousand bucks to a confirmed long-shot gambler—a plunger.

"A grand, winning at thirty-to-one returns thirty-one thousand clams. Lay it off on ten bookies, and you have a three-hundred-thousand-dollar win. Lay it off on a hundred bookies, and you have a *three-million-*dollar-plus win. In cash. In old bills. Tax-free.

"Okay, back to the payoff, which is where we always thought our heaviest muscle could be brought to bear. He goes to the bookie, he's had a thirty-thousand-dollar win. Threat is brilliant, but he is also streetwise. He knows there are vultures that hang around bookie joints waiting for a guy with a bankroll he's just won, to walk away, and then rob him. I suggest to you that that was exactly what happened to Mazzie and Garth stretched out up in Morrisania Hospital right now. Threat picked up his winnings and when they tried to move in on him, he wasted them. But—" Murdoch paused and looked at Solomon. "What was, and how do you explain, the label with his name and address on it? Why did he rip it off a manila envelope and throw it into the gutter?

"He's had the payoff figured from the very beginning. The label the criminalistics lab is going over right now, downtown, was a decoy. He shoved his winnings into a prepared manila envelope with two addresses. One with his name, Tonio Vega, Riverside Arms—on the top—*in case anybody should see it!* Because he knew he was never going back to the Riverside Arms. The manila envelope with his winnings inside was mailed to another address, concealed underneath." Murdoch paused. He looked around. "I suddenly feel foolish," he said quietly.

"Why? I believe it went down just as you said it. Absolutely," Solomon said.

"Yeah," Murdoch said, "so do I. But what was the second address on the bottom?"

"It could be anyplace in the city," Spain said.

"Or the country," Andonian added.

"In the city." Murdoch was emphatic. "I don't think he would let too much time go by—separating himself from that much money. The city. He's mailed it to himself, here, in the city."

"Okay," Solomon said. "But where?"

"We could talk to the girl again," Murdoch suggested.

"Or," Spain observed gloomily, "we could get lucky and pick him up."

"I believe," Murdoch said, "that he's planned everything else, and he's got this planned too. If the mailings are here in the city, and he mailed them yesterday, they would be delivered Monday. And once he gets his hands on the money, he changes back to whoever he was before, and phisst! He's on a plane—and gone."

"Okay," Solomon said. "This is Saturday morning. If there are as many envelopes as you suggest there might be, each one stuffed with thirty grand in cash, just any mailing address wouldn't work."

"Why not?" Spain asked.

"Can you see your average mailman making a delivery of that many heavy envelopes? The post office would probably call him up and tell him to come get them."

"So?" Murdoch asked.

"So!" Solomon was bursting out with a sudden driving energy that made Karl and Fitzgerald jump. "We call every post office and have them check and see if they have a bunch of manila envelopes to be delivered to Tonio Vega!"

"How many post offices are there in the city?" Murdoch asked.

Andonian had already started to move, snatching at the Manhattan phone book, while tossing the Queens directory to Karl, the Brooklyn listings to Fitzgerald. "We need a Bronx and Staten Island," he said, rushing out of the office into the huge central squad room, yelling at the top of his voice for everyone's attention.

Within five minutes every phone in the Seventeenth Precinct was being used to call every post office in the city.

"And suppose he mailed them to Newark? Or a friend in Los Angeles?" Spain said.

"Don't even think it," Murdoch said.

Murdoch, Solomon, and Andonian, all three of whom had been up all night, left the search through the city's post offices to others while they slept.

At four the next afternoon not a single envelope addressed to Tonio Vega had been found. Informed of this in his Riverdale apartment, Solomon wanted to know if the examination of Eleanor's and Tonio's rooms at the Riverside Arms had produced anything. Nothing of any significance had been discovered.

Another blank wall.

The man who was the cause of a great deal of energy and money being spent had gotten up, showered, dressed, and had a huge meal in a Ninth Avenue café; stopped at a deli and bought some fruit, cheese, the Sunday papers and gone back to the Holiday Inn.

He made one call. He asked to be awakened at nine the next morning.

On Monday morning Solomon joined Murdoch in his office for coffee. Both men were exhausted, in addition to the midwinter pallor of New Yorkers, both had a slight puffiness under their eyes. Solomon indicated Vicky's empty chair. "Have you heard from her?"

"Her phone is still out of order," Murdoch said. "I sent her a dozen roses, with your name on the card, and a hot meal specially prepared here in the hotel and brought to her by one of the waiters. He was going to serve it—"

"And?"

"She wouldn't open the door." Murdoch shrugged.

Solomon sighed. "That's the hard part about my business."

"Any luck with the post office and Tonio Vega mail?"

Jesse Solomon sipped his coffee. He shook his head. "No."

"What now?" Murdoch asked.

"Why," Solomon looked up, and raised his eyebrows, "I keep after the son of a bitch until I get him."

"I meant the St. Cyr Tower."

"What about it?"

"You have the authority to evacuate, if you think there is still a chance of another bomb."

Solomon shook his head. "That's one of the reasons I dropped by this morning. I'm meeting with the mayor and Spain in his penthouse in five minutes. I thought you would want to be there. You know as much about this whole business as anybody."

Murdoch nodded. The two men struggled to their feet, finished their coffee, and started for the door just as Vicky Jason walked in. She was smartly dressed and bright-eyed. She gave Solomon a curt nod, but spoke only to Murdoch. "Good morning, Chris."

"Good morning, Vicky—" He hesitated a moment, wavering between welcoming her back and asking how she was feeling. He decided against both. "I'm going up to Mr. Spain's. I shouldn't be too long."

She smiled and started taking off her coat.

Murdoch followed Solomon out of the door. Neither of them spoke as they rode Spain's private elevator to the penthouse. Jimco met them at the door and ushered both into the game room where Spain and the mayor were having coffee.

"Find anything in the post offices with Vega's name on it?" Spain asked.

"Nothing so far," Solomon replied. "But we're still with it."

Spain sat forward, resting his elbows on his knees and studying the tops of his shoes. Murdoch had seen him sit in that position many times when he knew his employer was deeply troubled.

"Well, gentlemen," Spain said. "Threat has successfully pulled off the ransoming of my building and evidently gotten away with the payoff. What now? Do I close down my hotel, throw everybody out, and strip the walls and ceilings to make sure there aren't any more bombs?"

Tonio was awake when the phone rang. He grabbed it before it had finished the first ring. "Thank you, I'm up," he said quietly.

He sat on the side of the bed and smoked a cigarette and let the presence seep back in. It was here. The moment of fruition. All he had to do was pick up the Litho-Vu mailings, change his clothes, and it was over.

He did not think about it anymore as he showered, shaved, and scrubbed his teeth with the new toothbrush he had bought in Macy's, and when he was dressed, he began to prepare. He checked the room for fingerprints, wiping the surfaces down with a soapy towel and then checked the two hand grenades and the .38. He left the room after eating some fruit and cheese, swilling it down with ice water. He wished he had time for a cup of coffee at least, but he did not have that much time to spare. Soon there would be a lifetime of never having to rush, or be at an appointed place, or do anything at all except exactly what he and his brother wanted.

On Ninth Avenue he bought two of the largest GI duffel bags the Army-Navy store had, and two Yale locks to string the heavy metal grommets, securing the tops. He shoved a brown paper bag he had brought with him into one of the bags, and he was ready. He did not have to wait very long for a taxi.

"Sixth Avenue and Fiftieth Street," he said, and settled back. He glanced at his watch. Thirty minutes. It would be over in thirty minutes.

In the NYPD criminalistics laboratory, Lieutenant Diedrickson made an adjustment on the electron microscope and eased forward to the eyepiece. He blinked once, as was his custom, opened his eyes wide, set his focus into a fixed stare. He reached out with his left hand and without looking made a minute adjustment. His field of vision, the object of his focus, clarified. He stared, hard. And with his right hand began to write on a huge yellow legal pad, again without looking, what he observed in the field below him.

When he was finished he leaned back and rubbed his eyes very gently before reading what he had written on the pad.

He stared at it, puzzling. It made no sense to him. He lit another cigarette, and picked up the phone. He called Chief Solomon's office and was told that Solomon was at Mr. Spain's in the St. Cyr Tower. Diedrickson dialed again. The line was busy. He finished his cigarette, stared at what he had written on the yellow pad, and tried again. Again it was busy. He poured himself a cup of coffee and tried a third time. If he didn't get through this time, he decided, he would go get something to eat and try after lunch. He dialed, waited, and heard the satisfying ring of an open line buzzing in his ear.

"St. Cyr Tower, good morning."

"This is Lieutenant Diedrickson of the New York Police Department. I would like to speak to Chief Solomon in Mr. Spain's apartment, please."

"Just a minute, Lieutenant."

Diedrickson waited, and then Solomon's voice boomed in his ear. "Yeah, Lieutenant?"

"Chief, good news. The type on the label and the type on the Threat notes are identical."

"Hold on, Lieutenant," Solomon said. Diedrickson could hear him speaking to someone else: "It's Diedrickson, down at the lab. The type on the label and the type on the Threat notes match—it's Vega. Lieutenant?"

"Yes, sir."

"You've done a hell of a job, and I won't forget it."

"That's very nice of you to say so, Chief, but there is something else."

"What?"

"This guy used a silk ribbon—"

"So?"

"Well, a nylon typewriter ribbon has a tendency to blot the letters onto the paper. That's because the ink dries on the ribbon."

"Lieutenant, please, no lectures."

"Chief, listen just a minute. This guy used a silk ribbon. The ink comes off the ribbon easier because silk is a natural fiber, and retains its wetness much longer. Therefore it takes longer to dry. The label I've been examining was pasted over something, or put down on something that had typing on it, and maybe because it got wet, some of the ink on the bottom was transferred to the *back* of the label."

"Can you make it out?" Solomon asked tightly.

"Yes, sir. I have it written down. You want to hear it?"

"If you *please*, Lieutenant," Solomon said.

"It's just an address. Litho-Vu. Post Office Box 1278. Rockefeller Center, New York, New York. Zip 10020."

Diedrickson paused and waited. "Chief—Chief?"

Carrying two GI duffel bags, Tonio got out of the taxi on Sixth Avenue, glanced at the long lines of holiday moviegoers waiting to get into Radio City Music Hall, and walked into the RCA building. The Lower Concourse, lined with shops, restaurants, service establishments, was crowded as usual for that time of day. Tonio walked east as he had done so many times before, another anonymous figure in black leather jacket, blue jeans, boots, and knit cap; even then aware of the eyes of the people walking toward him as their eyes flicked over his face and the eye patch. He was not nervous, but there was a slight elevation in his pulse. It was not enough to make him think about control, or be concerned about showing his anxiety, but he was aware of it.

He walked, head moving, looking for the slightest underlying aberration of movement or sound indicating that things were not normal, or as they should be.

He did not pause as he made his observations. Tonio kept his pace even, steps firm, duffels under his left arm, his right hand in his jacket pocket holding a hand grenade. He arrived at the post office substation at twenty minutes to twelve and got in line behind the other messengers.

"You really got a load this morning, Tonio," the clerk said.

"Yeah, the boss said it was going to be a big one. That's why I brought the bags." Tonio glanced around. He saw no one suspicious. Six messengers in back of him. Joey behind the counter stacking envelopes. People passing by. Ordinary people.

"Biggest load you ever had," Joey said, helping him shovel the envelopes into the duffel bags. "Must be about a hundred and fifty of them."

The last envelope went in. Tonio slipped the Yale locks through the grommets and snapped them closed.

"See you, Joey," Tonio said, and started dragging the heavy bags across the pink terrazzo floor.

"Manhattan Off-Set! Next! Manhattan Off-Set, let's go!" Joey yelled at the waiting messengers. An old man shuffled forward.

There was no longer any need for him to be Tonio Vega and dragging the heavy duffels, he slipped into the men's room off the Lower Concourse, and as he expected, it was empty. Though it wouldn't have made any difference. He stepped inside one of the toilet cubicles and locked the door. He opened one of the duffels.

He felt no panic, but he moved deliberately and quickly. He removed the eye patch and flushed it down the toilet; he did the same with all ID he possessed for Tonio Vega. He removed the leather jacket and pulled on a bulky cardigan ski sweater he took from the brown paper bag, threw the knit cap onto the floor, and pulled on a bulky beret-type cap with a visor. He removed a small hand mirror from the paper bag, and sitting on the john with the mirror propped up on one of the duffel bags, began to apply an untrimmed three-quarter dark beard. When he was sure the beard was well stuck, he slipped on a pair of wrap-around sunglasses. He stuffed the leather jacket and knit cap into the brown paper bag, locked the duffel again, and stepped out of the cubicle after flushing the toilet. He shoved the paper bag into the dirty towel hamper and examined himself in the mirror.

A half-block more of the Underground Concourse, up a few steps, then on to the International Building, up the escalator to Fifth Avenue opposite St. Patrick's. A taxi—and finish.

He turned to the door.

Solomon, Murdoch, and Spain, trailed by a dozen cops, barreled through the corridors of the Lower Concourse knocking people aside like a special team on a punt return.

"Litho-Vu," Solomon barked at the startled Joey. "Has Litho-Vu been picked up yet?"

"Who the hell are you?" Joey demanded.

Solomon flipped his badge and glared. "Answer the goddamn question. Litho-Vu. Has it been picked up yet?"

"Yeah, yeah. Five–ten minutes ago."

"Who picked them up?"

"Why, Tonio, like always. What the hell is this?"

"Young guy, with a patch over one eye?" Murdoch demanded.

"Yeah, I tol' you. Tonio—a patch over his eye."

"Which way did he go?" Solomon demanded.

"That way—" Joey pointed toward the corridor.

"*Left* or *right?*" Solomon yelled.

"Who the hell knows!" Joey yelled back. "I got United States mail to handle, mister! And you're interfering!"

Murdoch turned to Solomon. "We got a half-dozen ways to go. Up the escalator to Rockefeller Plaza. Sixth Avenue. Forty-ninth Street. Fiftieth Street. Or the International Building, which comes out right on Fifth."

"International Building," Solomon said instantly. With the entire force of cops running after them, Solomon, Murdoch, and Spain raced the corridors again.

Traffic on Fifth Avenue was unusually heavy that morning; there were special New Year's sales at Saks and other shops along the avenue. There was a heavy clot of taxis, blocks and blocks of them, whizzing by Tonio as he stood at the curb with his two duffel bags, signaling. A sea of yellow cabs, all alike it seemed, and all of them occupied.

He stepped out into the street, was missed narrowly several times and then spotted an empty. He waved frantically and saw the driver look at him and nod, pull over, and swerve to the curb.

Tonio loaded the duffels inside hurriedly and got in. He leaned out to reach for the door and, as he did, glanced back toward the entrance of the International Building.

Murdoch, Solomon, and Spain, followed by the cops, broke out of the revolving doors and spread out.

Tonio glanced at the driver. The man was turned toward the traffic, waiting for an opening and did not see the cops.

Murdoch saw the taxi at the curb. He looked for the occupant in the backseat, but could see nothing; he saw something else.

Tonio had the duffels upright on the floor of the taxi. Murdoch yelled at Solomon and started running across the sidewalk for the taxi. Tonio pulled out one of the grenades. . . .

There was a lurch. Tonio was driven back into the seat as the driver caught an opening and spun expertly into the oncoming traffic, picking up speed, changing lanes, jockeying for position.

At Fiftieth Street they caught a green light. The taxi shot across the intersection and within seconds was lost, leaving Murdoch standing on the corner, waving his arms and pointing. Solomon and the cops stood helplessly and watched the taxi vanish amidst the thick avenue traffic, just one more taxi among hundreds.

Tonio looked back. The traffic closed in back of him. He smiled, and turned the other way, looking over his shoulder, uptown, and watched the black monolith of the St. Cyr Tower recede into the clear, bright noonday sky. He slipped the grenade back into his pocket.

He relaxed and lit a cigarette. He propped his feet up on the duffels. He knew to the penny how much was inside.

There were a hundred and forty-two envelopes, $31,000 in each one. $4,402,000. Cash.

19

"Joey, the mail clerk, checked his records later and told us there were a hundred and forty-two envelopes," Murdoch said to Vicky. Later that afternoon they sat in Murdoch's office. "If he bet a thousand with all the others as he did at Lou Whalen's, it comes out to four million four hundred and two thousand bucks. In cash. Old bills. No taxes."

"And no idea who he was—is? Or where he came from?"

Murdoch shook his head. "None at all. Another five seconds—ten at the most—and we would have had him. But! It would have taken a Marine Division to stop traffic on Fifth Avenue and go after him. And we didn't, unfortunately, have a Marine Division."

"And the girl, Eleanor Cassie?"

"Solomon's questioning her now, but I don't think they're going to get anything out of her. Nor any of the other kids up at the Riverside Arms. He pulled them into his charade, as he did everybody else."

273

"Think they'll ever catch him?"

"Oh, I'm sure of it. If they keep the case open, which I'm positive, with Spain's connections, he'll see that they do. Time is on their side. They'll find a slip, an error, some false move he made somewhere along the way, and nail him. Like he did with the penny that had your print on it. All of the others were wiped clean, except one side of that one penny. He *can* slip." Murdoch paused. "And there's something else that can't be dismissed—"

"What?"

"A very tough cop named Jesse Solomon."

Vicky shrugged her shoulders. "If he failed to catch Threat before, why suggest that he'll do better in the future? He's a bureaucrat. He carries a gun, but in the scheme of things, he's a second-rater looking for his pension."

"Now, now—don't be bitter." Murdoch grinned. "Karl and Fitzgerald, two of Solomon's best detectives, made a connection between the death of Roccaforte, a Vice cop who was shaking down the independent bookies here in midtown Manhattan, and Tonio—Threat."

There was a knock on the door. Murdoch frowned and stood.

"Being a cop is like belonging to a closed brotherhood. Even though Roccaforte was on the take, and a dirty cop, they can't let one of their own get murdered and the killer get off. Solomon will keep this case open. And if I had to bet, I'd take Solomon." He opened the door. "Yes?"

A bellman stood outside and handed Murdoch a small manila envelope. "This came for you, Mr. Murdoch."

"How was it delivered?"

"I don't know. I stepped away from my station to speak to Mr. Kosinski at the desk, and when I came back, it was just laying there. I don't know how it got there."

Murdoch smiled. "Okay," he said.

So, it wasn't over yet.

He handled the envelope carefully, and the cassette inside, but he did not really believe there would be any fingerprints on it.

He dropped it into his tape deck—and found himself shaking. He made himself a drink. He felt himself glow inside. It was the same anticipation he used to experience when he was a boy watching a Saturday-afternoon horror movie.

He snapped the Play button:

. . . Hello, Murdoch. I never wanted anything but the money, which I now have. There are no more bombs. The building is safe. Believe it, because I have no further use for Threat. But just in case Chief Solomon should get clue-happy and try to track me down, you had better play this tape for Spain first.

Murdoch recognized the sing-song New York accent of earlier tapes. He reached out and snapped the Off button. His hands shook. The ice in his glass rattled so hard, Vicky reached out and took his hand.

He took a long drink and snapped the Play button again and listened:

SPAIN: Hello, Governor. What's with our little deal?
GOV: Joe, I know you're going to scream like a son of a bitch,
    but there is no way, no way on this earth, that I can order a fix
    on that horserace and keep it quiet. The answer, Joe, is no fix.
SPAIN: Listen, you spineless bastard! I want you to know—
GOV: Don't call me names, Joe.
SPAIN: I call you what you are, you prick! Don't let this happen,
    Clay. If people die because of you—
GOV: No you don't, you sheeny bastard! You don't lay this at
    my doorstep.
SPAIN: I always knew you were an anti-semitic schmuck! You
    took money from me.
GOV: And that's what I get for getting mixed up with you sheeny
    connivers—
SPAIN: It's us sheeny connivers that figured out a way to finance
    your campaign without reporting it, and got you elected. And
    now I ask for something and you give me the shaft.
GOV: I've had enough of this. The bottom line, Joe, is no fix.
    Jacoby even tried with Anton Cabot. No deal.
SPAIN: Listen to me, Clay. I'll tell *you* the bottom line. You
    either fix that horserace at the Big A or Jimco goes right to the

state attorney general on that upstate utility deal Jacoby was so
hot to trade off for—

Gov: Joe, for God's sake, Joe—what're you saying!

SPAIN: But, you do this for me, Clay, and I'll send you all the
papers, everything, on the utility deal. You'll be off the hook.
And not that many people have to know about the fix. And
once the race is run and the bets paid off, who's going to be
able to prove anything?

There was a long silence. The tape recording was of such quality that
Murdoch could hear both men breathe:

Gov: Who knows about Threat's demand, Joe? I mean, how
many people?

SPAIN: Not enough to matter.

Gov: I'll get back to you.

SPAIN: Not good enough, Clay. You give me your word that the
race is in the bag, and I'll send Jimco over with the papers
right now.

Gov: You won't hold anything back?

SPAIN: I give you my word, ya schmuck. I don't do that unless I
mean it. And you know it.

Gov: I know that, Joe.

SPAIN: Well? You got my word. You give me yours?

There was another long silence as the two men breathed and Murdoch
listened. He thought they might have finished, and then he heard one of
them clear his throat:

Gov: Okay, Joe. When Jimco arrives with the papers, after I've
gone through them and I'm satisfied, I'll work something out
on the race.

SPAIN: We got a deal? On the level?

Gov: Yeah, Joe. We got a deal. On the level.

SPAIN: Jimco is on his way.

Gov: Are you recording this on tape?

SPAIN: Of course I am. Aren't you?

GOV: As a matter of fact, I am.

SPAIN: Good! Then we know where we stand.

GOV: See you later, Joe.

SPAIN: Yeah, take it easy. You're not so young anymore.

Murdoch waited for the two men to hang up. Two clicks, and silence.

Murdoch snapped the machine off. He drained his drink and immediately poured another.

"What does it mean?" Vicky asked.

"It means," Murdoch said, reaching for the phone, "that if Threat walked right through that door and admitted to everything, he walks out anytime he wants to. Even if Solomon were to catch him, when Spain hears this, and he tells the governor, the pursuit of Threat is ended."

He waited for Spain to answer, holding the phone to his ear. He looked over at Vicky. He smiled.

"What're you doing for dinner tonight?"

She looked up, startled, and then smiled. He felt his world begin to slip into another dimension.

"Dining with you," she replied.

2 0 The old man sat in the living room listening to David
Brinkley and the evening news and flipped the sound off
the commercial. He removed his glasses and rubbed his
eyes.

In that moment he could hear the roar of the trucks on the
Interstate more than four miles away. He had still not
gotten used to having the southern Indiana farm country's
silence jarred by the thunder of the Diesels. But there
were other sounds, too. Pleasant sounds of women chat-
tering, moving about in the kitchen as they put the finishing touches on supper; the dog barking outside as the
truck returned from town. He glanced at his watch. Right on time.

The truck doors slammed and he could hear the low murmur of voices
and then the heavy tread on the steps.

The commercial was over. He snapped the sound back on, slipped the
glasses on his nose, and watched the terrible tragedy of Southeast Asia

278

go on—he wondered how much longer it would be before peace and sta-
bility really came to that part of the world.

The front door opened. "Evening, Pa."

The old man nodded and continued watching the news.

The kitchen door swung open, the lights in the dining room were
turned on and Eleanor set a huge platter of pork chops on the table. She
looked up. "Oh—I didn't hear the truck."

She came forward for a kiss.

There were four cars and they had stopped a quarter of a mile down
the rural lane and turned out their lights. There were twenty men in all,
wearing bullet-proof vests and carrying many different types of weapons.

"Where is it?" Solomon asked the State Trooper captain.

"Straight up this lane."

"Okay, let's go."

On signal from the captain, the men fanned out, climbing over fences,
and moving in a flanking maneuver; they were all experienced hunters
and they moved quietly through the dried cornstalks under a cold No-
vember moon.

Murdoch and Solomon walked in back of the Trooper captain. In a
few moments they could see the lights of the house.

"Do you think he might resist?" the Trooper captain asked Solomon.

"Your guess is as good as mine," Solomon grunted.

Everything seemed to be normal as they moved in closer, with the
Trooper captain speaking in very low tones over his walkie-talkie, directing his men into a tighter and tighter ring.

"You going to tell me now?" Murdoch asked in a whisper.

"What?" Solomon grunted.

"How you found him?"

"Followed the money."

"But he took the money."

"The girl—Eleanor Cassie, in this case—was the money."

"But she disappeared—or so you said."

"She disappeared," Solomon said. "But Laura Roc didn't."

"Letters!" Murdoch said.

"We put a watch on Laura Roc's mail. It took eighteen months, but it finally showed up—all we needed was a postmark, and a zip code."

The Trooper captain eased back from the window. "They're all sitting down eating dinner!"

"Then we go through both the front door and the back door—hard," Solomon said.

The break-in was organized within a few minutes, and the circle of Troopers smashed into the farmhouse on command.

There was no time for the family to react. Within seconds they were staring into the muzzles of twenty guns.

Eleanor looked up and smiled. "Good evening, Chief Solomon."

Murdoch and Solomon looked at the twins, seated side by side, from one face to the other.

The two men continued eating and grinned.

"Which one is the man you want, Chief Solomon?" the Trooper captain asked.

The twins looked at each other and then slowly each raised a finger and pointed to his brother.

"He's the one you want," they said together.

AQUEDUCT RACE CHARTS

Friday, Jan. 2nd. First Day. Weather Clear. Track Fast.

Attendance 18,578
Track Pari-mutuel handle $1,109,788.
OTB handle $987,991.

FIRST: $10,000, cl. prices, $12,500–$10,500. 4YO and up, 7F (chute).
Winner, T. L. Cashman's dk.b. or br.f., by Simple Pleasure-Needn't Try.
Trainer. S. Kelly. Net $8,500. Times: 23 2/5; 47 2/5; 1:13; 1:25 4/5.

OTB STARTERS	PP	1/4	1/2	FIN.	ODDS
A-Steel Pit 1		1	1 1/2	1 3/4	30.00
G-Back Space 7		3hd	3hd	2^3	21.40
D-Last Page 4		7^3	7	3^3	6.10
B-Cutting Edge 2		4hd	4^3	4^3	2.50
C-Windmill Sy 3		5^1	5^1	5hd	16.50
E-Perfect Fourth ...5		6^1	6^1	6	11.70
F-Say Yes 6		2hd	2hd	7no	1.70

STEEL PIT ....(MARTINO)	60.00	29.20	16.40
BACK SPACE.......(SILLS)		25.70	12.20
LAST PAGE.........(VARGAS)	....		10.80

OTB payoffs, (A) 58.70, 27.00, 14.10; (G) 23.40, 10.50; (D) 8.80.

DOUBLE (4–1) PAID $41.00

1/1-5